STONES OF MIRETHI

THE LOST PRINCE

Gabriel Bradford

STONES OF MIRETHI: THE LOST PRINCE

ISBN: 9798391578208

First edition: 2023

Cover illustration by Katora Design © 2023

I dedicate this book to the following people:

ELISE: Thanks for your encouragement, the editing, and believing in this idea. Without you, this would probably exist as no more than a mess of incoherent ideas spanning seventy pages.

To my friend at Katora Design: Thanks for the art. More specifically, thanks for listening to my terrible idea and creating something good. And then doing it again.

TABLE OF CONTENTS

DELIVERIES

Broad wooden doors engraved with images of animals, real and mythical alike, had been the convention of the high market shops a hundred years ago and, to some extent, they had endured the test of time. The older buildings' window-frames bore heavily rippled glass from the imperfect methods of yesteryear's craftsmanship, which caused reflections to appear elongated, warped, and shadowy. These buildings had been built of reddish-brown brick and rough-cut wood. They were squat, square, and offered little ornamentation. *Content*, Ashan thought to himself as he stuck his tongue out at his own reflection.

In contrast, modern structures utilized white-washed adobe mortar, allowing for gracefully crafted round corners and smooth domed roofs, of which there was an abundance. These adolescent buildings advertised wealth with highly ornate paneling about their high-arching doorways and perfectly crafted windows. The words **UNITY** and **PROSPERITY** were painted in red, blue, or gold on many of the modern windows in the elegant, sweeping lettering of recent trend. Most doors displayed the black three-pronged crown to signify support for the king as well as country. These new buildings gave voice to the tale of the kingdom's recent economic renaissance and love of aesthetically pleasing architecture. *Look at our success*, Ashan imagined the buildings shouting to the world as he turned away from the window and headed down the street.

Down a few blocks, he spotted the cracked, faded and overly large double doors of The Misty Trail, which were painted cobalt and bore no ornamentation. While most of the older buildings had updated their door pulls to ornate bronze, nickel, or even silver elaborate affairs, The Misty Trail offered rusty, worn iron bars that had been hammered in at a sharp angle. If those short lengths of iron could talk, he like to think they would say *My owner is so cheap that he paid an apprentice blacksmith to make a handle out of the nearest-available piece of scrap metal.* The building had a faded red brick face without signage or advertising to inform passersby of the services provided within. The windows were so filthy that Ashan wondered if they'd ever been cleaned at all.

The aroma of aged paper and fresh ink hit like a torrential flood upon entering and a bell above the door sang softly. In a flash, Ashan's concerns were uprooted and washed away. He wondered about why that happened and concluded that the scents just had a calming effect on him; after all, he had heard people describe the same thing about bakeries on occasion.

The front interior was lined with sturdy wooden shelves, each filled with knickknacks, special books with blank pages, and an assortment of things Ashan wasn't sure what to call. *Decorations*? *Thingamajigs*? Surely some were functional items, but he hadn't a clue about such things. Beyond these shelves, there stretched rows and columns of darkly stained wooden bookshelves, each so tall that Ashan would require a ladder twice his height to reach the uppermost levels. The rear and side walls were lined with bookshelves from floor to ceiling and, in fact, there was a ladder leaned up against those. If he were to guess, he'd say there were a thousand books resting in this one building. He'd commented as much upon his first visit to The Misty Trail; however, Master Hank, the owner, had disabused him of that notion.

At present, there was a large gathering of finely dressed lords and ladies in the front section of the store. Loosely forming a line, they stood in small clusters of between two and five and they spoke in hushed tones. Were he among people of his social rank, Ashan would be looking around to see what had shocked people into such silence; however, lords and ladies were very different folk with very different rules regarding public behavior. Among their kind, being loud in a public setting was considered rude and the wrong tone could be taken as a grave insult. *Even the wrong words!* Beyond the walls of the high market, where people like Ashan belonged, people were quite the opposite. They yelled at each other openly, whether it was simply to call attention to something, to vocalize disagreement, or if they were merely engaged in a lively conversation.

The high-born had even more peculiar rules regarding their manner of dress. They wore clothing in every hue and style imaginable and they often dressed to match those with whom they traveled, married, or were actively courting. They clothed themselves in several overlapping layers with beads and lacing so that it was often difficult to tell where one article of clothing ended, and another began. Many carried parasols that matched what they wore to protect their porcelain skin from the early spring sun. *Loud colors,* Ashan thought as he scanned those in the shop. People like Ashan wore clothing made from scraps of brown or tan cloth that was often held together by coarse thread and soft only when compared to broken rocks. Beyond the city walls, he fit in just fine, but here in the high market he was considered barely better than a stinking bucket of manure.

"Good morning, Ashan." Master Hank offered a wide, toothy grin from behind the display case nearest the front doors.

Short, balding, and rotund, Hank had the most exuberant smile Ashan had ever seen. It downright bordered on being obscene, but the high-born rarely mentioned it above a whisper, which was considered polite. He stood before his record book, quill in one hand and a bottle of ink the other, before a man and woman in nearly identical turquoise attire. Beside his book sat a package wrapped in light tan leather, which Ashan guessed to be a bundle of loose-leaf paper. Only the finest papers were wrapped in leather at the time of sale. Ashan had heard Master Hank describe the types and purposes of paper on a handful of occasions, but he still did not understand the why of such things. *Paper is paper...why have so many types?*

"Oh, uh..." Ashan hesitated to approach. He'd noticed the many hands that had risen to noses. "I've got a few packages for you, Master Hank." Saying the man's first name instead of his surname still struck Ashan as being disrespectful, but Master Hank disliked it when people called him by his family name. He didn't quite care for the title of Master either but didn't protest about it often. People found that off-putting and disrespectful, but their opinions never rose above a whisper, and he politely pretended not to hear.

"Set the lot here, Ashan." Master Hank indicated the top of the display case at his side by pointing with his quill. Several of those waiting shifted back and away, making room for Ashan's approach, as their expressions became a mix of anger and disbelief.

"Disgusting!" a shrill voice came at just above a whisper.

"The nerve!" a man hissed.

"I apologize for bringing you here, Lady Voth." a man dressed in black silks offered to a woman in an emerald dress with a white stripe across the chest. "I would not have brought you to such a lowly place, but they DO provide the highest quality paper in the capital." His voice rose to what would be considered vulgar among the current group. In

4

an instant, faces turned toward the man, some displaying anger and others agreement.

"Not at all. It reminds me of my uncle's study. I try not to allow first impressions to deceive me. We have a saying in the south about things...and some people." She cleared her throat and spoke a bit louder. "You can't scrub away polished-in dirt and a fresh coat of paint just hides the travesty beneath the surface."

Let these high-born turn up their noses at this place, Ashan thought, fighting the urge to give the man a rude glare. *They still come here. They need this place.* He tried not to let his feelings show on his face, lest someone see and take offense to it.

"Lady Voth, you are too bold." The man's voice came loud and struck a shrill tone.

"Yes, sir." Ashan replied, wanting nothing more than to sit and read, to pick up some new bit of knowledge, as Master Hank so often allowed; however, with the looks he was getting, he felt that today was not the day to stick around. He carefully placed the three paper-wrapped boxes upon the display and fetched the delivery slip from his bag.

"Let me see now." Hank examined the scribbled text on each parcel before setting one aside with a widening grin. A moment passed in silence before the man in black broke the silence again.

"You reek of the sewers!" Ashan did his best to not react, but inside his blood boiled.

"The sewers are just tunnels to carry away human waste. No doubt, the boy carries the scent of things placed there by people...like yourself." Ashan turned in shock at the lady's words and a collective gasp filled the moment after. Hushed whispers came a few seconds after and then the line broke apart. People lowered their gazes as they hurried toward the door.

5

"I had just about given up hope that it would be found." Hank spoke, dragging Ashan's attention from the high-born people. He gave Ashan a quick smile and moved his hands tentatively over the box. He pressed somewhere Ashan did not catch, a soft click sounded, and the lid sprang slightly open. Slowly, Hank reached into the box with both hands and removed a perfect glass sphere. Ashan gasped and took a step back before he noticed the red and blue shapes within it and the white stone base that had been made to resemble clouds.

"Beautifully crafted, wouldn't you say, Ashan?"

Ashan glanced around and, finding the last of the high-born just exiting, spoke a bit more loudly than he had intended. "A magic orb, Master Hank?"

"A beautiful ornament, don't you think?"

"Ornament?" Ashan took a cautious step forward and examined the orb. Within it there was a tree and hanging from its one short branch were a red and blue dragon facing each other.

"Yes. I know dreadfully little about glass-working, but this is magnificent!" He chuckled softly. "It is fairly old and late in arriving to me because it was stolen. I paid a substantial fee to have the thief tracked down, but it was worth it." The man's smile practically fell from his face, his gaze drifted off one way, and a fog filled his eyes. *Magic sickness*, Ashan thought as he watched the color in Hank's eyes vanish.

"Hank?"

"I owe you...a debt...can't know...then it has...at the end..." Hank's voice fell to a whisper. Ashan quickly stepped around the display case and rushed to Hank's side. Hank began to sway, and Ashan grabbed hold of one arm to support him.

Hank's eyes were now entirely white. "Hank?"

"There's a man there...and the trees went out..." Ashan took the glass sphere from Hank and carefully returned it to the box before gently guiding Hank backwards to a short stool near the wall.

"Hank, can you hear me?"

"Just once more...it could fall apart..."

"It'll be okay, Hank. You'll be okay." Ashan glanced around the shop hoping to find someone he could ask to go find help but found the place entirely empty. He'd seen the man go into fits like this before, but rarely did Hank speak so much nonsense and he worried the man's sickness was growing worse.

"No... a trade in three parts."

"I'm here, Ashan." Galena, Hank's apprentice, was suddenly at Ashan's side. Startled, Ashan let out a gasp when she spoke and shivered in fright. *Why didn't I think to call for her? She's so quiet!*

"When did it start?"

"Just moments ago." Ashan stepped back as Galena knelt before Hank and studied his face with a fair amount of worry on her face.

"Is his magic-sickness getting worse? I've never heard him speak so much before."

"No, it is much the same as always." She replied as she put the back of one hand to Hank's forehead.

"Is he okay?"

"Yes, he will be fine."

"Isn't it a fine day though?" Hank asked a bit loudly and smiled.

Ashan bent down close to Galena and whispered. "Why does he talk as if to someone?"

7

"He...he dreams sometimes." she gave him a reassuring smile. "You can go now. I will take care of him."

"Yes, Master Galena." Ashan replied.

"Isn't it a fine day though?" Hank repeated, still smiling broadly like a drunkard might. Under normal circumstances, Ashan would find the whole thing unnerving, but it barely penetrated the calm that had taken him when he'd entered the shop.

"Yes, the day is fine, Hank." He agreed as he rose to his feet and rounded the display case to find his bag.

"I know, but are you certain?" Hank asked.

"Quiet, Hank." Galena said as she pulled him up to his feet.

"Are you certain of it?" Hank pleaded in a suddenly worried tone.

"I am certain. The weather is warming, and Galena is here to care for you." He gave Hank a smile in hopes that it might help calm him and headed for the door. Galena appeared even more worried as she raised one hand to wave Ashan farewell. He smiled, waved back, and pushed the door open with one hand.

The sun was a little more than one finger from the horizon when Ashan returned to the ramshackle building that served both as his master's warehouse and his...well, he wouldn't call it home. It was a squat patchwork building constructed half of wood, a quarter of rough stone and the rest of mismatching bricks. It leaned in general, some of the walls had cracks, and the roof had begun to collapse years ago. A building this ugly wouldn't be deemed fit for the high-market, the lower-city, or even the dilapidated outer rim of the city; however, all the way out here in the ancient warehouse district, it fit in well enough. People here didn't even notice it, not among the torn tents and shacks that could not easily be distinguished from the large mounds of trash. As bad as the outside appeared, the inside was much worse. The roof leaked, the floorboards had gaps large enough for the mice to get in, the walls were crumbling, and there was the perpetual stench of mold and decay. The interior was packed with shelves, tables and boxes of goods that overflowed all about the floor. Getting around inside was a challenge that required moving crates and climbing over piled up items. More challenging was when Ashan's owner needed a particular object found in a hurry. Finding the correct item could take days of searching through boxes, as there were no records of where anything had been stored and no method for locating items. Quite frequently, his owner would throw things towards the center of the main room from the doorway, as he was much too large to fit between the tall stacks.

Ashan spotted Erekej pacing back and forth across the low wooden porch at the front of the building. The white-washed wood planks cowered beneath the man, letting out loud protests with each thunderous stomp. Erekej was a middle-aged man with sparse, greasy, black hair that looked like half of a too-small wig about to tumble forward onto his round face. His cheeks were splotchy and massive, making his eyes appear tiny and too close together by comparison. The state of his clothing matched that of the building as if the two had been cut from the same cloth. He wore a plain white shirt with several holes and stains that could never be washed out.

Erekej wore a scowl the likes of which Ashan had never seen. He'd seen worry, common anger, and white-hot, murderous rage upon that face, but this was new. Erekej's thick fingers turned red as he leaned on and gripped the aged wood railing. Ashan's heart jumped, faltered painfully for a few beats, and began pounding wildly. A tingling cold shot down his arms, his fingers grew numb, and his focus blurred. His mind grew dull, as if preparing to throw up that wall between his mind and body. He told himself it was his body's way of protecting his mind from pain, but it was beginning to feel like a loss of control over what little was truly his in life. *What is mine? Am I even mine...even a little?* He'd seen other slaves flush white with fear before and he was sure he looked that way now. He felt suddenly disconnected from the world, like it was a dream. His thinking slowed and he was only vaguely aware that he was walking. How he kept his balance was a wonder to him.

"You've got **loads** of work tomorrow!" Erekej bellowed.

"Yes, Master." Ashan spoke loudly enough to be heard, but not so loud as to offer offense. Erekej's reactions were unpredictable, often shifting from calm to explosive violence faster than Ashan could blink, and anything or nothing could set him off. Ashan had spent years trying to figure out the man's rules but was no closer today than when he'd set out to find the answers. Speaking too loudly, not loudly enough, not showing proper respect, or showing too little fear... He enjoyed expressing himself with fists more often than not. A task left incomplete without being told to do it was often the reason for a sound beating.

"I'll not have any of your goldbricking tomorrow!" Ashan sucked in air to respond, but before he could utter a sound Erekej let out a guttural scream and kicked the railing from the risers. He hopped down to the ground and ran up to Ashan, face turning red.

"Yes, Master." Ashan replied as he turned toward Erekej without looking up. He'd learned long ago that locking eyes with his owner was a sure-fire way to set the man off on a tirade.

"Set out the moment it is bright enough for that damned ass to see where it is walking. No sooner! If it injures a leg stumbling in the dark, you'll be **walking** every delivery for a year to repay me!" Erekej screamed so loudly that Ashan's ears hurt, but he tried not to let the discomfort show.

"Yes, Master."

Ashan didn't see Erekej's fist come until he found himself spinning about and then hanging by his pack. It was everything he could do to get his arms free from the straps of the pack and fall to the

10

ground. Erekej dumped the pack out upon the ground and snatched up the delivery slips and the coins. He quickly glanced between the coins and delivery slips. Erekej stepped forward until he was looming above Ashan and snarled. For a long moment, it appeared as though a sound beating was coming, but suddenly a look of deep satisfaction appeared on the man's face. The red faded from Erekej's face in an instant and there came the hint of a smile. The unexpected did not bring the slightest relief; rather, it increased Ashan's anxiety about what a calm Erekej meant. Erekej was far crueler when he seemed calm than when angry.

"Master Hank did not pay?!"

"He had a spell, Master."

He considered it a moment. "Wash yourself! You smell like death itself!"

"Yes, Master." Silence. Erekej glared down at Ashan for a long moment, maybe minutes. He locked his gaze upon a pebble in the dirt and waited, trying not to breathe too loudly. Erekej turned and stormed off without another word. This was so unusual that it put Ashan on edge for the next hour.

After putting the donkey into its little shed, feeding and watering it, Ashan set out to clean himself. Aside from the first spring rain a week before, this would be the first time Ashan had been allowed to properly wash himself in a moon...perhaps longer. The nearest well was a short distance down the road, and he had two buckets with which to fetch water. He didn't have a proper place for bathing, but the space between the donkey's shed and the main building provided some privacy and a large rock as a seat, not that anybody would be walking about so late.

He considered the rumors he'd heard that some slaves, ones used as house servants or the like, were required to be clean and smell good to not offend the high-born they served. He had never met one to ask, let alone seen one to know what they looked like. For all he knew, they were a myth created to give people like him hope, but he figured that if they did exist, they kept away from the less fortunate slaves. They were hated by people of Ashan's station. *Maybe for good reason.* He started scrubbing his face, ignoring a faint memory of his mother teaching him that all proper baths began with a proper scrubbing of the face. He pushed the memory to the back of his mind and considered those mythical slaves, wondering if they considered escaping their lives the way he did at times. He pushed that thought away with all his might, grabbed a scrap of cloth, and began to scrub the caked-on dirt from one arm. For a time, he wondered about what sort of foods those fortunate slaves were given.

Once he was clean, he headed into the building, where the stench of fresh rat leavings assaulted his nose and almost caused him to vomit. When he opened the door to the room in which he slept, he discovered that his blanket had been shoved to the corner to make space for three empty wine bottles and a crate of cloth-wrapped goods with a note resting on top. As he read the note, he caught the scent of fresh urine and red wine. He was not surprised to find that his blanket was soaked. It took an hour to haul water, scrub the floor, and to wash and hang his blanket outside. He was not surprised in the least.

When Ashan settled down to sleep, he focused on the memories from before he had become a slave. They had become increasingly difficult to call up, lost behind the years of overwhelming dread, heartache, physical pain and repetitive days of labor. He had to repeatedly push aside memories full of anger, fear, and anguish put there by Erekej and protect the old ones from intrusion. He focused on his favorite one, pulling it from the darkness, wrapping himself in it, and letting it become a dream.

He was sitting on a blanket that was sometimes red and sometimes a mix of red and black squares. There were trees everywhere he looked, but being unimportant, they were blurry globs of color. To one side, there were meat pies, freshly picked berries on a white plate, and a large plate piled high with steaming meat covered in a light brown gravy. Laughter came from his mother and father as he snatched up two handfuls of food and stuffed his mouth greedily. It was almost flavorless now, but there was a hint of a memory of what it had tasted like that warmed his heart. He turned toward the laughter and found the smiling faces of his mother and father. She had vivid blue eyes, long white hair, and...and nothing. Her face was a blur that shifted between oval and almond. His father had short brown hair, green eyes, and perhaps a beard. Occasionally a horse snickered as it walked to and from, its body brown and legs far too long. It didn't have a head, but there were ears in the right place, and he felt a fondness for the animal. The dream was dying, but it kept him company through the night.

The next morning, Ashan arrived at the alleyway alongside King's Wall, the innermost wall of the city that kept the undesirables away from the homes of the wealthiest lords and ladies. He grabbed his pack, patted the old donkey on the head, and moved from the main roadway into the alley. Along the way, he admired the massive white blocks of King's Wall, each of which were five strides long and taller than him by two hands. The wall stood a stone's throw higher than the tallest buildings outside it, or much more than that if the gods had made you weak like Ashan. He had heard that the wall had been built by giants a thousand years back, but he wasn't sure he believed that story. If anybody were to ask him what he thought – which nobody would ever do – he would have said it might have been humans using magic.

The door markings switched from numbers to mixed letters – not words, but random letters – that didn't have an obvious pattern. He took note of each door's marking, trying to find some sort of pattern, but some held three letters and some four. The sound of metal grinding against metal broke his focus and he found that a door he'd just passed had opened outward. Out stepped a man in a dark robe and a lantern in one hand. He was tall and his face suggested that he was very lean under the too-big robe. His long, crooked nose stood out on his otherwise normal face like a sore thumb. He turned to face Ashan with a look of disgust and eyed him up and down quickly.

"This way." he said with a hoarse voice.

"Yes, Master." Ashan pulled his pack off to retrieve the package.

"No. You must deliver it. Only...only my master can receive deliveries."

The man turned in place and walked slowly forward with a shuffling that suggested he had a bad leg. The large wooden door slammed shut as soon as Ashan entered the building and he found nobody there to have done it. *Magic!* A cold chill ran up his spine. The man continued without looking back, his lantern illuminating the brick-lined hallway just enough so that Ashan could see cobwebs above.

"Don't dawdle." the man sounded impatient.

Ashan followed the man down a bricked hall for a hundred strides before they stopped at a small door on the right, which offered no handle. The man turned and gave Ashan a stern look before speaking. "You'll go up the stairs and wait at the top." He gave the door two soft raps, backed away, and closed his eyes. For a minute, Ashan thought the man was going to go to sleep, but then there came the sound of a bolt being moved on the other side of the door. When the door lurched inward, there stood three starkly white, curious faces.

The three ancient men in their threadbare shorts were so pale that they almost seemed to be ghosts and their limbs were so frail that Ashan had to wonder how they managed to move at all. He could see

14

their ribs and the shape of their bones. The only real color about their bodies was the blue lines beneath skin and their eyes, all of which were blue. They stepped back and bowed deeply.

"Take him to the stairs." the robbed man demanded.

They didn't speak as they turned about with shuffling feet and began walking away. He moved to follow them and was startled by the door shutting loudly as soon as he had cleared the doorway. Ahead, one of the men was carrying a torch held high, which Ashan hadn't seen before. Whatever room they were in was so large that he could see no walls or a ceiling at all. Some forty of Ashan's paces later, a narrow door appeared, and, upon arrival, they set themselves to pulling the iron bar upon it. It seemed to take all their strength to pull the thing open.

"Up." One said in a barely audible whisper.

Beyond the door was a spiral stairway. He barely had time to study it when the light vanished with the closing of the door and plunged him into utter darkness. He took a cautious step and felt something crunch beneath his foot. *Just rocks,* he told himself and took a deep breath while he tried to remember how far it was to the first step. The same crunch came with each step, as if the stone itself were crumbling beneath his weight. He couldn't help but imagine that the stairs were littered with the skeletal remains of mice. For a spell, he considered turning back to ask for a torch. *No, nobody cares. They'll just get mad.* He found the stairs and walked slowly, having to feel for each oddly sized step in the dark.

Now that he was alone, it occurred to him how strange the situation was. *Is this why Erekej seemed so happy yesterday? I thought it was because he pissed on my blanket again.* The stories of slaves vanishing without a trace came to mind, especially those in his profession. People often told stories of slaves being killed for their meat, served up to other slaves as a cheap replacement of other sources of meat during the winter. *No, it's not winter,* he told himself.

15

He stumbled at the top of the stairs when he raised his foot up for the next step and found nothing. He caught hold of a putrid aroma that made him think of a big cauldron of boiling oil, dead fish, and dirty socks. He waved his hand at his nose and stepped forward cautiously, hoping the smell was from something close by. A few steps later the smell was just as strong, driving him to hold his nostrils closed with his hand and breathe through his mouth. He felt blindly at the air with his free hand while walking and eventually found a wall, which he followed to his right. He almost yelled out when he felt spider webbing wrap around his face, but the idea of tasting the air again was all he needed to keep his fear in check.

"I would." A muffled echo came from directly ahead.

He stopped and studied the darkness carefully. He thought he caught a faint flicker of light directly ahead a good distance and considered what to do. He hadn't exactly been given clear instructions and the people to whom he delivered things could be quite particular. *Maybe this is where I'm supposed to wait.* A minute later, he heard a murmur and decided that it wasn't worth making someone angry by waiting instead of going to find someone to tell him what to do. *Maybe they're waiting on me.*

"-any number of curses."

"Legends tend to be vaguely accurate at best."

"Yes, yes. The very reason it has been brought in such a circuitous manner."

"Humans!" Someone spit the word like a curse.

"Yes, humans…as well as halflings, elves and goblins. All with no signs of any curses. We should be safe."

Ashan stood frozen a few strides from the doorway set in the wall ahead, which was only faintly visible. From listening, he judged that at least six people were gathered in the adjoining room, but they

16

spoke mostly in inaudible whispers. Through the doorway came a constant breeze of fresh air with a subtle aroma of honey and bread.

Tell them you're here. What are you doing? No matter how hard he tried to force himself to act, his body refused.

"You were careful to take care of all who carried it?"

"Yes. Each death will appear to be caused by wolves or whatever is reasonable for the area. This last one is a bound slave. Easy enough to make it seem that he was sold without proper report or murdered by street vandals. You really should trust that I can perform such mundane tasks at my age."

They're...they're going to kill me?!

Unlike the other voices, this one bellowed, rich with exuberant glee. *Madness,* the word came automatically. *I need to turn back. Run! Escape...* He didn't need to look at the rings on his arm, but he did just the same. His entire body shook, and his legs begged him to start running.

"Never forget! The Mad King must live. I want him to know that it is *I* who brought him to his knees. He must be the last to die! He will watch helplessly as we lay waste to his armies and burn his lands. He will watch me slaughter his servants, his children, and his wife." The glee in that voice faltered as rage rose in equal measure. "I will lay waste to everything he loves. He will beg for death!"

"Of course, King Hotar; however, first we need to confirm the item's legitimacy...which has just arrived."

A blinding white light cast away the darkness and Ashan turned to run but hit something with his foot and fell. He let out an involuntary yelp when his right elbow hit the floor. His eyes began adjusting and he scrambled forward on hand and knee, hoping he was heading back toward the stairs out of dumb luck. A hand wrapped around the back of his neck and pulled him off the floor. He began flailing for anything

17

to hold on to and a second hand took hold of his ankle. He went sideways and felt himself being lifted high off the floor just as he was starting to see basic shapes again. Realizing that he was being thrown, he screamed as loud as he could. He was thrown then and met something hard with his face and chest in unison. He tried to reach out for anything to stop his fall, but there was nothing yet again. He hit the floor on his side and tried to scream but found his body unwilling. The world began to spin as a throbbing rose between his eyes. He tasted blood.

The world came into focus slowly. First, he recognized a wall of small dark stones, and then the blurry form of a man in a crooked doorway. Beyond the man, he saw a group of people standing around a table in the adjoining room. One man wore a brilliant golden crown with three points upon his head, red and blue attire, and the rest were dressed in black form-fitting clothing or billowing black robes.

Ashan rolled over at an agonizingly slow speed, testing each limb to see if anything was broken. *Run. Run. RUN!* He looked this way and that and found there were no stairs. He was in a small, well-lit room. *Where's the stairs?* He carefully pulled himself into a sitting position and gave his surroundings a quick study. He leaned back against the smooth stone wall and considered things. *Something's wrong,* he noticed a sluggishness in his thinking. Across the room stood a man in dark, form-fitting clothing and a hard expression upon his face. His eyes burned with hatred. The stark contrast between the dark clothing and his too-white skin struck Ashan as familiar, as if he had seen this man before, but he could not place the face.

"Give me the package." His voice was eerily calm for having just thrown another person. Ashan found himself having to replay the man's words to himself in his mind before understanding their meaning. When he tried to respond, he discovered that he couldn't get his mouth to work. It was both dry and wet with blood and the taste of blood was growing stronger. He turned to look back into the other room. *Crooked doorway. Crown. The King!* "Hey!" the pale man yelled to get Ashan's attention. A wave of nausea distracted him for a moment after moving his head. "Where is the package?"

"You've broken him!"

Hey, I bet that's King Hotar! Ashan found himself smiling at the thought that he was meeting the king, but then he found himself drowning in pain and remembering that he had been thrown. As he tried to speak, he found his mind suddenly empty. He couldn't recall where he was or why he was in pain, but he was sure that he was in danger. He glanced down at his hands and wondered how he'd gotten here and why he hurt.

Loud voices came to his ears, but they wavered as if people were yelling from across a large pond. He glanced over at a group of people sitting before a grand table of darkly stained wood through a doorway and gasped when he saw a man with a golden crown. It occurred to Ashan that there were no doors or frames for the doorway. In fact, the doorway had no depth to it as though the wall was as thin as paper. As he studied it, everything within the doorframe rippled like a reflection on water once disturbed. Why was I thinking about the king? As he considered that errant thought, he forgot about the doorway. He felt the thought float away without a care. Terror rose in his chest then and he felt a smile fade from his face. It was the lack of caring about the thought that frightened him and made him grab onto the thoughts currently in his mind. What's wrong with me? Oh gods!

"Have the bond ready to break." A shrill voice rang out.

"Get your bag." A pale-faced man said loudly from his left side. Turning to face the man, he was shocked to see a man with skin as white as a full moon. "Get the package."

He felt a distant sense of urgency rise and fall away quickly, as it was consumed by a creeping numbness that he just noticed was swallowing him up. A void in the back of his mind was growing, swallowing up thoughts. It took a moment of thinking about it before he was able to move, and he found that his arms didn't want to

19

cooperate. He shifted slowly to one side and clumsily pulled his pack off and dragged it to his side. He studied it for a long moment and realized that he couldn't recall why he was staring at the thing.

"That's it. Get the package." the pale man he vaguely recognized said.

Where have I seen that man before? He felt the thought slipping from his mind and snatched it up to keep safe from the monstrous void inside. As he did so, he became aware of another thought slipping away into the darkness. Whatever the thought had been, he felt it didn't matter now. No, something else mattered. Something he meant to keep safe, but he forgot where he'd placed it. He opened the bag, and his attention was stolen by something wet and warm on his hand. Shifting his focus took what felt like a long time and he discovered a single red dot just below his knuckles. His vision blurred and, as he waited for his eyes to focus again, he felt something trickle down his forehead, run through his eyebrow, and follow the bridge of his nose. Another wet something struck his hand. A violent dizziness struck him, and he had to close his eyes to keep from vomiting. A muffled voice sounded but he missed the words entirely. His head began to throb then, and he heard drums beating slowly in the distance.

"You broke him!" Someone yelled. Ashan considered getting up and going to tell those drummers to cease with the noise. Erekej did not like loud sounds and would be angry if he were forced to endure such drumming. *Don't they know to be quiet? Erekej will be angry if he hears them being so loud!*

Ashan pushed the bag away and rolled onto his knees, pushing himself up with both hands...He found himself laying on his left side. Confused but sure that he had to stop those drummers, he rolled to his stomach, planted both hands upon the floor at either sides and pushed himself upward. He brought one knee up beneath his chest and... He was laying on his stomach, hands at his sides, with his face pressed against cool stone in utter darkness. He felt a spinning and... His was pounding and he heard people talking, but he couldn't understand what they were saying over the drumming.

ALONE

"It doesn't matter either way."

"It **should** matter."

"Your opinions differ. Leave it at that or go argue your case with him. As I said, either way it goes, I have a job to do, and I'll thank you to let me do it without distracting me with your arguing."

Ashan tried to ignore the voices intruding upon his peaceful oblivion, but they kept breaking through. Each time they did, he became momentarily aware of a great pain, and he ran from it, but each time was more difficult. The final time he heard the voices, his eyes shot open, and he began to scream from the pains all over his body. Several hands pressed down on his legs, arms, and chest, preventing him from flailing and trying to get up.

21

It took a moment to see through his pain and he found figures dressed in black and a pair of emerald eyes gazing back at him. His strength quickly faded away and he fell helplessly still on whatever it was he was laying upon. The emerald eyes were set in a soft oval face beneath blonde hair set up in a bun and above a calming smile.

"That will do it." The woman said loudly. "He will live."

"Almost didn't."

"Indeed."

Ashan found his vision a touch hazy, his mouth as dry as sand, and a dull throbbing between his eyes. His chest burned and stung sharply with each breath as if something were broken inside and the muscles in his neck felt dull like he had somehow managed to pull them. He gave his arms a try and found them too heavy to fully lift from his sides. Memories of what happened came to him and, in a panic, he tried to sit up and find something with which to defend himself.

"Calm yourself." A deep voice came from the group in robes and a large figure stepped forward from the others. He came up to Ashan's side and leaned in close. The man wore a smooth, white mask that appeared unfinished with only the two holes cut for him to see and no face painted on it. Cool blue eyes gazed out at Ashan. "We dragged you back from the very edge of death. You will live, but only if you are careful not to exert yourself for a time. You will mend soon."

"Any signs?" A woman with a sharp voice questioned. Ashan couldn't tell which body belonged to that voice.

"If the thing cursed him, we may not know for some time." The blue-eyed man spoke. "Healing his body took from him as much as from me. There is nothing to do now but wait and watch."

"And fill him with food and medicine." The emerald eyed woman's voice chimed in.

"Is it necessary to feed him so well?"

"Yes!" the blue-eyed man snapped viciously. "Unless you want to explain to the king that the boy died. He was malnourished to begin with and any of you over-fed pigs would demand much more intense treatment to restore your health."

"Very well. We will see it is done as you say." the woman with the sharp voice replied.

Ashan tried to speak, but his throat was dry, allowing only the softest wheeze to escape his lips. The group did not pay attention to him; instead, they turned and began walking away and out of sight. Unable to move or talk, he set himself to the task of gathering and sorting out his memories. *I wasn't thinking right... I passed out. Someone threw me. I was bleeding.* When he recalled blindly hitting a wall, he shuddered at the thought of being thrown so easily. He'd never seen someone strong enough to do such a thing and wondered if that pale man had used magic to do it. He caught the memory of the feeling of his head hitting the wall and wanted to vomit when he recalled the dizziness. Fortunately, there was nothing in his stomach now. He recalled hearing murmured words but couldn't recall what they were. Then the drumming came to mind, and he considered it a long while. There shouldn't have been drumming underground... *No, I went up some stairs to get there. Maybe there was a field nearby where drummers were practicing. Yes, that must be it.* He lay as still as he could for a long while and sifted through his memories with a sense that there was more, he couldn't quite snatch from the abyss. Eventually, he gave up on the task and let himself fall back to sleep.

When he woke again, he found himself laying on his back again, with a cold, wet cloth upon his forehead. He glanced about and found himself alone in a small room. His eyes focused a bit slower than normal as he examined his surroundings, but not so much as to be concerned. *I'm just tired,* he told himself. Lifting his head was easy enough and his chest didn't hurt much as he dragged himself upright on shaky arms. He spotted a folded gray blanket at the edge of the room right before a wall of bars. Next to that, there sat a large wooden bowl with thick steam rising from it. Sitting up fully, he spotted a small cup, an entire loaf of golden bread and a large silvery decanter.

He scooted himself to the edge of the stone slab, tossed both legs over the side, and carefully evaluated his legs. They held his weight but only just barely and his sense of balance was bad. He swayed terribly as he walked over to the bars to examine the food and found a bowl of partially mashed beans, a chunk of yellow cheese larger than a fist, fifteen slices of mildly spiced meat he didn't recognize, and a bowl of some sort of brown mash he could not identify. The smells made his mouth water immediately and he used the bars to lower himself to the floor. This was a feast vastly superior in quality and quantity than any he had ever been given by Erekej. He picked up a slice of the meat and brought it to his mouth before pausing. He placed his face against the bars of his cell and glanced both ways along the hall for a solid minute. He saw only darkness in the distance and empty cells similar to his own. Closing his eyes, he listened for a few minutes, but all he heard was his stomach protesting the delay.

He turned his focus to the food and considered the last time he had been offered more than scraps for a meal, how that meal had turned his stomach inside out for a full day, and how Erekej had laughed over that for days. He was certain that this meal was another such trap. Should he eat without permission, there would come a beating he would not soon forget or perhaps he would spend the day vomiting. *No, Erekej isn't here to set a trap. I'm in a dungeon cell.* He reluctantly searched for the link to Erekej at the back of his mind. If he dug at it long enough, he could sometimes get a glimmer of Erekej's mood and that could be a valuable clue to what was happening. He swept over that spot and found nothing.

He opened his eyes and looked at his arm. The three interlocking metal rings that should have encircled his forearm were gone. *Gone?*

Ashan woke to the sound of metal striking metal repeatedly. He sat up and, glancing about quickly, found that nothing had changed since he had fallen asleep. Moments passed and the clanging came again. He pressed his face against the bars but could see nothing new. The sound came again and again. A minute went by like this before a rising cacophony of displeased voices drowned out the clanging. Several minutes later, a guard walked into view holding a short sword. He raised his sword as if to bang it on the bars of Ashan's cell, but paused when he saw that Ashan was awake. He nodded to Ashan approvingly and walked on. The yelling died down a few minutes later and silence fell again.

A few minutes later, there came a great scraping of chains over stone. Ashan pressed his face against the bars and glanced left and right along the hall. The sound stopped for a minute, but returned, lasting just as long. In the distance, the flickering light of one torch flickered out, leaving a small dark space between torches. Then the red torchlight was replaced with a steady soft glowing yellow light that was much more intense than the fire's light. The sound of metal grinding over stone returned then. Soon, another torch's light flickered out and was replaced with the soft, unnatural yellow. One by one, the lights replaced the torches in a slow march towards Ashan and he watched closely. The nearest torch's fire finally flickered out and there was a long moment of silence before the sound of chains being dragged over stone came again. The soft yellow light came and, when he saw that the light only faintly revealed three figures, he rolled away from the bars and cowered against the back wall of his cell. The fire's light just outside his cell went out and the silence came. An orb of soft, steadily pulsating light appeared from nowhere, bobbing as it moved through the air. When Ashan's eyes finally adjusted to the brightness, he discovered that it was being held in a hand. The light slowly revealed an arm attached to the hand, an elbow...a shoulder.

Finally, three unnaturally tall, deeply hunched, sickeningly thin men stepped out from shadows that clung to them like ivy to a tree. Slowly the tendrils of darkness released from the man holding the orb and retreated from the light. The man stepped forward and hung it from a hook on the bottom of the sconce on the opposite wall. The men turned away from the wall in unison, reached down to the floor, and grabbed at the air just above the stone floor. They lifted in unison, moving as if they were lifting something heavy up to their shoulders, and stepped forward once. The sound of dragging chains filled the air and Ashan had to stick his fingers in his ears. Three labored strides forward and they were close enough that Ashan recognized them as the same men who had delivered him to that stairway. *Where does the sound of chains come from,* he wondered as he crawled to the edge of his cell.

When the three stopped at the next sconce, they dropped their unseen chains and bent down, resting with their hands upon their knees as if exhausted. Though they made no sound, they heaved their chests as if catching their breath for a long moment. Not thinking, Ashan snatched up his remaining meat and the bowl of half-eaten beans and slid them through the gap at the bottom of the bars. He tried to speak, but his voice refused to come. He whistled instead.

Their heads spun in unison, and they studied him for a while in silence. Finally, two slowly approached his cell, their eyes locked upon his offering while the third watched passively. They wavered when they bent down for the food. This close, Ashan saw that they all had very similar features. Deep blue eyes, skinny noses, the same big ears, and the same parting in their white hair. The third stood a bit taller than before, wiped his hands upon the front of his leggings, and watched as the others made quick work of the food.

Once the food was gone, they lowered themselves down upon their knees, and bowed until their heads touched the floor. They remained like that for a few seconds before raising with tears in their eyes. They reached through the cell bars, grabbed Ashan's hands, pulled them to the bars, and kissed the tops of his hands once. They used the bars to pull themselves back up to their feet, turned, collected their invisible chains, and departed into the darkness of the hall.

Ashan watched them disappear and then turned his focus upon his own body, which he was surprised wasn't broken or heavily bruised. More interesting than the lack of bruising, was his missing bonding rings. *They're really gone! But for how long and why?* He had often imagined that the skin beneath would be sensitive to the touch, maybe even raw from rubbing against the metal of the rings, but there was no difference he could find, aside from the almost white skin from not having seen sunlight. *No more Erekej.* He let himself smile and revel in the joy of his freedom without worrying that Erekej might sense his good mood. *No more beatings, no more deliveries. No more moldy bread and no more trying to figure out the unspoken rules Erekej lives by and... No, there will be new rules here. New faces, new fists. No more sky, no more books to read in Master Hank's shop.* His smile faded and tears came. The small measures of freedom were gone now. *I will die in this cell. Maybe from old age or the next visit from that blue-eyed man.* Alone in his mind for the first time, he was able to think his thoughts and feel what he wished without having to pour his will into blocking Erekej's probing mind. His limited freedom was gone, but he had gained the privacy of his own mind. For all this, he cried.

"Wake up."

"Yes, Master." Ashan opened his eyes and rolled over, expecting to see Erekej. Seeing that it was a man in leather armor and a metal cap reminded him of where he was. He planted his hands and gingerly

27

pushed himself upward. There was a small pain in his chest, but not as much as he had expected. On his feet, he faced the guard but was careful not to make direct eye contact.

"You say guard instead of Master here. You understand?"

"Yes, Mast-uh, guard."

"I see the blow to your head that I was told about didn't break your mind. That is good news." The guard produced a set of keys from his pocket and unlocked the door. "If you attack me..." he held up a short sword and gave Ashan a grimace. "Do we understand each other?"

"Yes, guard."

"You'll be cleaning floors."

The guard removed Ashan from the cell and marched him down the hall with his sword drawn and at the ready. What the man thought Ashan could do against him was beyond his understanding, but he did try to imagine what someone could do in that situation. He imagined that some men who knew how to fight might be capable of wrestling that sword away from the guard, maybe jump forward and spin in the air to put some distance between them and at least be facing the guard. Perhaps, if a man was quick enough, one could spin and tackle the guard before he had time to respond. He tried to imagine doing those things, but each imagining ended with him dead on the floor from a stab wound or missing his head entirely. *Those men,* he warned himself, *would have to be very skilled and mighty, which I am not.* They arrived upon a large door with two guards standing before it, each with a matching short sword drawn as if ready to fight.

"New prisoner. Assigned for cleaning." the guard leading Ashan said.

"Right."

"I bet you he won't last the week." the guard leading Ashan said as the two stepped away from the door. They laughed and one of them pulled the door open.

"How much you wanna bet?"

"Look at him." The guard smirked. "One lunch ration."

"Come on, Allen. Look at his eyes! He's got spirit!"

The guard gave Ashan's eyes a good looking for a second. "I don't see it, but two copper?"

"Deal!" They shook hands and parted for Ashan to pass.

"Hurry up." The guard took Ashan by the arm and pulled him out into the mid-morning sunlight and fresh air.

High walls of dull gray stone rose all around, offering shade, indirect daylight, and a gentle breeze of fresh air. The floor was a crisscross pattern of black and cloudy white squares three hands wide like game-board he had seen somewhere. In the center of the floor, there stood a shallow square pool lined with brilliantly white rock and a three-tiered stone fountain resembling a flower that was nearly as tall as Ashan. At each corner, stood a black statue of a robed figure facing outward in a different pose. Careful detail had been given to the folds of their robes, their hands, and even their feet; however, their faces were unfinished. One's hands were clasped in front of its chest, and it was upon one knee as if begging. The second's hands were in fists, and it was in a pose as if about to fight. He'd have to cross to the other side to see the other two faces. Tables covered in white cloth stood in rows along the left and right and upon each was one dimly glowing orb. The chairs were darkly stained wood with white cushions with gold thread embroidering and the black silhouetted crown.

Along the far wall, there were large windows of the purest glass that offered a generous view into what seemed a feasting hall with a table so long he was sure he had never even dreamed of its equal. There were well-dressed people moving in that room, some in all black and some in all white clothing, but the design of their clothing was alien to him. *House slaves?* He wondered if maybe they were free servants instead.

29

"You will remove the lights and store them there." The guard pointed to a large decorative trunk along the wall nearby. "The tablecloths you will fold neatly and stack by this door." He pointed to three buckets near the water fountain. "You will scrub the floor with water from the fountain. Rags and soap are in the trunk. Do not leave this area. Do you understand?"

"Yes, guard." Ashan replied as he took in the courtyard. It was easily sixty strides wide and a hundred long.

"Do well, do not complain, and you may be put to this task each day. Consider it carefully today while you work. There is sunlight, fresh air, the fountain's water is safe to drink and there are far more unpleasant tasks I could assign you. This is a pleasure compared to cleaning horse stalls, cleaning laundry, or latrine duty."

"Yes, guard."

"Good."

The guard turned, sheathed his sword, opened the door again, and left, leaving Ashan to stand there taking in the majesty of the courtyard. The fear of being seen not working and getting punished his him after a time and he rushed over to the nearest table. He shivered as he glared at the orb of light upon it, but he grabbed it after only a short hesitation. He wondered how the magic of it might hurt him as he carried it to the large trunk and pushed away memories of his last experience with Hank. He put it at the bottom of the trunk and gazed at it for a long moment's study. The light within was faint, no more than a flickering speck now, driving him to consider how the thing worked. There were sixty orbs placed around the courtyard, some dim and some giving off no light whatsoever.

Once he had gathered those, he set to work gathering, neatly folding, and stacking the tablecloths next to the door to the dungeons. The softness of the material was shocking, reminding him of high-born clothing in the way it moved in the gentle breeze. It was so soft that he feared he might rip it if he wasn't careful handling it.

30

Lastly, he set to work cleaning the floor. In the trunk, he found an empty bucket, a bucket of salt, and a stack of thick white rags. Even the cleaning rags were soft! Scrubbing dirt, bird droppings, and what might have been dried sauce quickly became grueling work for which his body was ill prepared.

"Lunch." Someone snapped quickly.

Ashan jumped at the voice and let out an embarrassingly loud yelp of surprise. He took several deep breaths before tossing the rag into the bucket and climbed to his feet slowly, fighting a stiffness that had settled into his lower back from being on his hands and knees so long. On his feet, he spotted a man in black sliding a large wooden serving tray upon one of the tables along the wall to the left and he did his best to hurry after. The man pulled out a chair and sat, allowing Ashan a view of what food had been brought for him.

Immediately, he noticed three thick slices of bread with jam slathered upon them and a yellow apple. Then there were carrots, mashed potatoes, slices of white bird meat with gravy on them, and heaping pile of cubed red meat. Lastly, there was a bowl filled to the top with a white creamy liquid with reddish-brown meat visible just under the surface. This was a feast unlike anything he had ever seen in his life. *Surely, this is not for me. I'm mistaken somehow.*

He stopped dead in his tracks and wondered if maybe the man hadn't been talking to him at all. Maybe the man had spoken to himself out of excitement for all that wonderful food on the tray. "Sit." The man barked the word and pointed to the chair to his right. Ashan took the chair quickly, barely able to take his eyes off the food as he went.

"How goes your recovery?"

Ashan's heart jumped when he looked upon the man. In a heartbeat, he felt his skin go cold and his body lock up. That barrier between his mind and body was suddenly there, getting into place, and he remembered the blinding white light and the pain that had followed. The taste of blood and the clouded, fleeting thoughts he had had were

31

strongest. Something had been wrong and magically healed by that woman with the emerald eyes. He suddenly felt a powerful urge to urinate and feared that, seeing the pale man, he might not be able to hold it in.

"Don't stare. It's rude." the man said sternly. "I can understand your trepidation in seeing me again, but manners make the man." Somewhere off in the distance drums began beating slowly.

"Have you heard voices or seen things that were not there?" His calm voice sent a shiver up Ashan's spine.

"No, master." When he finally got his mouth to work, his voice wavered terribly.

"Have you felt any abnormal sensations? Smelled something that wasn't there? These things can happen after a blow to the skull. The brain can become damaged if violently jarred. The senses can be altered, the mind broken." His casual demeanor did not match his face, which seemed too still, as if he were trying not to move it at all.

"No, master." His fingers grew cold, and his face suddenly felt very hot.

"Do you...fear me?" He slowly leaned forward in his seat, his face a mask of indifference. The eyes didn't match the face, for they were a raging fire.

"Yes, master." His mouth grew dry, and his heart raced.

"It is wise to fear me. Only a fool would not. Your hands shake, your heart races." Ashan balled his hands up at the mention of his uncontrollable shaking.

There was a glimmer of emotion that crossed the man's face, but it was too brief to understand. "Your survival instincts are functioning. Do you notice that pungent odor that wasn't there before I arrived?" He sniffed the air and glanced in either direction, moving only his eyes. For but a second, his face showed anger and annoyance,

32

but returned to the mask when his eyes came back to Ashan. Ashan gave the air a quick sniff but caught the aromas coming from the tray of food.

"I myself cannot, but I am told that some can. Ash, oil and the scent of a body beginning to decay? That's the description I have been given. Do you smell it?"

Ashan sniffed several times before finding it. "Yes."

"My kind does not notice it. I suppose because it is natural to us just as you do not notice your own smells, such as the smell of your own feet after a day's hard labor. The nose grows accustomed to what is always there." A slight look of disgust touched his face, and he turned his head away as if he had heard something. For a second, Ashan thought the man looked ashamed...guilty even, but when he turned back, his face was the mask again. "You reek of fear as pure as that of a small child upon waking from a nightmare." He grimaced openly as though angry and studied Ashan for a moment before sniffing at him. "It's normal. What is not normal is the fact that you do not carry the scent of someone who is angry." He leaned back in the chair and studied Ashan with those hard eyes for a long while. "Do you have no anger for me? Are you so beaten and cowed that you would walk to your slaughter without protest like a lamb?" From a sleeve he produced a small, slender knife and tossed it upon the table before Ashan. Ashan looked at it and then back into those burning eyes. Sitting there with that calm face and fiery eyes, the man seemed a snake just waiting for a reason to strike. "Hand me my knife."

Ashan slowly and carefully pushed himself up from the chair, being careful not to move any part of himself quickly. *Strange,* he thought, *even now I don't want to die. I suppose my life is all they have left to take from me.* He took the knife by the blade and held it out for the man. The man looked at the blade for a second and then up into Ashan's eyes. Ashan stood there for a while just holding the knife before he began wondering what to do. If this was a test, he surely hadn't experienced one like it before and, try as he might, he could find

33

no right answer. After a moment, he set the knife down upon the table before the man, making sure to point the handle towards him for easy access, and returned to his seat. Terrified, he said nothing.

The man's hands clenched tightly upon the arm rests of his chair, bending the top support, and he pushed down so the risers snapped apart. At the same time, his face twisted slowly into a blend of rage and some emotion Ashan had never seen. Determination filled his eyes, and his face went halfway back to calm before flying back to rage. It was a quick thing, but the expressions were so wildly different that it terrified Ashan to the point that he pushed himself as far back into his chair as he could manage, looked away, and closed his eyes. *He's going to kill me!*

"You are so broken. You could have stabbed me and run. I gave you the opportunity and a weapon. You could have fled."

"You'd kill me." Ashan whispered as he opened his eyes again.

"You are certain of this?"

"You almost did before."

"I see." His calm voice was like a trap, luring Ashan into a sense of comfort. In an instant, his face twisted, and he let out a snarl as rose to his feet quickly. He took a big stride forward, coming right up to the edge of Ashan's chair, glared down at him with such fury that Ashan gave an involuntary yelp and jolted in his seat. The man reached down with one hand and wrapped it around Ashan's throat. He pulled back and grabbed the man's wrist out of instinct, but he barely managed to budge the hand. He pulled Ashan from the chair with such ease that Ashan was suddenly certain he knew exactly how the great city walls had been built. He reared back with a balled-up fist and... let out a primal scream as he released his hold of Ashan's neck. Ashan landed on his side and curled up instinctively, blocking his ribs with his arms in case this man started kicking him the way Erekej often would once on the ground. The man walked screamed again and walked over to an empty table nearby, took hold of it with both hands, and threw the thing

34

into a portion of the wall where there were no windows. The glass portion of the table shattered, and two legs snapped free, one of which struck another table and caused the glass top to shatter as well.

Finally, the man strode off without speaking and Ashan did not dare to watch where he exited the courtyard. Moments later, three guards appeared, gave him a quick looking over, asked if he were injured before returning him to his cell.

"Out of sight, out of mind, as my mother always says." One of them explained along the way.

"I think that invalidates our bet." Another replied.

"New bet?"

"Sa'teshka kills him in the month. Four coppers!" They laughed and Ashan welcomed the safety of his cell.

Ashan spent the following days in a constant state of fear that the man would return to kill him, and his nights were filled with nightmares of the man as well. Eventually, the fear faded, and he began to look for things to occupy his mind. He began with counting the bricks in the walls of his cell and trying to strike up conversation with the three old men when they came to exchange the torch with the orb of light each night, but they never spoke back to him. He also tried to start conversations with those people wearing robes and white masks when they came to deliver food, but they were only interested to know if he was seeing, hearing, or smelling things that weren't there. Each morning, the guards would take him to clean the courtyard, berate him for not doing a good job, and toss him back into his cell. They didn't want to talk either.

Certain that they would not feed someone of his rank so well forever, Ashan began to wonder when it would all end. He wondered if it would be the pale man, one of those masks people, or the guards. He wondered if they'd starve him to death, behead him in the cell, or use poison. Surely, poison would be the least messy option, but he had heard that people often emptied their bladders shortly after dying and that could get messy. *When will they be done watching me? It must end eventually!* Of course, he also considered the possibility that this was what life was going to be like forever. He was still young and useful. They could have him replace the three old men replacing orbs or just have him clean the courtyard for the rest of his life. The thought of being used for those tasks for the rest of his life filled him with dread and eventually replaced the nightmares about the pale man.

One afternoon, Ashan sat with his back against the rear wall contemplating while studying the bricks of one wall. A grey brick with a red splotch that was very close to being a perfect circle was his favorite and he wondered how it had come to be as it was. *Maybe they keep checking on me because they have me moving those light orbs. Waiting for the magic to kill me or break my mind?* He considered Master Hank's spells and hoped that he would be fortunate enough to die before the magic of those light orbs made him experience something similar. As good a person as Hank was, Ashan did not wish to experience the other side of what he had witnessed. He did not want to drift in and out of the world, missing things without warning. Of course, he didn't have money or friends who could take care of him, and he figured he'd likely meet his end without even knowing it was coming if he ended up like Hank. *Not that I have a choice in handling those orbs though. They'll get bored of watching me. They must! It's been weeks! Months?*

Wanting something else to focus on, he picked at a scab on his left knee and tried to guess the time. Midnight? *My hands are getting stronger from scrubbing those tiles.* He searched for the link to Erekej, looking for the smallest sign that it had once existed, and found nothing for the hundredth time. He rubbed his arm where the three metal rings had been and wondered who had removed them and for what reason. *I guess I don't belong to Erekej. Maybe they purchased me.* Between the object he had delivered, and the light orbs he handled each day, he was beginning to doubt that magic worked the way he had always heard. *Maybe magic items are made by magic people and can only do specific things...like a hammer.* He wondered on it for a time before giving up on the idea of solving that puzzle and focusing on a problem that felt...solvable.

I do everything they tell me, and they still say I do terrible work and hit me. At least they don't beat me often. Not like Erekej did. There must be a reason!

He ran through the tasks and what he'd tried to do differently so far in attempting to appease the guards. He'd been told he had used too much soap, too much water, not enough of either, left behind soap scum, didn't scrub hard enough on a few tiles, did the work too quickly, and took too long. Some days, the guards would show up at the end of the day and return him to his cell without comment and other days they would beat him, throw his food upon the floor, or just scream at him that he was an idiot.

Eventually, the frustration began to give him a headache and he slammed his fist upon the ground, scowled angrily at the bars of his cell, and barely held back a scream. *Erekej was easier to please than these guards!* The sudden wave of anger that ran through his body was shocking. He found himself breathing hard and wanting something to punch. This was happening more frequently, and it always got his heart going fast, which he supposed was because he had always had to hold his emotions in, keeping them from Erekej, and now he didn't have to do that. Unrestrained, they seemed to come more randomly and with greater intensity.

There must be an answer!

Try as he might, he never came to an explanation that fit perfectly. *Beatings make me slower, less effective! I could try to work faster, mind my details, use more salt and a lot cleaner water? Maybe the trick is to scrub in circles? There must be an explanation!*

"It doesn't matter. Nothing matters."

He was a bit startled at hearing his own voice. The words just came out of his mouth like in a dream and he felt an enormous sense of comfort having said it. The words rang true in his heart in a way he had never known and, as that truth settled in, something in the back of his mind began to move. Like the main cog in a clock, as that thing moved, so did another...and another. As he stared at the brick with the little circle in it, he felt a bunch of things move in the back of his mind where he rarely looked. It quickly became a swarm of parts moving around, flipping over and spinning before colliding. Fitting together and building something. He slowly became aware that he had been slowly realizing but that he had been fighting this moment for years. He hadn't wanted to face it. Hadn't wanted to know this thing. *What doesn't matter? Answers? Questions? Me? Anything?*

He was still feeling the realization come together when a guard arrived before his cell, which he only noticed when the sound of jangling keys caught his attention. The guard opened the cell door and gestured for Ashan. It seemed to take a greater effort than ever before for Ashan to climb to his feet. He turned toward the doorway and found his legs to be quite heavy, almost like he was wearing heavy armor. When he reached the hall outside, he felt all his willpower seep away in a single weary exhale.

Those things in his mind were swarming like mad hornets and he remembered how he had ignorantly placed them in the back of his mind one at a time over the years. He hadn't seen how they fit together along the way and had never checked. A part of him had known life was going to be easier not putting all these parts together, but now he didn't have the strength to stop them assembling there in the back of his mind. Faster and faster, they were finding where they fit. *Almost complete now.* He could almost see the meaning. There came an overwhelming desire to see the thing assembled.

Some strange curiosity urged him to look left and right, to see the other prisoners sitting or lying in their cells. To know, for reasons beyond his understanding, ...something. Hardly anybody spoke to each other in these cells and so he knew none of their names or voices. Sure, he knew one snored and one talked in his sleep...otherwise, they were all strangers here. Those in the cells to either side were seated, backs against walls, faces turned down. They did not stir even when the guard yelled and pushed Ashan. "I said, move!" He let his legs carry him forward if only to prevent himself from falling. He felt an important part of who he was being pushed out of place and something new fitting into that spot. It felt like death's icy grip upon his heart, but...there was something more than that. There was the promise of rebirth, the hope of being something better, and a necessity so deep that he wanted to die a little. *Just a little.*

"Why?" Ashan muttered, surprising himself. *What a stupid question. I know why. To go do work!*

...Why?

For clean water and sunlight!

...Why?

To live.

You aren't living. You are...surviving. The difference was suddenly clear for the first time ever.

"What?" The guard gave Ashan a hard shove. Oddly, the spike of fear that Ashan always experienced when force was used, even in the slightest manner, didn't come.

"Why?" Ashan was surprised at how loud his words came.

"Don't talk back!" the guard pushed him again.

"Why?" He found his voice came without the usual fear-induced wavering and hesitation.

"MOVE!" The guard screamed.

"Why?"

Footsteps and the clanking of metal on metal rose in the distance. The guard pushed Ashan, urging him forward, but he found that he couldn't walk. No, it wasn't that he couldn't walk, but that he cared not to do so, for he was not motivated to see to a task that would be of no suitable benefit. Two guards appeared ahead. They slowed once close and, lowering their weapons, waited in silence as they watched.

"Move!" the guard behind yelled again.

"Why?" Ashan replied flatly.

The guard pushed Ashan so hard that he fell to the floor. He landed hard on one elbow and yelped in pain. Laying there waiting for what he was sure would come, he noticed the face of the man in the cell before him rise. He saw sorrow in the man's face and wet cheeks but for a moment before the man's face turned back to the floor to stare at the space between his bare feet. The man turned his feet inward and wrapped his arms around his legs tightly. The man was covered in dark bruises. Something struck Ashan's shoulder and pain rose; however, as the pain rose, there came too an odd sensation he had never experienced. The pain shrank down as they met, like a cat suddenly faced with a group of dogs. In that moment, Ashan glimpsed the fullness of the thing in the back of his mind.

"Get up!" one guard yelled.

"Do your work!"

Ashan shuddered as that small part of himself became a memory of who he was, murdered by the realization that he had shied away from knowing so long. He knew he would miss that part of who he had been,

40

but he would no longer be served well by it. His following thoughts were both terrifying and comforting.

"I'll give you something to cry about!" one guard yelled.

These are broken people. Something struck him in the side, and he was vaguely aware of words being spoken. The words of a man telling him to comply with the rules of their system, which lacked order and never seemed to be the same from one day to the next. He had thought it a broken system or just too complex for him to understand; however, he now saw that it was not broken at all but worked as had been intended. He had ignored the parts that he hadn't understood and, in doing so, had missed the point entirely. It motivated people like him not only to comply, but to work harder, to find solutions, to check details...to do the best job they could. This system was akin to Erekej's, which had shaped him into a good slave, always improving his work without having to be told to do so. Fear had made him pliable, reliable and easy to handle. It was about motivation through fear, and he was no longer afraid of being beaten.

Ashan belted out in laughter. Someone rolled him over and punched him in the mouth. To his own surprise, he didn't care who had done it. Instead of looking for a face so that he could remember, hate and fear that person, he gazed up at the ceiling. *I would not hate a stone that I stubbed my toe on. I would remember to look where I was going.* He laughed again. A kick to the side came exactly when he expected it and he bellowed. One of them stomped him in the stomach as another kicked his side. The pain came and Ashan attacked it with laughter. They could kick him all they liked, but it would not make him fear them or do the work they wanted done. *Powerless.*

"What is wrong with you?" someone yelled. Ashan laughed so hard that he had to roll to his side and hold his stomach. A kick landed in the middle of his hands, and he was sure that several fingers had broken. He laughed harder at it. *Powerless!*

"Do your work!"

"No!"

"What is wrong with you?" One of them screamed.

"I will not obey!" The kicking came harder. "Kill me...and I...am free of you!"

"What is wrong with you?" A guard screamed at the top of his lungs. They continued kicking him and he continued laughing.

"You...have...no power!"

A CERTAIN KIND OF FREEDOM

Ashan awoke to pain. He gasped in shock at the amount and number of areas that pained him and was wracked by an uncontrollable coughing fit, which brought on excruciating throbbing in his ribs, chest, and entire left arm. He tried to shift away from something that jabbed his lower back; however, it followed him, and he soon realized that it was a hand plying at his ribs. He tried to turn and look for who was touching him, but his vision was heavily blurred so that all he found were vague shapes of different color. He attempted to speak, but his jaw wouldn't work at all due to swelling. The hand moved up along his spine to his shoulder and branched off to the side. A moment later, the hand was removed and placed on his stomach, slowly pressing here and there as it moved upward. When it climbed to his ribs, he knew that something was broken by the pain and the sensation that things weren't where they usually were. The hand then pressed against the left side of his stomach, and he found himself screaming involuntarily. He tried to roll away, but another set of hands pressed down on his chest and kept him in place.

"Broken ribs, several ruptured organs, broken ankle, dislocated knee, collapsed lung, internal bleeding. From the discoloration, I think he's been in this state for hours." a man's voice explained dispassionately.

"Any sign of magic?" a woman replied.

"No. Fetch Sa'teshka and the healer."

"But last time-"

"Ta'elyn!" The man snapped. "He is beyond my ability to heal alone. Go get Sa'teshka and the healer! I can keep the boy alive long enough for them to arrive." The man's hand suddenly returned and stretched out upon Ashan's stomach. A deep cold poured into Ashan's stomach and the world went black.

"They will suffer." A whispered voice full of venom in the dark brought Ashan from a dreamless sleep.

The pains were still there to greet him. His ribs ached such that it was agony to breathe, both hands hurt at the slightest movement, his jaw felt as though it weren't properly attached, one eye was too swollen to open, and his head hurt beyond words. Immediately he thought about screaming from all the pain, but his chest prevented him from filling his lungs even halfway and he lacked the energy to do so. He lay there panting for a long while before the thought of looking around came to him. One eye was swollen to the point that it wouldn't even open a sliver and the other barely opened. He saw a soft flickering light and felt that he was laying on something substantially softer than the stone slab of his cell. He wondered where they'd moved him, but then he recognized the almost perfect circle in one brick. The need to yawn came and he fought to hold it at bay for a minute before it won and

44

then he found himself whimpering and shaking from the pain it caused in his chest.

"You're awake?" a soft voice sounded from his side. He recognized the shuffling of paper followed by the scraping of a chair's legs on the floor. A second later he was met with a pair of emerald eyes and dangling locks of red hair. No, her hair was blond but some of the ends were red. Fresh, wet red. The woman wore a concerned expression, which he found confusing and a bit comforting.

"Blink three times if you can understand me."

He blinked his one eye three times.

"Good. I trust that I do not have to tell you to take it easy." Her hand appeared with a wet rag, which she placed on his forehead. She said something he didn't understand as words and suddenly the rag grew cold. The coldness spread into his forehead much too quickly not to be magic and the comfort it brought him reminded him a bit of that which he experienced when entering The Misty Trail. He wanted to panic at the thought of magic being used on him, but his body refused.

"That should be helping you to think a bit more clearly. Do you remember who you are?" Three blinks. "Very good."

She moved out of sight and there came a scraping of metal against stone followed by a weak groan. "No. Stop." a man's voice demanded weakly. There came a thud and then a soft clanging. Ashan tried to turn his head to see what had happened, but his neck refused him. "Help." The man's voice called softly in panic and shuffling sounds rose gently. Something metal struck the floor, shuffling feet, the snap of a bone breaking and then a humming sound filled Ashan's ears. The man began wailing in pain, but it was a muting yelling as though he were already half dead. A red light illuminated the ceiling and, a moment later, the wailing became a gurgling choke. Then there was a moment of silence and Ashan's heart refused to beat faster to match the panic in Ashan's mind.

"Right. Please dispose of the body, Farek." the woman's voice came.

"Of course." a deep baritone replied. There came the sound of something being dragged, followed by the all-too-familiar sound of Ashan's cell door being shut, then more dragging moving into the distance.

"You might like to know that he slept longer than you." The woman reappeared with a glowing red orb in hand. "He was only struck in the head once, whereas the three of them spent a good while kicking you in yours. I know many people would like to know this so they could tell the story later and gloat about it. Personally, I think it just means you were lucky." She explained, seemingly unaware of the blood dripping from her hand. "Anyhow, they wanted you dead for reasons I hope you can clarify later. When you're back on your feet, I mean. Which brings me to this." She nodded at the glowing orb. "Do try to relax and not move. I'm going to heal your injuries, but it will hurt. If your luck holds out, you will simply pass out from the pain. With your injuries being so severe, you will not enjoy this. Ready?"

He began to blink but was swallowed up in agony and a vivid awareness of what was wrong with his body. First, he became aware of the many broken bones in his chest, some of which had broken through the skin like knives stabbing out from the body. Second, he realized that he had been given medicine to numb his body, but he now felt it sort of evaporate from within, allowing sensations to reach his mind. Then everything became so much worse. He suddenly felt that he was missing the middle finger of his right hand, which was swollen up and larger than he would have considered possible. The left side of his face ached and throbbed agonizingly with every beat of his heart, his right leg was folded forward and up, now resting on top of his other leg.

As he sucked in air to let even the gods know of his agony, he felt the bones in his hand shift, the fingers splay, and a fire come to life therein. His elbow followed suit with its own fire a moment later and then his leg jerked, straightened out with a kick, and his neck craned

46

violently so that he was suddenly facing the wall. Three screams later and he was ready to beg for death instead, but he couldn't stop himself from screaming to do so. His body rolled to the side, and he felt his ribs shifting about madly, the muscles pulling unnaturally, and a hundred little stings spread across his torso. He was vaguely aware of vomiting for a moment, but the pain was such that he didn't even notice how long it lasted. The darkness swallowed him up some time later.

"Wake up." A gentle voice pulled him from a dream of vast green fields and birdsong.

He opened both eyes without issue this time, but a white cloth blocked his view. He found himself wearing a grin that didn't want to leave his face and he felt disconnected from the world with only mild pains about his body. He cautiously tested his arms and legs and found it remarkably easy to move them. He then took a carefully controlled breath in and found his chest, while pained a bit, functioned almost normally now.

He reached up and pulled the cloth from his face and found himself in his usual cell. He sat up, that smile spreading wider and wider, and examined the room. All along the opposite wall were stools covered in candles, oil-burning lamps, and glowing orbs at peak brightness. Directly in front of him, sat a woman upon a short stool wearing a bloody sleeveless white shirt, loose-fitting brown shorts and plain sandals. She had her long blond hair done up into a bun at the top of her head and her emerald eyes studied him intently. She was washing her hands in a bucket sat upon a stool before her. No, there was no stool. It was floating. He gave her a smile and continued examining his surroundings. *What?* He turned back to face her and studied the floating bucket. Yes, it was definitely floating in the air. She smiled at him and he, unable to stop himself, smiled back cheerfully.

"I gave you some Dog's Breath root so you would sleep and some Day Nirvana for the pain."

"What does that mean?"

"Dog's Breath makes you sleep no matter the pain. I expected you to flail for a moment, but you went on and on about it. Day Nirvana...well, it dulls the mind greatly. No doubt you are starting to notice its effects on you already. A few more hours now and you'll be right back to your old self. Until then, however, you're going to be a right happy fool like a drunk."

"I thought you were torturing me. Then I dreamed about fields. There were all these singing birds...no, not birds, just their songs." Ashan threw a hand over his mouth to stop himself from talking. The woman gave him a knowing smile and continued washing the blood from her arms. "Where's that blood from?" Ashan heard himself muffle through his hands.

"You, mostly." She spoke. "Some is from that guard, but not much."

"You killed someone!" The memory of what he had heard came slowly, as if trying to recall a dream from a moon ago.

"I did. Sa'teshka would have tortured the man for a long while before killing him and-" She stopped suddenly and glanced from the bucket to Ashan quickly with a look of surprise on her face. "I killed him to save you. Since he was one of the men who did that to you, I judged it as fair. He would prefer death over the other option, I assure you." Her expression turned stern, but only for a moment.

He dropped his hands and looked about the cell and wondered "How long have I been asleep?" and slapped his hands back over his mouth.

"Two days now. How do you feel?"

"Great!" He practically cheered and utterly failed to keep from grinning like an oaf. "I mean, sore."

48

"A fair bit less broken too, I would wager. I am a great healer." She said with a beaming smile. She forced the smile from her face for all of a second before it returned. She grabbed a small towel and began drying her hands. "I dare say I must've spilled some Day Nirvana on myself. It can have the unnerving effect of causing one to speak any stray thought that crosses the mind. Not to worry though! That part of it fades quickly." She pushed the floating bucket aside, stood and crossed to one of the stools along the wall, where she began rummaging through an assortment of small glass vials. Ashan watched the bucket float over, bounce off the wall, and begin slowly heading back towards the woman.

"This is a good way to feel. I wish I could feel this way all the time."

"I would not advise that. Day Nirvana is addictive. Most people kill themselves when they become addicted and run out." she explained as she examined one of the vials. "I didn't give you enough for that though! I am very careful."

"Who are you? Why did you heal me?" Ashan felt that he should be worried about what he was going to say next, but the ability to worry was a strange concept to him in the moment. It was like trying to figure out how a dog might be able to breathe under the water or ride a horse. *Silly thoughts*. Then it occurred to him that he didn't know how to ride a horse.

"I am Sophia, and I healed your injuries because-" She stopped herself with some visible effort and returned to her seat. "No, I don't want to tell you that." She gave a sigh of relief and cleared her throat. "Dangerous stuff, that Day Nirvana! I only hope I have enough left to use on Sa'teshka. It is very expensive stuff, you know." She gasped as if frightened, eyes going wide. She tried to frown, but the smile returned quickly.

"You are friends with that man?"

"Yes!" She beamed at him. "Well, no. No, not really. He doesn't have friends that I know about." She pursed her lips and Ashan could tell

49

she was straining to keep herself silent. She studied him intently for a long moment and placed her hands in her lap and smiled worriedly. She continued in a soft tone. "I'm sorry."

"Sorry for what?"

She snapped her fingers, spoke a word Ashan didn't understand, and moved her right hand as if throwing something. Whatever it was, Ashan saw nothing, but he felt something softly tap his chest and then the world started going dark. "I must stop talking and I'm simply no good at that part of life. You'll wake up in a few minutes. I'm sorry, dear."

HOUSE KAIRN

Anvindr entered his father's study with a wobbling stack of books and letters in his arms, closed the door with a gentle kick, and lost his balance. He had to spin about twice to keep from spilling the entirety upon the floor and then quickly deposited the lot upon his father's massive oak desk. He crossed the room to the spilled items, snatched them up, and removed his formal dining coat before returning to the desk. With a deep sigh, he sat down and pulled himself up to the edge of the desk, where he mustered up the will to begin what would surely be a full week of careful work.

He began with the large accounting ledger from the top of the stack. He quickly found the page with the most recent entries and fetched his bottle of ink and a quill from the top left drawer. With an assassination attempt having been made against the high-king and the subsequent announcement of war, he needed to write a great many letters to all manner of people in the week ahead and little time to do so while seeing to the usual matters of his family's estate. The usual calculations had to be run first and then he could begin running the expenses to cover the demands high-king Hotar had laid out in the recent letter regarding the war efforts. He needed to increase food production by half, which meant he needed to acquire more workers, which would take a fair amount of time and money since they were easiest to acquire from the far south territories. He required at least twenty more smiths to arm his soldiers, but he had to do so without taking them from other lords and ladies to avoid entering into lengthy negotiations to avoid angering some of them. Somewhere in his pile was a note with last year's number of people from his lands suitable for conscription to war, which needed to be gone over and updated so that he could have conscription letters written and sent. It was a task he dreaded, but necessary in order to provide the number of soldiers the high king had demanded of him. A year wasn't long, but many things could happen in that time that meant a man was no longer suitable or eligible for conscription and people did move and age. He'd have to hire people just to update that list. With no official timeframe given, he could only assume he had months to get all the tasks completed.

"One thing at a time." He scolded himself as he opened the bottle of ink and began reading from the ledger.

So far, this had been the best financial year his family had managed in the last twenty by a fair margin, which was saying something given how the family estate had grown in all those years. While his father would have been pleased with that fact, he would have forgone praise in order to focus on what further goals that success had provided. Anvindr had to pause and think about that for a long moment, which was difficult with how tired he was; however, the big picture eventually came into focus, and he began to plot. He wouldn't have to increase food production as rapidly as he had been considering all day; rather, he could use his surplus money to purchase food from allies and negotiations could be arranged to exchange skilled farming labor for lumber. Checking his ledger again, he saw that he was beyond storage capacity as it was, and that construction of more storage barns was behind schedule. If he didn't deal with that problem soon, he would be dealing with the problem of having lumber sitting out in the rain. He pulled out the small booklet and searched until he found a note scribbled concerning allies in need of lumber. There in the corner was the note regarding two allies with severe shortage of lumber due to forest fires that had consumed great swathes of land late last summer. Of course, those allies had not been advertising that fact, but Anvindr knew through his network of spies.

He scribbled down numbers for estimated costs for the training of soldiers and paused to consider if he was forgetting something. Somewhere there was a book in his father's library the next room over that described all manner of war expenses, which included an extensive record of past wars, a chapter on predicting inflation, and an extensive plan for war-time profiteering, but he didn't want to read it now. Besides, all those calculations depended on gathering the information of what existed currently and then plugging them into complex equations and he didn't have the mental focus for that now. Worse still, those equations made the core assumption that said war was semi-local. A war between different royal houses could be very complex and often didn't even appear to be an open war at all; meanwhile, Anvindr had to plan for a war between different empires, which meant he had to find one of the hypothetical war books down in the basement library.

"No, focus on the now. One step at a time."

The letters offering employment to soldiers and smiths were of the highest importance now. You could always find good soldiers, but a good smith was a different story entirely, as being short on armor and weaponry could spell disaster. After double-checking his ledger's numbers, he began making two lists: the first being which local smiths he would attempt to hire and the second was the best towns in the south from which to recruit soldiers and laborers. Southerners were known for their predilection for conflict, foul dispositions and lack of decorum; however, through years of experience, Anvindr had learned that their attitudes could be mostly remedied by applying extra coin, strong drink, and following a more southern set of rules in respecting people. He'd need to mix them in with his local forces and set strict expectations to minimize in-fighting.

According to his father's research, ninety-one percent of any job offer made would be accepted and rough estimates suggested there were ninety-thousand unemployed people looking for work in the largest city in the southern territories, which meant he could expect almost eighty-two thousand workers to answer the call. A sizable force to add to his already existing forces. Of course, he had to assume that only one-quarter of those were suitable for combat, half could be regular workers and the other quarter could be trained in a skilled trade. Of course, he needed seasoned tradesmen, but gathering them required far more work. He would need to send letters of notice clarifying his intention to recruit said workers to the lords and ladies of each southern territory as polite notice. At the same time, he would send requests to the heads of trade guilds, and, after negotiations, they would sort out which members to send him. Hiring seasoned professionals in the north was much easier and faster, but he didn't want to waste time in an environment with such high competition.

"Lord Kairn?"

Looking up from his work, Anvindr found his newest maidservant sticking her head through the door. She was young – too young for working in his opinion – but her father had been adamant about her working. It was common practice for young kids to be exchanged between allied and to serve such a role for some years before being elevated to serve a higher role, but Della couldn't be ten yet. Of course, Anvindr had been sent off to another house to work even younger than that and it hadn't been terrible. Mostly, she had been sent to serve in Anvindr's home because her father knew that he did not employ corporal punishment on those under his employ like so many others did. Della was a diligent servant but very shy for her age and the short time she'd been serving his household. She smiled at him but then forced the smile away in her effort to appear less childish, something her father had lectured her on when delivering her into Anvindr's care. Her father favored an austere resolve in others, but she was still young, and he didn't not enforce such rules, for there were still years left for her to enjoy being a child. "Yes, Della?" He offered her a smile to encourage her to stop frowning so much.

"There's a man come to see you, Lord Kairn."

"At this hour? Who?" He set the quill aside and capped his bottle of ink.

"Lord Sa'teshka, my lord. Shall I see him up?"

"Lord Sa'teshka?" *Why would he wish to see me?* "Are you sure you heard rightly?"

"Yes, Lord Kairn."

"Tall, pale man with a stern face and plain black clothing?"

"Yes, Lord Kairn."

"See him up."

She turned and ran down the hall to the stairs. He quickly worried over the hand full of times he'd heard about Lord Sa'teshka visiting nobles over the years, each more an open assassination than a social visit. Why, it was rumored that when he'd made a social call on House Raskell, he'd slaughtered them at their dining table and then lay waste to every servant and guard of the house with no more than a fork. *Just rumors and wild speculation,* he lectured himself as he picked up the small bell at the far end of his father's desk. He gave the thing two rings, set it down and stood up to straighten his shirt and stretch his weary legs. His younger brother Aklyn appeared in the doorway a few moments later with a silver tray, two cups and the small white tea pot their mother had always favored using with company.

"I assumed coffee, Anvindr." Aklyn gave a wide smile as he crossed the room to the far end and set the tray down upon the small table before the fireplace.

"Where's Alma tonight?" Anvindr asked as he approached. He felt a pang of sorrow at the sight of the two plush chairs on either side of the little table, which he had done well to ignore for many days now. Unfortunately, this had long been the place his father entertained special guests and held serious talks with family. His family would expect the tradition to continue lest he insult the memory of their father. It was in these chairs where his father had given him the "growing up" talk, which was more a lecture on the how's and why's of becoming an adult. There had been similar events for each new layer of responsibility his father had put upon his shoulders, and he knew it was the same for his siblings. Why, his first heartbreak and taste of brandy had been with his father in these chairs.

"Her daughter finally went into labor."

"Hertina?"

"Yes."

"We should do something special for them." Anvindr immediately began thinking about how he could make time to find a special gift for their family.

"I cleared my schedule tomorrow to see to that task. You've already got enough on your plate, Anvindr."

"Ah. Well, thank you, Aklyn. Very...good of you."

The healthy coloring and fullness of Aklyn's face caught Anvindr off guard then and he smiled. It hadn't yet been two moons since his spies had discovered Aklyn in an alley one night and brought him home. How long Aklyn had hidden his addiction to Bliss wasn't clear, but, judging by the near-white of his skin upon discovering him, he had been very near the end. He'd spent that first week tied to a bed moaning in pain, screaming incoherently, and sicking up anything he was fed. The team of doctors Anvindr had hired had initially counseled the family that Aklyn was unlikely to survive the first few days of withdrawal, but here his brother stood. Not wanting to remind Aklyn of any of it, he didn't bring it up.

"Anything else you need?"

"I think that will be good, Aklyn. Thank you."

"You're welcome." Aklyn turned and walked out of the room with a small glimmer of the care-free stride he'd always had before the Bliss.

Moments later, he heard the thumping of heavy feet upon the stairs accompanied by the much quicker and lighter steps of Dalla. Anvindr straightened his shirt, brushed the worry sweat from his palms onto his pants and took deep breaths to calm his nerves. A moment later, Della came into view, stopped outside the doorway and announced proudly "Lord Kairn, I bring Lord Sa'teshka." She waved the tall, pale man into the room with that serious look upon her face and ran back the way she'd come.

Lord Sa'teshka wore his constant plain black attire, which consisted of flat pants, an undershirt that barely showed at the neck, a long-sleeved over-shirt with buttons painted black as night and rugged soldiering boots in black. Although his clothing bore no symbol of house, military rank, or station emblems, the overall look was neat, and each component was pragmatic. People talked about his manner of dress all the time, often wondering if he owned more than one pair of anything; in fact, there were running jokes that he owned only one pair of socks and that he spent each night washing that pair over a bucket in his bedchambers worrying that they would get stolen. Of course, people also said he had no taste or fashion, but his clothes did have a certain utilitarian style to them. Compared to the extravagant affairs most lords and ladies wore, Sa'teshka was something approaching invisible or poverty-stricken in his appearance.

"Welcome, Lord Sa'teshka." Anvindr said and gestured for the man to take one of the seats near the fireplace.

"Good evening, Lord Anvindr Kairn." Lord Sa'teshka strode forward with a determined gait. There was preciseness to his overall demeanor that most would assume to be caused by bitter annoyance, but instinct told Anvindr that there was something else there. The man marched across the room like a soldier, examined the two chairs, turned and sat down. Lord Sa'teshka took the nearest cup and began preparing himself a drink.

"It's just Kairn, Lord Sa'teshka." He instructed as he took his father's seat and waited to prepare his own drink.

"Just address me as Sa'teshka."

        The corners of Sa'teshka's mouth turned down sharply and then returned to their previous state so quickly that Lord Kairn almost thought it hadn't happened at all. The thought of how long he had been awake crossed his mind and he hastened to get himself a drink. He reached forward for the white pot and, taking hold of it, noticed a slight shaking of the cup Sa'teshka held. The man sniffed at his drink a moment before taking a sip. There had not been whispers of Sa'teshka suffering any illness and so Lord Kairn made a mental note of the shaking but did not ask. He prepared his own drink, sat back in his father's chair, and blew softly to cool the liquid. Sa'teshka's eyes were on his cup for a long moment as he took small sips. Then he shifted his focus to look Lord Kairn dead in the eyes. There was a burning hatred in those eyes, one Lord Kairn had seen in the eyes of men who carried old grudges that had long ago become insatiable. Suddenly, Lord Kairn did not feel safe.

"What brings you so late, Sa'teshka?"

        Sa'teshka's lips tightened ever-so-slightly, his eyes narrowed a fraction and hardened tremendously. The fire in those eyes grew threefold and Lord Kairn was suddenly certain that Sa'teshka was about to attack him. He casually moved his left hand to the chair's arm in preparation to fetch the concealed knife therein and took a deep breath.

"I have observed you for quite some time now."

"To what end?" Lord Kairn moved his hand a bit closer to the knife and brought his cup to his mouth at the same time to distract Sa'teshka from that hand. A slow sip gave him time to consider which of his many legally questionable activities might have garnered such attention. Given that almost all his covert actions were legal, he had to assume it had something to do with his spies. Of course, getting caught employing spies wasn't that big of a deal, usually resolved by paying a fine and apologizing to whoever was offended.

"You are a paragon of order, a careful planner, and a fair man. Most importantly, you care for the well-being of other people."

"I thank you for the compliments."

"Ordinarily, I would not give a man like yourself a single thought. You are uninteresting and predictable."

"Are you here to insult me?"

Annoyance crossed Sa'teshka's face in a brief flash. "Pay attention to what I said, Lord Kairn! I didn't take you for one of these weak gold-bloods who takes anything that doesn't worship them as an openly hostile insult."

"I suppose I must then ask what it is that I have done to garner your concern."

"Nothing." He swallowed hard then and turned his attention to the fireplace. "The situation with the dungeon has become unacceptable."

"How so?"

"Gross mismanagement." He paused and took a long draw from his cup. He pursed his lips and his nostrils flared as he took a very controlled breath in. When he continued, it was much more slowly, as if he was having trouble planning his next words. "It was recently discovered...that Lord Harik had been allowing guards to...mistreat prisoners. This led to the discovery that he was stuffing his pockets with funds that were designated for the care of those who resided in the dungeons. Given the severity of these crimes, he has been...relieved of command."

"Relieved of command?"

"I tore his arms off." His nostrils flared wide, and he took a deep, unsteady breath.

"Are you asking me to take up the command?"

"You will bring order to things." It sounded more a command than a comment.

"I have some trouble believing that King Hotar would suddenly begin to care for the living conditions of those he chooses to throw into his dungeons."

Lord Kairn refilled his cup with one hand. It was a bit of an open tell to leave his other on the arm rest, but he dared not give up any slight advantage possible. He tried not to imagine how terrified Lord Harik must have been when he realized he was going to be pulled apart by horses. Lord Kairn had seen it done once in his teen years and didn't care to see it happen again.

"He cares for the theft and the disrespect."

"There are many other lords and ladies who would jump at the opportunity this provides to be in King Hotar's company. The way I heard it, Lord Harik was at the castle most days and found every opportunity to ingratiate himself-"

"He was a sycophantic bastard." His face twisted with disgust for a moment but was quick to return to neutral or as close to neutral as he could manage. At the same time, his free hand gripped the arm rest tightly, giving away his impressive strength.

"He may have been, but there are others who would be very pleased by the opportunity you are offering."

"King Hotar has made it clear that the success or failure of the next person to take the position will reflect upon me personally."

"So, it's personal for you now?"

"Yes."

"Perhaps you should find someone more willing to take up the task." Lord Kairn sipped at his cup and watched Sa'teshka carefully. The man shifted his gaze to the fireplace quickly and glared unblinkingly for a long while. "I am not interested in the work and might do a poor job."

"Are you not tempted to be near the high king at all?" he asked without looking at Lord Kairn.

"No. I already have a life over-full of responsibilities. To take on more would cause me hardships I would rather not contend with at this time. As you know, I have a few siblings and a sizable population to look after. With the coming war, the king has given me quite the list of things I must supply. Let me show you."

Lord Kairn sat his cup down and rose slowly. He'd feel safer with fetching the small hidden knife but left it undisturbed in favor of better options. Sa'teshka rose and followed him over to his desk. Near the top of the pile was the decree of war with the long list of supplies high-king Hotar had demanded of him. The number of soldiers was followed by a long list of supplies ranging from arrows, bows, swords, and various foods listed in hundreds of barrels each.

Just under the war decree was the decree titled "The Allowance and Forgiveness of Mystics and all Related Craft-works New and Old". It was a lengthy document dissolving all laws that had outlawed magic items and magic use outside the High-king's direct control and demanding their use in the coming war. Most importantly, it provided total forgiveness to those who had hidden away their enchanted items, abilities, or servants, which was likely all lords, ladies, and a great many merchants. Looking at the decree, Lord Kairn recalled his own secret stash of small, enchanted items. He would still have to make time to tear down the wall hiding that room in the basement and hire a mage to document what the items there could do.

"As you can see, King Hotar has demanded much from me."

Sa'teshka didn't speak but took up the paper and studied it at length. As Sa'teshka considered the list, Lord Kairn walked around his desk and began rummaging through the pile of books and papers. Here, he could make a stand, as there were glass vials of acid in one drawer, a short sword hidden behind books on the shelf behind him, and there were a number or mid-sized daggers within a large false book on the corner of the desk. Sa'teshka scanned the papers on the desk and took up the sheet with Lord Kairn's latest notes.

"Hiring from the far south regions will be time-consuming."

"Yes, but there are a lot of people there needing work." Lord Kairn replied as he fetched the sheet with that information and handed it over.

"You could supplement your workforce with slaves much faster."

"House Kairn does not support slavery or indentured servitude."

"So, buy slaves, free them, and hire them."

"I will as I can, but many other houses won't sell to me because of that very thing."

"You lay a lot of problems at my feet." Sa'teshka sneered, sat the papers down, and walked back to the chairs to refill his cup.

"I will find solutions. I always do."

"I can offer the blacksmiths you require." he sipped at his cup and locked his gaze upon Lord Kairn's eyes. "Half the grain crops at best and most of the carpenters you require."

"In exchange for what?"

"We can settle after the war."

"I prefer not to have open, vague agreements, Sa'teshka."

"I do not intend to swindle you, Lord Kairn. If I was a man bent on profiting, I'd have come prepared to barter. As it is, I need you to take the task at hand."

"It seems like you are very invested in this."

"Let us just say that King Hotar is not a forgiving man. I do not want to repeat the mistake that was Lord Harik."

"Still, why me? There are plenty of other people who could be honest and orderly."

"Of those recommended, I disliked you least of all."

"I suppose I will take that as a compliment."

"Report to the castle tomorrow." Sa'teshka sat his cup at the edge of the desk and placed the papers on top of the nearest book and turned around.

"I didn't say I'd do it."

"You'll do it."

"I might."

"You will." Sa'teshka left the room.

A KEY

Ashan gave up attempting to count the passing of days and, for a time, counted his meals, and tried to guess how much time passed between them. When he realized there was no pattern to the arrival of his meals, he moved on to counting how many times he saw the same guard, how many different ones he saw, and which days they worked. There emerged no pattern and he moved on to humming songs and trying to recall stories he'd heard; however, having heard so few songs in his life, he began to create his own. By the time he memorized one of his own creations, he was certain that the gods had not intended for him to become a bard.

Ashan was singing loudly when the guards delivered a prisoner named Larren to the cell next to his. Larren was a petite woman in her late twenties with dark hair and an impressive resolve to scream profanities at the guards for much longer a time than he would prefer to listen. Of course, when the guards weren't around, she was polite, a bit formal, and soft-spoken. She told him how she had been having an affair with a nobleman, who had promised to divorce his wife and marry her in the Spring; however, when their child had been cold-born, the man accused her of murder out of spite for his delayed promise. There had been a short trial and she had been sentenced to serve a year. That was just over two years ago now. Ashan and Larren were equally overjoyed when a blind man named Sarko was delivered the following week. He claimed he was serving six years for fighting and nearly killing a city guard. How a blind man could pull that off, Ashan was unsure, and Sarko didn't give details. Overall, Sarko didn't seem to mind being locked up, often commenting that he ate better here than he had as a free man and that the only down-side was the lack of sunlight making him feel a constant coldness down to his bones. Ethar, who couldn't be older than nine, but claimed to be twelve, arrived a few days after. He was serving eight years after having been convicted for the crime of summoning a demon and attacking city guards, but he said that it had been a genie that he'd been found with and there had been no attack; rather, high-king Hotar had discovered that he had found a genie and locked him up so that people wouldn't know the truth of the matter.

A week after Ethar's arrival, the guards finally deposited a man in the cell across from Ashan. As they departed, the man shook his cell door violently and gave it a firm kick. When Ashan turned to face the man, he was shocked to find a man three times his age and in remarkably good health. He shrugged when Ashan looked at him and simply said "Had to check. You never know what chance fate will give you." he explained.

"I'm Tark." He glanced along the hall a moment before looking back at Ashan. "I haven't seen you before. You new? Why are you here?"

"I delivered something to the king. It was cursed and they're waiting to see what it did to me. You?"

"Boring story." Tark replied.

66

"Maybe." Ashan said. "What do I have but time though?"

"Fair point. I nearly killed some rotten kid related to a lord who didn't take kindly to it. He was trying to have his way with a woman and I just...lost myself behind my fists." he sighed and took a seat at the front of his cell.

"Sounds heroic." Ashan commented.

"Nah, boy. It was just rage I had in me finding a target. Perhaps a worthy target but that's not for me to judge. It was wrong." He shrugged and looked down. "I'm no hero. I was drunk and angry. It didn't help that I was a high-ranking officer at the time who should have had more self-control." He sighed and glanced about the hall. "I was a wreck. Had been for a long time. I turned my own life to shit with anger and drink. Lost my home, my wife, friends... I belonged down here."

"You don't now?" Tark did not respond for a long while.

"You look right shit, boy. They not feeding you?"

"They feed me. Mostly scraps of bread now."

"Well, you look like you just lay there all the time. Frail as a twig. You don't work your body?"

"They don't let me work anymore." Ashan explained.

"Let you? Boy, you can work your body right there."

"What do you mean?"

"Do you think people get strong only because the gods bless them to be so?"

"Ye-what?"

"I never met a man who woke up strong one day after asking the gods to make it so, but you go ahead and beg them for strength if you like.

As for me, I *MAKE* my body strong with good food and exercise. Or whatever food I can get."

Blasphemy! Ashan backstepped in shock. He almost ducked down to avoid the bolt of lightning he expected to come shortly after, but then thought better of it since he was in a cell with a roof. He found himself even more surprised to find a part of himself wanted to hear more. He considered the man's words a long moment and found himself certain that the man's words were truth. *The strong are in charge! The gods gave them strength so that you would know your place!* Erekej's favorite saying crept up from the back of his mind, filling him with doubt, but there was a ravenous curiosity in his heart as well. "Tell me more." he said at last.

It took little time to realize that the guards were separating prisoners by temperament, taking those who were willing to work somewhere that was disconnected from those in this area so that no information could travel between the two groups. Unlike his previous neighbors, who had cowered at the mere sight of a guard and had never spoken to him, these people spent their waking hours talking, singing, or playing games as if they were free people gathered at some normal social event. Laughter had quickly become normal.

Ashan was exercising with Tark while half-listening to a story Larren was telling Ethar, but he was distracted by the screaming of guards in the distance. It was so normal to hear, that it no longer struck Ashan with fearful imaginings that they would come to beat him next. Whoever was being beaten by the guards gave out a few pained yells, but, like most in this area of the dungeons, mostly screamed out a taunt about how weak or powerless they were. The guards never went so far

68

as to break someone's bones or kill, but they had lost their previous dispassion entirely.

"Who wins?" He asked Tark.

"What do you mean?"

"This battle of ours. They don't kill us, but they are growing more and more angry. When will their leader let them start killing us?"

"They use us as workers. You once cleaned the royal courtyard...now someone else does. I was used for cutting firewood and hauling water. They are trying to get us back under control."

"It's not working. Especially now that we're being fed well again."

"The screaming and beatings won't work. We just have to keep our spirits up until the next thing happens."

"How do you stay in such good cheer?"

"For a long time, I wallowed in self-pity and anger while I just laid about on the floor. I got weak and bored, but one day I asked a guard if he could sneak me extra food if I polished his boots and he said yes. The next week, another guard wanted his boots polished and I agreed. Before they moved me here, I had a stockpile of food, extra clothes, and tools in my cell. I sharpened blades, mended clothing, and even wrote letters for the less-educated guards to send to family."

"Things won't go back to how they were, will they?" Ashan strained to pull himself off the ground with the highest bar at the front of his cell but failed to get even halfway. He tried a second time and a third before dropping to the floor and let out a frustrated groan.

"No." Tark pulled himself up on the bars of his own cell with only one hand. "Push the ground."

"I'm tired."

"You are tired because you spent so long doing nothing. This is how you make yourself not tired, boy. Unlike counting the bricks of your cell wall, this also won't drive you mad."

Ashan watched Tark do five more one-handed pull-ups before lowering himself to the floor. Pushing himself off the ground repeatedly seemed silly but, as Tark said, it was far more entertaining than counting bricks. In fact, he'd already forgotten much of the pattern and the total number of bricks since learning the blasphemous teachings from Tark. Though, really, he had learned that he'd been lied to by Erekej his entire life about...well, so much.

"Do you think they'll kill all of us when they have enough new prisoners to replace us?"

"No. They would have to answer for that, and they have no good explanation for what has happened here already."

"What happened here?"

Tark gave a slight smile before answering. "Something destroyed the illusion of control everyone thought they had."

Tark switched to pushing himself up again and they fell into silence for a while. Where Ashan could barely push himself off the ground thirty times before the task grew difficult, Tark could do so fifty times with only one arm before switching arms.

It was then that the prisoners wearing white shirts arrived with food, as had been happening for a short while now, and Tark ceased his working out to attempt to engage them in conversation. They refused him as they always did and went about their work of delivering food to each cell. Ashan was too excited by the tray of food he received to attempt speaking with them himself, but he also didn't know what sort of information Tark was after. They went about their work quickly and slowly vanished in the distance.

"Why don't they speak to us?" Ashan asked once they were beyond sight.

"I assume that they know we are being beaten for refusing to work and are afraid to be seen sympathizing with us."

There was a soft thud in the distance and Ashan pictured someone practicing falling, as Tark had taught those within sight and, in turn, they had taught to those beyond. The same had been done with punching and kicking techniques. You basically fell backward, not letting your head or elbows hit the ground so that when a guard pushed you, you avoided the annoying broken finger, dizziness, or serious head injuries. *You need your head to think and your fingers for making effective fists.* Ashan repeated the mantra Tark had taught him.

"There is always hope." Frezz, the newly arrived farmer who was arrested for poaching, called from a few cells down. How he could hear their conversation was a wonder.

Tark laughed and called back. "We can also hope dragons will fly from the pages of books, burn the king to ash, and set us free." A dull thud sounded again.

"Hope is a friend in the dark." Frezz replied.

"We should never let ourselves become stuck as men with nothing to lose. There's a dark path there I've seen soldiers travel down. Remember that." Tark said more quietly to Ashan, his face growing suddenly serious.

"Good evening, Edrick." the voice of the guard pulling sentry duty echoed from down the hall. Ashan recognized Edrick's name from overhearing the occasional conversation between guards, but that meant little to him. "How's the wife doing?"

"Well, time for the guard rotation. How very exciting." Tark said with a smile and a tone suggesting he was excited. There came a tinkling, a scraping of metal grinding softly against metal, and then another dull thud. A moment later there was a murmur.

"I bet you an apple the guard has gas." He gave Ashan an excited smile.

"You don't have an apple. Besides, they always have gas." Ashan gave the man a smile.

"Someday I will have an orchard full of the biggest apples you have ever seen!"

"And what exactly will you do with that?"

"I will make them into pies and sell them!"

"Soldiers make pies?" Ashan laughed. "Can you even cook?"

Ashan heard the faint shuffling that made him wonder if the guards were changing or sorting through a small pile of clothes and then hushed whispers. He looked at Tark, but Tark was just frowning at him as if thinking of a clever retort. "I will find myself a wise woman, make her my wife, and she will teach me to cook! You just watch!" Ashan rolled to his feet, quietly stepped up to the bars of his cell, and pressed his face as far through as he could. Most of the torches had burned down low so they offered pour lighting now. He heard something being dragged in the distance, the creaking of a cell's door, and then silence again. A moment went by before he heard the soft jangling of keys and a lock being worked. He turned and found Tark signaling for Ashan to remain silent. Not as skilled in moving silently as Tark, Ashan did not move other than to turn his head so he could look back down the hall. He quieted his breathing and strained to catch the slightest sound. Somewhere, far off in the distance, drums began beating. He imagined a field of soldiers training before a set of giant drums and dismissed the thought for the many questions it suggested. Tark stalked across his cell to the pile of clothing he had ripped into long strips. Quietly, he wrapped one hand and then the next to protect his knuckles, as he did each day before he set to work punching the brick wall at the rear of his cell.

"Tark?" a voice wafted through the air.

"That way." Another voice replied.

A few moments later, two men appeared from around a corner. One man carried a lantern with a low flame that gave off just enough light for them to see where they were going. As they drew nearer, Ashan saw that the man holding the lantern also carried a long knife and the other carried a sword. He glanced over and saw that Tark was stretching his arms, as he always did when he was expecting to fight with a guard. "Tark?" one of the men called softly. Now only a few cells away, Ashan saw that these men wore only tattered shorts. Their faces suggested that they were nearly Tark's age, but they weren't warriors like him.

"I am here." Tark announced loudly, obviously not feeling the fear that had Ashan's heart thumping along and his knees wobbling.

"You are Tark?" They stepped up to the cell and raised the lantern to shed light on Tark's face.

"I am. Who are you?"

"I am Leatto, a common thief."

"I am Ulreth. I killed men for money."

"Do the guards send cutthroats now?" Tark replied angrily. "Are they such cowards?"

"No. The guards are slain." Leatto explained and shifted the lantern to illuminate his knife. The blood was fresh.

"I am Tark. I am...no, I WAS a soldier who attempted to murder another soldier." he replied. "That is who I used to be."

Ulreth did not hesitate. He stepped up to the cell and slipped in key after key until the lock gave way. Together the two pulled open the cell door slowly. Tark stepped out and, glowering, spoke: "Give me the keys." They complied without speaking. Tark made three

73

powerful strides to Ashan's cell and began trying keys. This close to the man, Ashan was overcome with a sense of awe and fear. There was a look of cold dedication in the man's eyes he hadn't seen before. This was a man who wanted something and was willing to move mountains to achieve his goal. The look in his eyes said he knew the mountains were already preparing to move because he was coming their way. When the door swung open, Ashan just stood there glaring at it. "Come."

"How did you come to be free." Tark asked them.

"Keset. She flashed her pretty eyes upon a guard this last week." Ashan had difficulty understanding the man's accent. Leatto held up a hand to Ulreth and Ulreth nodded to him.

"She pretended she was interested in a guard and the fool opened her cell. She killed him. She set me free first and gave me the keys. Told me to free others and to find you."

"She said she would do this thing, but we did not believe." Ulreth added.

"A man named Ar'ran told us where to find you."

"Ar'ran? Is he a prisoner here?" Tark asked, shock clear on his face.

"He is and he said to tell you that everything is water under the bridge."

"Water is always under the bridge. This man is Ot in the head." Ulreth said with a chuckle.

"I told you it is a saying here."

"Take they keys and free everyone you can." Tark said to Ashan.

Whispers grew in the dark and, before long, there were clusters of people in the halls wearing the bloodied armor from slain guards.

Some had taken up daggers, swords, or make-shift clubs that had been the legs of chairs. Most gave Ashan a quick nod of approval when they came upon him to gather those he had freed. Each person he freed gave him a quick hug or a whispered thanks before joining into or forming their own group.

He traveled down one hall and then another before spotting a boy half his age with another large ring of keys and a group of younger men helping him to free people. The boy gave him a smile and went about testing keys in the cell door he stood in before. Ashan waved back and continued until he found a hall where there were occupied cells and set himself to freeing those people.

Some time later, after he had doubled-back on nothing but empty cells, Ashan came upon a massive room filled with tables, brightly burning torches, and an army. It was an army of malnourished people dressed mostly in tattered clothing, holding few weapons, but it was an army none-the-less. The place appeared as though it might have once been a communal feasting room, but it had the look of having fallen to disuse some years ago. He found himself standing at the back of the crowd watching clusters of prisoners arrive. After a short while, an older man carrying a sword came and gave a wave that Ashan interpreted to mean there were no others coming.

"Slaves!" Tark rose above the crowd as he climbed upon a table, and everyone turned to face him. "Beggars!" He bellowed so loudly that Ashan was certain down to his bones that guards heard his words all the way from King's Wall. "Thieves, murderers, innocent people who were lied about, and children! My name is Tark and, as a soldier who nearly killed another soldier, I deserved to be sent here for what I did. Some of you also deserved to be here, but this has not been a place of justice; instead, it has been a place of arbitrary cruelty and starvation." The people cheered at these words and many raised fists into the air, their expressions turning angry or determined. "People starve to death in the streets and if they dare to take as little as a loaf of bread, they are thrown into this hellish pit of despair and inhumane torment for years!

I say we must end this tyranny! I say we must fight against those who oppress us. I would rather die than to live without justice!"

"Justice!" One voice rang out in the crowd alone.

"Yes!" Another came.

"We must have just laws that serve us all equally! Not laws that permit lords and ladies to trample us with carriages and then jail us for damages and injuries to a horse! I may smell as bad as a horse's rear end, but I am a person! I own me!"

"I own me!" The words were called back by several people immediately and then again by more. On the third shout, it seemed nearly everyone was yelling those words.

The little army departed the room through a single door on the far wall that opened to stairs. Through the crowd, Ashan barely caught a glimpse of a set of doors swinging open before he heard the clang of steel and a loud scream. At the top of the stairs, the army surged forward along a wide hall. When he reached the top of the stairs, he discovered three dead guards and a growing puddle of blood. Whatever weapons or armor they had possessed before death were missing now. He gave them a silent prayer, that they might find peace in death, and jumped over the bloody pool.

Clanging and screaming arose in the distance as he entered a dark hall with glowing orbs hanging from sconces on either side. The little army slowed for but a moment before surging again. He came upon a set of wide doors at the end of the dark hall and found five corpses there. Four guards and one man in rags who might have been seventy years old with a cut upon his stomach and an open wound in the middle of his forehead that suggested he had been stabbed by a sword. He gave these men a prayer and passed through the doors to find a grand hall filled with bright sunlight that hurt his eyes.

This room was full of darkly stained wooden chairs with cushions, small tables, and paintings hung all along the wall. Atop the small tables sat silver serving trays, pure white pitchers, and bowls of sliced fruits. To his right was a wall of glass and through it was the all-too-familiar royal courtyard. A number of people grabbed handfuls of the sliced fruit as they crossed the hall to a set of decorative white doors that appeared to have been torn from their hinges. Excited shouts rose from ahead and the little army gained speed.

When he crossed through the doorway, he found what had caused the commotion. The little army had entered yet another feasting hall. There were five rows of tables pushed together to appear as one long table with nearly a hundred high-backed chairs set at the ready. Red streamers stretched from the walls to the center where a great chandelier hung with soft white orbs of light dangling from it. Upon the tables, plates sat piled high with still-steaming meats that Ashan didn't recognize. Cups sat full, candles burned, and about half the placements were prepared with silverware. *They are setting up for a feast*, Ashan thought as he turned toward the nearest table. People were already shoveling food into their mouths. Some took handfuls of this or that and moved on toward two massive doors at the other side of the hall while others stood or sat at tables to get their fill. Ashan wanted nothing more than to eat and he saw the same in the faces of those around him.

He made his decision and ran for the nearest table. He snatched up a handful of sliced red meat that was covered in a dark brown gravy and scanned the table for something to drink. A flicker of white in his peripheral vision caught his attention and he was startled by a sudden change in the rhythm of those far-away drums. Looking up, he scanned the crowd for what had caught his attention and caught a glimpse of a pale face through a gap between people that closed quickly. *Sa'teshka*, the name came to mind unbidden, and his heart jumped.

Sa'teshka turned, studying the crowd, and their eyes met. Sa'teshka's eyes widened in recognition, and he was motionless for a second. Then he screamed, face contorting into rage, but his words were lost behind the sound of pounding feet, clanking plates, and the shouts of the little army. He moved.

Sa'teshka tackled Ashan and, as they fell, Ashan recalled Tark's teachings on controlling a fall. He balled his hands into fists, threw his arms and head forward to keep them from slamming into the floor, and forced the air from his lungs. After landing, Sa'teshka quickly sat upon Ashan's midsection to pin him into place and let out a vicious snarl. He placed one hand around Ashan's throat and the other took hold of one of his wrists. He repeatedly slammed Ashan's hand upon the ground, stopping only when Ashan's hand went numb, and he lost hold of his food.

"This food isn't for you!" Sa'teshka screamed.

Ashan tried to buck Sa'teshka off himself, but the man held his position firmly. He released Ashan's wrist after a second and reached over the edge of the nearest table. He returned with a large pitcher and poured the thing out onto Ashan as if to add insult to injury. His stomach growled angrily and, without realizing it, Ashan began to strike the man in the face. Sa'teshka didn't even seem to notice the strikes as he grabbed another pitcher and emptied onto Ashan. This time, some of the liquid got in his eyes and Ashan had to stop striking the man to rub it away so that he could see. Once he could see again, Ashan began looking for a knife or fork he could use to stab Sa'teshka.

Pallid, quavering hands swept across Sa'teshka's face. The bony fingers pressed deeply into his cheeks, and he froze. His eyes shifted to those too-thin fingers and he turned in place before yelling angrily. "Get away! Don't touch me!" He released Ashan's throat and stood. He flailed at those thin arms, batting them away, but after a moment, one hand closed its fingers around Sa'teshka's neck. A second later, a second hand joined the first and Sa'teshka wailed as if in pain. He kicked at them and clawed at their arms, but they did not respond. The third man appeared as if from nowhere and took hold of Sa'teshka's flailing legs. Together they shifted him about in their hands and slowly stepped away from where Ashan lay on the floor. Then, all at once, they heaved Sa'teshka across the hall. He crashed face-first upon the far wall with a sickening crack. Then he fell, leaving behind a smear of blood, and settled upon the floor motionless. The three men watched for a moment before turning to face Ashan.

"Ashan." They moved uncharacteristically fast and without the sounding of their invisible chains. Kneeling at his side, each looked to him with pleading eyes. "Ashan." Whichever one spoke he was unsure. Their mouths all moved in unison, but the sound seemed to come from nowhere. "Flee. Do not fight." Together they lifted Ashan from the floor and set him on his feet. "This way is death." One of them took one of his hands and placed in it a silver ring with a single black stone upon it. "Take this to Isirdost. Tell the high king that the danger is great."

"What is this?" Ashan asked as one of the men took the ring from his palm and slipped in onto Ashan's finger.

"A curse and a blessing. Go back. Go with Frezz." They pushed him softly and a moment later his legs took over. He did not look back.

It was only when Ashan reached the familiar halls of the dungeon that he let his mind wander a bit and slowed to stop the pains in his legs. He crossed the area where the little army had formed and considered what danger they were heading into that those three men had just saved him from and begged for the gods to spare as many as they could. *Why spare me?* He looked down at the ring, which was barely visible in the darkness of the dungeon and wondered why they'd given it to him. *Perhaps it means something?* Just then, he stopped and glanced about. His cell was just down a few more halls and he knew no other manner of escape. *There must be other doors that take people out of here.* He closed his eyes and listened, hoping he would hear footsteps and that they would lead him to Frezz.

"STOP!" Ashan glanced backward and saw a guard step out from a cell not far behind him. Spotting the guard's sword, Ashan swore at himself for not grabbing something to use to defend himself and ran.

A moment later, Ashan came to a split in the hall. He glanced left and right and found only cells and low-burning torches. "Frezz!" he yelled as he turned back to find that the guard was approaching quickly with his sword drawn. *This was a mistake,* he screamed at himself. *Run! We'll die!*

"Ashan?" As if summoned, Frezz stepped out from a nearby cell. Somewhere the man had found himself a tall walking staff and a water-skin.

"Frezz! Guard!" He pointed. Frezz walked with the casual stride of a man asked to look at a rock upon the ground. Wondering if the old farmer had lost his wits, Ashan turned to face the other hall and immediately spotted two guards approaching.

"Down!" Frezz shouted.

Instinct took over and Ashan found himself diving to the floor with reckless abandon. Along the way he recalled his falling lessons, closing his hands to protect his fingers and emptying his lungs, and he gave Tark a silent thanks. Looking up at Frezz, he let out a shout of surprise as the end of that staff sprouted numerous little flames. The flames danced about unnaturally and grew as if the staff's end had been doused with oil. A heartbeat passed and the flames stretched out, engulfing the end of the staff and stretching outward furiously. Frezz yelled and the fire leapt from his staff. A gust of air hit Ashan a second later, forcing him to close his eyes for a long moment. When he opened them again, all he could see was fire. He rolled over until he found a wall and glanced about for an escape route but found only flames. As quickly as they had appeared, they vanished without a trace. He scrambled up to his feet and found that the lone guard lay dead and blackened upon the floor no more than three steps away. Frezz's staff still burned as he approached.

"Retreat!" Someone yelled and when Ashan turned, he found the other guards were no longer approaching. "Call for reinforcements! He uses magic!" The forward guard hissed.

The rear guard stepped forward, raised a hand bearing a knife, and drove the blade down into his companion's neck. He turned and twisted the blade quickly before removing it in a quick motion. Then the guard lifted his companion's arm, stepped under it as if to support his fellow, and began walking the dying guard forward. Ashan couldn't help but to compare it to all the times he'd seen a drunken person being helped along the roadside in just this fashion. The guard tried to elbow his assailant, gurgled, and spewed up blood twice before jerking and slumping. The living guard walked over and carefully dropped the man he had murdered on top of the guard Frezz had killed and knelt at his side. For a second Ashan thought the guard was going to say a prayer, but then he took the coin bag from the guard's belt and began cleaning his blade on the guard's shirt.

"What's with all the yelling, kid?" The guard stood and gave Ashan a smile that reminded him of the one Erekej often gave when he thought he was being clever, but the guard's eyes lacked malice. There was something else there, but Ashan couldn't place it, but the way the man smiled at him made him want to trust him.

"Did something go wrong?" Frezz asked. "Are more coming with you? Any more guards?"

"I don't think anybody is following me." Unsure, Ashan glanced down the hall to be sure. "He saw me just a bit down the way. Those three old men, they said to go with you. They said to go to Isirdost."

"They're not coming with us?" the guard asked incredulously.

"It appears not."

"They were coming?" Ashan asked.

"I'm sure they have their reasons. They always do."

"They are too stubborn. Lead the way." Frezz frowned, but the guard smiled.

"Right. This way, kid. Timing is crucial and we may need to do some fighting."

"What time is it?" Ashan asked as the guard turned and began walking quite quickly. He grabbed the fallen guard's sword and hurried to follow behind Frezz.

"Late in the day. Later than I would like, unfortunately." he replied.

"Later than you would like? What does that mean?"

"We don't want anybody to hear us." Frezz spoke softly as he placed a hand on Ashan's shoulder and pulled him to his side. "We walk far enough behind him so any real guards we encounter won't know we're all together."

"He's not a real guard?"

"No."

"But-"

"I will explain later. For now, keep an eye out for anybody following us."   They trailed a good thirty strides behind and paused at each intersecting hall while the man checked for guards. When he returned, they would move along in whatever direction he led them. On two such occasions, Ashan thought he heard fighting in the distance, but Frezz gave no sign of hearing the sounds or concern. After what felt like hours, they came upon a door that opened to a stairway that led up for a hundred strides. Ashan waited with Frezz as the man went up the stairs and passed through a door at the top. Only moments passed before the man opened the door and waved at them to follow. He shut the door and Ashan followed Frezz up the stairway.

Just as the man had told Ashan, it was late in the day. The world was eerily quiet and the air crisp, like winter was only a few moons away. Ahead lay a stable at least twice the size of any Ashan had seen before and to his left and right were large, fenced areas, where he assumed horses would be trained or exercised. Nothing in the far distance appeared familiar, save the wall, but he could not tell which of the walls it was. A moment went by before Frezz nudged Ashan forward and ran toward the stable. Their sudden arrival spooked several horses near the entrance, which caused several horse heads to pop into view. Frezz waved for Ashan to follow, and they continued directly through the building. After the smells of the dungeon, the smell of horse droppings was almost pleasant and the soft straw beneath his feet was a sore reminder of his lack of footwear these past...*months?*

At the opening on the other side, Frezz paused to study the world beyond. Beyond the doorway, there was a fenced in area and beyond that there was a short white wall and houses stood just on the other side of that. Tall houses in white that all leaned against each other to appear as one large building with many doors.

"Take slower breaths. Focus on controlling your breathing." Frezz said, finally turning to face Ashan.

"Where's your friend?"

"Checking the way ahead."

They ran to the short wall, climbed it quickly, and ran to the nearest space between buildings. They kept to the alleys as they traveled, halting at each intersecting street to check for people, and whenever Ashan needed to catch his breath or rest his legs. The further they traveled, the more guards and people they spotted in the streets. They crossed ten large streets lined with nearly identical buildings before Ashan realized which wall it was that he had seen. *We're in the center! We'll never get out!* The realization nearly caused him to run directly into a large stack of empty crates piled up at the end of the alley, but Frezz caught him just in time. He pictured how far it was to the outskirts of the capital and all the strength left his legs, causing him to fall to his knees.

"Are you well?" Frezz knelt in front of him and handed Ashan his water-skin.

"We're-" He took a moment to drink and catch his breath. "We're in the center of it all!"

"Breathe. Calm yourself. We will be fine. We have planned for this."

"You planned it all out? You were a prisoner. You were locked up. You said you were jailed for hunting-"

"I didn't tell you the truth. I will, but we need to keep moving or we will miss our easiest opportunity to get beyond the wall." Frezz offered his hand for Ashan.

As the crowds grew, so too did the number of city guards. As they crept slowly nearer to the wall, a fear grew inside Ashan that he had not expected to ever experience again. *Erekej could be here somewhere. Anywhere! He could have been looking for me this whole time! He could have hung up reward posters! Anybody could recognize me! He could put the bond back on me! He could own me again!* A trumpet blared nearby, someone yelled angrily, and he heard faint drums begin beating. Anger rose inside him, and he forgot the pain in his side and the burning in his chest. *I'd rather die!* Fear reminded him that the rewards for stolen or lost slaves were often substantial, but he bashed it away with all the anger he could muster. *I. WOULD. RATHER. DIE.*

"So sorry, madam." Someone said.

"Just a plate, my dear." a woman replied.

"That trumpeter really startled me."

"Me too, dear. No worries." Ashan glanced around the corner to see who was talking. He caught a glimpse of a woman dressed in white, huddled down to pick up pieces of what had been a stark white plate.

"Ashan." Frezz pulled him back into the alley and gave him a look of warning. "Focus. Whatever thoughts that you are suffering, put them from your mind. Focus on controlling your breathing." Ashan only now realized that he was breathing harder than when he had been running.

"Yes, m-uh, Frezz."

More twisting alleys followed, and they came upon the largest and cleanest road that Ashan had ever seen. Unlike the lower city, there were no market stands or older buildings along this street. Each building was made of the same material, built in the same design, painted white and bore the silhouetted crown upon the front door. The roadway was almost perfectly flat with a slightly raised stone walkway on either side and there was nothing that Ashan could call trash anywhere he looked. The people he saw were, judging from their fine clothing in every color and parasols, nobles. The wind carried heavy aromas of fresh food and his stomach growled audibly. They were very near to King's wall now, with a gate and guards only a few blocks further up the big street. *So close!* Then he looked at himself and realized how quickly he would be noticed if he stepped out onto that street. He looked over at Frezz and saw him studying the sky.

"Where is your friend?"

"Behind you."

Ashan nearly screamed in freight at the sudden words in his ear. He spun in place and almost yelled yet again at the sight of the solder. The man now wore a purple sash across his chest, gold-gilded armor with and a slightly different helmet that bore three golden dots at the front. Ashan didn't know the significance of the dots, but he assumed it meant a great level of authority. The man pressed a bundle of black cloth into Ashan's hands and then tossed a similar bundle to Frezz. He smiled and gave Frezz a deep bow.

"A little over-dressed?" Frezz asked as he unfolded the cloth, revealing it to be a black robe with a big hood and a golden crown embroidered upon the chest and back.

"Priest clothing?" Ashan asked.

"One must dress appropriately for their role in the play."

"The plan was to be discrete." Frezz said sharply. "This is not discrete."

"A high-ranking lord can be discrete!" the man protested playfully. "Besides, we don't have time now to change anything. Our gate captain will be replaced any time."

Ashan pulled the robe on with as much haste as he could and marveled at how soft the material was. There was also a pleasant aroma that he could not identify, but thought it smelled of flowers and fresh dirt. He pulled the hood forward as much as possible to hide his face and waited for Frezz to do the same.

"Priests and those training to become priests..." the man paused and adjusted Ashan's cloak at the shoulders before continuing. "That's you, kid. They often take vows of silence, which means you do not say anything at all. Even the guards at the gate can't command you to speak. It's a great role for a first timer like you!" He gave Ashan a big smile and then marched toward the street.

Frezz motioned for Ashan to go ahead and began pulling his robe on. To Ashan's surprise, they marched right out to the middle of the road and turned left. He kept his eyes glued onto the back of the guard and waited for a signal, wondering what would happen at the gate. Normally when passing through a gate, Ashan had to show a letter Erekej had given him to be allowed through or the guards would turn him away angrily. Sometimes, they would search through his goods first, but the event usually meant waiting for more important people to get through first. Lords, ladies, soldiers, other guards, merchants, and workers of all levels were more important than he had been.

"Lord Grathson!" a voice called from behind.

"Yes?" Frezz's friend spun about in place on one heel and began walking backwards without slowing.

"Did you hear there was trouble in the dungeon earlier? An escape and an attack aimed at our king!" Ashan instinctively turned to find the source and found an old woman shrouded deep beneath a heavy black cloak atop a wagon pulled by two oxen. The youth of her voice did not match the age of her face by several decades.

"News travels like the wind. Full of flies and hot air."

"Not quickly enough, I'm afraid." She gave a stern nod and then Frezz pushed Ashan towards the wagon. Ashan almost asked where he should sit but remembered what the man had said to him about being silent at the last second. Frezz joined the woman on the bench and Lord Grathson walked alongside the wagon. As they approached the gate, Ashan slumped and pulled his hood as far forward as he could manage and fixed his eyes on his own feet.

"Out of the way!" Lord Grathson began shouting. Startled, Ashan looked to Frezz first for direction.

"That fool!" the woman cursed under her breath and Frezz hummed his agreement.

Ashan watched in horror as Lord Grathson cleared a path up to the gate, bellowing curses at anybody too slow to remove themselves from his path. The high-born, offended by his obscene loudness, glared at him as though he were dragging a dead body through the street and intentionally spreading guts and blood upon every surface possible. Ashan cursed inside, certain that this scene would soon develop into a fight, but he remained seated. *This is our only way out, you fool!*

"Captain Veylin! You sour dog!" He cheered as if having seen a friend for the first time in months.

"Lord Grathson." A man called back. The crowd parted and through them walked a slender man in black hide armor and a short sword in hand. His long black hair clung to his face, and he sweated as if just interrupted in the middle of a sparring session. The coloring of his face suggested that he had either recently lost his lunch or was about to and

87

his voice wavered in a way that was all too familiar to Ashan. *Fear*. "Need I remind you to keep the peace yet again?" Ashan picked up on the threat, but wondered if Lord Grathson would notice.

"Veylin, I must get these priests to safety. Murderers have escaped from the dungeons. So, blast the peace and make way." he screamed with a venom nearly equal to Erekaj's.

"An escape? From the dungeons?"

"Yes. Clean out your ears and open this gate. The high-king would not be pleased to hear that a priest and his student were slain because a gate-captain spent valuable time telling a lord to mind the peace."

"Open the gate." Veylin shouted.

"Good man." Lord Grathson said as he headed back towards the wagon. Veylin turned towards the gate and took two steps before he suddenly stopped and turned back, his face determined. The wagon lurched forward.

"Pardon...Lord Grathson, but." His face was growing almost white. "But you did say that when you saw me today that you would...settle our little...debt."

"Ah. Right you are." He reached to his belt and worked free a small coin-purse in a flash of finger-working that Ashan couldn't follow. He placed them into Veylin's hands and spoke softly. "If the real Lord Grathson makes an appearance, say it was Lord Vasktok who you saw."

"What if Lord Vasktok comes about?"

"He's dead." Lord Grathson replied.

Veylin's eyes shot wide in sincere surprise at those words. He worked his jaw, tears formed in his eyes, and choked out the words. "My sister is avenged. Thank you."

"You are welcome, friend."

The second gate required nothing more than a shouted "Let us through." and on they went without so much as a second glance, but the ease of their going did not lessen Ashan's worries. As the sun sank, there came to be more soldiers in the streets than civilians, and he saw that people were being stopped for questioning at many intersections. Fortunately, the guards and soldiers gave them only a quick glance before moving on. The streets eventually emptied of people, shops became shuttered and all the while, Ashan repeatedly imagined seeing Erekej running around every corner. Eventually, the only people left in the streets were the bound...people not important enough to protect from any emergency.

By the time they reached the eastern slums, it was well and truly dark out. They departed the big road and traveled south a way before coming to a dilapidated three-story building that appeared nearly ready to fall in on itself. The windows were shuttered with wood planks of varying size and age, there were several holes in the exterior walls, and the roof sagged terribly. By the side of the front door, there stood just one off-white stone pillar tall enough that it might have once supported a porch that didn't exist now. There was no sign of another pillar and Ashan imagined that the others had been stolen ages ago. People who lived in the slums were known for theft and finding uses for anything.

"Why didn't they come?" The woman questioned as she jumped down to lead the oxen into the building. The large doorway was a bit slanted, as if the entire building had slowly leaned one way over the years. He wondered if the thing might just fall over on them once they were inside.

"I don't know yet." Frezz answered.

The inside of the building looked even worse than the outside. Someone had added mismatching planks of wood to support the roof and walls here and there, but they had warped over time, and many had come free over the years. Looking up at the underside of the roof, Ashan was certain that the thing was about to break apart into several sections that would each fall their own direction. Inside, there were two pens for keeping animals and a large mound of hay in the far corner, which gave the air a comforting smell compared with the dungeon; however, the real comfort came from being out of sight, where even if Erekej came walking by he wouldn't see Ashan. The old woman and Frezz freed the oxen from the wagon and placed them into separate pens. They then pushed the wagon towards the corner opposite the hay.

"You didn't get to ask them?"

"No. Ashan here said that they sent him after. I guess they decided to stay." Frezz explained.

"Maybe they were too afraid of the risk."

"Perhaps."

"You don't sound pleased about it." She replied softly.

Ashan jumped out of the wagon and started heading over toward the large, slanted opening to look out at the world. Lord Grathson appeared in the doorway at that moment and appeared to be working at the straps of his armor.

"He's not happy because I altered the plan." he explained.

"You changed the plan without letting me in on it." Frezz snapped.

"You changed the plan?" she and Frezz walked over, and both began helping him out of the armor he wore.

"Yes." he gave the woman a big grin.

"And what, exactly, was wrong with our original plan?"

"Nothing. It would just be easier to reveal Frezz as a spy. It worked well too. They immediately trusted me, and that trust allowed me to move about freely. Hell, I didn't have to sneak about at all. People were

90

so happy to meet the new guard who caught a spy on his first day to question why I was in certain places." He explained with a laugh.

"Yeah, and I had to spend the entire time in the dungeon in this illusion." Frezz complained.

"They couldn't have beaten you that much. Probably not even as bad as I was treated in Del Mor'vast!"

"Del Mor'vast was entirely your own doing, my love." the woman kissed the man quickly on the cheek and gave him a stern look.

"I-" he paused a moment and sighed in annoyance. "Yes, but you left me there a whole moon!"

"You deserve it again after this!" Frezz pulled off his priest's robe and dropped it to the floor. "I need this off now."

"Right." the woman turned to Frezz, who bowed at her deeply. She reached out to his head and began searching through the hair at the back of his head.

"Ashan, you might want to brace yourself." Frezz said.

"Don't be scared, kid." Lord Grathson added with a wink and a smile.

Eventually, the woman pulled a small cord out from Frezz's hair. She pulled at the cord with one hand while untangling knots with the other. A few moments later, she pulled free a small glowing object that let out a brilliant white light from within a knotted mass of hair. She quickly cut it free with a small knife and Frezz rose with a pained groan. "Thanks." His lips became a blur of color as they moved and when he brought his arms up to his face, they left behind a trail of pink smoke.

"Don't worry, kid." The woman said. "Just a little illusion magic wearing off." She gave him a comforting smile.

Frezz rubbed at his face with both hands and a swirling mass of pink dust flew out like a bursting cloud. "You nearly ran out." The

91

woman explained as she tucked the small object up a sleeve. Frezz waved his hands through the building cloud and stepped through it. The creature that appeared then was not the man Ashan knew as Frezz – it wasn't even entirely human. His face was like that of a lizard's made almost human by the gods and his scaled skin shifted from one green to another as he moved. His ears rose to sharp points like those of an elf and his bare feet were like a bird's, with three long toes at the front and two short ones at the back with black claws. The claws on his fingers were much shorter but appeared just as dangerous. He walked about in a wide circle, the image of a human breaking apart and floating away as smoke and came to stop before Ashan.

"This is the real me." Frezz said at last.

"You're a... a lizard-man?"

"Dragon-blooded." Frezz said.

"So, part dragon?"

"Sort of."

"I take it our investigation is over?" the woman asked.

"It is for me. I will share what I know with those of my order, and they will devise a plan. For now, I can do no more. You and Martokal should leave this place as soon as you can." Frezz said.

"You know our history with the brotherhood." She waved her hand as if swatting away a bug.

"We know the risks." Martokal said as he stacked the armor up along the wall.

The woman reached into the front of her robe and withdrew a silver chain with a small glowing rock on the end of it. She undid the clasp, pulled it free, and tucked it away into her sleeve. Immediately, her long gray hair began to climb up from the bottom of her shoulders to just below her ears and darkened. The wrinkled, sagging skin upon her face pulled back, smoothed out and darkened, leaving only a small haze in the air of dark pink dust. A scar stretched across her face from the left peak of her forehead, across the left eye, over the nose, and ended just below her lips. While her eyelids bore faint lines, the eye itself appeared undamaged. She couldn't even be thirty years old.

As she ran a hand through her hair a few times, Ashan saw that she was missing the small finger on that hand. There was also a thick black triangle and some form of writing forming two circles within it, which he had heard southerners used to mark criminals, but he didn't know the language. She gave Ashan a reassuring smile and turned to face Martokal, who smiled back at her.

"I wish you would be more cautious." Frezz said. "Monarchs do not form alliances with the brotherhood lightly."

"I thank you for the concern, old friend." She smiled at him. "Will you be staying a while or heading out directly?"

"Ashan and I will head to Isirdost tomorrow." Frezz replied.

"I'll make a stew." She replied.

"Take these oxen and wagon. They are well rested and strong. We've had it loaded with supplies in case we required a quick escape." Martokal said.

"Thank you." Frezz said.

"You're taking me to Isirdost?" Ashan asked Frezz as the other two turned and headed outside.

"Do you have something to stay for?" Frezz asked.

Ashan considered the question for a long moment before answering. "No."

"You will like Isirdost." Frezz patted him on the shoulder and made to follow his friends.

Overwhelmed by fear of being seen, Ashan buried himself in the hay and found it a marked improvement in comfort over his cell's stone floor. He closed his eyes for a long while and tried to calm himself but was plagued by images of soldiers finding him. Each time he pushed these thoughts aside, he remembered his cell, the beatings, and his few interactions with Sa'teshka. After a while, he stuck his head partly out from the hay and watched the world with suspicion. The world was quiet and dark until a fire was lit outside and there came the sounds of someone cooking.

Some while later, the woman brought a very wide and deep wooden bowl to Ashan. "Stew." She said as he sat up in the hay. "Eat up. You'll need your strength tomorrow." she gave him a smile as he took the bowl with both hands and sniffed at it. "It's beef stew. Very good for growing boys."

"Thank you, Lady..."

"Sielya." She offered him a wide smile. "Just Sielya. There are no lords, ladies or *masters* here. Just us. Just people." Ashan was suddenly reminded of Hank. It was her smile that, while nothing like Hank's, was the same.

The stew was as a gift from the gods compared with what Ashan was used to eating. It had a pleasantly biting spice that tingled on his lips and gave the hint of burning on his tongue which he had never experienced. It soothed his nerves and melted what felt like an ice-blade running through his center. As soon as he emptied the bowl, Frezz was at his side with a second. They traded and Ashan watched Frezz return to the fire outside before digging into it. Frezz made a gesture to Sielya as he sat and she turned to face Ashan, giving him a smile and a nod. As he chewed his first bite, he was reminded of his childhood. A quiet night around a roaring fire had been normal events

94

and, though he could not quite recall his parents' faces, he found a measure of comfort in the moment.

The flash of lightning in the distance woke Ashan just in time to discover Erekej stepping through the crooked doorway. Holding in a scream, Ashan silently dug himself deeper into the hay. *No!* His heart thrummed and he screamed in silent terror. Thunder rumbled through the air, shaking the building, and causing Ashan to tremble. Erekej turned slowly in place, searching up and down carefully. He sniffed at the air like a hound, each breath ragged. He'd seen Erekej at this point of rage only once before and the beating had left Ashan unable to walk properly for weeks. *He's going to see me! No, I'm not hiding. I'm just resting after working all day. This is where I'm supposed to be. He won't be mad if I am where I am supposed to be!* He plead to the gods for Erekej to miss him, to move on, to see that Ashan was in his proper place and that all was well. He curled up into a ball, hoping Erekej would just leave whatever scrap of food he'd brought and leave like he so often had before. Erekej turned in place so slowly that the sun rose, set again, and a great storm blew in from the horizon by the time he came to face the pile of hay. In the darkness, his eyes were alight with dancing red flames that illuminated his rage-twisted face.

Lightning struck nearby and a gust of howled loudly as it shook the old building. The wind clawed its way inside and began blowing the hay so that it swirled around Ashan and exposed him. Thunder clapped so loud that Ashan felt it deep inside and, in it, he heard the mocking laughter of a cruel god. Erekej's eyes locked onto Ashan then and he bellowed madly before charging for Ashan. The wooden paddle with the grooves, holes, and metal rivets appeared in Erekej's hand then and Ashan screamed.

Erekej swung and Ashan cowered before the mighty paddle, too afraid to even brace for the pain he expected. The blow sent him rolling over suddenly rocky terrain that poked and cut at his flesh. "I'm sorry, Master!" he screamed, and thunder filled the air. He climbed to his feet a moment later and found Erekej charging him again. Ashan turned to run and twisted his ankle on the very first step. He rolled twice upon the jagged rocks before stopping himself and looked back to Erekej. "Please, Master!" Erekej's body turned black, broke apart, and blew away in the wind like dust. The world tilted and he began to slide across the hard ground. He grabbed at the ground for anything to slow his fall, but only managed to cut his palms on the sharp rocks there.

"I wish I could tear your throat out." A man's voice rose above the thunder, and he slammed into flat ground.

Ashan rolled to his back and found himself in the room where Sa'teshka had thrown him against that wall, where he had nearly died. He lay in a corner a bit away from where he had been when the event had taken place and saw himself also scrambling across the floor blindly. *No, there had been a bright light,* he scrambled to his feet and ran to help his other self. He grabbed at himself but passed through that body as if it were a ghost and almost fell.

Through the doorway came that bulbous, massive man with the golden crown upon his head. He walked quickly over to the stumbling other Ashan, reached down with a great big smile upon his face, and took hold of the back of that Ashan's neck. He lifted that Ashan, grabbed a leg with his other hand, hefted him up over his head and threw that Ashan at the wall.

"There. Now fetch my property from it." High-king Hotar demanded as he walked back through the strange doorway and took his seat at the table therein.

"You've broken him!" Sa'teshka screamed as he ran into the room.

Ashan's copy moaned and shifted slowly upon the floor. He pulled himself into a sitting position clumsily with a groan of pain and began looking about the room with his head tilted one way. He leaned

96

back against the stone wall and took a deep, shuddering breath. Ashan walked over, knelt at his own side, and gasped when he saw that his head was misshapen in this version he was watching. He grabbed his own head and felt for any sign of lasting damage but found nothing.

"Have the bond ready to break." Someone said from the other room.

"Get your bag." Sa'teshka said. A long moment passed, and the other Ashan looked up at Sa'teshka with confusion clear on his face. "Get the package."

"Where is it?" Ashan turned and found a second Sa'teshka was also in the room and was addressing him. He glanced back and saw that the copy of himself and the first Sa'teshka were quickly being swallowed by darkness.

"I'm dreaming. This is a nightmare." he said mostly to himself. Even as he said it, he became aware of the sensation of stalks of hay poking at his sides and neck. It was a faint, but comforting, sensation. "I'm asleep."

"After a manner." Sa'teshka twisted his face and threw out one pale hand. The fist caught Ashan on the nose, and he was thrown back. He hit a wall and rebounded off it. "Dreams can still hurt though. Some more than real life. Tell me where it is!"

"Where is what?"

"The amulet."

The world turned and he fell upwards. Ashan jolted violently and raised both arms to brace for impact but found himself deep inside the hay. The two oxen nearby snorted and stomped in disapproval of his sudden movement. He crawled out from the hay and climbed to his feet.

"He's up." He heard Frezz's odd accent announce from outside.

It was a dream!

"I told you he needed sleep." Sielya said.

"How are you?" A middle-aged, balding man clearly dressed as a blacksmith, complete with apron and hammer walked into the building.

"There is more stew, if you want." Sielya appeared as the elderly lady with which Ashan was already familiar.

"It all really happened." He said more to himself than them. He reached up and felt his bare arm again to make sure. He checked the back of his mind for the link to Erekej. Again, nothing.

"Yes, and today we leave this place and all of that behind us." Frezz's voice came from the old blacksmith, who gave him a smile. Ashan assumed the man was attempting to reassure him, but when he smiled the false image of a human face stretched outward, almost into the shape of Frezz's real face.

"Don't do that, Frezz." Sielya said, giving the man a soft punch in the arm. "You'll scare people."

"Why? Was it not the right expression?"

"I've told you before..." she sighed. "Practice your human expressions in a mirror. You need to learn the differences between a happy smile and the smile of something that just found someone to eat. Besides that, every time you smile, the illusion stretches wrong, and it looks very weird. Almost scary. I need time to learn how to modify the spell to work on you correctly." She illustrated by grabbing her false nose and stretching it out. The image was nauseating to behold.

"I don't eat people."

"PEOPLE don't know that."

"Eat well, Ashan. I am going to check the gate to see if they are letting people out. I'll return soon." He turned away without another word.

Sielya watched in silence for a minute before turning, giving Ashan a once-over and clearing her throat. "So, Frezz tells me you had quite the day yesterday."

"Yes, Lady-er, Sielya." She turned and gave him a wave to follow. Ashan followed but kept his head down when they reached the outside world. There were now four logs around the fire pit, where a pot hung above a small fire. She quickly served him on a rough wooden plate, sat and gave him a warm smile.

"Don't let the bad times weigh you down. You are free now. Frezz will see to it that you make it somewhere safe. He can seem rough at times but know that he means well and always has your best interests in mind." She explained. Ashan didn't know how to respond and busied himself with eating.

Nearly an hour later, Frezz returned with a large sack of potatoes thrown over one shoulder and a mostly empty bag at his side. Sielya and Ashan were atop the wagon, rearranging supplies to disguise the wagon as that of a merchant. She threw shovels, wooden buckets, pots, pans, bags of apples, and a ton of empty crates on top. Ashan tried not to look at the bags of apples because it made him wonder if Tark had survived or been killed in the battle he himself had fled. Frezz tossed the potatoes at the rear of the wagon and offered the other bag to Ashan. "Change into these." he said.

"How's it look?" She asked.

"Easy. It seems there was a disturbance at the docks this morning and most guards and soldiers have been drawn there."

"Probably Martokal. He's been talking about sinking one of the big ships there as a distraction for weeks."

"Yes, I'm sure he would enjoy doing that. There are a few guards at the last gate and soldiers are hanging wanted posters." He gave what Ashan guessed was a chuckle.

"Are they accurate?" Sielya asked.

"Fairly."

"Weapons are at the bottom." Sielya said as she jumped down.

"Thank you."

"I'll follow you as far as the gate. If there is trouble, give me a sign and I'll create a distraction."

Ashan peered into the burlap sack and found a clean white button-up shirt with long sleeves, a green tunic, a pair of rugged brown shorts, and a pair of brown leather boots. He quickly ducked behind the wagon and changed. Everything was a bit large on him, but comfortable and soft.

"Ashan," Sielya called. "I'll see you again soon." she smiled.

"Yes, Lady-uh, yes, Sielya. Thank you."

"Take care of yourselves until then."

They traveled east and north for four uneventful, yet terrifying, days before Ashan's nerves were shot and he was forced to sleep for more than an hour at a time. When he woke on the fifth day, it was morning and they had escaped what he had always considered the unending city. Lush, green fields of food-crops stretched out in every direction, and he could see only a few structures. For maybe an hour he watched in silence as he tried to come up with what number of people it would take to properly tend to the amount of plant life he could see at any given moment. He knew almost nothing of growing food, aside from that it needed watering, keeping safe from animals, and that someone had to spread manure on the ground to make it grow new food each year. He imagined people shoveling animal leavings into carts and then shoveling it out onto the ground elsewhere and was thankful he hadn't been used for that sort of work. *How many would it take?* Of course, after the food was grown, it had to be picked and transported to the different marketplaces to be sold. Such work took people. *Slaves.* Wherever there were slaves, there would be owners and out here in the growing lands there would also be hired guards, or so he had heard. He kept a keen eye out for people in those endless fields.

"Do free people work these fields or are they all like me?"

"I believe it is mostly done by slaves in this kingdom." Frezz replied.

"Do farm workers have to do something to manure before putting it on the ground for growing things?"

"How do you mean?"

"Do they just gather it from where animals live and throw it on the ground here for plants?"

"I'm not certain. They may let animals graze the land, so they do their business here as they walk around. They may also employ magics to spread it about or just for the growing process." Frezz explained.

"You can use magic to make food?"

"Not to make it, but to help it grow, keep it from getting diseases and to keep it from going bad."

Ashan tried to imagine how any of that worked. "Why won't anybody help us?"

"You mean all of the slaves?"

"Yes." Ashan figured there must be thousands of slaves just to tend to the fields he could see currently, and perhaps only hundreds were needed to gather and distribute manure. The idea of using magic to make plants grow made him want to vomit. *Have I always been eating magic-grown food?*

"Slavery is profitable. This kingdom has three million slaves that don't have to be paid to work. One high-king rules supreme and no individual or group holds enough power or advantage over the others to challenge the system. One voice alone could do nothing but get itself crushed."

"There are three million slaves?"

"At best guess."

"That's a lot more than I thought were even people."

"Veysor is a large empire."

"What is Veysor?"

"The name of the lands your king rules."

"I thought that was Katora."

"Katora is just the capital city you lived in."

"That's just a city?"

"Yes, but it is one of the largest cities I've ever seen." Frezz's nonchalant explanation was difficult for Ashan to understand. *All I have known was just one city?*

"What about where you are from?"

"The Isles of Fire are free lands. No person owns another."

"Could they help?"

"Perhaps in time, but our elders fear your king. Alone, he is dangerous, but he has made an alliance with the Brotherhood of Blood, which makes him worse than dangerous."

"What is the Brotherhood of Blood?"

"Vampires obsessed with turning everyone else into their docile food supply."

"What does docile mean?"

"Obedient. They would love nothing more than for everyone else to be too scared to fight them. Aside from the threat they pose, the world is a big place and there are problems everywhere. Many seek a solution to the problems here, but nobody wants to invite a war with vampires."

"Is slavery normal?"

"Throughout most of the world in one form or another."

"I wish we could free them all."

"You are not alone in that desire, Ashan." Frezz clamped a hand down over Ashan's left shoulder and gave a soft squeeze.

"Couldn't someone just buy them all and free them?"

"It has been attempted a few times in a few places. Most of those who are freed quickly fall back into debt and will be working these fields again in a few moons. You know how this works?"

"I've heard stories."

"Are you familiar with why slaves rarely become free?"

"Yes. I owe my master three-thousand gold marks. More than I could ever hope to earn. He charges me for clothes, food, housing and medicine so that the debt keeps increasing."

"How did you gain debt in the first place?"

"I don't know. I was little."

"And your parents?"

"I... I don't know. Mast-...Erekej told me that they owed him money. They were supposed to pay him to get me back, but they disappeared."

"I am sorry to hear it."

"It happens to many."

"Indeed."

As he considered Frezz's words, he studied the world around them, and worries seeped into his thoughts. Though they hadn't seen another person for quite a while and he knew they were far from where he had always lived, he imagined Erekej suddenly appearing around every small rise in the ground on horseback with soldiers to recapture him. Out here in the wide-open world with no buildings, there seemed no place to run and hide, aside from the tall rows of green stalks, but those were off a fair bit farther than he could run easily or quickly. They went on in silence and Ashan tried to enjoy the view without thinking of the slaves that likely worked the fields or his parents.

Shortly before sunset, they arrived upon a wall of trees with a large sign standing before them that read "White Rock" in faded black lettering on a white background. The road turned gently to the left going into the trees for a good sixty paces and veered sharply to the right just before they came to a round clearing a hundred paces across. The outer perimeter of the clearing was lined with short wood buildings that almost seemed to have been built for children. In the center stood a white stone pillar twice as tall as Ashan and wide enough that it would take two tall men to reach around. It was surrounded by wide a bed full of red and blue flowers. Ashan examined the town carefully, noting that the signs hanging above doors didn't have words to name the businesses as he was accustomed to seeing; rather, they provided pictures to depict what sort of work was offered. There was a spool of thread with a needle on one, a butcher's knife on the next, and a hammer on the third. There was a space between buildings on the opposite side of the clearing that was just wide enough for a single wagon to pass that lined up with a path in the trees there. Through that, he saw several more buildings and either a large pond or a very small lake, but he wasn't sure how large a body of water had to be before it changed from being a pond to a lake.

They went around on the left side of the pillar and Ashan was surprised to find it bore no holes or markings of any sort. *Strange*, he thought as he tried to sort out its purpose. *An odd thing to name a town after,* he considered as he returned his attention to the road ahead. Beyond the gap, the dirt roadway split north and south just before the pond and wrapped around in a wide circle. There were, perhaps, fifty buildings within sight, each unevenly staggered around the pond with walkways leading from front doors out to the dirt road. There were small shacks, big houses, a long building with twenty doors, and several large patios. These buildings did not line up with each other and some even faced different directions. There was space between some of them that had been left unused and could have accommodated a few houses. There were only a few stone walkways, and he couldn't find a single street sign. Some of the houses had flowerbeds full of red, some yellow, and some had short shrubs instead. Some shared basic designs in small ways, such as the general size or relative distance to the road, but some had rectangular doors painted blue or round windows. Overall, it was a confused mixture of design, direction, and color. *Beautiful.*

They turned south and passed ten houses and a large warehouse before the road turned back to the east. He considered how easily he could identify one house from the other by its look – no address needed. *I don't do that job anymore,* he scolded himself. They came to a stop beside the building with twenty doors and Frezz climbed down from the wagon slowly and began to stretch his arms and back with several deep yawns. A second later, one of the doors opened and out strolled a group of men wearing plain clothing and wielding a cudgel, sword or ax. They walked casually, faces curious, but their weapons set Ashan's heart racing. Their skin was far more darkly tanned than what he was accustomed to seeing in the capital and he wondered if they were farmers. They eyed Ashan and he turned to face Frezz, wanting to say something but fearing to say anything at all.

Frezz walked casually around the wagon and gave the men a short wave. They faced Frezz and hefted their weapons either upright or onto a shoulder as if preparing to attack, but their faces were passive. *They could be guards. They might recognize me!* Instinct drove him to

105

check his surroundings for Erekej. After a few words, the men shifted into more relaxed stances, waved hands as if swatting a fly, and then gave a collective stare at the wagon for a moment.

"You're mad!" one of them practically shouted. It was followed by a collective nodding of heads and several loud guffaws. "Or a mad fool."

"It's a cheat, sir. What's wrong with your oxen? Water sickness?" The group approached slowly and eyed the two beasts. One of them seemed to eye Ashan more than the wagon, his eyebrows furling judgmentally. With a gut that hung over his belt by two hands, a bald head, and deep frown lines, he reminded Ashan of a trader who liked to scream as much as haggle to whom he had frequently made deliveries. He immediately wanted to dislike the man.

"I ask for five gold or five gold in value on trade." Frezz said, tone almost flat.

"You're joking. Did Gregor send you to vex me? Everyone knows his livestock has come down with the Dying Worms! I already told that old fool that I'll buy if he gets them back to health, but not sooner!"

"I am relocating south. Better trade opportunities. Time is crucial and I can make better time without having to stop at every town to feed and rest these beasts." Frezz said to the bald man.

"Relocating? Where you heading?"

"Whitetail River. Got family there."

"Didn't you come from the capital?"

"Yes, but the taxes and fees for trade there are outrageous." Frezz exclaimed.

"I hear ya! Damn king keeps raising taxes like we have all the money in the whole of creation!" the man turned to spit angrily.

"That's why I'm heading south." Frezz said.

"Well, can't say as I blame you. Lower taxes and I've heard trade is picking up." the man gave the wagon a long looking over. When his eyes met Ashan's, however, his brows furrowed deeply, and his expression turned sour. Ashan couldn't help but shift his gaze to his feet. "Now, listen here, stranger." the man swiveled on one foot and set his eyes upon Frezz. "We here do not permit the use or trade of slaves within the lands of Lord Turley. If you want, you can head up north two days to Turley Keep and he'll buy the boy's papers off you. The rate is ten gold and I suggest you take it for your own safety. If people find you with slaves in Turley lands...well, let's just say that you better be good with a sword."

"The boy is free." Frezz replied. "Though, if I may ask, why would your lord pay ten gold for any slave?"

"It's a courtesy. Sell or die, as we say here." The man turned to Ashan quickly. "Are you free, boy? You can speak honestly."

"Yes, ma-uh, sir."

"A shy one, huh? I believe you, but not long by the looks of you."

"Not long, sir."

"We need a room for the night as well." Frezz announced.

The room was four times larger than Ashan's cell had been. There were two beds separated by a small table, the walls had been recently painted a stark white, and the was even a window in the front wall that faced the pond. The air inside carried the faint hint of flowers and pipe tobacco, but the thick, soft bedding smelled cleaner than any he had ever known. *This must be what it is like to be rich,* Ashan thought as he wrapped himself in one of the blankets.

While Frezz slept on the other bed, Ashan ate his fill in apples and dried meat and, feeling safe for the first time in a long while, just enjoyed the silence and safety of the room. Once Frezz awoke, he sorted through the many bags they had hauled in from the wagon, laying out numerous knives on the bed before changing clothes. He put on a pair of black pants with a long-sleeved shirt, a thick coat that fell to his knees, high boots, and then began stowing all those knives about his body. Three went up each sleeve, one in each boot, and the rest were tucked into either side of the inside of his coat. He then fetched small glass vials from another of the bags and put them into several small pockets inside his coat. If it hadn't been for the serious way Frezz moved, Ashan would have made a joke about how much gold a man must have to require a coat with so many pockets.

"Frezz?"

"Yes?" He stopped, fake human face contorting with an odd expression, and he cocked his head to the side a bit farther than a human could. The image of the human he hid behind sort of crumpled up on itself like folding cloth.

"What are you doing? You look like you're preparing to fight someone."

"It's almost dark. Vampires cannot travel in daylight, but they're fast. We will have little time before they arrive." Frezz explained.

"Vampires?"

"Yes, they've been following us."

"How do you know that?" Ashan shot upright as the image of Sa'teshka came to mind.

"Whenever you've slept, I have gone and checked behind us. I am certain they found us last night, but too close to sunrise to risk an attack." Frezz explained.

"They cannot travel in daylight?"

"Sunlight burns at their skin like fire." Frezz explained.

"Sa'teshka was in the daylight once."

"He would have been using magic to temporarily protect himself." Frezz reached into one of the bags and pulled out a clear orb. He set it on the bed before Ashan, placed a single finger upon it, and spoke in gibberish. "This is your defense for tonight. All you must do is place a hand upon it and it will give off a light that will harm them, but only use it if they find you. The power in it is very limited." he explained.

"You want me to use magic?" he practically jumped backward, and half fell to the floor.

"It is safe. Always keep a knife or sword on you as well."

"Shouldn't we just run?"

"We cannot outrun them. Their bodies don't tire as quickly as yours."

"How many will come?"

"A lot if they're smart, but I don't think they know who they're following yet."

Leaning against the exterior wall beside the door, Ashan watched Frezz walk off into the forest. When he was out of sight, Ashan scanned the road while repeatedly lifting and dropping the tip of the white sword Frezz had given him into the dirt between his feet. Three men appeared a short while later with a wagon full of metal poles with curved tops and several hooks in them. They followed the road, stopping every ten feet or so, and stabbed one of the poles into the ground at the edge nearer the pond. Behind them, though moving a bit more slowly, another group of three hung lanterns upon the poles.

109

Guards passed by in five-minute intervals, each wearing mismatching leather jerkins, tall leather boots, and carrying a sword, ax or club. They were nothing like the guards to which he was accustomed, as the city guards wore perfectly matching uniforms, meandered aimlessly, yelled a lot, and were as corrupt as the day was long. To his surprise, these guards ignored Ashan, marched hurriedly about as if needing to be somewhere urgently, and seemed rather pleasant. One of them even waved at Ashan as he went by the first time. *Are all small towns this quiet? Is this small? There have to be sixty buildings. Is that enough to make a proper city?*

Perhaps an hour passed before one of the guards caught Ashan's attention. He wore darkly stained boots that rose to his knees and carried both a sword and a spear as he walked, but that wasn't what caught his attention; rather, it was the fact that the man came marching between two houses from the East instead of arriving by road. He waved and stopped two guards in the road, met with them there for a moment, and then parted from them. He stopped where the road curved to the right suddenly, stabbed his sword into the ground, and walked into the darkness between two houses. *Probably relieving himself behind a tree,* Ashan thought and turned to look the opposite direction.

Just as he looked to the south, a guard emerged from the space between two houses where he was looking. He walked out to the center of the road, knelt and picked up an ax laying in the dirt. He stood, glanced around, and began walking at an alarming speed. At the next space between houses, he knelt in the center of the road, rose without the ax, and strode off into the darkness again. He was gone for only a few moments. Again, he took up the ax, walked to where there was another dark gap between houses, and set the ax down there in the road. *What is he doing?*

Looking back to the other guard, Ashan found that he was now doing the same thing, only stabbing his sword into the ground so that it stood upright. *What are they doing?* He watched carefully as both men drew nearer, and, in the soft lantern light, he noticed that either

110

man carried a sack at the waist. The guard with the ax reached into his sack as he walked into the dark space between buildings again, but Ashan could not see what the man did in the darkness. On and on they went until they met up in the street directly in front of Ashan.

"Anything?"

"No, but that wizard is sneaking around on the West side of town. I just pretend not to notice him. Not sure what he's doing."

"He might get in the way. Tell the others. Lord Turley won't be happy if some outsider gets hurt in this."

Gets hurt in what? Does everybody speak in riddles?

"I'll let Lord Turley know we have an extra on the field."

"What about him?" They both looked at Ashan.

"He's just a kid. I wouldn't worry about him. How many more do you have?"

"Maybe eight, but I think-"

A scream rang out from across the water. Both guards spun and raised their weapons in unison. The darkness between two houses across the pond was broken by a fountain of fire and illuminated at least five figures, but the flames winked out before Ashan could gather anything further. Another scream came a few seconds later and another eruption of fire pushed back the night. In the momentary light, Ashan saw the silhouette of a man with great black wings in a group of six other silhouetted figures. Again, the light went out before he could get a sense of what was happening, but the scream of pain that followed gave him some idea.

"Damned wizard! He'll ruin it! Go tell Lord Turley!" Both guards ran. *Ruin it? Ruin what? Does everyone always know what is going on but me?*

111

Ashan ran out to the edge of the pond-lake, stopping when the water rose to his knees, and studied the darkness. Again, flames came and went in the same space between buildings, and he caught only a glimpse of people. It was difficult to know, but he thought there were only half as many as before. "Frezz!" he screamed as he tried to estimate which direction around the pond-lake was shorter. When he reached the dirt path, he caught a flash of bright white in his peripheral vision. He spun in place and found only darkness. Another flash of light came from only halfway around the pond on his left side and he found himself blinded. He pictured himself stumbling in that room right before Sa'teshka had thrown him. This blindness wasn't the same, but the memory drove him into a panic.

"Boy!" a voice came from behind him and was followed by heavy footfalls. "Get yourself to safety, young man!" A massive hand clamped down around Ashan's left shoulder and spun him about. "You can't fight vampires without armor. What are you thinking?"

"I heard screams. Someone needs help."

The man's laughter was a powerful baritone Ashan felt in his own chest. His eyes adjusted and he found the shape of a man so wide of shoulder that he would need an extra arm's length to reach about the fellow and his hand was almost large enough to wrap around Ashan's entire head. His green eyes and bulbous nose seemed overly large for his face and his thick black beard hung nearly to his stomach. Judging from the size of the man's legs, one kick would take the fight out of much better men than Ashan. As large as he was, he wasn't all that tall, standing only a finger's width taller than Ashan. He wore thick hide armor stained black with overlapping plates of flat metal affixed at the chest and he held the handle of a massive ax in one hand so that it rested upon his shoulder. He wore no helmet, leaving his bald head exposed, which Ashan thought was odd given what the man had just told him.

"What you heard were the screams of vampires falling into our True-light traps."

"True light?"

"Get back to your room, kid. Let us see to the fighting." He gently pushed Ashan in the direction of the room he was supposed to be staying in. Across the pond-lake, another wave of fire crashed against the ground.

"Fool wizard best not burn anything down!" the man said as he nudged Ashan onward.

A horn bleated twice, and a wave of soldiers appeared in the north just beyond the furthest houses. Turning, he also found a wave of soldiers charging out from the trees in the East. "Hurry now!" the large man sounded urgent and pushed Ashan to move faster. Each soldier wore black-painted armor and carried an ax or sword, looking like a properly equipped army. The difference between these soldiers and the ones with mismatched armor and weaponry stood out as very strange to Ashan.

As if they had timed their charge, a hundred white lights erupted across the little town, banishing all of the night in an instant. Ashan ran the rest of the way to the doorway to his room and, upon arrival, spun around to watch. The large man turned and ran away to the West, quickly joining with a group of twenty soldiers as they followed the road south and around the pond-lake.

A minute passed before that horn let out another set of sharp blasts and the many lights suddenly began to languish and flicker like a flame being blown out. Yelling and screaming rose at the same time as clanging of metal against metal, but he couldn't see where any fighting was happening from so far away. The drumming became frantic, and Ashan thought that perhaps the drums were actually being used to communicate something to the soldiers, but all he could see was the overall pattern of movement in that sea of black-armored bodies. *Maybe faster means danger?* He began to wonder how long it would take to learn the meaning of the drumming as he noticed soldiers gathering around houses. Some of the lights flickered out then.

"YOU!" a voice called out from nearby and Ashan jumped at it.

At first, he saw nothing, but then he found a man standing in the darkness provided by a large tree twenty paces away. Far from one of the lights, the man would have been difficult to spot in his black clothing if it weren't for his sickly white face. "Where is the amulet?" Sa'teshka suddenly appeared behind the man as if he'd been invisible.

Ashan nearly jumped at the sight of the man. His knees grew weak, and a cold numbness spread through his face and hands. He stepped back slowly and tried to think of what to do. His first instinct was to run away and hide in the forest, but then he began imagining how far he would get before one of them caught him and threw him against the side of a building or a tree. It seemed to take forever to gather the idea of shutting the door and he felt himself moving very slowly when he did exactly that.

With the door shut, he turned and ran to the back of the room. *No! They've found me! How?* His eyes fell upon the orb that Frezz had left and, glancing at the door several times, he hovered his free hand above that unnaturally smooth, glassy surface. He registered his increased panic more than the sound of the door slamming against the wall and breaking free from its hinges. A pale-faced man appeared in the doorway a second later, but Ashan couldn't hear the man's laughter over the sound of his pounding heart. The man wore nothing more than a pair of pants and his chest was covered in blood that seemed to have come from his mouth. His hands were half covered in charred skin and an arrow was sticking out of his leg. He said something that Ashan couldn't hear and waited a few breaths before his face twisted with rage. He screamed in a rage that made the hair on the back of Ashan's neck stand upright suddenly and ran toward Ashan.

Brilliant white light filled the room in a flash and the man's eyes shot open wide as his expression turned to horror. He skidded to a halt, backstepped and turned while flailing his arms. In that time, the skin on his face turned beat red, his chest followed, and finally the skin on his back did as well. It was like watching watered down ink flowing

114

down paper, except there was the wailing of agony. He stepped toward the doorway twice before he fell to the floor and began clawing his way across the floor. A second pale-faced man appeared in the doorway then, but he screamed and darted out of sight to the side with a howl of pain. The skin of the man upon the floor blackened, cracked apart to reveal a wet redness, and his hair burst into flames. He screamed again and the black layer began to slide off the surface of his body. Blood poured out and white fatty tissue began to turn dark. A finger disconnected from one of his hands and suddenly began to move even faster, but then another finger tore free. Still, he flailed his arms and pulled himself closer to the doorway. "No." He howled. His left leg stopped moving then and he slumped down upon the floor as his right arm ceased moving. Then the hand on his still-moving arm fell off and splattered upon the floor and he didn't even scream. His chest rose and fell four more times.

Looking down if only to not see the grotesque scene, Ashan found that he had touched the glassy orb, from which the light was pulsing. He looked at it for a long moment before remembering Frezz's warning to use it sparingly and removed his hand quickly. The world outside suddenly grew loud with shouting, the clanging of metal against metal, and screams of pain. It took a moment to understand that the sounds of fighting were growing nearer.

"I understand that you're afraid." That familiar voice came from just beyond the doorway. "You want to live, and I will let you. Everyone will think that you died. I don't need you to die – that was Hotar's desire. All I need is the amulet.

"I-uh-you...you tried to kill me." Ashan barely managed to speak above a whisper.

"That was Hotar, but he's not here now. Tell me where you've hidden it or toss it to me now if you have it and you can run off to wherever it is you're going."

115

In a flash, that pure white hand came into view in the doorway. It cast a cloth bag halfway into the room, which struck the floor and sent coins scattering all about the floor. Without looking directly, Ashan guessed there were at least forty gold coins there – the larger ones worth three of the small gold coins he's seen only a few times in his life – and he knew it was a fortune. *A hundred coppers make a bronze, ten bronze makes a silver, twenty silver makes a regular gold and three regular gold make the triple-gold coin. Now they're trying to pay me for something I don't even have?*

"I would guess that you're heading north to Isirdost. Of course, you did hear part of the discussion about going to war with Isirdost." He paused a moment. "I would recommend that you go south instead. South beyond the city of Bal Keth, you'd find life easy. No slave-trade, a flourishing economy, and great weather all year long. You'd have little trouble finding a place to live, learning a trade, and doing well in life. I only need the amulet."

Freedom. A fortune at my feet. Ashan glanced at the gold for a second and imagined what kind of life it would provide him. "I don't have it." He considered where the thing could be. He had made his deliveries as usual that day, had never left his pack unattended for even a moment, and then they had captured him. *If they don't have it, who does?* He considered it for a long moment before realizing that Erekej could have given him an empty package to deliver that day. He had never known Erekej to steal a package before, but that seemed the only possibility.

"Maybe my owner has it." He suggested as he found a sudden wave of anger filling his chest. *Maybe he traded what little I had, even my life, for some amulet.* "I never open packages. I was a bound slave! What would I do with jewelry?" He found it difficult to say anything more. Tears welled up in his eyes as he considered how little he had been worth to someone else. *That man threw my life away for some...some...TRINKET?* Ashan suddenly found it difficult to breathe

116

and his chest burned as if he'd eaten something spicy. His knees then grew weak, and his left hand began to shake.

"How many people will your war kill?" The thought came from nowhere.

"That's not your responsibility. King Hotar will attack with or without the amulet. He's already gathering both armies. You're just an escaped slave. These things are bigger than you. Take the trade and go be free. We'll forget all about you and you can forget about us. You can go live a nice, quiet life."

Both armies? Why two distinct armies? Wouldn't you gather all your fighters and call it just one army? His left knee gave out and he hit the floor. The sword slipped free from his suddenly weak hand and his vision blurred, darkening a touch. He tried to speak, but his lips barely moved. He tilted forward and fell, face down, onto the bed. He glanced around in a panic, his head moving only vaguely as he intended, and a heaviness settled upon his chest.

"Take a moment to consider this trade. If you don't take it now, there won't be another opportunity."

Ashan slowly slid backward off the bed and fell sideways upon the floor before he could get his arms to budge. He rolled onto his chest and dragged his arms up. He pushed himself up from the floor slowly and pulled his legs beneath himself. He was terrified at how sluggishly his limbs obeyed his commands. When he finally stabilized himself on his knees, he grabbed at his sword but missed the first two times. He dragged it in one hand and almost screamed in panic when it tripled in weight. *No! Wait, the orb! The light!* He dragged the sword upright, so the point was on the floor and then, using it like a cane, pulled himself up off the floor. He swayed wildly on his feet and turned in place very carefully so that he was facing the bed again. Shifting his focus from the floor to his free hand seemed to take forever. *Why am I so slow?* Even his thoughts seemed like a toy boat stuck in mud.

117

"No." Ashan was alarmed to hear the single word dragging on with a slur like a drunk's.

"Get it!" Sa'teshka yelled.

Turning his head to face the doorway seemed to take an eternity. Two pale-faced men appeared there, and one came directly for Ashan while the other jumped upon the bed. The orb flew to the corner with a kick and Ashan screamed. He stumbled backwards away from the vampire upon the bed and both his knees threatening to give out under the strain. Using both hands, he brought the sword up and pointed the end at the other vampire. The weight of the thing was such that his fingers were numb and threatening to fail. The coming vampire looked at the blade but smiled as he continued onward. The blade sank into the man's stomach, and he didn't even flinch; rather, an amused smile formed on his face, and he grabbed Ashan by the throat with one hand.

"Where is it?" he demanded. Ashan looked about for the second man and found him rummaging through Ashan's pack, throwing one item at a time to the floor. "Give it to us!"

A red, flickering light weakly illuminated the room then and someone screamed. A thud sounded and then the man who hold Ashan against the wall suddenly jolted upright and his face twisted with pain. The man's eyes shot open wide, and his forehead shifted, angled out at the center with an audible crack, and split apart. Blood gushed out and a blade stretched out from the wound a hand's length. The man's eyes flashed white and his hold on Ashan's throat eased greatly. They fell to the floor.

Ashan sluggishly turned his head to look up and found a man wearing a suit of armor standing above him. He tried to scream but croaked weakly. The armor wasn't like those he had seen before. Normal armor was usually a patchwork of metal parts strapped to the wearer, often with overlapping layers tied together with strands of leather and with small gaps here and there so that you could see the person beneath was wearing thick cloth material he didn't know the name of. This armor appeared to have no gaps at all, and nothing seemed to overlap anything else. The surface was black, but hadn't been painted, as it shined and reflected its own red lights, which emanated from many glowing symbols all over the thing. *Magic*, he cursed as he tried to push the dead vampire off himself, but all he managed to do was shift its weight slightly for a moment.

The armored man turned and swung a massive black sword with matching red symbols sideways. There came not the slightest sound of metal grinding against metal as the massive suit of armor twisted at the waist. Then it stepped forward, swung again, and someone screamed before a thud sounded. The armored man turned, stepped back twice, and raised his sword up at his side. The movement revealed another pale-faced man standing in the doorway with wide-eyed shock upon his face. The armored man stepped forward quickly and swung his blade, which sliced through the pale-faced man with what seemed no difficulty whatsoever.

A moment later, the armored man turned back around and peered down at Ashan in silence. Finally, a massive, armored hand reached down at Ashan's legs and Ashan tried to scream but croaked meekly instead. The hand lifted and carefully moved one of Ashan's legs. It took everything he had to move his head to see what the man was doing. When the man set Ashan's leg down, he discovered there was a small dart with yellow feathers protruding from the inside of his right leg halfway between knee and ankle.

"Lucky I was near." A deep voice boomed from the armor, but without the high-pitched ring as from a man wearing normal armor. The face of the helmet was a single smooth surface, polished so that it was almost a mirror, and Ashan could find no eye holes. "It's not poison, but a paralytic. You'll be okay in a few hours."

"Lord Turley!" A voice called from outside. "They are retreating."
"Almost had the bastard!" the armor cursed. "Do you feel well, boy?"

"Y-yes, sir." Ashan tried to move, but now could barely shift his head.

"Relax." The armored giant reached down with one hand and pulled the dead from atop him. "I'll post guards outside to protect you until you recover. Don't try to walk for a few hours and don't eat anything. You could bite your tongue badly or fall and hit your head. I've seen it happen." The man turned and side-stepped through the doorway in a hurry. There was a faint thump from each step, but far too quiet for the size of the armor. *Impossible! No, magic!* He screamed inside as he tried to move and failed.

"I know a cart of dung when I smell one."

The armor was even more terrifying in the light of lanterns the soldiers had placed about the room. The entire thing seemed to be a single piece of metal, but it moved everywhere a real body moved and the chest heaved as the man inside took breaths. *Magic,* he repeatedly cursed as he studied the thing. Seated upon one bed, this Lord Turley was an imposing figure. He had hard eyes and the look on his face gave Ashan the impression that the man's only hobbies were being angry and slaughtering vampires. Lord Turley had removed the faceplate of his helmet before arriving, which seemed to have been no more than a square in the front of the helmet, and Ashan could not tell how it was secured into place.

Three men sat on the opposite bed dressed in regular clothing, as if they were civilians, but Ashan was sure they were more than that with the way the soldiers outside served them drink and food on silver trays with no more than the wave of a hand or a nod. There had grown a large crowd of soldiers outside who watched through the doorway in silence. There was also some sort of medicine man around, who had come twice already to have Ashan drink some warm liquid he had made that tasted just like tea with honey added to it. The man had said it would help counteract the stuff from the dart that had taken his ability to move from him, but it seemed to be working very slowly.

Ashan stopped studying the onlookers and looked at the vampire at his side. Looking at what Lord Turley had done to the vampire made the hair on his neck stand up and his stomach turn. *He shouldn't be alive!* Three knives rose from his stomach, two fingers had been cut off one hand, and his leg had been sliced open from the hip to the knee. It wasn't the first time Ashan had witnessed someone get tortured for answers, but those had been men and the torture had been a sound beating or maybe even a broken finger or nose. This was an entirely different sort of torture, and he did not want to see it again any time soon.

The vampire sat quietly now and listened as if this were a casual meeting between friends, expressing not even a hint of pain or discomfort. They hadn't harmed Frezz or Ashan so far, but he did wonder when that would change, as this Lord Turley fellow seemed to be growing tired of the answers Frezz had been giving. He wondered how long they would torture him before believing that he knew practically nothing about anything whatsoever.

"We are just traveling south. I am-" Frezz began.

"I have heard this much." Lord Turley blurted angrily. "Fleeing increased taxes in the capital, selling cart and oxen to travel south by foot with a newly freed slave in tow. No documentation of purchase conveniently. Right on the heels of an assassination attempt against high-king Hotar and the dungeon escape too." He gave the barest hint of a smile.

"I paid for the boy. He is free to-"

"Do not piss on my leg and tell me that it is raining." He shouted. "I saw." He rose and pointed at Frezz's human face, only a few inches between fingertip and nose. "I may be old, but my eyes and mind do not betray me. Not yet. You spew fire and disguise yourself with magic. The timing is too great a coincidence. You are either escapees from the dungeon or the would-be assassin!"

"The same could be said of you." Frezz replied flatly.

"How do you mean?"

"Wearing Shadow-plate, armed with a Whispering Blade." Lord Turley's eyes narrowed. "I learned quite a bit about this kingdom while they had me locked up. Magic has been outlawed in these lands unless your high-king controls it, but, perhaps, I was misinformed. Should we call upon the authorities to determine if I am an assassin? Once accused of being this assassin, I am sure the king would be interested to hear which lord hired me. Why, I could speak any name that I wished, Lord Turley." A long moment of silence fell before Frezz continued. "The number of True-light orbs used in this little town alone...why, I bet the high-king and his...allies would find it rather interesting."

Lord Turley glanced to the three men seated upon the other bed for a moment. They did not appear surprised by anything they had heard, and each gave him a short nod after a long moment of consideration. Lord Turley turned to face Frezz a moment later and let out a deep sigh.

"Who would believe a thing like that? News travels like the wind. Full of flies and hot air." Frezz shifted, glancing back and forth from Lord Turley to the advisers a few times and worked his mouth as if chewing for a moment.

"Not quickly enough, I'm afraid." Silence hung in the air a long moment before he continued. "Where are Sielya and Martokal?"

What? This is the same conversation he had with...IT'S A CODE! Do they know each other? From the way they had captured, chained, and thrown Frezz into the room, it sure seemed they did not. *But it's the same conversation I heard before.* Lord Turley's expression became that of a man making a difficult decision, torn between two options, calculating outcomes. It lasted only a moment before

122

determination settled upon his face. He stood, raised his sword hand directly over his head, and brought it down hard.

"NO!" Ashan screamed and closed his eyes. CRACK. Something wet splattered across his face and he yelled out in panic.

Opening his eyes, Ashan first checked himself for injuries and then faced Frezz. Frezz appeared uninjured, but Ashan's eyes were drawn upon the vampire who had been between them. Not only had the vampire's skull been cleaved in two, but the sword had cut all the way down to the floor. The sight turned Ashan's stomach and he had to look away quickly to keep from vomiting.

"Not a fighter?" Lord Turley asked, his voice eerily calm.

"Not as yet." Frezz replied.

"We have much to discuss." Lord Turley said.

"Send him to wash and change." Frezz said.

Five soldiers escorted Ashan to the pond-lake. As he pulled off his blood-covered clothing, an older soldier with a head of messy, graying hair grabbed a twig, walked over to the nearest man's lantern, and set the tip on fire. He then untied a bag that hung from his belt and removed from it a tobacco pipe and set about stuffing it with tobacco from the bag. A minute later, he lit the tobacco from the twig and took a draw from it as a contented smile spread across his face. A young soldier came from near the larger group, set himself at the edge of the water and began untying his boots. He hit the water just as Ashan was pulling his bloody socks from his feet.

He was surprised to find that the water was rather warm compared to the water from the well where he had always retrieved water for bathing. He walked out until the water was at his waist before he began trying to wash away the blood. A minute later, he heard splashing and, turning, found that several soldiers and a rather large

123

man were walking out into the water. In the darkness it took a moment to recognize the large man as the soldier that had stopped him and returned him to his room earlier. The large man wore tan shorts and carried a lantern in one hand and a pole in the other. He walked right up to Ashan, stabbed the pole down firmly and then hung the lantern upon a hook at the top. The man's chest was a mix of scars and tattoos, which were difficult to see in the dim lantern light. He first recognized a snake and a boar and then a bunch of words forming a square with an eye in the center.

"Soap?" the man held out a thick white rectangle.

"Thank you, master." he replied instinctively as he snatched the bar of soap. While it looked small in the man's palm, in Ashan's it was awkwardly large.

"Gravar." He gave a little head tilt and began splashing water onto his chest. "I hear you got a kill."

"What?"

"My men say you stabbed a vampire right through the chest." A young boy who could barely be a year older than Ashan came splashing over with excitement clear on his face.

"I, uh-no, he stabbed himself. I was just holding my sword out. I don't think it even hurt him." Ashan explained. "Then that guy in the suit-"

"Lord Turley." The young soldier offered eagerly.

"Yes. He cut the vampire's head apart.

Gravar smiled wide. "What I'm hearing is that you held a vampire in place while Lord Turley finished it off." He gave Ashan a wink.

"No, the vampire was holding me by the neck when that happened. I couldn't even move."

Gravar sank down into the water and began to scrub at his long beard. "That's what I like to call teamwork, which is vitally important during battle. So, by my reckoning, it still counts as your kill!" he gave a short chuckle. "What's your name?"

"Ashan."

"Were you scared or terrified?"

"Terrified."

"Everyone is their first time going into a battle."

"Even you, General Gravar?" the young soldier asked.

"I pissed myself, to be honest. My brother was there, and he never let me forget it." He chuckled.

"I feel like everyone knew what was going on but me." Ashan explained as he lathered the soap in his hands.

"Sometimes things just look that way. None of us knew what your friend there was doing sneaking around in the woods. We forgot about him when the vampires came until we saw his traps going off.

"Traps?"

"Tripwires and vines that grew up suddenly to grab their legs. Kind of ruined our plan to surprise attack them when they reached the center of town. Then he didn't realize that we were trying to capture him until we already had an ambush set up."

"You were waiting on the vampires to attack?"

"Lord Turley received a message about them heading this way."

"Who sent the warning?"

"We're not sure. It was a messenger bird. I figure it's one of your friends looking out for you."

"I-I don't have friends."

"Your friend's friends?" General Gravar responded and then dunked his head under the water and scrubbed his beard and face. When he came back up, he gave Ashan a questioning look.

"I suppose so."

"You don't know?"

"No. I don't really know him that well. We were in the dungeon together, and he helped me escape and-"

"You were in the high-king's dungeon?" the young soldier interrupted excitedly.

"Yes." Ashan thought of everything that had happened there and was about to start telling the story, but he felt a sudden fear that he was telling too much already and stopped himself.

"How'd you get out?" the young soldier asked gleefully.

"Some prisoner killed a guard she tricked, and we freed each other after that." *They don't need to know about the ring.* "I went with him. His friends gave us the wagon and they stayed behind."

"I thought all the people who escaped the dungeon had died." The young soldier said.

"No, not all of them." General Gravar said. "Our spies in the capital say that nearly half of them escaped."

"You have spies in the capital?" Ashan asked as he scrubbed his face with the soap.

"Of course, he does! All high-born spy on each other. How do you not know that?" The young soldier said incredulously.

Ashan thought about it for a long moment. "I guess because I have always been a bound slave for a merchant?"

"Ah. That does make sense. My aunt's new husband was the same and he says that the hardest part of free life is learning all the things he didn't know that he didn't know."

"All the things he didn't know that he didn't know? What does that mean?"

"You know. It's the stuff you don't know, but when you know it, you realize you didn't know it! So, it's the stuff that you don't know that you don't know." He gave a short laugh. "Like...uh...you don't know if someone wants to hit you until they hit you, but then...well, there you are knowing they wanted to hit you and realizing you didn't know."

"Okay, but how could they tell you the same day it happened when it took us days to get here? Ashan asked as he tried to recall if anybody had passed them on the journey.

"Messenger birds, of course!" he laughed.

"How do you get birds to send messages?"

"I know exactly how it's done! My cousin trains them!" he began excitedly.

"I hadn't realized that securing the dungeon for a full moon was that difficult a task, Anvindr."

Lord Kairn knew his sister well: Koraine had intentionally worn metal-shod heels because she knew *exactly* how annoying, distracting, and bothersome she could make her steps. They were too loud to be worn in polite society, but high-king Hotar allowed such improprieties while in his company; in fact, he seemed to enjoy things that ruffled the feathers of others, so long as he could watch.

Lord Kairn dreaded the next hundred steps, not simply because the sound of her steps agitated his headache, but because he knew what was coming. He wanted to make up some reason he could politely leave the window to wait for the family carriage alone, which would give her another thing to complain about, but he could not. Unfortunately, she knew his schedule and, besides, delaying the inevitable only made it worse in the end.

If the gods were in a merciful mood today, the boy he'd sent for the carriage had made good time and the thing would arrive quickly. Why, if he had any luck at all, she could be away in mere minutes to continue her search for a new husband. *Anything to replenish your personal coffers,* he thought. She'd had plenty of offers from suitable bachelors in the past moon, but none had been to her liking so far. *Financially.* Not that it mattered much to him when exactly she got to the business of getting married again, but the business of courting, becoming engaged, and preparing for the actual marriage usually meant she would forget about pestering him for several months and he was looking forward to that part of the whole thing.

"I'm still investigating what happened." Despite his best efforts, his voice came out strained instead of calm.

"The keys just walked off? Is that really the story you're going with, Anvindr?" Koraine spat.

Clang. Clang. Clang.

She sighed, and then spoke again, softer. "This would have been easier if you had just emptied the dungeon, on your terms, instead."

Kairn gave an involuntary sigh and took a moment to admire the hall. Large, colorful paintings of summertime fields, the finest tiling from ceiling to floor, and the highest quality stone statues lined either side of it from end to end like they were soldiers standing guard.

They were characters from the old stories, each posed as if in deep meditation, but they reminded him of soldiers just the same. There were a few small tables crafted of brilliant white stone full of glittering flecks and upon each sat a golden bowl filled with light-stones with rubies covering them so that they gave off a gentle red glow. Although it wasn't to his taste, it was an impressive sight just the same. He hated to think what the cost to maintain just this hall would be if the grounds weren't kept up by prisoners and slaves. He pushed those thoughts off and gave his sister an inquisitive look.

"You know I wouldn't have chosen that."

"An hour is all it would have taken!" She almost yelled the words. She took a measured breath then and let it out slowly. "You are like father. You spend too much time thinking and never act." She pursed her lips in obvious frustration. She clearly had more to say, but just then they had arrived before their carriage. Her face twisted with disgust, and he admired the beautiful craftsmanship.

"Have a good evening, dear sister." He spoke before she had an opportunity to bring up her obvious displeasure with the old carriage and pulled open the door. The driver was there a moment later with the stool. She climbed in and waited for the door to shut before speaking in a very flat tone. "I wish you luck on your journey, Anvindr."

Kairn watched until the carriage was out of view before turning around and heading back up the hall. He took the fifth door on the right, went up three flights of narrow, twisting stone stairways, and then traveled along the most cramped hallway he had ever seen. If a second person had come along, they would have had to brush their chests together to pass each other. Twenty strides later, he took a left turn, opened the last door on the right, and climbed a few stairs to a door. On the other side of this door was the high-king's war room. Therein he discovered many soldiers in heavy plate armor, the war council, and one of the high-king's advisors. The soldiers stood along three of the room's walls while the war council and the advisor sat at the massive table in the center of the room. The sight confused and alarmed Lord

Kairn, but he took a deep breath, shut the door, and gave the group a deep bow.

"Warm welcoming, Lord Kairn." the advisor announced softly.

"The same to you, Advisor Narn. And to the war council." Lord Kairn walked up to the edge of the table but did not take a seat. He knew he would be off in short order and the seats were reserved for more highly respected lords and ladies.

"I presume that High-King Hotar explained to you how you will proceed?"

"I am to take soldiers and find the escaped assassin, who was just spotted in White Rock."

"I mean more...specifically." Advisor Narn's blue eyes burned with anger as always and Lord Kairn wondered for the hundredth time if the man disliked him specifically or if he was this way with everyone. If Advisor Narn were half his current age, Lord Kairn would still think him too old to challenge to a duel and so he ignored the hostile expression the man gave.

"I know nothing more than this, Advisor Narn. To be honest, I am surprised to see soldiers wearing heavy armor when our target is so far away."

"Understandable, Lord Kairn."

Advisor Narn, in his advanced years, had to place both hands upon the table to pull himself from his chair. He then used a cane to walk from his chair to a chest against the wall. He checked several pockets before finding a ring of keys. He motioned one of the soldiers over and had the soldier lean down to unlock the chest and pull open the lid. Inside lay a sphere that swirled with blue and purple smoke. "Wake up!" Advisor Narn spoke loudly at the thing before turning to face Lord Kairn. "The king has spared no expense in finding this old relic and he is entrusting you with it for this mission."

"What is it?" Lord Kairn stepped over to get a better look at the thing, but he already knew that all manner of magical devices had been crafted with a crystal ball as the material component and that there seemed to be no two that performed the same action. Why that was, he was uncertain even after years of study. Though, really, there wasn't much material left in all the lands to study and most of it was just about useless drivel having to do with telling the weather a day in advance or how to avoid certain illnesses that were extremely uncommon.

"A shadow-construct. Much like a person, but with flaws in the intelligence it was given. It will take you and these men to White Rock." Advisor Narn gave the sphere a smack with his cane and shouted to it with visible effort. "Come out here now!"

A thick black smoke rose from the sphere and Kairn jumped back in surprise. The smoke rose to his own height and began to solidify, after a fashion, into the shape of a man. Looking at the thing was difficult because he found his eyes wanting to see through the smoke and focus on the wall behind it every other second. The top formed a head which immediately began to turn this way and that, seeming to take in the room's contents and, after a moment, Lord Kairn thought he saw the outline of a set of eyes and a nose, but his eyes kept focusing on the brick wall instead.

"Ras'vetra," Advisor Narn spoke in a demanding tone. "This is Lord Kairn. You will do his bidding until I tell you otherwise."

"As you command, Advisor Narn." Lord Kairn had not expected a voice to come from the shadow at all, let alone a human one.

"Ras'vetra, take them to White Rock." Advisor Narn turned to Lord Kairn then. "This manner of travel, albeit quite remarkable, is exceedingly unpleasant. Dizziness and vomiting are to be expected and I should warn you-"

Suddenly, Lord Kairn fell. He instinctively reached out to catch himself with both arms, but his arms weren't there. The ground wasn't there. The world wasn't there. He tried to scream, but no sound came.

131

He tried to look down to find his body and found only darkness. He then fell to his right and began spinning like a child's spinner toy. He felt himself wobble as if the momentum of the spin was almost gone and then nausea hit him hard. He wanted to vomit. The spinning changed direction and accelerated twenty-fold. He thought to pray to the gods to be released, but as he tried to decide which god might be the right one for this situation, the world came back. He crashed into dirt and grass on his left side and rolled over three times. He didn't have time to take anything in aside from that which was directly before his face. He dizzily rolled and pushed himself upward just in time to avoid vomiting on himself blindly. As his stomach neared empty, he began to hear other men retching as well. Someone yelled a curse a few moments later.

Once his stomach was empty and the dizziness faded, Lord Kairn stood weak-kneed with the soreness and unsteady feeling that only a day of hard work and forgetting to eat caused. He found himself in a grass-covered lull between three small hillocks. Around him, the soldiers were just beginning to rise as well, some removing their helms and others frantically glancing about. He climbed to the top of the nearest hillock and scanned his surroundings quickly. The grassy hillocks went on for quite a distance before meeting up with a vast forest, behind which rose mountains. There were no signs of civilization.

"Is anybody injured?" he yelled as he counted the men from this vantage point.

"They'll be fine." At the nearby voice, Lord Kairn spun around to find the shadow at his side. He tried to determine if it was looking at him, but it was impossible to tell. Out in the sunlight, the thing was much more transparent than it had seemed in the war room.

"What did you do?"

"I moved us through the un-place."

"The un-place?"

132

"Yes, the place that isn't this place." His tone was jolly.

"Where are we?" Lord Kairn glanced about again, hoping to see smoke from a house or the slightest hint of a road.

"On a hillock."

"I can see that much, but I thought you were taking us to White Rock." Lord Kairn explained.

"And so I did, Lord Kairn."

"This is not White Rock. There's no town here at all."

The shadow stooped down quickly and rose with a small, white pebble held between two shadowy fingers. He held it out as if proudly presenting it to Lord Kairn. "White rock. Right here, Lord Kairn."

"This is **a** white rock, not the **town** of White Rock." Lord Kairn recalled that Advisor Narn had told him the thing's intelligence was flawed and considered how to move forward for a long moment. "Do you understand the difference?"

"Pardon my error, Lord Kairn." Lord Kairn thought he saw a faint smile on the shadowy face.

"Well, take us to the town of White Rock."

"Certainly, Lord Kairn." The shadow turned and began walking.

"Where are you going?" Lord Kairn caught up quickly. The upper half of the shadow's body twisted at the waist, so it was facing Lord Kairn while the legs kept carrying it onward like a demented nesting doll. Looking back, he saw that the armored soldiers were falling into two staggered lines behind and catching up rapidly.

"Why, I am leading the way to the town of White Rock, Lord Kairn."

"Don't **lead** us there. Take us there with magic the way you took us here."

133

"Oh, I am afraid I cannot do so, Lord Kairn."

"How so?"

"You see, it is not safe to travel in the un-place frequently."

"What? You just took us all through it. Why is it dangerous now?"

"They will be watching now, of course."

"Who will be watching? There's nobody else out here."

"There's birds, Lord Kairn."

"Birds? Answer my question!"

"I have answered your question, Lord Kairn. The birds will be watching."

Lord Kairn took a deep breath to calm down. So far, this shadow was reminding him of the game his sister Aydreis often enjoyed playing when they were still kids. *Of course, Aydreis only loved that game because it annoyed me so much*, he considered. "Do you not understand my questions?"

"I enjoy your questions, Lord Kairn." This time, Lord Kairn was sure he saw smile-lines in the thing's face.

"But your answers do not make sense." Lord Kairn commented. The thought occurred to him that restructuring his questions into commands might yield different results. "Tell me why it is not safe to traverse this un-place."

"The living are not permitted there, Lord Kairn."

"How is that different now than it was before?"

"They weren't watching before, Lord Kairn. Now they will be paying attention."

"Okay. Tell me, how far are we from White Rock?"

"A few days, Lord Kairn."

ALL GREAT PRINCES

Lasashu ate and drank until he ached dreadfully. He unbuckled his belt, pulled it free and dropped it to the floor. Several people had watched his break in decorum, but their eyes darted away quickly. He knew that nobody would say anything about it – not here and certainly not in front of his father. Hell, he could just about go nude without causing a scene, but he wouldn't...not after last time. The only eyes that didn't dart away were those of his father at the other end of the table. He was also giving Lasashu a stern expression of disapproval, but it was as fake as the look of innocence that Lasashu returned. Luckily, his mother had missed the event. Had she noticed, she would have been very vocal about her displeasure and, in doing so, she would have caused an even bigger scene than he might have. She likely would have yelled and scolded him and the guests at the table would have found it improper. Certainly, talk of her behavior would travel far and wide, as it often did. His father always called it her fiery northern temper. Most would just say it was something in the blood and leave it at that.

He lazily studied the veranda while sipping his wine. To him, there was nothing spectacular or extraordinary about the place, but he was trying to understand another perspective – one that itched at the back of his mind. White tablecloth, dim lantern-light, standard tableware, sixty or so identical chairs, common chandeliers. Outside, he saw the capital stretching out to the east and south against the coast as far as the eye could see. The view was average in his estimate. Anybody could walk on the shoreline and get the same view of the ocean and the docks. Average food, average wine, and average clothing. Yes, everything was perfectly average, but, just the same, that little something in the back of his mind just wouldn't leave him be in peace. *Those bastards did this to my mind,* he cursed silently. *A curse! I want my peace back! I deserve it! I am a prince!* He kept his expression neutral. Nobody here had to know that his blood boiled or that he was plotting murderous revenge even as they sat here discussing building a new route for trade. No, none of these kings, queens, dignitaries or their relatives needed to know that Lasashu was plotting murder in an area with the lowest crime rate for the past fifty years.

"Father." Lasashu rose quickly, faking a drunken sway, and slammed his cup down upon the table. Silence took the room as everyone turned in shock.

"Yes, son?" His father's soothing voice brought such calm that he almost sat right back down and forgot everything he'd been thinking. *Damn you!*

It would be nice to sit back down and live the life he always expected to live. He could just ignore those things the witch had planted in his mind until they faded entirely and go about the life he had already been living. *That's the problem! Those bastards think I'm spoiled! They think I'm worthless! They think they are better than me! Better than me? I'm a prince!* He had to take several deep breaths to

138

calm himself. *I will lead this empire. I will make the law. I AM the empire!* Another three breaths.

"Father, I have decided..." The hours of planning exactly what he would say all seemed wasted now. He didn't want to tell his father the truth. *No, you'll convince me to forget it. Hell, I've nearly convinced myself to a hundred times today.* The truth would take too long to explain, and he would miss his chance. *I am NOT afraid! I can do **anything** I want! They are peasants!* "If you'll excuse me, I think I shall retire for the night."

"Of course, son."

"Thank you. My apologies to the council and all our honored guests." He announced. "I promise I shall be better company tomorrow night." *Unless I leave. No, it's a trick. They weren't serious. They are liars.* He kept his rage caged as he bowed to show his respect to the southern dignitaries and then headed off towards murder.

Across the castle, Lasashu opened the room to his private quarters by kicking it – a good way to alleviate the stress that had been plaguing him all day. He would love nothing more than to get into a fight at a pub to really take the tension away, but there was no time for distractions. He shut the door and practically ran across the room to the far side of his bed. He knelt, reached under his bed, and grabbed for the bag of poor people's clothing he had collected earlier that morning. His hand found nothing, and he had to take a knee to lower himself to look. There was no bag but there were a pair of bare feet on the opposite side of the bed. He shot bolt upright and found *her* standing there with a smile spread across those thin lips beneath icy blue eyes.

Blasted, arrogant, brazen woman!

"What are you doing here?" he hissed at her, almost letting it become a full yell.

Every time he met the woman, she was dressed up in a different disguise. She was dressed as a beggar this time, but he recognized her

139

despite the thick dirt smeared across her face, mud on her withering dress, and the fact that she appeared to have doubled in size around the middle. Were it anyone else, he would tackle them to the ground and beat them before calling the guards and having them lock her up. Unfortunately, as he had learned a moon ago now, she was clever and very fast. Well, maybe she wasn't clever, but she was always ready with a hand of dirt to throw in your eyes or some foul thing to do to escape an honest fight. There would be a man from her group in the next room or a cart of hay set out to catch her fall if she needed to jump out a nearby window to escape death. With her, Lasashu would not be surprised to find that there were twenty carts of hay waiting around the castle already. He would find great pleasure in throttling her, but he was certain that he had already walked into one of her traps.

"You know why I am here." The fact that she did not acknowledge his being a prince was outrageous.

Not taking his eyes off her, he reached for the knife in his belt. He found the empty leather sheath. She gave him that annoying smile and reached behind her back with one hand and presented him his knife. She gave it a quick twirl before tossing it on his bed.

"I will teach you to respect royalty, you bitch." he growled.

"Young Lasashu, there are **many** things that I respect in this world. I respect clever little foxes, stubborn mules, and cats who knock things down because it's just their nature." She gave a little giggle and smiled, but her smile faded quickly, and her face grew hard. "Most of all, I admire the mistreated servants who pray for their employer's son to become a good man capable of caring and treating them with even the most basic of respect instead of praying for that boy to find a quick death so that they might be free of his spoiled, arrogant, greedy, vindictive ways."

She turned away and strode over to the edge of the large open window and peered out. "Unfortunately, you are a lowly cockroach. You are not worthy of the respect you demand. Under all that selfish,

140

deluded personality you've got going on, you don't even respect yourself. Not really. Honestly, you've been-" Lasashu quit listening and quietly grabbed his knife from the bed and stalked towards the woman as quietly as he could. "Yet, my associates believe there is a way to salvage you." He timed his steps with her words so that she wouldn't hear him. *This is it! I'm finally going to kill the bitch!* "Why, *Rangar even believes that you don't intend to murder me.*"

"What?" He stopped and looked up at her face.

He'd been so focused on her midsection, where he intended to drive his blade, that he hadn't noticed her head turn so that she could see him. She leapt up onto the ledge, turned in place and smiled at him. As he charged, she jumped backward into the open air. He leapt after her and thrust the blade into her stomach. Feeling the blade cutting into her flesh sparked joy in his heart. He twisted the blade, released it, and pushed her away as hard as he could. He knew how far she usually placed those carts of hay and had already planned this carefully. The hard push he gave her would prevent him from flying too far out. He would land in the cart and she on hard ground. He saw the terror upon her face and smiled back. *You're dead now!* Looking down, he spotted the cart full of hay below...about twenty paces further out from the building than he had ever seen it placed before. The ground came up to meet him before he had a chance to scream.

Someone slapped Lasashu across the face twice and a cold liquid was poured over his face. When he tried to roll, his ribs burst into pain. He screamed in agony and blinked his eyes rapidly to clear the liquid. Alcohol by the smell. His vision cleared as something was shoved into his hand and when he looked, he found that it was the thick handle of one of his larger tankards that he had broken just a few days before.

"Listen, you bastard." a man's voice came and, turning to face it, he found the woman and one of her men standing above him. He thought to take a swing at the man, but the pain he felt made him want to remain as still as possible. Something was broken, but he wasn't sure of what

141

or how badly and he knew from his tutoring that moving could worsen many injuries to the point that they never healed correctly.

"You're a right sorry bastard." The man knelt and spoke in a calm voice.

"Rangar!" Lasashu attempted to give the man a rude gesture, but when he tried to move his left arm, he felt only pain.

"Make your decision quickly."

The woman began to gather and pull her dress up and Lasashu thought that at last she was showing how lost her mind really was; however, under the dress she was wearing long shorts and a bloodstained off-white shirt. Around her waist she had two big leather wine skins with twine holding them in front of her stomach. She smiled at him as she gave one wine skin a squeeze, which caused liquid to squirt out from a thin hole. She began working the knots in the twine.

"I lost a good shirt tonight, but..." She reached behind her back and brought out his knife. "I did gain this fancy knife. Life is give and take. You'll have to forgive me for what you, no doubt, consider the theft of your knife. You see, I have a rule that if you attempt to harm me with something, that thing becomes mine." She cut the twine and dropped the punctured wine skin to the ground.

"We made you an offer and you've just thrown it away trying to kill one of us. Sadly, this means I am left with no choice but to give you this final offer. As soon as your pampered ass is well enough to travel, you will travel to the great wall up north, as is tradition among you royal bastards. If you refuse, I will kill your mother and father. After that, I will kill some person you know each time you act like a spoiled brat or mistreat your people. Do you understand me?" Rangar spoke calmly, as if he didn't even have emotions and his face was a mask of utter calm.

"I will kill you!" Lasashu yelled, causing a great pain to rise in his chest and sides.

142

"That would be an interesting thing to witness." The two turned and walked away.

Not only did the guards respond immediately to his screams, but they also had been well-informed and intelligent enough to not send a summons to the nearest town healer; rather, they interrupted the festivities in the veranda to ask Princess Adelaide, a visiting noble renowned for her skill in healing, to assist. The soldiers made quick and careful work of relocating Lasashu to his chamber bed, where Princess Adelaide set to work on mending his body. While she worked her magic on him, he came up with a lie that he had been drunk and had fallen from his window. The worst of the pain came when she began mending his many broken bones, which had him screaming in pain for nearly an hour. Maybe it was two. Afterwards, he was left alone with two servants who served him alcohol and changed his clothing.

He then had a few hours to start putting together a plan to murder the woman and her men in a different way. He would hire every spy and assassin in the capital to discover where she and her men had gone and slaughter them as soon as was feasible. The contracts would be expensive, and the guilds would likely ask him to pay those debt in a few years when he rose to high king, but those were concerns for the future. Having that woman's head hanging in his room was a delightful thought that made all the pain tolerable.

When he woke next, his body felt as if nothing had happened. He jumped out of bed, opened the door of his chamber, and was immediately surprised to find not a single servant waiting for him. He thought to yell for one of them, but could not recall any of their names, which only irritated him because he wasn't supposed to know their names. *They are supposed to be here!* He rummaged through the drawers of one of his dressers and found suitable attire for the morning meal and headed down to the great hall. He found the place deserted. *The veranda,* he thought. *Yes, everybody was drinking that strong wine last night, so they'll want fresh air this morning. A very good choice.* He took the most direct route across the castle to reach the veranda and found it empty as well. There weren't even guards posted at the door, which surprised him. *Poor people could get in here and attack me!*

From there, he took the quickest route to the castle's front entry, yelling for servants as he went, but nobody came to him. At the front entry, he considered that, perhaps, everyone had moved down to the gardens at the foot of the grounds, where his father would routinely hold what he called *The Public Talk,* where any person could come and speak with the king directly. *Yes, that's why all the guards and servants are missing!* The commoners loved it when the king held this event, but he hated it himself. There would be a feast and all of the best sweets, but he also had to deal with the smell of commoners! Begrudgingly, he returned to his chambers and changed, with some difficulty finding things, into better attire.

By the time he had traveled down the hill to the northernmost garden entryway, he had worked up a heavy sweat and his legs were exhausted. Thankfully, his suspicions were confirmed by the presence of hundreds of filthy commoners. They sat at every bench in sight and upon checkered blankets in the grassy areas. Most of them, however, walked along the many stone walkways, taking in the view of the many statues, the fish in the shallow ponds, and even himself with amazed expressions. He didn't care much for the gardens himself. *Average.* If he was high king, he would have the whole plot of land cleared for a new castle to be constructed instead. *Maybe training grounds for the guards. Anything aside from these useless gardens.*

He followed the pathways that seemed least crowded to the centerpiece of the gardens. According to his tutors, many hundreds of years ago, the great kings had commissioned the best artists and the most skilled builders to fashion flat black stones into the ground here and to carve into the face of each of them a different, elaborate scene.

Many of them were of battles being waged, farmers tending their fields, and people fishing in the sea. On one side sat the high-backed, plain black marble throne and rising from the grass behind it stood the hundred or so stone pillars, each representing a living member of a royal family. It was said that there had originally been only four stone pillars but that the gods had so admired the gardens that they had remade the pillars with their great magic. Each was different in shape, color, and size. His own pillar, which had climbed from the earth on the day of his birth, was a tall rectangle of tan sandstone and rose only as high as his own waist. His mother's pillar was circular, pure white, and came to a sharp point at the top. Set into the face of her pillar were five glowing, red, round gems.

There was no telling what the differences or changes in the pillars meant exactly, as the gods worked in mysterious ways; however, everybody which one was his father's pillar and what the most important feature meant. It stood at the center of the lot, directly behind the stone throne, and was twice as high as any other. It was triangular, primarily black, with a white stone crown at the very top. There were thin glowing white lines of stone that ran from the base to the crown at the top. High king was always signified in this manner.

His brother's pillar was off at the far left of the lot of them. It was a hand shorter than his own, fully black, and looked more like the blade of a sword rising from the ground than anything else. It seemed to fit his brother's love of combat arts, which Lasashu thought of as more dancing than fighting skills, but he let his brother have it in silence.

Beyond these pillars was the *Wall of Names.* It stood twice as tall as Lasashu, ran fifty feet, and was three strides thick. The black stone had a mirror polish and was unmarred by time, save for the names of great leaders that the gods would occasionally inscribe upon it. The names upon it were so small that they could not be read from more than a stride away, but there were many. To Lasashu's current vantage

145

point, Wall of Names seemed to have only a faint discoloration at the upper left corner.

Lasashu stepped off the pathway into the grass to admire his pillar from the opposite side. He imagined the day when his pillar would light up, grow the sacred white crown to signify that it was his time to ascend to his father's current position, and smiled to himself. It would be a grand day, surely, but he gave a silent prayer that it would be a day far, far into the future. When it happened, there would be great feasts for a week, and he would have wizards light up the sky at night as was commonly done on the new year's celebration. He prayed that it would only happen after his father had died of natural causes. *Peaceful. In his sleep, please,* he begged the gods. He looked to his father and admired the man's health. Yes, that day had to be very far away. His father still sparred with his trainers, could work all day without experiencing fatigue, and didn't suffer the usual health concerns of other men half his age. *Anybody would be lucky to age as gracefully.*

His attention was pulled suddenly then by a bright flash of light. Turning, he saw that one of the pillars was glowing brightly and the din of the commoners suddenly died down. Changes in pillars were very rare events and, of course, heads were turning. There, in the back, he found that his brother's sword-shaped pillar had changed from pure black to dark gray. He gasped with the crowd and wondered what it could mean for a long moment before he began to search the crowd for his brother's face. All he knew for certain was that his brother was still alive because the pillar had not turned to dust.

"Fetch the priests!" Lasashu's father yelled as he stood from the black throne. Even yelling, that voice seemed calmly powerful.

"Father." Lasashu called out in his best impression of his father's deep, soothing tone, but failed.

He made a quick mental note to practice more and raised one arm up into the air. He stepped forward and pushing aside a man so

146

filthy that he considered ordering guards to take the man to a bath house right then and there. He stopped himself only after recalling his father's fury the last time he had done exactly that. He reached the black stones in a few strides and gave his father a quick smile.

"Father, I can go and fetch the priests, but I will need my guards for protection. Guards!" He scanned the crowd for guards quickly. Six would be plenty. "Get a move on it!" he yelled when none appeared to move.

The crowd's eyes were on him, and he cursed himself for not taking the time to dress better. *My servants will certainly learn not to abandon me on such an important day again!* "We need to round up several runners to check my brother's usual haunts." Everybody was staring at him in silence and none of the guards had moved. "GUARDS! MOVE IT!"

One of the guards shifted his gaze to meet Lasashu's and Lasashu found confusion there. Then he realized that the man hadn't been looking at him. The guard was looking past him. His blood boiled in anger. *I was not wasting my breath! I am a prince!* Then Lasashu realized that the commoner standing next to the guard was looking past him as well. Lasashu scanned the crowd and found face-after-face wearing concern or terror and not one person was looking at him. *Father!* He spun around quickly and found his father standing before his great throne with his head turned toward the pillars.

"Father." He stepped forward and scanned the pillars. "I think that-"

Following his father's gaze, he froze in horror at what he spotted. The top third of his pillar sat upon the dark stone tile flooring. Shards of it had broken off and were scattered about in a wide arc around where it had landed. A dark something sat upon the center of the still standing portion of his pillar and he had to stare at it for a long while before he understood what it was. *Hollow.* His pillar was hollow. *Broken.* Something shook his shoulder and the blur of colors that made up the world outside his focus changed.

"You know what this means, son."

"It's broken..." Lasashu heard himself mutter.

"and... found... now." Another voice came in and out of his attention.

Lasashu saw a black stone wall in his mind and heard the clomping of a horse's feet. "It's broken." he said.

"Yes, it is broken, son." his father's face came between him and his broken pillar. "And you know what this means."

"It's broken." His mind raced to find meaning. He knew he knew the answer, but he couldn't find it. "We have to fix it." This was almost the truth, but he could feel there was something missing. "We fix it."

"You have to go to the wall, son."

"We   fix   it."
"Yes, the wall is how you fix it, son." He focused on his father's face and found sadness there, something he had rarely seen. "You must go, son."

"Go?" A flicker of that black stone wall came to his mind again. "No, father. We must fix it. You must fix it."

"Son, you must go. You know what this means. It's your brother."

"He can't fix a pillar."

"I'm sorry, Lasashu. I have failed to be the father you needed. I thought I had more time to work with you."

The wall came to his mind again. *No*, he pushed the thought away. Then he remembered what a broken pillar meant, and he felt his life fall apart. Everything suddenly meant nothing. He was not a prince, he was not rich, he owned nothing. The woman would not die because he didn't have two copper to rub together to pay the assassins guild. He had no power, no family name to give weight to his promises, and there would be no favors granted him. Worse, should he ask for a favor, he

148

would be branded a coward. Not even the poorest beggar would have anything to do with him. He could never climb higher in society than the most poor, unfortunate soul in all the land. He considered his brother. His father had mentioned his brother. It took a moment to recall his lessons and when they came to him, he gasped in horror. His brother would have to deliver him to the wall in only a few short days or die. *The gods did this to me! They've taken everything! They blackmail me with my brother's life!* His blood boiled.

"No, it's a mistake!"

"You must go, son. There is no choice."

"They can't do this to me."

"They are gods, son. Trust in their wisdom."

"No." He whispered and considered what he could do. "DAMN THEM!"

"Damn them all you like, but what is done is done."

"THEY CAN'T DO THIS TO ME!" Lasashu screamed. "I DON'T DESERVE THIS!"

"LASASHU!" He felt his father's baritone voice deep in his chest.

His father's hands released his shoulders and he suddenly stood upright. Anger had replaced worry on his father's face and Lasashu felt as small as a mouse. His father's mouth fell agape as though he were about to speak, but Lasashu could see that his father hadn't yet thought of the words. The look on his father's face vanquished all the rage from Lasashu's heart.

"You are an impetuous, capricious **CHILD!** You care for nothing, and you treat others poorly. You curse the gods with one breath and say that you do not deserve their wrath with the next. You are a constant thorn in the side of your family, those who tend to your every need, and every stranger you cross paths with! If you fail to go to the wall,

149

your brother will pay the price." He took a quick, ragged breath and continued a bit more slowly. "Were it possible, I would take his place to protect him from you."

Before he could recover from the harsh words of his father, two soldiers took him by his arms and dragged him away. Off they went through the crowd, all eyes on him, without a word from the two men. Each time he opened his mouth to demand they release him so he could go and plead his case with his father, he got stuck and couldn't think of how to begin. He couldn't command them to ignore what his father said even before his pillar had broken, but, more importantly, he didn't know where to restart the conversation with his father. The soldiers took him out from the garden onto a public street and followed it west and then north as it turned. Over a hill, they arrived at one of the buildings soldiers called a rotation house. They took Lasashu into where the horses were kept and sat him down on a stool. Other soldiers gathered and there was a fair bit of discussion, but he couldn't force himself to listen.

After a while, an old soldier knelt and handed him a large bottle of what turned out to be brandy. Low quality swill compared to what he usually had, but he devoured it just the same. *Time. I need time to plan. They can't send me to die. My pillar was hollow...* He kept picturing it in his mind. *This can't be the gods. They wouldn't do this to me! Hollow? Stone isn't hollow! Real stone is solid! It must be a fake! Yes, that woman must have moved my real pillar! She must have hired a wizard to move it. Clever bitch! I just need to reach the spy's guild and have them find her and then find out where she put my real pillar. Yes!* He stood, walked out to the street, and looked about to get his bearings. They'd taken him much further than he had noticed. *I can cut across the alley and take that street directly south to the lower market street and then it's only-*

"Sit back down." a large soldier stepped in front of him. He almost punched the man for the tone he had used, but when he looked up at the man's face, he knew sitting down was the better option. The man did not leave him be after that and Lasashu began considering whether he could outrun the man. Unfortunately, he had to conclude that the answer was no and so he set about considering the option of bribing the man instead. Technically, that was a crime, but he figured maybe the man didn't know what had just transpired. A demand should work, but he had to compose himself first.

"Hurry!" The voice broke Lasashu's focus, and he turned to find one of his father's advisors coming up the street at a dead run. Fifteen mounted soldiers trailed after him at a casual pace.

"Finally! My father has come to his senses!" He stood with a smile.

The advisor was an overly thin man in his middle years who kept a clean-shaven face, was overly eager in general, and rarely smiled. Egan or Allen or whatever his name was ran up to the two guards standing watch at the corner of the building and spoke with them quietly. They headed in toward the horse stalls at a jog and the advisor headed over to Lasashu. As he approached, Lasashu thought he saw a hint of satisfaction on the man's face, but it vanished as soon as the man locked eyes on Lasashu.

"You've arrived just in time." Lasashu announced to the man with a smile. "I have reasoned out the truth of what has occurred. If we hurry, we may be able to find my real pillar and the culprit of this grave injustice."

"Pardon?" The man furled an eyebrow at him.

Arlen didn't give him a proper bow or even address him with the proper honorific, but Lasashu let it pass without chastisement because of the dire situation. "Hurry back and tell my father that we have no time to waste. We must set the city guard on high alert and mobilize every soldier at our disposal! Go!"

Arell turned to face the mountain of a soldier and gave the man a small nod. "Good to see you, Landrik."

151

"You as well, Commander Rabbel."

"Please remove this man's possessions for the journey ahead."

"What?" Lasashu protested. "Did you not hear me? There will be no journey! We must correct this injustice! Go and tell my father quickly, as we have no time to spare. She'll be headed to the border already."

The soldier began patting Lasashu's pockets as the advisor watched, both quietly ignoring his pleas. A minute later, the two guards that had vanished returned with a bundle of brown clothing, handed it to the advisor, and returned to their positions at the corner of the building. When the guard finished checking Lasashu and stepped away, the advisor tossed the bundle of clothing at his feet and gave a very pleased smile. "Change." he said.

"Into these rags? I think not!"

"Landrik, I need you to... motivate this man for me."

"Happily, Commander Rabbel."

The soldier punched Lasashu in his stomach with remarkable speed. The only thing more surprising than the speed was the force behind that fist, which caused Lasashu to fall and roll over. Had he eaten, Lasashu was certain he would have had to empty his stomach immediately. He wanted to come up swinging but knew he was no match for the mountain of a man and so he took a moment to breathe and calm himself. *With a man this big and dumb, I have to fight with reason and logic.*

"The pillar was a fake." he said as he stood and began dusting off his shirt. "We must act quickly-"

"Quickly. Yes, you are correct. The sooner you reach the wall, the sooner we will know that our prince's life will be spared by the gods."

"There's no need for that. This is all a clever ruse to get rid of me." Lasashu explained.

152

"Change." the massive spat at him. "Or do you need more motivation?"

"You are speaking to a prince!"

"Your pillar broke. You aren't a prince. Change!" the advisor said as he drew his thin-bladed sword. "I will not ask again."

"How dare you draw a sword against me!" As Lasashu yelled, he spotted his brother among those on horseback. "Reginald! You will listen. We must hurry. There is a plot against me! We must put the city on high alert!" His brother jumped down from his horse and approached quickly. "We need to find this woman and the men she travels with. Sell-swords and thieves, you know. They will have hired a wizard to move my real pillar and replace it with that junk that broke. I bet the wizard made it to break when there were people nearby or just me. She's tricky like that, you see."

"Brother," Reginald took hold of Lasashu's shoulders and looked him in the eye. "Change your clothing. You know how this works."

"But, Reginald, I just told you what is going on."

"I heard you, Lasashu. If what you say is true, we will find her. You can tell me about the details along the way."

"No, she will escape. She wears disguises! Nobody will recognize her but me."

"No disguise will work against a wizard, Lasashu. We will find her."

It was humiliating enough to be forced to change in plain view of the public, but what made it worse was the plain, low quality, brown uniform he was given. To be dressed up as a fledgling soldier as if he were some commoner was an insult he would not soon forget. *That advisor picked these clothes just to humiliate me! Allen will pay for this!* Dressed in smelly, itchy clothing, he was presented a horse. He waited for a minute for someone to help him up, but the mounted men just glared at him expectantly. He watched how Reginald climbed into the saddle and did his best to mimic it, but it took him four attempts before finding success. Atop the horse at last, he sneered at those who refused to help him, dedicating each face to memory for later.

"My lord," Arlen said to Reginald with a tone of concern. "Custom dictates that only two go."

"The gods have allowed greater numbers to make the journey, Commander Rabbel." Reginald replied.

"Commander Rabbel," one of the mounted men spoke up from the back. "Lord Reginald has our allegiance, and we would not see him go alone. I, myself, owe a life-debt."

"Forgive me, Lord Reginald. I do not intend to question your judgment."

"There is nothing to forgive, Commander Rabbel. "Relay my brother's concerns to our father. If what he says is true, he deserves justice. I will send you what information he gives me once we reach the wall."

"Good luck to you all."

Lasashu's horse moved unprovoked, falling in behind his brother's horse, and the others fell in behind him. *These things follow each other. I thought this was going to be difficult!* Lasashu began to think. *This is perfect. We can leave the city and come back at night. Yes, that woman will hear the rumors and think that I am gone for good. She won't see my assassins coming!*

They took the most direct route through the city heading north. Beyond the heart of the capital, Lasashu noticed that the common folk suddenly stopped taking notice of his group and not even one of them gave the proper respect as they passed. Were he not dressed like a commoner, Lasashu would teach every one of them to show him the respect he was due. How Reginald tolerated it was beyond understanding. *Perhaps he is drunk, and I didn't smell it over this putrid uniform.*

"Brother," he tried pulling the horse's reigns and kicking it to get it to maneuver over to the side of his brother's horse, but his horse gave an annoyed snort and continued as it wished. "I have a new plan. It's brilliant, if I say so myself. She'll never expect it!"

"Who is this woman, Lasashu? And why does she vex you so greatly that you suspect her of going through such efforts?"

"She leads a group of sell-swords and thieves. They've been plaguing me for months. I let the insults pass, thinking I had run into a drunk here and there, but they stole my coin-purse and threatened me. I changed where I did my drinking and they found me again. I have tried having them apprehended, but they work in teams to distract the guards to escape. She has stolen over a hundred gold from me so far and now this business with my pillar."

"And what is this plan?"

"Take me out of the city and spread word to the commoners that I am off to the wall so that she'll hear it. She will think we fell for her little ruse. Then sneak me back in so I can speak with the spy and assassin guilds and have them hunt her down. She won't expect it and we can recover my real pillar!"

"And what of the mage who she hired to move your pillar and make the fake?"

"It has to be one of the elders in the order that studies the pillars. Nobody else would know how to pull the ruse off."

"And how many years of your soul would you trade for her life?"

"The assassins cannot ask for more than three and the spies will take gold and secrets as payment."

"I see." Reginald raised a hand and stuck one finger up and spun it in a circle. Immediately, the next soldier in the line came forward alongside his brother. "Go and see what dealings my brother has had

155

with the spy and assassin guilds. Report your findings to Commander Rabbel."

"Yes, my lord."

"There's no need for that, Reginald. You can ask them yourself when we meet with them tomorrow."

"We are going to the wall, Lasashu."

It took two days to become accustomed to the stench of the horse and the constant itching caused by the poor quality of his new clothing. Either was easy compared to the terrible food he was given, which he flat-out refused to eat after the first day. Of course, once his hunger grew, he had no choice but to eat what was given, even though he was pretty sure the lot had gone bad. *Dry, flavorless, plain bread! No honey or even jellied fruits. No duck liver or even beef!* To a man, none of his brother's personal guard could cook worth a damn. All they cared to catch were rabbits or snakes and even that they cooked too long and barely seasoned. Worse yet, the wine had run out just hours into the journey and his brother refused to turn back for more. If he had money, he would offer to pay them, but he was penniless and even his promises were of no value to them. *First the gods curse me and now they won't let me be in peace!*

*A vast f*orest appeared upon the horizon late into the second day and he had expected to enjoy the shade within, but he found that it only added terrible humidity to the heat. He poured sweat like he was ill and quickly developed a headache, for which nobody offered any medicine. Yet, it got worse as they dove deeper into the woods. He developed a rash on his inner thighs, a spider bit his left shoulder which itched to no end, a branch scratched his neck, the trees smelled like rot, and nobody cared. *This is why your pillar changed colors!* He thought angrily at his brother. *You stopped caring!* They slept on the bare ground and Lasashu had to use his shirt for a pillow, which had developed quite the rank odor, but he had no other choice since nobody had offered him one of their spare shirts or blankets.

"It is too hot for this." He complained to his brother as they mounted their horses on the morning of the third day. He wanted nothing more than to sleep after that horrid breakfast of overcooked rabbit with no spicing and stale, plain bread.

"So, you have said...four times this morning, Lasashu." His brother didn't look away from the path in the woods.

"I don't think it is wise to push the horses in this heat. They could fall ill."

"The horses are fine."

"Perhaps it would be better to find a town tonight instead of sleeping on the ground again." Lasashu suggested.

He recalled having been told that there were only a few towns between the wall and the capital, but so far there had been none along the way. There wasn't even a road sign, which worried him. He wondered if his brother was taking them along this old, ill-used path to intentionally avoid perfectly good towns along the way just to deprive Lasashu of good sleep and drink. *Who knows what you'll do since your pillar changed.* He eyed his brother suspiciously. If he were home, he could call on the men who studied the pillars to find out what was wrong with his brother and what had caused the change. *Can I even trust you as a brother?*

"The nearest town is Denhald, and the detour would cost us three days, which we don't have."

"What is three days in exchange for a soft bed and good ale, Reginald?"

"I don't have three extra days."

"You don't know that."

157

"Nobody knows when I will fall dead. The gods may have given me years, but I will not gamble with my life to sate your frivolous desires." Reginald spoke flatly, as if commenting on the color of a tree, but Lasashu could tell that his brother was both worried and annoyed by the way he held himself in the horse's saddle.

"First, that woman plots to make it seem that the gods have cursed me and now my own brother refuses me the smallest of comforts. What a fine few days indeed!"

"Listen to me, Lasashu." Reginald turned in his saddle, locked eyes with Lasashu, and took several deep breaths. "Were you not my brother, I would cut the tongue from your mouth here and now. I would beat you black and blue and you would walk barefoot the remaining distance."

"You are a heartless bastard!" Lasashu yelled. *I must escape tonight!*

A REASON FOR LIES

By the time White Rock came into view, Lord Kairn had already grown to suspect that the town was on high alert. Every traveler heading away from it had kept their distance from his forces and wore expressions of worry or outright fear. Traders heading away were well-armed and traveled with far too many soldiers their common wares could ever justify. Unfortunately, he hadn't been able to get clear answers from those he had stopped along the way, for they all gave cryptic answers or refused to stop for him. There were large groups of heavily armed soldiers patrolling the town's perimeter when he arrived, and they reacted quickly upon seeing his force's arrival by forming up into a defensive wall at the pathway into the town. When his men arrived before that wall of soldiers, they waved him to enter the town, but nobody came to speak with him.

As they passed beyond the first few houses and neared the water, Lord Kairn paused at a striking sight. Two white houses stood astride a large patch of charred grass. For a long moment, his mind refused to work the sight out and he had to focus his mind on it like a drunkard before noticing that the charred area formed a sloppy circle. Though it was a good distance away, he saw signs of a battle there. A chunk of wood was missing from the corner of one house and there was a sharp gouge in another place that must have been from an ax. In the center of the charred grass, there was a patch of bare dirt where someone had dug down half a finger deep and removed the topsoil. He aimed himself at that scene and noticed a large group of soldiers come into view from the north. No, they were forming up, not coming into view. *I need rest. My eyes are playing with me. Or coffee. Yes, coffee and then rest.* With the banner of House Turley raised on a pole at their front, they began to march while still forming up. They were impressive in their speed and silence, letting out only a few clangs of metal on metal. Lord Kairn marched to the edge of the burned grass and waited for them in silence.

"House Turley welcomes House Kairn to White Rock."

While the common soldiers wore white adorned with a bright red wolf on the chest, this man wore a sharp uniform of half black and half red with a sunburst that spanned his entire chest. A high commander if Lord Kairn remembered the odd insignia of House Turley correctly. The man walked out from the others and greeted Lord Kairn with a smile as he approached.

"We appreciate the welcome." Lord Kairn replied. He wasn't interested in this high commander as much as the expressions on the soldiers beyond. Most appeared bored or tired, but there were a handful who wore expressions of shock – the usual expression of soldiers after seeing their first combat or death. No, it was something more. A few of them stood too close to their compatriots and held their weapons with white-knuckled grips. *They've seen worse than some regular battle and death.* The high commander came and offered his hand with a generous smile.

"Your men are very welcome here, Lord Kairn. House Turley will be pleased to accommodate you at the manor up north."

"Thank you, High commander. Is that the direction the assassin headed?"

"It's just captain...Captain Reskar, Lord Kairn."

"My apologies, Captain Reskar. I'm not very familiar with House Turley's ranking system. Seems to be a well-guarded secret."

"Yes, we change uniforms regularly to confuse any would-be spies or infiltrators. What assassin do you speak of?"

"The assassin who tried to kill high-king Hotar that has escaped some days ago now. I was sent to capture him. King Hotar informed me that he'd been spotted here in White Rock. I would have come sooner, but we ran into issues."

"I know nothing of an assassin, Lord Kairn, but that might be why my company was ordered to White Rock. Perhaps this assassin was spotted here by one of King Hotar's spies, but we were not informed of such, or we would have assisted in capturing the villain. Unfortunately, we've had our own excitement and without knowing what this assassin looks like, I could not tell you in which direction he traveled. I could have my men ask the townspeople. Do you have a description?"

"I do not, but I have that...creature." He pointed out Ras'vetra, who seemed entirely uninterested in the gathering of soldiers as he walked towards the water ahead. "What excitement have you had?"

"A small group of vampires, Lord Kairn. As you can see, it caused quite a disturbance. Almost lost both these houses to fire and one on the far north side of town as well. Luckily, only a few were injured, and nobody was killed. It was fortunate for White Rock that my company had arrived just before sunset that day. We could have lost the entire town." He gave a very proud smile.

"Very fortunate indeed."

161

Lord Kairn looked over Captain Reskar's soldiers quickly and found that none seemed bothered at the sight of Ras'vetra as he walked out into the water, but they were watching. This was a secondary concern for him now though, as it was more alarming that the man was lying about the fire almost destroying the two buildings. Lord Kairn has seen a few houses that had caught fire before and a few seasonal brush fires, which had driven him to study how fires spread for a summer. This fire hadn't caused anything more than superficial damage to either house; further, the fire hadn't been fueled by the grass, as there was plenty of green in the burned areas. So, it hadn't been fueled by the grass or anything on the ground here. He guessed that the fire had been projected downward as if from one of the fire-breathers that were part of carnivals or perhaps through magic. This close, he spotted tracks from a cart that had been used to haul something out of the area, which suggested that they were hiding something. Wherever that topsoil had been moved to, he guessed there would also be blood and maybe even the bodies of whomever had been slain. He wondered if stories were right about vampire bodies turning entirely to ash upon death as he looked to the north. He did not see another such area of burned grass or any house with fire damage.

"Where are the bodies?"

"Burned two days ago, Lord Kairn."

"Did you capture any alive?"

"We slaughtered all that we could. Best guess is that there were three survivors from the group, and they headed back east into the forest." The captain's eyes shifted a bit, and his smile became forced. *What are you worrying about?*

"Any idea why they attacked?"

"It's a smaller town. It only attracts large numbers during trade times. Luckily, this was a slow week for trade. We figured they planned to feed on the townspeople but didn't know my company had arrived. We struck camp just north of town. I've heard vampires usually watch

162

towns for a few days before attacking. Perhaps this group was starving to the point of madness."

"Would you mind allowing us to share your camp? My men are rather exhausted from the days of marching and carrying heavy armor."

"It would be my honor, Lord Kairn. I do believe that you'll be the first member of the Kairn line to visit Turley territory in four generations."

"I think you may be correct. I believe it was my great-grandfather Dolin who was on speaking terms with Jeremiah Turley in their youth."

"Then it will be my great pleasure to relay the news of your visit to Lord Turley."

North beyond the trees, the first thing Lord Kairn spotted was a vast expanse of sun-bleached tents arranged into rows and columns with banners standing here and there with what he assumed were platoon insignia. Near the camp's heart, he saw six tents big enough to seat twenty soldiers comfortably and then ten nearly half that size on the north end with one large flag waving gently in the wind with the House Turley sunburst in gold on black.

Some hundred or so soldiers were occupied with training exercises on the East side of the camp. They were broken into clusters of people performing different exercises with those running forming a circle around the lot. Across the road to the West, there was a group of maybe forty people working over fires and cauldrons. The smell of spiced meats made Lord Kairn's stomach erupt with violent protests, reminding him that he hadn't eaten in nearly a day now. In total, Lord Kairn counted at least two-hundred soldiers within sight, but there were at least three times that number of tents by his quick estimation.

"I would recommend that your men toss their things down now and grab chow before those soldiers start forming up. You can accompany me to my tent. They always bring several meals worth for me and whatever company I have. I also have some fine southern rum, if you'd

163

care to partake, Lord Kairn." Captain Reskar explained in a jovial tone as he began walking a bit faster.

"That I would, Captain."

Lord Kairn turned a moment to wave his men to do as suggested and continued alongside the captain. When they reached the first row of tents, he took note of the paths between and around them, where the ground was almost barren. He considered whether the captain had lied out of the habit of concealing his company's movements or if there was some conflict brewing with a neighboring territory's soldiers he meant to conceal.

They passed through many rows in silence before arriving upon the six large tents at the center of camp, where they were greeted by three soldiers standing guard before the first. Others stood guard before the other five tents and still more patrolled the whole lot, which made Lord Kairn wonder just what valuables required so many soldiers to guard. Captain Reskar dismissed their salutes with a wave as he passed them. Lord Kairn gave the soldiers a wave and followed the man into the tent. Inside, he found the tent lined with big tables piled high with all manner of general supplies. Crates full of bottles of alcohol, swords, spears, writing implements, socks, shoes, shirts, coiled ropes, reams of paper, and bulging sacks of flour, sugar and coffee beans. In the center of the room was a large flat table with a map and near the rear was a slender table covered in food stuffs. The captain headed directly to the table and began pouring himself a cup of clear rum and once done, grabbed a hand of meat and shoved it in his mouth with a sudden look of desperate hunger on his face. He waved Lord Kairn over, mumbled approvingly at him, and chewed quickly.

"Pardon my manners, but it's been a busy day on top of a busy week. I've not yet eaten today. Help yourself, Lord Kairn."

"Thank you." Lord Kairn found a stack of oval white plates and silverware in the far-left corner of the table almost hidden by a stack of books. He grabbed a plate and fork and began piling it high with

164

food. Once the plate became heavy, he poured himself a cup of rum, which was about as clear as water. Southerners were partial to light spicing in strong rum, which wasn't to his taste, but he found it pleasing now. "My men could use with a washing as well, if possible."

"Ah. Well, I dare say that your men are in for a pleasing surprise. We currently have on loan a mage who can draw water from the ground and heat it." He smiled as if at fond memories, stuffed his mouth, and then frowned. "Uh, recently found, of course."

"Of course." Lord Kairn agreed with the lie by offering a smile and a wink, as was customary.

"Oh...I guess I don't have to lie about that with the change in law on that matter. I just got the news yesterday." Captain Reskar snatched another big chunk of meat and popped it into his mouth with a big smile. "I apologize if that offends you."

"Not at all." He took a swig of the rum and began to work on his food.

"Kind of odd that you were sent to hunt down an assassin with heavy armor, if you ask me."

"That shadow-man was supposed to take us to White Rock by magic."

"How do you mean?"

"A terrifying and vomit-inducing manner of travel. We were in King Hotar's war room, and, without warning, everything went darker than night. At first, it felt like falling and then rolling down a hill in a barrel at incredible speed. I couldn't even see my own body or scream. The spinning seemed to change direction after just a moment and...and then we were back in the world again. I remember falling, but perhaps no higher off the ground than a wagon bed. In those moments, we had traveled what would have taken us days by foot."

"Incredible." He downed the rest of his cup and returned to the bottle eagerly. "So, you had a destination before White Rock?"

"No. That shadow-man misunderstood where to take us. It took us to a small white pebble in a field between Taln's Bend and Red River and then said it couldn't do the same trick again. I was told that it isn't terribly intelligent." Lord Kairn stuffed his mouth with food and studied the tent's insides carefully.

"Sounds both astounding and terrifying."

"It was a bit of both."

"I wish I had one. If I could move troops that quickly...well, I can't really imagine how productive that would make things. OH! Imagine if it could move grain during harvest."

"That would certainly be something, but he hasn't been able to reproduce the feat in four days."

"Sounds terribly unreliable."

"Indeed." He considered what to do about Ras'vetra's performance issues as he chewed another big bite and examined the tent. "So, are you hoarding things to prevent theft?" He waved at the room in general.

"No, we had another tent for this stuff, but it got a big rip during transport. Should be repaired in a day or two. Until then, I will be sharing my space. Officers don't really need this much space anyhow. It's all for show, if you ask me."

"I see." He stuffed his face again and examined the contents more carefully. There wasn't anything out of the ordinary as far as he could see.

"I can resupply your soldiers with most things before you set back out. We have plenty of supplies and whatever we don't have here, we can find in White Rock. Trade has really picked up here in the last few years. That's why we came here. Normally, we would get our supplies from Turley keep directly after sending requisition requests and waiting a moon."

"I appreciate that. Can you arrange for our heavy armor to be sent back to the high king? I think if I try to make them march with that stuff another day, they'll hang me up from the nearest tree."

"Certainly."

"And I'll leave a letter expressing my gratitude with you for Lord Turley as well."

"That may take a while to get into his hands. The last thing I knew; Lord Turley was traveling to the capital. Besides which, he rarely inspects my company. Says I run a well-oiled machine."

"It does appear as such."

Lord Kairn spent the next two hours drinking, feasting, and discussing whatever subject Captain Reskar brought up. Luckily, Captain Reskar possessed a sharp wit and an animated sense of humor. In another life, the man could have been a jester or some such in a traveling bazaar, but he'd managed to find himself here instead. The man enjoyed discussing four things in life: finances, combat tactics, the proper care of a sword, and the woman he was going to marry. Her name was Mayla, and she was a petite blonde with big blue eyes, daughter of a minor lord and the youngest of six siblings. She was a rebellious, foul-mouthed woman who didn't care for wasting words or time doing anything she wasn't enjoying, which had often meant that she could be found reading, drinking, or hiring bodyguards to take her deep into the wilderness in search of the unknown. That was how Captain Reskar had met her and, subsequently, found himself both in love and in a prison cell four years ago. It turned out her father hadn't appreciated Captain Reskar assisting his daughter in her venture into the forest when he had expected her to make an appearance at a celebration, but, as it turned out, she would rather be hunting for lost artifacts and such instead. They shared two years like that: adventuring, being caught, and then him spending a few hours in a cell with her father berating him. Things had changed recently though. Mayla turned twenty-seven, graduating from spinster to thornback and her father had suddenly declared them engaged. They'd be married shortly, but first he had to see to the construction of their home, which was about half done currently.

In the morning, Lord Kairn made the walk to White Rock alone to see what he might discover for himself. He followed the road south into town, circled around the water twice and then headed south to the cluster of buildings that encircled the tall white pillar after which the town had been named. His father had been interested in this stone and had numerous drawings and paintings of it in a book filled with stories of its origin and purported meanings. Some stories said the rock had fallen from the sky and others said that it was left there by whomever had built the ring-walls of the capital – a discarded leftover never seen to by those ancient builders for unknown reasons. Whatever the case, he found himself there wondering at it for some time.

He considered the shape of the town, the path of the roads, the pond, the ring of trees growing around the town and began planning how he would attack the place. He worked out several strategies to defend the town and began running through different scenarios. Time and time again, he ran into the same problems. Most worrying was the fact that the soldiers were camped north of town and had been there longer than Captain Reskar had claimed. *They would have seen the camp...why risk alerting so many soldiers?* If he had been leading the vampires, he would have wanted to begin his attack from the north side of town in order to prevent any patrolling soldiers from escaping and alerting greater forces. None of the soldiers he had seen so far carried horns, which would their ability to audibly alert the camp. A scream or the clanging of metal might do the trick, but horns were quite commonly used when such a distance existed.

If the vampires attacked from the east, why is there only the one large, burned section of grass on the west side of the water? Perhaps they wanted something from inside those houses? Perhaps the fire was a distraction? Knowing little of vampires, he wondered why they would cluster up and make a stand in the face of such a large force? *Surely, they would have seen that camp and planned for a tactical retreat. There should have been human casualties regardless of who set the fire though. They must have come from the west instead and thought themselves undetected.*

"Ras'vetra." he spoke quietly.

"Yes, Lord Kairn?" Lord Kairn nearly jumped with the suddenness of Ras'vetra's voice at his side. It took several deep breaths to calm his heart.

"Don't sneak up on me like that." Lord Kairn nearly yelled.

"You called me. I assumed it was urgent."

"Just walk up like people do."

"I will try, Lord Kairn, but it is difficult to learn your strange customs."

"Do try." He glanced around to see if any of the patrolling soldiers were nearby before continuing. "Can you tell what happened here?"

"Can you be more specific, Lord Kairn?"

"With the recent battle. That Captain is hiding something."

"A group of vampires came and were ambushed. Most of them were slain."

"Ambushed?"

"Yes."

"How can you tell?"

"I watched it happen."

"You were here?" Lord Kairn tried to keep his voice down, but the shadow-man was really testing his patience.

"No, Lord Kairn. I was with you."

169

"You can see that far?"

"I can see no further than you."

"Then how did you see it?"

"Birds showed me."

"The birds show you things but won't let you travel through that dark place?"

"Of course not, Lord Kairn."

Lord Kairn rubbed his temple and sighed deeply to keep himself from outright screaming at the thing. "Can you tell which direction the assassin went?"

"The man you are seeking went East."

"Will you take us to him with magic yet?"

"No, Lord Kairn."

"How long do birds watch you?"

"Depends on the bird, really."

"Can you tell why the captain is lying about what happened?"

"I cannot."

"You really are about useless."

"Thank you, Lord Kairn." the shadow-man's voice sounded very pleased.

"What about the vampires?"

"They went back West."

"Well-wait, what? Back West?"

"Yes, back west."

"They didn't come from the east?"

"No, Lord Kairn. They came from the west and returned in that direction."

"Did they catch the assassin?"

"They did not."

WITHOUT LIFE

After days of practicing the stances and swings Frezz had taught him, Ashan was sure that he had learned all there was to know about getting blisters from swinging a sword and a little of how to treat them. Overall, he was sure that the only thing he had learned about using a sword was that he knew almost nothing about using a sword and that realization had stoked a fire in him to learn all he could. To think that some goo from the inside of a plant could relieve his pains simply by smearing it on his skin was a wonder and he hadn't believed it at first; more so, Frezz had explained that it would help his skin heal as well and, currently, he didn't believe that. *There's a lot of things I don't know,* he reminded himself as he slashed through a thick cluster of vines and stepped forward. The pain in his hand was a constant reminder to hold the white rusty sword with a more relaxed grip, which went against his instincts. *Everybody knows more than me,* he thought

173

as he began pulling the larger dead branches free of the wagon's path in the roadway.

For a while, he imagined how his life might be now if things had gone differently. He had not escaped the dungeon, been freed after a time, and become a free person. In his freedom, he had found a job, earned money, lived in a small house, and spent his free time reading books in Master Hank's bookshop. *No, I would buy books and read them in my own home.* In that life, he would have become an avid reader, perhaps reading an entire book each moon, and would live in a clean home. There would be clean clothing, regular bathing, and good food. *Friends would be nice too.* His imaginings were pleasant distractions from the hard work of clearing the road for the wagon, but he kept having trouble picturing himself working. *I know how to make deliveries and care for an old mule. How does that make money? What else could I do?*

Fierce drumming broke the tranquil near-silence of the forest. Startled, Ashan dropped the dead tree limb he had been dragging and shot upright, searching for the source of the drumming. *Soldiers use drums!* He recalled the drumming from White Rock and during the escape from the dungeon and his heart began to race. The drumming almost felt like an attack all on its own. He caught a dark flicker of movement from the corner of his eyes, but when he turned to face it, he found nothing. He raised the sword up and over his shoulder so that he was prepared to swing at whatever might come, but then remembered Frezz's teachings on stance and adjusted himself to the first stance that came to mind. He turned so that his hip faced whatever enemy might come with most of his weight on the leg further away from an attacker. As he re-positioned the sword, he spotted a man dressed in loose-fitting black clothing that seemed three sizes too large and worn thin. He weaved left and right around trees as he charged toward Ashan. Heart racing, Ashan imagined it was a vampire. *No, it's daytime!* When the man reached the road, Ashan found that he was wearing some sort of leather mask. The man reached into his coat, pulled out a knife, and threw it.

Ashan half swung his sword at the knife and dropped to the ground at the same time with a shout. The sound of metal striking stone caught his attention and it took a moment to realize that he'd released the sword as he'd dropped. He rolled over and away from where the man had been, imagining the man might try to attack where he lay, and climbed to his feet. He began stepping backward as fast as his feet would allow and searched for the sword and the man at the same time.

"Get down!" Looking, Ashan found Frezz halfway between the wagon and himself approaching at a fast walk. He held a staff raised high in one hand with a red glow emitting from the top and a knife in the other. His human disguise was melting away as he moved as if being blown off by a wind that wasn't there.

"My sword!" Ashan yelled as he stepped toward it.

"No!" Frezz thrust his staff forward and a stream of fire spewed from it.

Ashan dove to the ground and rolled away from the stream of fire. The masked man dove to the side to evade, but the stream of fire struck its leg, causing it to rotate in the air. Ashan rolled all the way to the dropped sword, grabbed it with both hands, and climbed to his feet clumsily.

"Move!" Frezz shouted over the roar of fire. Looking back over his shoulder, Ashan saw that the fountain of fire was shifting towards him. He dropped back down and rolled under the fire again. "Watch out!" Frezz shouted. The man came from above the fire at a terrifying speed and slammed a foot in the center of Ashan's chest. Ashan hit the ground, felt his grip on the sword falter, and rolled several times.

"Retreat!" Frezz shouted.

Ashan rolled onto his back just in time to see the masked man leap into the air. In the air, the human form melted away, the black cloth twisting around and stretching out until it resembled a snake instead of a man. It wound around another fountain of fire and

175

continued until it arrived upon Frezz. It snaked around Frezz's staff and latched onto his wrist. Frezz dropped his knife and clawed at the thing, but it continued snaking up his arm unbothered.

Ashan fetched his sword and ran over, not knowing exactly what he could do to attack the snake without injuring Frezz. By instinct, he grabbed at the snake with one hand and prepared to cut with the sword carefully. He was surprised to find the form wasn't solid; rather, the mass was made of strips of frayed, oily cloth that smelled so horridly that he almost began vomiting immediately. The frayed bits snaked between and around his fingers like a thousand worms wriggling to escape. He clasped and tore at the mass, but each handful of oily wormy stuff slowly wriggled through the air to the larger mass and rejoined in the movement up Frezz's staff and arm.

It progressed slowly, but surely. When it reached Frezz's neck a frantic minute later, Frezz raised his arm straight out before himself and uttered something Ashan didn't understand. The thing jolted violently twice and then froze suddenly as a dull light arose from deep within its core. Frezz then slung his arm down and most of the mass flew from him and splattered upon the road. A heartbeat later, a soft hissing arose as black tendrils of smoke began rising slowly. Ashan turned the sword over and drove it through the center of the smoking mess. Black liquid splattered everywhere, but it did not respond otherwise.

"It was just cloth and oil?" He withdrew the sword and poked at the pile carefully.

"It was a shadow."

"A... shadow?" Ashan turned to check that his own shadow was still normal.

"A creature created by magic."

"What did you do to it?"

176

"A purification spell." he answered as he began picking bits of oily cloth from his sleeve.

Ashan studied the mass for a moment, wondering if he should offer it a prayer for the dying so that the gods would take it to a better place. "Were you scared?"

"Not of that. I thought I sensed something more though." Frezz gave the mess a quick look, turned his attention to the forest around them, and began to sniff the air. "Do you smell that?"

"Just burning cloth." Ashan quickly scanned the forest.

"It's very quiet."

Why did the drums stop? No, the drums were still there, but they'd grown more distant and had slowed greatly. "Very." Ashan closed his mouth so he didn't have to taste the air and focused on what he could smell. After a moment, he caught a hint of rancid oil and ash which reminded him of Sa'teshka. "Would vampires make a thing like that? I smell something like Sa'teshka."

"I doubt they could. From what I have read, vampires have great difficulty with practicing magic. I thought I sensed something that would be dangerous though."

"That seemed plenty dangerous to me."

"It would be dangerous for the ill-equipped."

"Someone like me who can't use magic?"

"Well, yes...and no. You could have made easy work of it with the right training or even with just enough salt."

"Salt?"

"Yes, many dark creations like that react violently to salt. Just mix salt into water and wet your blade and it will cause devastating wounds to such things...usually."

177

"Does that work on vampires?"

"No, vampires aren't dark creations."

"Maybe this is why people say the forest is haunted." Ashan offered.

Frezz closed his eyes and sniffed the air slowly for a minute before speaking again. "Quick lesson time. There's nothing you can do to fight a ghost, so if we do happen to come upon one and it comes for you just start telling a story or singing. Many of them will become enchanted by such things. The undead can be frightening and disgusting, but they will cease being animated if you cut off their heads. Easy work, but don't let them gang up on you. Run if there are too many getting close to you."

"What does animated mean?"

"Like being brought back to life, but without the mind of the person they were."

A second later, the oil and ash odor grew substantially stronger, carried by a gentle breeze from the South. Ashan faced the gentle breeze and watched the forest, leaning this way and that to peer between trees. After nearly a minute, he caught a glimpse of motion between trees. He shifted to one side and discovered that there were two figures approaching this time. "Two." he said and began to wonder if Frezz could take on two of those things at once as easily as the one.

These two did not break out into a run like the other and, after watching for a long while, he noticed a limp in the stride of a man covered in mud. Behind the first, there came a short, slender woman in what must have once been a long, flowing gown, but was now a darkly stained and shredded mess that barely covered her torso. She moved as if each step might be her last. His instinct was to run to her and offer help. The wind suddenly picked up and Ashan had to take a quick step back and cover his nose to block out the increased intensity of the putrid odor. Rot and advanced decay struck him mightily and a cold chill ran through him.

"Sick people!"

"Undead." Frezz hissed and stepped forward. "Keep an eye out for someone who is alive." He spun in a circle and began speaking words Ashan didn't know.

Ashan spotted six more people shuffling out in the distance – all with the same clumsy gait and state of clothing. A slender, aged, black human in black clothing with a plain blue trim appeared in a group a minute later, which caused Ashan to gasp audibly in shocked recognition. The man's lanky frame, short black hair with a hint of white above each ear and the scar running across his forehead were unmistakable. He recognized the man from the hundreds of statues, paintings, and murals he had seen his entire life as high-King Catora. Unlike the others, he was dressed in clean clothing and his face and hands were cleaned as though he had just been bathed. *I thought they cremated your body!* A black scabbard with gold trimming hung empty at his side and a short, silver knife protruded from his chest, but there was no staining upon the clothing he wore. One of his hands was missing.

"King Catora!" Ashan yelled.

"They're undead." Frezz flung his staff about wildly and the little, red stone atop it began glowing brilliantly. "Try cutting their heads off and do not allow them to surround you." Ashan felt sick at the prospect of doing the former king's body damage. *Well, at least I'll die free, Ashan* thought with a weak smile. "We hold here. Let them come to us and then retreat as needed."

Ashan raised the rusty white sword and tried to count the shuffling bodies. Beyond the shuffling corpse of King Catora, there was a man barely older than Ashan with a large chunk of his neck missing who appeared to have had his midsection cut open and the insides removed. Not far behind that man, there was another wearing a priest's dark brown robe with six arrows sticking out from his chest. Three were clustered together directly behind the priest wearing plain

179

clothing and bearing no obvious blood stains, arrows or knives; however, their faces and arms appeared much older than their semi-clean clothing, almost as though they had died of old age, and someone had dressed them up in newer clothing. Ashan thought it odd that whoever was creating such monsters might be concerned with modesty.

A wall of vines shot up from the ground and wrapped around the three in the back, causing them to fall to the ground. They did not yell in surprise the way Ashan expected; rather, they clawed at the ground as if trying to continue moving forward and worked their mouths as if angry. Ashan drew up the sword and watched in silence, wondering if they would break free or turn their attention upon their restraints. A few seconds passed and the air rippled at their feet and slowly expanded. He looked to Frezz to ask what the man was doing, but then decided not to interrupt whatever it was. When he looked back that the three, half their bodies were gone and the rippling in the air was just swallowing up their heads.

"Your illusions will not serve you here!" Frezz shouted. Ashan turned just in time to see Frezz thrust his staff forward. The fountain of fire flew forward, met the rippling in the air, and fanned out like water hitting the ground. A moment later there came a loud boom and then a sudden gust of wind slammed into Ashan, carrying an even more vile stench that turned his stomach and made his eyes water. Those drums were suddenly close, but this time there were at least six and the beat was frantic. He heard Frezz speaking sharp, unfamiliar words in what seemed both anger and surprise. He blinked rapidly to clear the tears from his eyes and saw that the rippling in the air was gone, now replaced by at least twenty shuffling bodies. Fire erupted from the ground here and there at Frezz's utterances, and some of the bodies were flung back or set ablaze. The rest continued walking forward.

"WOAH!" Ashan shouted and jumped back when a wall of fire sprung from the grass at his toes without any warning.

Vines wriggled up from the earth to wrap around the legs of the nearest undead and the smell of burning flesh quickly filled the air. In the moment, it was difficult to believe what he was seeing happen. The nearest undead fell because of the vines upon his legs, but he began pulling himself forward with both arms. The vines were too late and too slow to catch the second undead and it came directly at Ashan with arms outstretched and hands grabbing. When it was close, it let out a menacing growl like a dog and lunged at him. Ashan barely managed to jump backward and out of reach.

Ashan turned left, thinking to run away, and stepped backwards with one leg at the same time. This resulted in him tripping over himself and falling backwards to his left side. He yelled in fright at his mistake, looked up at the man, and helplessly watched him step forward and lean down toward him.

"Ashan!" Frezz came between them, his hand closing around the undead's neck, and let out a terrifying growl. The undead man raked his fingernails across Frezz's face as Frezz lifted and tossed him toward the fire as if he weighed nothing. Frezz turned, took Ashan by the arm and dragged him to his feet. Ashan was surprised to find that he had kept hold of his sword.

A scream arose in the distance then and Frezz released Ashan to turn back towards the oncoming undead. To his horror, Ashan found that the undead were closing quite a lot faster than he had originally understood. Frezz stepped back and thrust his staff out with a yelled word that sounded like half a word interrupted by a roar. A small ball of yellow fire sprouted from the end of his staff and flew quite fast until it struck one of the undead in the chest and cast it backward into several others. A wall of fire shot up from the ground a good ten paces ahead and stretched out a good ten strides wide. The undead didn't seem to care at all, stepping through it as if they weren't aware of its existence.

"Their heads!" Frezz yelled as his free hand rose to check the scratches on his face. There were three small bleeding lines on his cheek. *Red*

181

blood. Just like everything else, Ashan thought as he raised his sword and faced the coming enemy. The others were getting close, and they all glared at him with a strange hunger in their eyes.

"Be careful." Frezz ran forward and thrust his staff forward like it was a spear. The blow knocked a man back off his feet and sent it rolling into the wall of fire, which seemed to be shrinking rapidly.

"Yes, Master Frezz." Ashan followed Frezz forward and jumped over what was left of the wall of fire, raised his sword overhead, and brought the blade down between the eyes of the nearest undead. The skull split with a sickening crack, the man ceased moving, and began falling backward. Ashan was pulled forward by his sword, which refused to come free of the undead's skull. Just as he lost his balance, he released the sword to keep from falling upon the body and fell at its side instead. He rolled away from the thing, scrambled to his feet, and studied it to make certain it wasn't...alive still. Then he took the blade in both hands and rocked it back and forth to free it.

He hefted the sword upright again and checked his surroundings. Nearby, he spotted Frezz, who kicked one undead in the midsection, backstepped, and thrust his staff out at it. The ball of fire engulfed the undead and it flew back as if kicked in the chest by a massive horse. "Ashan! Wagon!" Frezz turned and ran toward the wagon. The vines here and there suddenly fell to the ground and the last flames vanished in the blink of an eye. Thunder sounded somewhere in the distance and a streak of white light cut through the forest a moment later. It branched off to strike an undead and a tree near to where it stood and winked out. *Lightning?!* Ashan turned and blinked his eyes rapidly to get them to adjust after the brilliant white of the lightning. Thunder sounded again and he closed his eyes in preparation for the flash of light.

Something touched his shoulder and ran down halfway to his elbow. He jumped away, turned, and opened his eyes to a large man who might have once been a soldier from the size of his arms. He scrambled to raise his sword and back away from the man at the same

182

time, but tripped over something and went down. Instinct told him to brace his grip upon the sword and roll further away from the man and he let that guide him. He felt sticks break beneath him as he rolled and flew to his feet after three rolls. He raised the sword halfway, spun around, and used the momentum to attack the creature, only needing to angle the blade up at the thing's neck. Passing over its arms by a thumb's width, the blade struck true, but cut only halfway through the undead's neck. It must have worked though, because the thing suddenly went limp and fell to the ground, half tackling Ashan in the process.

"Frezz!" He pushed the undead off his legs, fetched his sword, and ran towards the wagon.

It took two breaths before he found Frezz lying on the ground with black smoke rising from a dark spot on his back. He screamed and ran as hard as he could. The back of his clothing had a black burn in a rough circle about as big around as one of Ashan's hands. "Frezz!" He dropped the sword, grabbed Frezz by the shoulders, and rolled the man over. His eyes didn't open but he groaned weakly. A snarl came from behind and, turning, he saw one undead coming very much faster than the others.

Ashan grabbed his sword and jumped to his feet. He found himself in a stance without having thought about taking it, and only just then decided that Frezz was right that they would become instinctive after a time. He waited for the undead and swung the sword with all his might, hoping to take the head off at the neck. He missed by several inches, was dragged to the side by the sword's weight, and had to jump back to escape the undead man's reaching hands. He reset his feet, realizing now that he shouldn't put his entire body into an attack as he just had, and waited. The undead man came again, and he waited for it to get closer this time. *Much closer.* He swung and closed his eyes at the same time and felt the resistance of flesh and bone.

Thunder rumbled through the forest. Remembering the direction from which the lightning had come previously, Ashan turned and hoped it would miss him. The streak of white came in an instant, burning at his eyes and making everything else seem dark. At first, he thought that it was heading towards a tree a good thirty strides to his right side, but then it shifted course directly towards himself. He screamed, raised his sword, and slammed his eyes shut. *Isn't lightning faster than this?* Every hair on his head stood and he screamed again, certain that he was about to die. Something collided with his sword, and he had to redouble his grip not to lose hold of the thing. Opening his eyes, all he could see were parts of his arms and a brilliant white light that hurt to look at.

The sword shifted left and down as if somebody had yanked on the end of it and suddenly the light vanished. The world was all blurry splotches of color not even vaguely in recognizable shapes and he prayed to the gods that his vision hadn't been ruined forever. *Please, let me see again.* There came thunder again and the sword shifted to his left and up on its own accord right before that brilliant white light filled his vision again. *Doesn't thunder come after lightning?* The sword shifted to his right slowly, as if someone were gently pulling it by the tip. *Doesn't metal let lightning flow to the ground? Doesn't it always make its way to the ground no matter what is in the way?* He couldn't remember where he had heard these things. *Magic,* he hissed to himself. *Frezz lied about this sword!* He wanted to be angry, but the fact that the sword was currently saving him from what he could only imagine was a painful death twisted his anger into gratitude.

He realized that the movement and pressure of the sword was like that of a fish pulling on a fishing line. He remembered, for a moment, fishing with his father. They had been seated upon a checkered blanket at the edge of a lake and his father had explained to him how to judge the size of the fish from the sensations coming along the line. Whatever was on the other end of this bolt of lightning was moving, walking, getting closer one step at a time, and it was much larger than a fish.

He thought of Frezz laying upon the ground nearby and wondered how he could protect the man from the remaining undead who were, no doubt, still approaching. He glanced to the side, expecting to be so blind that all he would find was a blurred color. He expected not to be able to tell which splotch was the wagon; however, he found that his eyes focused almost immediately when not facing the white light in front of himself.

"Frezz." he yelled when he did not find the man.

Then the lightning vanished, and he found the undead were quite close now. He began slowly walking backwards as he considered the situation. Beyond the undead, there appeared a middle-aged, portly woman wearing a black cloak clasped at the neck with a single golden leaf pendant. Under the cloak, she wore a black dress with blue lace trim three fingers thick, and a high neckline that Ashan found both familiar and strange at the same time. Her dirty blonde hair hung in gentle curls halfway to her elbows. It took a moment to realize that the chest of her dress was covered in thumbnail sized green gems that formed the shape of an eye. She held a short white stick in one hand as she marched directly towards Ashan. Behind her, there followed a thin figure in white cloth bandages covering every bit of its skin like a leper.

"This is MY FOREST!" Her voice came strained and shrill.

Ashan dodged an undead woman, raised his sword, and brought it down through the thing's skull. After, he had to plant a foot on the back of the thing to wiggle and pull the blade free. Why nobody had ever mentioned swords getting stuck in bodies during battle, he was unsure, but he silently cursed his luck at having never heard of that fact. *Maybe I'm doing this wrong,* he considered as he ran from the grasps of three that came at him in unison. He positioned himself and waited patiently for another to come for him. When it arrived, he cut the thing's head clean off and didn't even lose his balance.

All the while, his attention kept returning to the woman in the black cloak, whose face grew angrier with each undead he dealt with. As she grew closer, he noticed that she wore rings on several fingers, her ears supported several bejeweled items, and several necklaces dangled from her neck. "You will pay dearly for trespassing in my forest, boy." she called.

Behind her, the leper collapsed against a tree and crumpled into a ball upon the ground. A glimmering upon the leper's right arm caused him to pause a long moment in confusion. When he realized that the leper was wearing bonding rings, his blood began to boil, and he found himself suddenly unable to care at all that he was using a magic sword and the tiredness of his arms no longer mattered.

"That's a well-crafted sword." The woman said with a smile. "I might just keep you alive long enough to learn how you enchanted it."

She casually waved her white stick and a ball of fire burst out from its tip. The odd burning sphere was almost as large as Ashan's head and moved quickly, giving him just enough time to brace himself and close his eyes. The thing struck him square in the chest and he felt the ground come out from under his feet.

"NOW!" The woman screamed.

Ashan spun and twisted before landing and then rolled over the ground several more times. He found himself unarmed and trembling as he pushed himself up to his knees slowly. He saw that his attackers were now behind him and pivoted on one knee to face them. He looked left and right before finding where the sword had gone and sluggishly rose to his feet despite how much effort he tried to put into moving quickly. The leper was there a moment later to kick him in the chest and knock him back to the ground. He landed well, all things considered, and the leper came down upon his chest. A hand came for his throat, and he tried to squirm to the side and push himself out from under the leper but wasn't nearly fast enough. He reached out with both hands and pushed the leper away, but his limited strength failed him. Panic rose when the hand clamped down and made it difficult to breathe.

"I'm sorry." A young woman's voice whispered.

186

"Get off me!" The other woman screamed, and that familiar sound of rushing fire came.

His attacker shifted to look behind and he grabbed the hand at his throat, found fingers, and pried at them. He felt a momentary loosening at his throat and tried to suck in air, but the fingers clamped down again just in time to prevent him getting even the slightest bit of air. A moment later, the hand pulled away and the woman's head came in close to his ear.

"Kill me while she's distracted!" Ashan pushed her with all his strength, and she fell off him. He rolled away from her and climbed to his feet quickly, finding her laying there on the ground looking up at him. "Kill me and you might survive. Please."

Ashan glanced to the screams of the other woman and his heart lifted when he discovered Frezz squaring off with her. They circled around each other as a wall of flame rose to surround them. Through the flames, he watched as they began flicking their wands at each other, exchanging blasts of fire and streams of blue light in turn. Some vanished at a wave of a wand before reaching the other person, but some landed and caused one or the other to yell out in pain.

"Please, you must hurry! She's distracted but that won't last long! Kill me and she will be weakened! I'm sure you will survive her then. She might just flee."

"You want me to *kill* you?"

"Yes!" She inched closer upon her knees, and he saw her blue eyes through small slits in the fabric that was wrapped around her entire head. There were tears.

"Aren't you bound?" Ashan turned his attention back on the two who were fighting. The undead were heading towards them now and he wondered what would happen when they reached Frezz.

187

"Raise the fallen!" The woman screamed as she sent a blue light towards Frezz.

"No!" The leper screamed mournfully as she shot up onto her knees and arched her back beyond what Ashan thought was normal.

The leper threw her arms up and the ground shook violently as if something massive had fallen nearby. The grass at her knees suddenly turned a sickly brown and began to wilt as if a flame were being held too close. The wilting grass spread out in a circle and leaves began to fall from the first tree the circle reached after only breaths. Branches shriveled, fell apart, and the bark cracked audibly.

"RUN!" the girl screamed. The undead Ashan had dealt with began to rise.

A pained shout drew Ashan's focus back to Frezz, who was now backing away from the woman with one hand at the opposite shoulder. Frezz no longer attacked but seemed to be focused on deflecting the blue lights fired at him, and the lady was moving faster than before. He limped backwards, seeming to struggle to keep up. *He's losing!* He watched the undead begin walking, now much faster than they had been before, and some of them were tearing flesh from themselves as if undressing. *Don't just stand here! Do something! Do what?*

Frezz screamed in pain – *or was that a growl?* - when one of the blue lights struck him on the right shoulder. *I don't even know what that stuff is!* He looked back at the leper, who had collapsed upon her side and had hidden her eyes behind her wrapped hands. *I won't kill a slave.*

"Kill me." She wailed.

He ran, snatched up his sword, and tried to figure out which of the undead he should start with. Hatred welled up in his heart as he considered what the leper had told him. "Take his life!" The woman fighting Frezz screamed. Turning, he found the leper rising to her feet and looking his way. She rose suddenly, ran to him, and grabbed him

188

by the front of his shirt. He tried to pull her hands free, but she pushed him backward, slamming him into a tree. *I thought she was exhausted!*

"I'm sorry. So sorry!" she sobbed.

He tried to push her to the side, but found his strength was barely enough to nudge her an inch now. Red tendrils of smoke rose from her hands at his chest, swirled around as they rose, and then began snaking their way up her arm. One small tendril rose and floated over to the center of his chest, and he suddenly felt his strength begin to diminish. Pushing against her, he looked to Frezz and saw his friend still retreating slowly.

"Your bodies will join my army." Frezz's attacker laughed.

Never! Ashan would have yelled the thought, but he was overcome with a hatred he had never felt. His heart beat faster, he let go of the sword, and pushed the girl to his left side with a renewed strength. She reacted to his pushing by placing one foot backward exactly as he had anticipated. He grabbed the front of her clothing just below her neck, planted his right leg out a bit, and yanked her towards himself just when she pushed forward against him. He twisted at the waist and threw her to his right side, releasing once he felt her legs collide with the one he had planted out a bit to trip her. With nothing holding him back, he took up that sword, ran, and flung the thing with all his might.

UNTIL LATER

Refreshed and supplied with lighter armor and horses, Lord Kairn and his soldiers traveled much more quickly upon departing White Rock. Captain Reskar had made a proper farewell ceremony of it, bringing his entire company and most of the town together, and giving a lengthy speech about cooperation, honor, and integrity. The way he put things, one would have thought that the tension between house Kairn and Turley was at an end and a time of peace and prosperity was about to fall upon the whole of the empire. The man's speech left Lord Kairn wondering if he was a captain simply because he was running away from the purpose the gods had set before him and simply hadn't been found out yet.

Lord Kairn led his soldiers south for a while and turned west once they were far enough away not to be noticed by the townspeople; of course, he expected that Captain Reskar had someone following so that his subterfuge would be discovered shortly. Given his mission, that was of little concern. What concerned him were the obvious lies he'd heard from Captain Reskar concerning the events that had transpired in White Rock. Why vampires had come from the west and why they happened to attack when the assassin was there was a curious mystery that nagged him like a thorn in the side that was too small to remove. Worse still was the fact that he had had to conclude that either Captain Reskar's forces had been camped there at just the right time or that they had known to expect vampires to attack and that troubled him more than anything else. While Lord Kairn hadn't discovered any fresh graves, he found it difficult that not even one of his soldiers had fallen in the battle, even if they outnumbered the vampires dramatically. *Not even if they were well-armored and knew what they were facing.*

They eventually came upon tracks left behind by a heavily laden wagon and followed them for a day before reaching a pathway newly cut through the forest. A few hours later, they came upon a pile of dark, sticky cloth and a dark burn on the old road not far from it. Unable to identify the sticky substance, he considered that the assassin had changed his clothing and soaked these old garments in some odd concoction to hide his scent from dogs, which suggested that the assassin knew he was being hunted. Lord Kairn had his men search the area and they quickly discovered several bodies nearby, which appeared to have been dead for many months. The troubling thing was that there were no signs of decay where those bodies lay and some of the damage was certainly done recently. Tracks in the forest suggested the bodies had been carried and dumped here.

Troubled, Lord Kairn halted the men for a mid-day meal to give himself time to consider things. Several soldiers began digging graves for the deceased while others built a fire and set themselves to cooking a proper meal. Most of the rest lay up under a tree to rest in the shade.

Lord Kairn broke out his small book for notetaking to read, packed his pipe of tobacco, and took a seat against a tree far from the nearest body. It was times like this when he wished he were one of those brilliant minds from old stories, where someone could look at a situation or set of facts and realize what was missing in only a moment. Some considered him exactly that type, but he knew he was average at best, but that was why he had the book of notes. *Sometimes the most brilliant people you know are just people who have taken the time to examine things and dared to ask not why but how.* His father's words came to mind unheeded as he began reading from the book, sticking to the notes he'd taken in the last few weeks.

The vampires had to come from the west, passing at least one village for notice to be sent. But then that person had to recognize them as vampires and know where to send word to Captain Reskar. Or to send word to someone who did know...but that would require more time. So, the vampires came from further west than the nearest village. The camp wasn't new though. He recalled the worn paths between tents and tried to guess how long it had been there.

After eating he decided to follow his gut instinct to follow the trails southward. He wanted to believe whatever had happened here to be unrelated, but the coincidence was much too great to ignore. The usual reason to be hauling dead bodies through a forest was to dispose of them in a graveyard or somewhere nobody would think to look. Given that the forest had been forbidden for so long a time, he suspected murderers. Perhaps bandits even. *Why would such people be hiding bodies this far out from the nearest village though?* He half-expected to discover a den of thieves and murderers, put a quick end to them, and then return to chasing after the assassin. As far as the importance of the two, murderers would be a happy little sidenote in the story, but his mind kept returning to the fact that whoever he was following was using a wagon with beasts of burden. *Slow traveling for someone on the run,* he considered.

A few hours later, they arrived upon a great clearing in the forest, in which stood a small log cabin barely large enough to house a person, a bed, and perhaps a table. There were dead bodies strewn about, a large garden, and an assortment of wagons and carriages. It was the carriages that really stood out. Such a large gathering of wagons was normal for lords and ladies at celebrations, but here it was strange beyond saying. There were wagons of low quality, which likely belonged to farmers or very poor merchants, but there were also fine wagons with obvious care having been given to the details when built. The dead here wore clothing ranging from the lowest quality to that only lords and ladies could afford.

Lord Kairn dismounted his horse, called for his soldiers to watch for an ambush, and began searching. The first body had been a man in his thirties, possibly a farmer from his build, who had died from a blunt object striking the back of his head. The second was a young girl, perhaps only ten, dressed in what would have been considered high-quality silks had they not been ruined by time, weather, and the blood that had stained the material when her throat had been cut. The third was a man whose clothing was in tatters and flesh so decayed that it was impossible to glean further information about how he had died or his age. The next few bodies were in advanced levels of decay as well, possibly having died as much as five years ago. The biggest pattern he noticed was that most had been older when they'd died. He continued checking them, trying to find another pattern. With no signs of decay upon the ground, he had to conclude these too had been moved from wherever they'd been murdered and dumped here recently.

"Captain Hamish, search outward for more bodies." he called without looking.

Finally, he pulled out his sword and marched over to the small cabin. Three soldiers came rushing toward him and pulled their own swords as they arrived. He waved them to follow as he approached the small cabin's far corner. Around that corner, he found the door wide open, and the floor covered in blood. Inside, there was a small straw bed in the nearest corner, a small cookpot resting in the center of the floor, and a hundred stacks of books standing waist high. The interior was well lit in flecks of differently colored light. That's when he looked up and gasped. The entire ceiling was covered in bottles of every size, shape, and color imaginable. It took a long moment of study trying to figure out how they were hung there and what light they were reflecting before he realized that he was looking up at the floor. The bottles were sitting upright on a floor rather than hanging and sunlight poured in through a window above. In turn, they reflected the light down into the cabin. It took a moment to realize that the sunlight coming in through the window above was coming from below. He stepped back, turned, and walked to the other side to check what was reflecting the sunlight. He found nothing but grass on the ground and then noticed that the cabin had no window on the outside. He returned to the doorway and gave the scene a long study.

"My word." One of the soldiers at his side almost whispered.

"The light's all wrong." He observed.

"Yes, my lord." the soldier replied. "Entirely the wrong direction."

"Ras'vetra!" Lord Kairn hissed.

"Yes, Lord Kairn." the shadowy figure called from a good fifteen feet away.

"Come look. Tell me what this is."

"Certainly, Lord Kairn." He walked over very slowly and peeked through the doorway as if frightened when he arrived.

"A witch's study, I would say."

"Yes, I gathered that much. I mean that!" Lord Kairn pointed.

"Another room. Somewhere else."

"Somewhere else?" the nearest soldier hissed. "A magic doorway in the ceiling?"

"Exactly." Ras'vetra replied.

"Do you know what happened here?" Lord Kairn asked as he stepped into the cabin and studied upside down room above.

"No, but these things are temporary. I suppose that you nearly caught someone, and they made this to escape." Ras'vetra explained as he entered the room and began sniffing the air. "Smells like necromancy in here."

"What do you mean it smells like necromancy?"

"The blood and the plants."

"Plants?"

"The other place has plants close to the way. I recognize the smells."

"Can you tell where the other side is?" Lord Kairn asked as he walked across the room to try to see out that window above. He saw green grass through the window and re-positioned himself until he saw the sun's reflection in one of the glass bottles. "Upside down from here." He considered how the thing might work. If he jumped, would he fly up to the floor there?

"No." Ras'vetra began sniffing at the nearest stack of books.

"Is it a dangerous thing?" Lord Kairn raised his sword slowly up into the air, expecting to find some barrier there to stop him.

"Extremely, Lord Kairn. I wouldn't-"

With a loud pop that hurt his ears, the other room disappeared, replaced by the sloped ceiling of the cabin in which he stood. He lowered his sword and turned to face Ras'vetra with a question already forming, but then he saw that Ras'vetra was reading from one of the books. *This thing is intentionally not helpful,* he cursed inside. He gave a sigh and lifted his sword to put it back in its sheath and saw that a hand's length of it was missing. He brought the tip up to his face and examined the cut. He was suddenly glad he hadn't had someone lift him up into the other room as he had been considering. He searched the floor for the rest of his sword but found nothing other than the pool of blood.

"You could have warned me earlier." Lord Kairn said as he sheathed what remained of his sword.

"I did try, Lord Kairn."

"What are you reading?"

"A Theory of Life and Death." he said as he flipped a page.

"You mentioned necromancy earlier." Lord Kairn examined the room.

"I did."

"We almost caught a necromancer?"

"I think so."

"Can you reopen that thing so we can go after it?"

"No, Lord Kairn. That is not within my power. It is not something that can be opened again. It is as though it never existed in the first place." Ras'vetra closed the book and tossed it carelessly across the room.

"So, this necromancer is beyond our reach now? Do you think it will return?"

"I would say yes. This is a lot of research and I hear books are expensive."

"Why'd it close...or vanish so suddenly?"

"It was a trap. You set it off with your sword. I would guess they wanted to know who had nearly caught them, which they could have figured out with the top half of your body or just your head." He picked up another book and opened it.

"Okay. We'll burn it all down." Lord Kairn faced the soldiers waiting outside as he considered how much time to spend. "Prepare wood and a small fire."

Turning back, he strode over to the nearest stack of books and picked two up. Opening them, he saw that the writing was of a different hand in them. One was large, clumsy handwriting like a child's while the other was small and neat. The first letter at the beginning of each page was much larger and stylized differently than the rest and had neat flourishing. He grabbed another two and found entirely different handwriting in them as well. "It looks like several different people wrote these. The binding, paper type, and sizes are all very similar to what I'm used to seeing. Can a necromancer use magic to keep rain out of a shabby cabin like this?"

"Yes, Lord Kairn."

"Can you find me the oldest book in here?"

"Easily." It almost looked as though the shadow-man smiled. It jumped on top of the stacks of books and walked toward the back of the room, sniffing all the while. "Yes, it's here. Not very old, really."

He took a knee and began digging into the books, tossing them aside as if they were worthless. Watching it throw books made Lord Kairn's blood pressure rise, but he didn't say anything; after all, while he loved what books represented, these were books on topics that were best kept away from people. Lord Kairn began checking the backs and insides of books in search of maker-marks or any other clue that might tell of their origins but found nothing in the first few. Necrotic Ailments, An Urging for Blood, Avoiding Plagues, To Bind a Mind, Sicknesses of Bone, A Jolly Chant of Death, Dark Tidings, Forbidden Ritual, and The Cost of Life all appeared to have been made by practiced hands but bore no marks. *Of course, no reputable scribe would want to be known for copying such works.*

"Are these all books about Necromancy?"

"No. There are also books about medicine, gardening techniques, and cookbooks as well."

"I do like learning more about cooking." Lord Kairn offered with a smile.

"I didn't take you for a cannibal, Lord Kairn."

"I'm not."

"Oh, in that case, you may not want any of these cookbooks."

Ras'vetra walked back over and held out a thick book that was entirely black as if someone had soaked the jacket in ink. "Here you are."

Flipping it open, Lord Kairn found the inside of the jacket was also straight black. The next page had a simple crow painted in the center with one leg curled up and the other outstretched, almost gripping a human eye. A line ran down from the bottom of the eye as if the ink had run and then there were two small letters below that. T. and L. *A maker's mark!*

"Can you tell where these books come from or who made them? I mean magically." He asked.

"No, Lord Kairn."

"Is there anything you can tell me about this place and what has happened here? Magically or perhaps by the birds?"

"Birds would not be here. I wouldn't be here if it was up to me."

"It is a right dreadful." One of the soldiers commented from the doorway.

"I think I would agree with you in that." He took the old book and then seven more and headed for the door. "Search for any unusual books or anything else odd and bring me whatever you find."

Back at his horse, he removed his ruined sword and hung it from a saddlebag before depositing his books therein. *If you want to understand a criminal, examine his home,* his father's advice crept up and he began to scan the scene in general. Off in the distance, he spotted a tree that seemed to have a worn ring about as high as his knee and headed that way. When he arrived, he found that there was a chain wrapped about the base of the tree with manacles at the free end. He pulled out his small book and made a quick sketch of the area and wrote a few thoughts about it. Oddly, he found many small bits of cloth in the area. Dirty burlap, as it turned out. He gathered a few samples and stowed them in his pocket for later examination.

With nothing else standing out, he headed to the garden, which was large considering the size of the shack. *Large enough to keep two people busy, but not large enough to produce enough food to feed two people all winter.* There were many plants of all sizes, shape and color there, but he recognized not one of them as something that produced food. He checked the area for remnants of burlap but found nothing.

"Ras'vetra."

"Yes, Lord Kairn." The man simply came into existence in front of Lord Kairn, causing him to reach for his sword out of instinct.

"What are these plants?"

"I do not know their proper names, but I believe they are all used in necromancy."

Lord Kairn frowned to himself, turned, and walked onward. He circled the camp twice before returning to his horse, where he met three soldiers with arms full of books. "What have you found?" He repacked his pipe and considered the dirty burlap. The necromancer had had someone chained to that tree and perhaps the burlap had been repurposed as clothing for that person. That would fit well with the location and the small bits and pieces. *Perhaps, the burlap was used to haul food here and then burned as kindling?*

"These seem to be about magic. Lots of drawings of body parts and symbols none of us know."

"Right. Load what you can into my saddle bags and set fire to the place. We have an assassin to find."

Lasashu tried desperately not to hate his brother, which was quite difficult now with the burning, sharp pain in the bottom of his right foot spiking with each step. He could handle the leg cramping, the growing knot between his shoulders that wouldn't fade, the sweat burning his eyes, the general soreness of his jaw from the numerous fists his brother had placed there, and even the tender cut above his left eye. The fact that his brother had stripped him naked after beating him and was currently forcing him to walk barefoot the last full day of their journey was tolerable. *Barely.* What he could not endure was how that woman had done something to his pillar to put him in this situation and how even that had not been enough. He now knew that she had also bewitched his brother's pillar as well and it had changed Reginald into a moody, violent man who could not listen to reason and simple facts. Lasashu had allowed the beating and the current disgrace of being marched naked for Reginald's sake alone. *The man cannot see that he is her pawn, cursed out of his wits,* he reminded himself as resentment rose for a moment. *Find clothing, escape, return to the capital, find the...No, I have to put revenge off until I find a magician who will fix my brother's pillar. Free my brother of this curse, fix my pillar, then get my revenge on that accursed woman.* The plan was...incomplete. He still hadn't reached the great wall, of which he knew almost nothing, which still posed yet another obstacle in his way. He would have to learn the layout and plan his escape carefully, which would take time she was surely using to flee. *A bath!* He lost himself in imagining a nice, long, hot soak for a few minutes. *No, first a healer!* He could plan better without pain distracting him from every other thought. It would also make travel easier.

The forest ended abruptly, as if the gods had drawn a perfectly straight line upon the world and told the trees not to grow beyond it and gave way to a field of golden-stalked grass as tall as a man on one side and short, leafy plants that wouldn't touch Lasashu's knees on the other. In the far distance, he spotted a few large ponds, several clusters of reddish-brown buildings numerous enough that they could have been a town, and the great wall. From this distance, the wall looked awfully short and useless; though, he had heard it was quite tall and impressive up close. Though he couldn't see the entire thing from this vantage point, he vaguely recalled hearing that it ran from one ocean in the West to the other in the East – some three or four days by horseback. *They will have horses for my return trip!*

Hissing disrupted Lasashu's thoughts and instinct caused him to jump backward and immediately scan the dirt path for a snake. Finding nothing, he shifted his gaze to the tall grass alongside the dirt path and wondered what manner of snakes might inhabit the area. A moving dark blur in the corner of his vision drew his attention and he discovered two hulking Novaes exiting the forest a good twenty strides off to his right. There came several excited snorts from the horses and one man's horse reared up at the sight of the creatures. It took no longer than a second to assess how dangerous the Novae could be and Lasashu couldn't blame the horse for its fear. He had always assumed that the paintings and drawings he had seen were exaggerated versions of the creatures, but now he saw that they had been exactingly accurate reproductions of their size and brutal physique. Not knowing the history of the Novae, Lasashu assumed that the gods had altered large felines until coming up with what he now saw. Each stood a hand higher than the tallest war-horse in the group and were half-again as long at least. Their smaller front legs were six times thicker than any horse's and the rear legs were easily twice that size. They were covered in deep black, sleep coats of fur, which made their emerald eyes appear

202

to glow in comparison. They eyed the horses with an obvious hunger in their eyes and they hardly made any sound as they walked.

"Hold your ground, men." Reginald spoke loudly, a tone of concern in his voice. "We must hold and wait for them to pass."

"What if they do not pass?" Lasashu gazed back at the soldiers and saw more than one face turning white.

"They will pass." The fact that Reginald sounded so certain annoyed Lasashu. *I hope you do not change much more before I can free you, Reginald. Much more change and your own men will turn on you before long.*

"Give me a sword, brother."

"No."

"You would deny me my right to defend myself?"

"I deny you nothing that you could put to good use."

"In that case, give me a sword."

"No. You are incapable of putting it to good use. Whatever you believe yourself capable of doing...your actions would cause all our deaths. Ask again and I will have you crawling the rest of the way." Reginald replied flatly, eyes locked on the two Novae. The beasts turned a bit, angling for the wide-open north, but did not immediately take their eyes from the group. A moment later, the group's predatory stride changed to something very similar to the way a cat walked when it was acting as though it had never been up to anything at all. "Let us be on with it."

They set off upon the dirt trail a bit faster than before and though the Novae never looked back, Lasashu noticed how their ears moved about every few moments. If he understood correctly, the two creatures were listening and keeping track of where Lasashu's group was, which worried him. He imagined them turning about and attacking suddenly and the only attack that seemed useful in his mind was stabbing at their necks. He figured the beasts would be far too fast for that to work and he wondered if they played with their prey the way alley cats often would. He shuddered at the thought and tried to keep his focus on the world ahead.

When they finally arrived upon the wall, Lasashu was surprised to discover what appeared to be a small town. The little town's buildings stood in small clusters of red, gray, white, and green like groups of friends who were hesitant to meet with other groups of strangers at a ball. The reddish-brown brick roads separating them were wide, even, and formed a neat grid, which was starkly different than the aimless, wandering affairs back home. The westernmost cluster of buildings were red and there appeared to be a large array of livestock pens and two big barns. The next cluster was gray and there were training grounds there with stray dummies and large fenced in areas that seemed to be for horse training. The cluster painted in white had the largest building in the whole of the town and he assumed it was a hospital, but the symbols on the outer walls were foreign. In the unpainted wooden cluster at the center, he saw a blacksmith's shop, a butchery, and a carpenter laying out boards near a tannery. *By the grace of the gods!* Past the carpenter, Lasashu spotted a wooden sign with faded wording and a pair of overly large wooden cups dangling from it. *Wine may be asking too much from a place like this, but at least they have SOMETHING!*

He guessed that there were almost fifty buildings and nearly three-hundred people in sight now. Most wore plain trousers and once-white, long-sleeved tunics with deep V-necks. He was surprised to find laces in places where he was accustomed to having buttons and made a mental note not to forget to request buttons instead. Wooden buttons would be acceptable. At a quick estimate, he figured that one out of every fifty people, wearing leather bracers and brigandine, were soldiers or guards – if there was a difference here.

As they entered the town, people stopped whatever it was they were doing to glare openly at Lasashu's forced nudity. The fact that they didn't even attempt to hide the fact that they had noticed enraged Lasashu; in fact, several of them dared to laugh and point as well, which drew further attention. He quickly set to memorizing faces and considered delaying his escape long enough to get revenge on them. Once he memorized ten faces, he abandoned the task. *I cannot spend so much time teaching manners to such lowly people. I must undue my brother's curse before he gets himself killed!*

They followed the first road they came upon until it came to the great wall and turned east onto a much wider road that created a gap between the wall and the nearest buildings. They passed eight buildings before coming to an open area that formed a half-circle off the wall a good forty strides across. There were short shrubs along the walls of the buildings in the two clusters on either side of the clearing, and a few dirty, off-white stone benches here and there. It was almost a good start to what might one day become a public garden, but there were no plants or water fountains in sight. Instead, there were two short pillars of smooth white stone with flat tops about as high as Lasashu's midsection and decorative stone laid out upon the ground – well, it had the appearance of having been abandoned halfway through being built and then finished later by someone who didn't care for continuing with the design. *Lazy.*

Six guards stood before the nearest of the two pillars dressed in matching black uniforms and holding short swords of nearly identical design. *Guards! Help is finally within reach!* They stood together facing a seventh man who wore only dark brown trousers that fell just above the knee. The man possessed the frame of a blacksmith and the deep tan of a farmer, but he also possessed a dull expression that marked him as a lay-about vagabond or a dullard. Whatever the man had done to attract so many guards, Lasashu hoped they would be done with the matter shortly so he could have them guide him to a hot bath and fresh clothing without too much delay; of course, watching a beheading take place in the pursuit of justice would be an entertaining event to behold. *And a healer,* he reminded himself. He couldn't imagine that the witch had managed to bewitch the people here before his arrival.

"Prince Reginald!" One of the soldiers called out.

The soldiers' gazes rose from the vagabond to Lasashu's group in a flash. Smiles were replaced with serious expressions as recognition swept over them and they began to sheath their swords. The vagabond, however, turned slowly in place and scanned Lasashu's group with the blank expression of a dullard. He didn't salute or bow like the soldiers, and, in fact, he didn't even seem to take notice of the fact that Lasashu was naked. Lasashu almost cursed at the man for such disrespect, but wondered if the man was more than just a dullard instead.

Reginald's men climbed down from their horses, handed their reigns to a single man, and, strangely, began to remove their swords. One-by-one, they walked over to the soldiers by the vagabond dullard, handed over their sword, gave a quick bow, and returned to their horse. When the last man had surrendered his sword, the whole lot of them turned and began leading their horses away from what Lasashu imagined they might call a courtyard. "What are you doing?" Lasashu called angrily. "You have yet to announce us! Get back here!" They ignored him entirely.

When the last one was gone, Reginald stepped up beside Lasashu and cleared his throat meaningfully. He found his brother standing tall, stiff, and with his head held high, as he usually would when he was attempting to impress their father. Such attempts had never worked and Lasashu found the display particularly obnoxious now. *Don't be such an apple-polisher!* Reginald gave his pants and shirt a quick dusting off and set to work tucking in his shirt so that the wrinkles weren't so terrible. The soldiers ahead stood in the manner Lasashu had heard called "at attention" and watched silently, as if awaiting orders. Lasashu glanced back and forth between those soldiers and his brother several times before frustration overtook him.

"What are you doing, Reginald?" He hissed.

"Waiting."

"For what?"

"He's busy thinking." Reginald spoke at almost a whisper, not turning to face him.

"What?"

"Be quiet and wait."

"I am a king! I don't wait on people – people wait on me!" he protested loudly and looked back at the guards. *Who is thinking?* The guards were attentive, obviously waiting for someone to give a command and he could see nobody of importance anywhere else in the courtyard. The vagabond dullard's eyes were unfocused, gazing somewhere upon the ground between both parties now – obviously not much going on there now. "Are we waiting on the Asp to get done thinking? Surely, he is not employed here as an attendant!" The guards suddenly shifted hateful gazes upon him, but he paid them no mind.

"Don't use that word!" Reginald's voice came with venom, and he closed his eyes tightly.

"Enough of this waiting. One of you go and fetch me a healer and the commander of this little town." Lasashu demanded.

"Lasashu, you damned fool." Reginald cursed at him quietly.

The Asp man suddenly came to life with rapidly blinking eyes and a deep breath, as if he hadn't been breathing the entire time. He glanced about quickly as if he were surprised to find himself where he was, turned to look at the soldiers behind him for a moment, and then brought his gaze back to Lasashu and Reginald. "Ah, Reginald." The man's words were devoid of tone and his face didn't alter expressions in the least. *An Asp!* It would have been proper to smile when greeting two kings, for they were the bringers of peace in the world, but Lasashu had better things to do than to berate an Asp for showing improper signs of respect.

"I apologize sorry for interrupting you, Mandeep."

"Why are you apologizing to a commoner? He was the rude one for not acknowledging us!" Lasashu spat and gave the Asp his best contemptuous glare, but he seemed not to notice.

"I hope you do not take offense with my brother's words." Reginald said.

"I have carefully evaluated numerous rumors regarding his personality and was anticipating such statements." The Asp's tone was remarkably flat.

"That sounds like something you would do, and I appreciate your understanding." Reginald replied with a smile.

"Directly to the point?"

"If you please."

"What point?" Neither man paid Lasashu any attention.

"I understand you see great urgency in the moment, but I request some of your time after your use of the Communion Pillars."

"I welcome a conversation." Reginald replied.

"You're going to seriously waste time speaking with an Asp, Reginald?" Lasashu inquired as he wiped sweat from his forehead and tried to remain calm.

"Do not be rude, Lasashu."

The Asp man and the soldiers turned then and strode off a short distance before turning to watch, their faces a mixture of curiosity and concern. Reginald then strode forth quite quickly to the nearer pillar and waved for Lasashu to go to the other. As he walked casually where Reginald indicated, he tried not to find offense in his brother taking the nearer one. *Selfish! You have boots and I've walked barefoot all this way!* He almost protested but decided to be the bigger man about it; after all, it wouldn't be fair to himself to get all upset and hold what was happening to his brother against him.

When he arrived at the pillar, he discovered that the top of it bore the impression of a hand five times as large as his own. The pillar was a ghostly white stone with a thousand small cracks running through it, which reminded him somewhat of the low-quality diamond he had stolen from that vile witch the night he had met her. He tried to recall what he had heard about these pillars, but all his memories were hazy with alcohol and centered mostly around the fact that his tutor for that subject had been angrily lecturing him to pay attention. "You might need to know this stuff one day!" the old codger had yelled on several occasions.

He looked to his brother for guidance and Reginald gave him a firm nod and serious look as he slowly planted his hand into the imprint upon his own pillar. Reginald closed his eyes and moved his mouth in silence, likely praying to whichever god had put these odd pillars here in the first place for permission to use them towards whatever purpose Reginald had in mind. Lasashu hesitantly placed his hand into the imprint of his own pillar and watched Reginald for what to do next. A moment later, Reginald gave a jolt as though surprised or struck in the face suddenly.

"I am Reginald, brother to Lasashu." Reginald called loudly as he glanced up at the sky.

"Are we speaking to the gods?" Lasashu asked. *If these pillars send my voice to the gods, maybe I can ask that they fix this whole mess? Maybe they can tell Reginald that this is all wrong, that it's a trick. Surely no curse will prevent him listening to the gods.*

"Just say your name! I can't believe you haven't read about this!" Reginald hissed.

"I am King Lasashu." He looked at the pillar and then to the sky. *Where else would the gods come from but the sky?* The pillar warmed under his hand, and he looked back down. The heat grew a fair amount and then slowly faded. Then nothing. "It got warm for a moment. What happens next, Reginald?"

"Just wait. They will light up to indicate what is to happen."

"They light up? You mean the gods won't come?"

"No. The gods aren't coming here. Why would you even think such a thing, Lasashu?"

"I should think that they would show up to explain themselves, Reginald."

"Explain themselves?" Reginald's pillar suddenly illuminated with a bright red light from within. Reginald's mouth fell open and his face twisted with confusion. "Mandeep!" he turned in place to face the Asp man. "What does this mean? I've not read anything about a red light!"

Panic in Reginald's voice made Lasashu's heart jump, and he tried to step away from his own pillar, but nearly fell when his hand refused to come free. He turned towards it, planted his other hand on its edge and pushed against the stone. His hand remained stuck. "I'm stuck!" He planted a foot against the thing and pushed, which only managed to cause his wrist to hurt.

"This makes sense." Mandeep replied calmly. "Do you seek an explanation of this phenomena, or do you seek the solution?"

"Uh...both, I think, but try to make it short, Mandeep." Reginald said as he leaned down to investigate the stone.

"Someone help me!" Lasashu tried pushing the pillar to knock it over, but it did not budge. The stone grew warm under his hand.

Mandeep took a deep breath. "It is documented in the book Traveler Tantiri's Seventh Attempt at an Abridged Explanation of the Functions of the Communion Pillars at Saveth's Wall-"

"Much shorter, Mandeep." Reginald said. "Just the essence of information, if you please."

"Ah, yes. You have previously indicated your affection for fragmentary information. Concise, I believe you called it."

"Shut up and help me!" Lasashu screamed while kicking the stone. A terrifying thought occurred to him in that moment, and it made his heart race. *What if what that witch did to Reginald altered him so that the stones don't recognize him? He could die just the same as had I not come here. He should have listened to me!*

"You are not the person who was to deliver Lasashu." Mandeep explained as he approached Reginald.

"But I am his brother, Mandeep."

"Traveler Tantiri's hypothesis, which is widely supported among academic minds in the relevant fields of study, suggests that the relation must be of blood; however, there are three documented cases where the chosen has been delivered by someone not related in blood. I am afraid-"

"Does this mean I'm going to die for defying the gods?"

"My apologies, Reginald. I phrased that poorly. It is difficult for me to communicate in the manner you prefer, as so much important information must be left out-"

"GET TO THE POINT!" Lasashu screamed.

"The red light indicates that you are not related by blood." Mandeep went on.

"I didn't think that would matter." Reginald replied. "We are brothers in all other ways."

211

"The gods do tend to care for what's in the blood. There are two known courses of action available to you now. The first is to apologize to the gods for your lack of knowledge...and to forswear your claim of relation and responsibility for Lasashu. If they are forgiving, they may allow the responsibility to fall back upon the person who should have made the journey and did not."

"His only blood-relative is our mother." Reginald's face twisted with worry.

"Is she not here?"

"No."

"The other solution is to accept a *Burden*."

"Stop talking and help me, you idiot!" Lasashu screamed as he considered cutting his hand off at the wrist. The heat was growing quite hot now and he thought he saw a hair on the back of his hand curl up.

"A burden?" Reginald's eyes shot wide open.

"Such is the only known solution to this particularly troubling conundrum. Are you familiar with this?"

"I have read some of the histories." Reginald replied softly as his gaze fell to his hand upon the stone.

"Do you recall the words you must say?"

"Not entirely."

"In that case, I shall assist you."

"Mandeep, if it costs me my life, please ensure that my parents are promptly notified and that I was thinking of them in my last moments."

"Are you seeking emotional reassurance, Reginald?"

"No, Mandeep. I fear how my death will hurt my parents. Tell them that I died painlessly...even if it is not so."

"You would have me twist the truth? What is your reasoning for this?"

"I would like for them to believe that I died painlessly and without regret." Reginald explained. "To ease their pain in some way."

"Ah. Yes, that makes sense."

"SOMEONE HELP ME!" Lasashu directed his scream at the soldiers who had not responded to him so far. "I will have you all hung!"

Mandeep stepped around Reginald's pillar and placed his hand onto to top of Reginald's. "We must begin by humbly requesting the attention of the gods." The Asp man looked up into the sky and Reginald did the same, both falling into a long silence. "We must ask them calmly, our hearts not overflowing with fear for what is happening in the moment." *Praying silently? How will the gods hear you?*

"Reginald!" Lasashu called. "Send the guards to find a wizard! We can't wait on this Asp's beliefs! He probably doesn't even know what he's talking about!" Reginald did not respond and so Lasashu redoubled his efforts to free his hand.

"Give me a sword, you fools!" He yelled to the guards but found that they had dropped down upon their knees and had their foreheads pressed against the ground.

Lasashu climbed atop the pillar, placed his feet on either side of his stuck hand, and pushed with all his might. The whole thing then shone in brilliant blue that was so bright he had to close his eyes. His hand came free a moment later and he flew from it. He landed on his side and rolled away from the pillar. *Victory!* He rose with a cheer.

"Fool!"

The Asp appeared then and threw a fist at his face, but Lasashu ducked under it easily. Before he moved out from under the Asp, he considered tactics. If he ran to his left, he could reach the guards with their heads pressed to the ground, from whom he could easily wrestle a sword and cut the Asp down in just a swing or two. If he ran to his right, he could get into the open away from the pillars and simply strike the Asp in the throat a few times to cut off his airway. The Asp's knee came up to meet Lasashu's jaw so quickly that he didn't even have time to move his arms to block it. Everything went dark for a moment, and he found himself lying on the ground with the Asp standing above him. Lasashu raised one leg up to his chest and kicked at the man's knee, hoping to break it. The man moved his leg quickly, stepped forward, and planted a foot upon Lasashu's throat. Lasashu struck the man's leg a few times, tried to push it away to the side as he had been trained to do in such a situation, but it did not move.

"Crucial learning opportunity." The Asp said.

"Get off me, you Asp! I will have you hung for this!"

"Your behavior suggests that you are unaware of your status here at Saveth's Wall."

"I am a king!"

"You lost that status when your pillar broke, Lasashu. From that moment on, you have held no greater status than any other person. You should accept your fate. You serve Saveth's Wall now."

"I am a king. Saveth's Wall serves me."

"Don't kill him, Mandeep." Reginald said as he appeared at the man's side.

"I would not murder a man such as this. His debt is too much."

"You question my manhood?" Lasashu yelled and began beating on the Asp's leg.

"Stop it, Lasashu." Reginald shouted. Unaccustomed to being shouted at by his family, Lasashu ceased his attack and glared at his brother. *Is it already too late for you, brother? What has that witch done to you?*

"Let me up."

214

"No." Reginald's voice dropped low, and he continued slowly. "You have neglected your education, Lasashu. You don't understand what has just happened or perhaps I am wrong, and you simply do not care."

"I know what has happened! I broke free!"

"Astounding lack of perception." The Asp commented.

"You were released from the pillar because I just took on a *Burden*. The only other option was to let our mother die."

"Nobody was going to die, Reginald. This whole thing has been a clever ruse to destroy my life. It's all that witch's doing, but-"

"No, Lasashu. You see what you want to see and nothing more. I hope that while you are here, you will come to understand that about yourself, but you'll probably run away to go chasing this woman. I don't know what you've go with this woman, but you need to wake up. Murdering some woman who spurned you isn't going to make things go back to the way they were."

"It is MY LIFE! She has taken everything from me, and you are blindly following her plans! This is all a trick! She has cursed your mind to turn you against me! Let me up!"

Reginald took a deep breath and looked up at the Asp. "Please send him away. There is little to be had from this conversation."

"You cannot dismiss me like a child!"

"I wish there was some way of reaching you, Lasashu. I wish there was more I could do to help you, but...that is no longer an option."

The Asp waved a hand, and the guards came running. They took hold of Lasashu's arms and, once the foot was off his neck, pulled him to his feet. Lasashu fought to free himself, but there were too many and he quickly relented. "Release me or I will have you all hung!" he screamed repeatedly, but they continued pulling him away.

He didn't notice the large, dark brown wooden door set into the wall until they were pushing him through it. They entered a large room with several doors along one wall and a flight of stone steps going upward. They took the third door and entered a wide hall, where soldiers immediately took notice of Lasashu's yelling, but they didn't seem at all surprised at the sight, as if kidnapping a king were a regular event here. They went a fair distance before stopping in front of a plain wood door with the words "Supplies One" sloppily painted upon it. One guard released Lasashu, gave the door a gentle knocking, and returned to help press Lasashu against the opposite wall.

"I will have you and your families hung for this!" Lasashu yelled. "First your children so that you can see the agony on the face of your wife." *I shouldn't have wasted so much strength on that Asp. He's really going to be sore when his brain finally catches up to the damage I did to his leg. I bet I broke the leg!* A moment later, the door ahead opened, revealing two older men in plain brown robes.

"Yes?"

"New arrival for you. Needs clothes and a wash."

"Sounds like he's a stubborn one." One of the robed men commented before turning and walking away.

"I also need a healer. Preferably before a hot bath." Lasashu announced, standing taller. "And none of these commoner clothes. I require buttons. Wood buttons will do for now." he explained. The guards removed their hands from him, and the remaining robed man gestured for Lasashu to enter the room ahead. "And somebody fetch me something roasted. I am famished."

"This way." The robed man said.

The room beyond was large, brightly lit, smelled of dye, and was cramped. All he could see at first were three long rectangular tables stacked high with crates and clothing with barely enough space between them for Lasashu to pass. The space beneath these tables was filled with boxes, crates, and remnants of cloth that appeared ready to topple. He followed the robed man in and found there were more tables beyond the three and they were piled just as tall as the first ones. One was covered in tall stacks of neatly folded brown breeches made from linen and each bundle was tied with thin white twine. The next table was similarly occupied by stacks of black breeches and the next with baskets of dark brown woolen socks, drawers, a wide assortment of work gloves, archer gloves, and other things he didn't recognize.

"We will start you off with breeches and a shirt for now." The robed man said as he grabbed a brown pair from the nearer table. "There's not much time before evening formation, so the rest of your clothing will have to wait."

"Evening formation?" Lasashu asked as he scanned the room for the finer clothing he wanted.

"Yes, there are several daily formations. You will find out which ones you are to attend later."

"As long as they're not too early in the day." The robed man turned and gave him a curious look. He checked the contents of a crate beneath the nearest table and found more socks.

"They're not optional, son." The man grabbed a shirt and began making his way over to Lasashu, careful not to knock anything off the tables as he went. "Here."

Lasashu grabbed the breeches and dropped them instantly, his hand recoiling at the feel of the material. "By the gods, what is that made of? That won't do at all. I wear silk!"

"Everyone wears the same uniform while on duty here."

"I wear silk!"

"Son, there's not a scrap of silk in all Saveth's Wall."

"Fine." Picking them back up, his skin recoiled in disgust at the roughness of the material, he wondered if he could just remain naked in his own room for a few days until proper clothing could be crafted. He wondered if the material had been made in a way to incorporate saw dust and sharp bits of glass or dirt.

"This way, son."

The man moved quickly through the tables away from the doorway Lasashu had entered through and Lasashu followed, ignoring the stacks he knocked down along the way. The path between tables took him left and right a few times before finally coming upon an open door where the man waited for him with an annoyed look on his face that made Lasashu want to strike him right in his old, wrinkled nose. He found that they had rejoining the second robed man he had seen before, whose expression was more hostile than simply annoyed and Lasashu's anger redirected towards this man. The adjoining room was the largest bathing room Lasashu had ever seen; though, it was also far from the prettiest. The floor and walls were all a dark stone that had a rough texture beneath his feet and the air wasn't as warm as he would have liked. There were four large bathing pools set into the floor that were of uneven size and there wasn't even a proper window or opening to let in the sunlight. Instead, there were candles set upon ledges along the wall and numerous softly glowing orbs here and there upon the floor or in the water that lit the room a bit. The place smelled of cheap soap and, worse yet, there were other men already bathing.

"How long will it take?"

"How long will what take?" the man stepped up and placed a rather small sliver of yellow soap and a rag in Lasashu's hand.

"How long will it take to have proper clothing made? I can't wear these common clothes for very long." he explained.

"That depends."

"Depends on what?"

"You."

The other man sneered openly at Lasashu and spoke in such a disrespectful tone that Lasashu very nearly dropped the soap to find something with which to stab the man. "Nobody here is going to be supplying or even crafting the clothes you are accustomed to having back home. The gods demanded you come here and here you are. You are no longer royalty." He locked eyes with Lasashu and let a moment of silence pass. "As such, you have no fortune with which to pay for the luxuries you desire."

"You don't know what you are talking about." Lasashu snapped at the man. Ordinarily, he would hit the man right in his mouth, but the prospect of a nice, hot soak was too enticing now. "Now, take me to my bathing chamber." Both men sighed.

A NEAT TRICK

Ras'vetra pretended to pick at the dirt beneath his fingernails with a small knife he'd stolen from King Hotar some time ago. It was an expertly crafted work of art with careful attention given to the finest details and Ras'vetra admired it. He wondered how long would pass before its absence would be noticed and hoped it incised the vile tyrant. Nothing delighted Ras'vetra as much as seeing the man lose his temper when he discovered Ras'vetra's little acts of defiance. *Wiggle room,* he liked to call it. As of late, his favorite activities involved irking King Hotar whenever possible and chortling at the man's futile attempts at retaliation, including his failed attempts to destroy him. Each new attempt was more entertaining than the last, but his favorite had to be the time that King Hotar had tried to stab him with a cursed knife.

Ras'vetra smiled at these thoughts and glanced around. He found one of the nearby soldiers watching him pretend to clean his fingernails with a confused expression. Ras'vetra smiled at the soldier, making his mouth open far too wide for the size of his head and made his teeth all sharp and long to scare the young man. The man's eyes opened wide at the sight and returned to staring at the dirt floor quickly. *Boring and incurious. Disappointing.*

He gave a slow sigh and grunted his dissatisfaction with the situation. The soldiers in the little once-house with him were excited or afraid; whereas, being stuffed into a small space with twenty humans, Ras'vetra was both annoyed and uncomfortable. It was a beautifully weather-beaten place that had been partially burned before being left to rot away under the pressure of weather and time. The frame leaned a bit in one direction, the glass windows had broken, and the wood was a dark gray, which gave it a wonderful, haunted look. The walls were cracked, the roof had holes, the fireplace had leaned fiercely away from the main structure, and the wooden floorboards produced the most satisfying of protests when the soldiers walked upon them. The whole place gave off the aroma of decaying wood and fresh moss, which was just lovely. If Ras'vetra were free to do so, he'd live in this place until it fell entirely apart. Thereafter, he'd haunt travelers for fun and to keep from being disturbed. The only thing he'd alter was the clearing that surrounded the little house, where someone had once tended crops. He would fill that ugly clearing with large trees and perhaps thorny bushes as well.

"Someone's in the clearing." One of the soldiers whispered excitedly. This would be a first battle for some of these young men.

"It's the assassin!" The excited tone of the young soldier only irritated Ras'vetra. *Were I allowed, I'd possess your body and punch your face with your own hand until you passed out from the pain!* He almost laughed at the idea.

"Calm yourselves." The eldest soldier said calmly. "Don't talk or move. It's supposed to be a *surprise* attack."

Ras'vetra didn't bother to look up from his fingernails. This wasn't going to be a surprise attack...well, not the surprise for which

222

these soldiers had planned. He'd been watching the three traveling for days and had estimated the time of their arrival with a high degree of accuracy. The young travelers would hang back, probably flee during the battle, while the warrior would provide distraction. *That's what I'd do.* The soldiers had the potential to win the fight with their enchanted armor without his assistance, but he'd been ordered along. Specifically, the order had been "Go and capture them. Don't let them die!" He'd formulated a plan of disobedience on the spot and was tempted to implement that plan right now; however, he wanted to watch a fight, or be in one, and these untested soldiers needed the experience to temper their arrogance. That arrogance had been far more annoying than their smell and he figured he might be able to fix the former just as easily as a rainstorm he'd conjured had fixed the latter.

"I know you're here. Show yourselves." the voice rang out across the clearing.

The soldiers stormed out of the house in a rush of clanging metal and excited shouts. Ras'vetra stood slowly, gave his arms a stretch, yawned, and tossed his stolen knife into a corner of the little place. *You'll never get it back now!* He smiled as he turned and departed the house at the pace that very often angered those who had been his master over the years. The soldiers tore across the field at such a rate that three of them fell halfway to their target and attacked straight away. One-by-one, they swung whatever weapon they possessed and were dodged easily.

"Surround him!" Lord Kairn had to yell his order six or seven times before the lot seemed to hear him and obey.

Eventually, they formed two staggered circles with no more than an arm's space between any two and...and then the order fell apart as three younger men broke rank. The dragon-blooded stepped forward and caught the first soldier's war ax just below the head, placed his second hand in the soldier's midsection, lifted, and tossed the man aside. The second soldier, having seen this, skidded to a halt with wide eyes, and held his sword flat upon his own chest in an instinctively defensive posture. The dragon-blooded took hold of that sword and yanked it free just as twisting green vines shot from the ground to ensnare the third man, who had also decided it was best not to charge in but had kept his sword at the ready. *Delightful! You've trained both in magic and martial combat! I wish you and I could have a fair fight.* He considered it for a moment, but faced the reality that the human soldiers would strongly disagree with such a thing. *Perhaps next time.*

As expected, the dragon-blooded's two young companions were making their way around the clearing, creeping along just inside the tree line. Ras'vetra smiled as he realized that his plan had just been consolidated for him. *The word heavily implies a group and there's only one group here now.* He smiled to himself as he watched the heavily armored soldiers get tripped, jumped over, caught up in vines, and generally fail in every attack. Watching them fail against one man wearing no armor was much more entertainment than watching two clumsy children tripping over their own feet and making a great racket in aiming for silence. Slowly, they ceased their initial tactic of each soldier rushing in, swinging with great might, and began coming in for the dragon-blooded's back side. *No honor at all in these men!*

"Attack in pairs!" Lord Kairn called out. "Swords first and use your skills instead of speed!"

Desperate faces turned to Lord Kairn, who was walking in a wide circle around the soldiers, and a bit of resolve settled into most of them. Three soldiers with swords approached the dragon-blooded at a controlled pace this time and they spread out so that each approached from a different angle. The new tactic should have been challenging enough for any intelligent person to call out for an end, to accept that he was bested; however, that was when the dragon-blooded began to fight in earnest. He leapt over one man, turning in the air, and planted his hand flag against the man's armor. The man jumped forward with a yelp, lost his footing and fell as the other two ran after the dragon-blooded with swords flailing wildly.

"Use your weapons! Stop flailing and chasing him!" Lord Kairn called out angrily.

What a joke. I've seen more invigorating battles in plays. Next time, I should try to convince Hotar to send bards and tell him that all dragon-blooded are fearful of music! He laughed hard at the show, which turned a few heads, but that wasn't abnormal. *I wonder if he'd fall for that.*

"Axes!" Lord Kairn called out and three soldiers with axes charged in.

The dragon-blooded charged forward at two of these men before they had spread apart, dropped to his knees so that he slid along the ground right between them, and reached out to tap either at the waist. Both fell a second later with surprised yelps. The dragon-blooded rose, turned, and charged at the third man carrying an ax, but the man immediately began backing away. Others were beginning to slowly retreat away from the dragon-blooded as well, all confidence drained from their posture.

"Retreat." The dragon-blooded's voice came blaringly and the certainty reminded Ras'vetra of someone he couldn't remember clearly. *Someone with red hair...or red eyes?*

Paying closer attention, Ras'vetra felt it when the dragon-blooded destroyed the enchantments of a soldier's armor with no more than a touch. Whether it was some sort of *Purifying Touch*, a dark curse, or if he could dispel the magic fueling those enchantments, Ras'vetra was unsure. Immediately after, that soldier crumpled to the ground like all those before him, which was expected given the amount of weight no longer being offset by magic. The dragon-blooded ran to another soldier and sent that man crashing face-first into the ground with no more than a tap on the shoulder. *Impressive,* he thought with a smile. Several soldiers chose that moment to turn and run, but the dragon-blooded had noticed and headed after them.

Ras'vetra had begun the morning with every intention of enjoying a fight he intended to allow to go on for a while; however, the

225

remaining soldiers, clearly having decided that an all-out assault was their only chance to win the fight, charged their target together. The dragon-blooded touched three soldiers before turning back to face the charging group and Ras'vetra felt that the man was preparing to use magic in a more aggressive manner. He set his staff aloft in the air, took a deep breath, and... magic swirled around him. A moment of thinking was all it took to realize that the dragon-blooded was about to remove the one variable that allowed Ras'vetra to disobey his current orders and he *shifted* himself to the man. "WOAH!" When he arrived, he sent a gust of air out against the human soldiers to stagger them, buying himself the time he needed. He grabbed the dragon-blooded's wrists and waited a moment for the man's shock to settle before continuing. The dragon-blooded blasted him in the chest with fire three times before stepping back and attempting to kick one of his legs. While he was impressed with the strength and power surging within the dragon-blooded, there wasn't time enough to appreciate that.

"If you'll pardon my interruption, I can't let you kill any of them."

"Shadow!" The dragon-blooded growled and snapped his teeth at Ras'vetra's face. The sensation of living flesh moving through his...shadow was akin to being lightly tickled, but that tickling was followed by the urge to vomit.

"That's just disrespectful, sir." Ras'vetra replied with a wicked smile. "I was very specifically ordered by High-king Hotar to capture some people and that none were to die. So, you see, if you kill any of *these* people, I'll have to capture you and your two friends instead." He dropped his voice to a whisper before adding, "I cannot allow that...it'd be exactly what the king wants."

"Ras'vetra! Traitor!" Lord Kairn screamed just as he swung his sword for the dragon-blooded's head. *What a pest! Smiling,* Ras'vetra opened the way into the *unplace*, designated who was to travel with him, and gave the *unplace* the required amount of magic.

226

The slight tingling sensation that washed over his body came only seconds before the world turned wrong. Lord Kairn watched the world vanish and relaxed his body in preparation for the fall he knew would soon come, glad that he had caught the subtle warning this time. He held his sword out to the side and thanked his lucky stars that they'd been waiting for hours after having had breakfast instead of eating shortly before fighting. Down became left and then up and finally returned to down again. Nausea swept through him, and he nearly vomited. A moment later, the darkness was replaced by green, and he landed on a soft, wet bed of thick grass. He waited a few long moments for the disorientation to pass before opening his eyes and sitting up.

"Ras'vetra!" He yelled as he cautiously rolled over.

It took him a good moment to calm his nerves so that he could get to his feet to examine the world around and, when he finally did, he found soldiers laying all around. Some were passed out, some were vomiting, and a few were helping each other to stand in their heavy armor. Not finding any signs of obvious injuries, Lord Kairn turned his attention to the world around them. All was farming fields aside from a grand wooden wall a hundred strides off with two massive white flags with red hawk heads at the center fluttering in the wind above the gates. "Shit." Hawk Harbor held a certain renown for being inhospitable even in the farthest northern towns. Its people had chased off all royalty some ten years ago and then chased their duke out of town under threat of death just five years after that. Now there was a council that oversaw the town – a council that every citizen voted into office every three years. The last lord he knew to have visited Hawk Harbor had been sent back to King Hotar dressed in rags and with a missing finger. Whatever happened to the soldiers the man had brought with him was unknown.

"Ras'vetra!" He pulled his helm free and threw it down.

"Yes, Lord Kairn?"

"This is Hawk Harbor! It'll take weeks to get to the capital!"

227

"Indeed, it shall, but I will deliver my captives..." He offered a wicked smile that reminded him of his younger sister. "Exactly as ordered."

"We are not your captives!"

"Did my owner not say to go and capture *them* and not to let *them* die? You are all perfectly unharmed."

"You were not told to capture *US!*" Lord Kairn yelled. "Take us to the castle NOW!"

"It seems to me that..." he paused, pretending to think for a moment. "...a week is a perfectly reasonable amount of time. Your king is a busy man, and I shouldn't bother him so soon after being sent away. Especially because I may have inadvertently captured the wrong group of people."

"Inadvertently?!" Lord Kairn yelled. He wanted nothing more than to run his sword into Ras'vetra's midsection, but knowing it would be a futile gesture, he took a deep breath to calm himself. "Why are you buying time for those who tried to assassinate our king?"

"I have been specifically ordered not to speak on the matter of the assassination attempt."

"Take us back now!" Lord Kairn screamed.

"Would that I could safely, Lord Kairn, but they were most certainly watching that time. They'll be right on us if I do it here and now."

"Birds?"

Ras'vetra glanced about a moment. "Most certainly, Lord Kairn. A fair number of them." His calm tone was a hot coal on the skin.

"You are about as useful as a broken hammer!"

"What a beautiful thought."

It occurred to Lord Kairn that there were several flaws in his thinking that may have been key to the misunderstandings with
228

Ras'vetra. Every time he had tried to get Ras'vetra to do his traveling trick, the man always brought up birds. Not this time though. *No, I'm making too many assumptions.* Ras'vetra had actually said "They're watching." and had agreed that birds were watching. After that, Lord Kairn was the one who kept asking about birds and Ras'vetra had agreed. Well, he vaguely agreed. He was vague, indirect, and frustrating, as if he were insane or they were not discussing the same things. *That is the key! Ras'vetra is...maliciously compliant...strictly speaking...like he's trying to find ways to be disobedient.* If his sister Aydreis were there, Lord Kairn was sure that she would quickly identify the game Ras'vetra was playing and likely find a solution. *He does answer some questions in a way that sounds very agreeable and open. But he took us to a white rock...* He pondered on that event for several minutes as he watched his soldiers milling about in silence. To a man, nobody liked Ras'vetra and with good cause, as he often used his idle time to annoy someone. At one point, he had lured a snake into camp, which turned out to be harmless, but it had caused a freight because it appeared very similar to a deadly snake. He also liked to just stare at people for long periods of time until they turned away from him. *Very much like a game Aydreis would have come up with.*

Lord Kairn was distracted from his thoughts by the sudden movement of a soldier. The soldier turned, scanning the world with sharp attention, and began marching his way with an air of urgency. With cardinal red hair a finger's length that almost stood straight up and a short, neat beard to match it, Captain Dousk was an easy one to spot. His pale face wore an everlasting smile that was almost as fake as his sister Koraine's love for her late husband and those eyes were almost always alight with a lust for power. He was also the sort of man who loved to interrupt conversations with orders to anybody he thought he could bully to feed his ego and bolster his own sense of importance. He was, perhaps, the fifth most vexing person Lord Kairn had ever met.

"Lord Kairn." Captain Dousk spoke with an almost musical lilt and a smile he seemed to think was welcoming or reassuring, but the man opened his eyes too much and there was a smugness to his smile that made Lord Kairn wonder if the man wasn't entirely right in the head.

"Yes, Captain Dousk?"

"I thought I might educate you on the situation in Hawk Harbor. I, myself, visited just last summer and found the people rather wicked and downright hostile. Why, it was-"

"Yes, I've heard the stories."

"Right." His smile faltered and his brows furrowed slightly until he was quite nearly frowning, but it lasted only a moment. He thought for a moment and cleared his throat before continuing. "Well...in that case, I would urge you to direct us to the north-west until we cross the river. I believe it will be safest not to stop until we reach the city of Bay's Hand, where we can catch a boat up the coast to the capital. It would certainly be the fastest option and my cousin Sarah lives in Bay's Hand, which would afford us a good night's sleep in comfort."

"Thank you, Captain Dousk. I will think on it." *Bay's Hand?* He had never heard of the place, but Captain Dousk had called it a city and he knew that this man only called the largest of places cities; in fact, there were rather large cities he had referred to as towns.

He considered the distance and time Ras'vetra had just given the assassin and was certain that the assassin would be beyond finding by the time Lord Kairn reached the capital. His luck lately had been turning for the worse and there seemed no way to turn it around. He considered leaving the soldiers behind to make the best time that was possible, but that would likely look even worse, and he needed at least two men to back up his story of what had happened. Heading directly to the north-east, would be a straight shot towards the assassin, but it was a great distance and... Well, he had no way of knowing if the trip would be in vain with Ras'vetra coming along. *Perhaps I could distract Ras'vetra? How does one distract a thing that you don't really understand? Swing a sword at it, pretend to only want to talk to the assassin? No, I will just have to return to the capital and explain this mess.*

"Ras'vetra." Testing a theory, he whispered instead of calling out.

"Yes, Lord Kairn?"

Ras'vetra appeared as a cloud of black smoke. At first, there was just a faint cloud of darkness, but it grew darker in the shape of a cloud. It took a few moments before it stretched out into the general shape of a person and nearly twenty heartbeats before Lord Kairn could locate the finer shapes of a face. He quickly considered his sister's favorite childhood games and set to work figuring out how to quickly work through their weaknesses.

"Use your magic to take us to the assassin."

"If but I could, my lord." Ras'vetra began. "Unfortunately-"

Perhaps I need to be more specific, he considered. That was often the key to his sister's most annoying games. "Use your magic to take us all to the assassin right now."

"Again, my lord, I cannot. Might I suggest-"

"Use your magic to take us to the assassin's last location now."

"I am unable-"

"Use your magic to take us all to the capital...right now."

"I am unable to-"

"Please, use your magic to take us all to the courtyard of the high-king's castle right now."

"I cannot-" Ras'vetra sounded frustrated, but Lord Kairn didn't bother paying attention. A few nearby soldiers took notice of what he was saying and began calling out for their fellows to prepare themselves, which elicited a great number of disappointed groans.

231

"Use your magic to take all of us to the training grounds east of the capital city...right now."

"My lord, are-"

"Use your magic to take all of us to the nearest safe place nearest the capital city right now." Ras'vetra's body became almost invisible for a moment and then began shifting between nearly invisible and almost normal like a candle's flame being blown in the wind. At the same time, his face was screwed up by a painful struggle.

"NO!" he blurted loudly. "It's not a safe place-"

Got you! You're finding some excuse to disobey! Something isn't safe according to some twisted logic you are using. I'm close! "Use magic to transport all of us to the assassin safely."

"I cannot take you to the assassin, my lord. The-"

He wants to distract me again. "Use magic to transport all of us to the high-king's castle safely...right now."

"Damn you." Ras'vetra cursed and his body faded away entirely.

Darkness swallowed up the world and Lord Kairn cursed in shock when the spinning sensation struck him faster and more intensely than it had previously. In the darkness, he tried to look around to get some sense of what was happening but found nothing but utter darkness. Moments later, a bright red light came into being and he slammed into something hard. He rolled once and skidded against that hardness for a moment before something heavy fell on top of him.

A hundred shocked screams filled the air and the thing on top of him shifted, rolled off, and groaned. He rolled away just in time to find the soldier preparing to vomit right where he had been. Lord Kairn rolled to his stomach, planted his hands upon highly polished black stone, and pushed himself up to his knees. He found a crowd of well-dressed people retreating, soldiers wearing purple sashes charging in with weapons drawn, and high-king Hotar sat upon his massive golden throne at the head of the room. *NO!*

"HOLD!" King Hotar's deep voice filled the room.

Lord Kairn scrambled to his feet so that the guards might see his face, recognize him, and not attack. "It's Lord Kairn!" Someone shouted from the crowd that was still retreating along the wall.

"Lord Kairn?" King Hotar shot up from his throne and threw his massive golden goblet to the floor. The look of shock on his face vanished in a blink and was replaced with rage as he stepped forward. His eyes scanned the room in a flash and then locked in on Lord Kairn's face.

"You return, but I see no captives."

"My apologies, high-king Hotar." Lord Kairn took a knee and bowed deeply. "I was..." He had to pause a moment to consider his words. "I failed."

"You have failed to capture the assassin?"

"Yes, your majesty. I find myself unable to command Ras-"

"I entrusted you with a powerful tool!" King Hotar stepped right up to Lord Kairn so that his legs brushed Lord Kairn's hair. "You return empty-handed and interrupt an important event merely to complain that you could not use my tools competently?"

"My apologies, your majesty. I could not-"

"Others would not abandon their duty and their king so weakly!"

ALONE TOGETHER

The forest became atramentous and languid. The birds ceased their singing, the sun was swallowed up in dark clouds, and the days lost their warmth. Ashan's dreams became nightmares that woke him repeatedly each night. Half his dreams were about sitting down to a feast and finding plates full of bizarre creatures that wriggled, hissed, and flailed at his face with little mouths full of sharp teeth or tails with stingers. In others, he found himself sneaking about in a bitterly cold darkness, knowing something was out there looking for him, and his clothing would suddenly burst into flames and the thing would see him. In a few, the shadow-man appeared out of nothingness, commanded his travelling companion to kill him, and laughed as she obeyed. She would tackle Ashan and pull colorful streams of smoke from his chest until he died. Each time, his efforts against her were utterly meaningless. Ashan often woke from these nightmares mid-scream and would flee. This was another such night.

"Ashan."

With an involuntary yelp, Ashan turned, pulling his sword, and took several steps away from the source of the sound. He spotted Argel limping towards him, her once white clothing darkly stained from sleeping on the ground, and her eyes were open wide in shock. Beyond her, he studied each space between trees and every shadow carefully.

"I need more rest, Ashan. I can't...keep up."

Ashan felt himself scowl even before he understood what she had said, but then his attention was pulled away by a movement off to his left side. He raised his sword defensively and realized that the movement had just been a branch swaying in the cool breeze. *Blast, it's cold,* he cursed.

"Please."

She took a few pained steps closer before stopping, tears rolling down her cheek, and began to cautiously lower herself to the ground. It looked like a difficult task with how she had to avoid putting weight on her swollen ankle. While she kept saying that it was no more than a bad sprain, he was beginning to think something was broken, but he kept that thought to himself. She had stumbled and rolled down a hill a little more than a day ago now and it didn't seem to him that it was getting any better. *If anything, it's getting worse,* he considered.

He turned away and pretended to busy himself with scanning the forest in all directions, but really, he had to breathe and fight the overwhelming urge to run. He also wanted to scream at her for having left him behind when he had tripped over an exposed tree root a week ago. He'd yelled out in panic, and he knew she had heard him because she had looked back, but she'd continued regardless. *No, it was a different situation then,* he reminded himself. *We heard those voices and were running.* In his head, he knew the situations were different and he felt shame for his anger at her, but he felt that anger in his heart.

"Sleep."

Though he tried, he could not take the resentment from his voice. He drove his sword into the soft ground and began removing his pack, which was doubly heavy since having absorbed what had previously been in Argel's pack and scanned the area in earnest. Every shadow at the corner of his eyes seemed to move until he turned to look at them and found nothing.

After a short while, his stomach protested audibly, reminding him that there was no food left in his pack. *If only Frezz were here,* he thought. Every living thing seemed to have fled the area shortly after they'd run away from the shadow-man and the soldiers, not that he knew how to hunt or trap anything anyhow, but it limited their options. So far, he had identified a few leaves that were bitter and one that caused diarrhea before settling on a few types of grass that didn't seem to have any ill effects. He was beyond hungry. Worse than the hunger was the exhaustion that had him considering leaving behind his sword and pack to make walking easier, but he clung to the sword out of terror and the notion of being able to attempt self-defense. He often thought that the sword might help in killing something to eat, but he hadn't seen anything larger than the strange squirrel-like rodents that dashed about in the tree branches overhead. They were too fast and out of reach, but that hadn't stopped him from wondering if they tasted good.

The whole situation made Ashan feel utterly alone, worthless, and angry. He felt a pang of guilt for leaving Frezz behind as he turned to face another shadow that had seemed to move in the corner of his vision. *I led him to his death. It would have been better if he had gone ahead instead of me...he could have delivered this thing.* He looked down at the ring and thought again about abandoning it. *He could hunt, find food, make a fire, navigate...use magic. We're just two useless runaway slaves. Can't even feed ourselves. We ran like cowards!* He tried not to replay the memories of that figure he'd seen. *He told us to go on without him. He knew what he was doing.* The attempt to soothe himself, to push away the guilt, did little.

237

Ashan studied the forest in silence until he heard the change in Argel's breathing, signifying that she had fallen asleep. He stepped away as quietly as he could manage, leaving his sword and backpack behind as a sign that he would return. He headed back along the way they had come before, walking slowly and minding the many dried sticks to avoid making any excess noise. After a while, he turned north and walked for half an hour before he came upon a clearing. Upon seeing it, his instinct was to avoid it at all costs; after all, the last clearing had led to disaster, and he was starving because of that event. Unfortunately, his grumbling stomach had other ideas. *Fewer trees could mean other types of things grow there.*

He made his way to the edge of the clearing and studied it at great length. On the far left, there were several piles of bricks and black remnants of wood from what might have once been a house that had burned down long ago. *Did the king's men burn down every house when they made it forbidden to live out here?* There was a stone archway that might have once been a doorframe, which leaned dramatically away from a pile of bricks. Near the center stood a heap of dead grass and twisting, thorny vines a hand taller than Ashan. The rest of the clearing was overgrown with slender stalks and grass that had already died and dried out in the cool weather. *Winter will be here soon. What will we eat then?* There were also a few small trees at the edge of the clearing, but nothing older than two seasons judging by their size.

He studied the place for a long time, seeing nothing and hearing only the occasional creaking of a tree swaying in the cool wind. When he did take to the clearing, he headed straight for the big pile with the vines, thinking to cross the area slowly and to hide behind whatever was available along the way. If there were soldiers, he would rather not just walk upon them. He crept to it, taking care with each step he took so that he didn't step on anything that would make much sound when broken, and kept himself as low as possible along the way. Once there, he crept around the pile slowly, studying everything he could lay his eyes upon as he went. A sound came and he dove to the ground, his hand going to his sword. He almost screamed when he realized he had left his sword sticking in the ground back at camp. *Why'd I do that,* he thought angrily.

Because you haven't been getting enough sleep.

He almost pounded the ground with a fist as he realized just how tired he was. He had stabbed the sword into the ground as a message that he would return, which was a fair idea if he were simply going to find a tree to urinate behind. *Yeah, that was...stupid. You've let your fear take control of you.*

He lay there for a long time, hearing only silence before concluding that he had heard nothing more than his imagination. *Not the first time.* With a sigh, he rose to his hands and knees and began to walk forward slowly, eyes searching for what had made the noise, if there had been a noise at all. Three baby steps forward and he felt something soft and cool pop beneath his right hand. Looking down, he saw that he had slid his hand beneath a thick thorny vine. No, the vine was under his hand. He couldn't make up his mind about what he was seeing and so he carefully lifted his hand and found that his hand either passed through the vine or the vine had been beneath his hand at the start. He gave the vine a poke, but his finger passed through it. *I'm so tired I'm seeing things.* Confused, he found another thorny vine to test and found that it behaved the same and so he began touching everything to determine what was there and what was not. He quickly found that none of the thorny vines were real, allowing his hands to pass through as in a dream; however, along the way, he did find real vines, but none offered thorns. They wound about in big loops and offered clusters of something soft that squished easily between his fingers. The smell was intoxicating.

"ARGEL!" Argel had to fight with all her might against her body to wake up. "Argel, wake up!" She would prefer to believe what she was

239

hearing was just another dream and ignore it, but his voice kept coming. Barely able to look upon him, Argel certainly didn't want to wake up and talk to him. For her, a deep shame filled every waking moment and she wanted to sneak away from him as soon as possible. Unfortunately, she never had the strength to keep going after he called an end to their day's walking so that they could sleep. Where she would go when she got the chance didn't matter, just so long as she went where Ashan wasn't. Once her ankle was healed, she would leave him no choice but to continue without her. She would never see her family or home again, but she knew she didn't deserve either after...

"ARGEL!" Ashan screamed and shook her violently.

When she finally opened her eyes, his face was inches from hers. Haunted eyes drove cold daggers into her soul, and she slammed shut her eyes and shifted sideways with a moan. She wondered if he even had it in him to survive the journey to the nearest village or wherever they might again find food or water. In some ways, he looked worse now than the day she had met him, and she wondered if it was a lingering effect from her having drained the life from him. *Some things simply cannot be refilled...*

"FINE!" He spat his words furiously. She tried desperately to shrink away, to hide somewhere deep within so as not to hear his voice. "You won't even **get up** to save your own life!" Silence came and she hoped that he had finally gone, abandoning her. *I deserve it*, she thought angrily as a wave of guilt and fear hit her. His arms came quickly, one sliding under her legs and the other forcing itself beneath her back. He rocked her one way and the other, adjusting her before grunting and lifting her from the ground. He sort of tossed her up with one arm and then the next, adjusting his arms beneath her, and then grunted. The world rocked back and forth, side to side almost like a boat, and terror filled her heart. "Frezz should have abandoned us both. We're practically useless. Yes, we'll probably die of starvation soon." He swayed one way near to the point that it felt like they were about to fall, but then he took a deep breath and things returned to normal.

"Doesn't mean I'm going to give up. I'd rather die free and hungry than go back."

Ashan did not speak again. He grunted whenever he stumbled or when climbing up a hill, but he remained silent otherwise. Argel wondered if he had finally lost himself in hating her the way she knew she deserved. *Perhaps he found a cliff. Toss me over the edge. Good for you. I'm just holding you back. With any luck, you will finally find food and freedom.* After what seemed an eternity, just when the rhythm of motion and the warmth of Ashan's arms were about to lull her back to sleep, there came a sudden light. Fear gave Argel the power to open her eyes and she found herself in a clearing. Even with full moonlight, Argel couldn't make out much of the world around herself aside from plants. A short while later, she was lowered to the cold ground and Ashan fell with a huff at her side.

"Raspberry patch." he mumbled. A second later, she heard him chewing and caught the rich aroma of berries. Her stomach protested, not caring for the guilt she felt. She waited a while before opening her eyes.

"Are-are they poisonous?" She was glad for the darkness, for he might have seen her tears and she didn't want that.

"I'd have already...figured that out by now."

Argel didn't wait for further assurances. She reached up and fumbled blindly until her fingers met her desired target. She filled her hands, stuffed the lot into her mouth and chewed twice before swallowing. She continued in this manner until she felt that she might burst.

Ashan woke from a nightmare with a start and blurted out a half-grunt, half-yelp of fear. His mind immediately turned to thoughts of running and fear was fueled by the realization of how far they'd traveled since Argel had injured her ankle, but he pushed these thoughts away and focused on calming himself. He rolled over and saw through blurry eyes that Argel was sitting up beside him. He cleared his throat, and she gave a start with a small squeak. She turned and he was startled at the sight of her face. She had removed the cloth wrapping that had concealed her face and now exposed, he could see that she was terrified. He sat up and rubbed his eyes to clear his vision. Once clear, he sought out his sword and began scanning the world through the mess of dead grass and thorny vines. Finding nothing of note, he crawled to the edge of the mound of dead plants, testing each thorny vine he came to in case there were real ones in the mix. *Real?* He ignored the thoughts that came to mind about the strange thing and crept to its edge.

Thump.

"I know I heard something." A booming voice proclaimed. "Show yourself!"

"You hear things." A second voice came.

"Again." A third voice offered.

"I hear true!" The first voice retorted angrily.

Ashan turned to face Argel and found she was glaring wide-eyed at him with an expression that suggested she was about to run. She'd brought her legs up to her chest, wrapped her arms around them, and was half shaking and half rocking in place. "They can't see us." he whispered.

"I don't see tracks."

"You are blind!" One laughed. "You couldn't track a heard of them in fields of mud."

"You scared them off with your foul breath." The first spat.

"You both scare the whole forest with your arguing. I'm surprised the trees haven't grown legs to get away from the two of you."

Just keep walking, Ashan begged silently as he searched for the bodies belonging to the voices. He waved for Argel to come to his side and crept to the opposite edge of the...*illusion?* Once there, he planted both hands upon the ground to stabilize himself and leaned forward slowly until he could get a good view of the outside world. Directly ahead at the edge of the clearing, he discovered three men standing together, each wearing only a loincloth and holding a roughly crafted club that was more a tree's branch than anything. They stood twice his height and looked like something from a jester's tale of giants with their bulging muscles.

"Do you smell that?"

The first sniffed several times. "What? Your breath?"

"Wild berries."

"I see no berries."

"Old wizard's hidden goodies still grow all over the forest."

"No. The witch killed him, and nobody comes for growing things now."

"Some berries grow again."

"I smell them too."

Almost in unison, the three bent and began carefully probing the ground at their feet and kept their eyes locked onto their hands. *They know what to look for!* As big as they were, he figured it wouldn't be long before he and Argel were found. He considered trying to sneak away at first but realized that was impossible with how big the clearing was. Fighting was out of the question, given that each of the giants was twice his height and could probably lift a cow without much trouble. Thinking, he looked down at his sword and wondered how much he could even injure ONE of them before being smashed. *I need a plan!* His eyes caught the ring he wore, and he considered how many people must live in Isirdost. He was supposed to deliver the ring as some sort of warning. *What is it they said? Is it worse than they thought? The king is worse than they imagined?* He couldn't remember the exact words now. Either way, it didn't matter in this moment, and he pushed the thoughts away. *Plan! I need a plan.* Drums sounded in the far distance. They weren't close enough to be concerning in the moment, but it put a little kick in his heart. *Great. Just what we need. At least I know which way to run.* He sat his sword down and removed the ring.

"Argel," He whispered. "You have to get this ring to the king in Isirdost. It's a warning. King Hotar is going to attack." He grabbed her hand and put the ring on one finger. It didn't fit and he went to the next bigger finger. "I will attack." He motioned which way he intended to go. "You must run. Maybe I will buy you enough time to get away from them."

"Isirdost. King Hotar." she looked down at the ring and then back up at him. Whatever she was thinking, her face twisted in fear and sorrow.

"You have to run that way." He pointed to clarify, hoping she'd heard the drums in the distance and knew what they meant.

Ashan ran, half-stumbling, out from cover and directly towards the nearest giant. He was surprised that they didn't notice him immediately or even react to the sound of his running, but they didn't, and he kept on a straight path. He arrived saying a silent prayer to whatever gods might be listening that his death would be swift and without much pain and brought up his sword and back with both hands. His target suddenly looked up, gasped loudly, and brought his massive club up and forward at a terrifying speed. Ashan's sword sank into the wood a finger's depth. Remembering how he had to lever the thing free from the skull of one of the undead so long ago, he didn't even have to stop moving; instead, Ashan tightened his grip, moved forward and veered to his right. The blade popped free with ease and, now behind the giant, he swung at its far leg. Again, the giant moved at the last second, shifting its weight and moving it's leg away from the sword.

"Hey!" the giant yelled as it jumped away and brought its club up overhead as if preparing to attack. It paused, surprise clear on its face.

Horns called out from the forest while the giant stepped forward and brought the club down. Ashan jumped to the side and barely escaped the thing, but he felt the sound of it thumping the ground in his bones. As he ran, he couldn't help but imagine what the thing would have done to him. Oddly, he found it reassuring to realize that it was unlikely he would survive such an attack long enough to know he was suffering pain. Without thinking and much to his surprise, he found himself running around the giant again, but a bit closer this time. The giant grabbed his club with both hands and lifted it much more slowly this time. Ashan reared back and slashed at the giant's midsection as he ran. The tip of his blade bit at the fatty tissue just above the hip and the flesh parted. It wasn't a deep cut, but the giant yelped and leaned away from Ashan.

THUMP. Another club smacked the ground just behind Ashan and he turned to look. This giant wasn't looking at Ashan as he expected; in fact, all three were focused on the spot on the ground where the second had just struck its club instead. The giant placed both hands upon the club and visibly struggled to lift it back up. They screwed their faces up as if surprised and then looked up as if only just realizing that Ashan had escaped the attack. Ashan turned about and ran back at the three and was surprised that they appeared shocked at his attacking them. The shock of it was short-lived though. They recovered and began lifting their clubs up high again.

Ashan veered to his right as soon as he was within striking distance and aimed himself at the giant furthest to his right. The giants reacted slowly to his change in direction. One brought his club down and to his right, slamming it into the head of the giant to his right, which caused that giant to drop his club as he shouted and brought his hands up to his head. The offending giant turned to his compatriot in

245

surprise just as the third giant swung his club down at Ashan. It missed by a fair margin and Ashan charged in as fast as he could. He drove the blade into the giant's side just above the cut he had made previously, and the giant screamed much more loudly than Ashan expected. The blade only sank a finger's depth before the giant released his club and, twisting, moved backward from the blade. The reaction to pain was much faster than expected.

Motion at the edge of his vision caught his attention and he looked left just in time to see the fist coming. It connected with his right, upper chest and the world went dark. He struck something hard with his right arm and hip in unison, felt himself rise and fall, and then finally came to rest on his back. He got the impression that he had rolled, but the pain was so great that he didn't give it a second thought. Light came in splotches of color, and he rolled, finding himself screaming in pain, but all he could hear was a rushing wind and a faint heartbeat.

RUN! He blinked his eyes rapidly, rolled to his stomach, and pushed himself upright. *Run where?* With each blink, the splotches took form. *Away, you idiot!* First, he spotted his sword several strides away and then the three giants, who stood together and were watching him with surprised expressions. *Yes, I'm surprised to be alive as well,* he thought at them. He stepped towards his sword, each step causing the pain in his chest to spike, but it seemed to diminish the sound of rushing wind he was hearing. He tried twice to lift the sword with his right hand before snatching it up with his left instead. Great. *The less useful hand,* he cursed.

A red light filled the forest behind the giants just then. Just as he wondered if the forest was on fire, a fireball crashed into the back of one of the giants. It yelled out in shock and pain and stumbled forward. The other two reached out to catch him but missed. *They're kind of slow,* he considered. They watched their friend fall, studied him in confusion for a second, and finally turned to face the direction of the attack. A second ball of fire struck one of them square in the face, sending it stumbling backward with a yell.

"Old wizard!" one giant shouted as it brought up its club and quickly stepped backward.

Ashan spotted movement in the forest beyond and froze. Frezz leapt from a high branch to the ground, vanished behind a tree, and reappeared a moment later around the side of a tree some distance further off. He stepped out, twirled his staff, and sent another ball of fire arching towards the giants.

"NO!" The bleeding giant took up its club and hurled it at Frezz, but Frezz darted behind a tree for cover.

At the same time, the other two giants began taking handfuls of dirt and throwing them at Frezz as well. After a few of them, Frezz ran from behind that tree to another, much larger one. As he ran, he made motions with his hands and a wall of flames suddenly erupted from the ground and encircled the giants. Compared to the last wall of fire Ashan had seen the man create, this one was twice as thick and seemed much taller.

"No more fire!" One giant screamed as he bent down, scooped up a handful of dirt and poured it on the flames. The other began striking the ground with his club. Neither seemed to influence the flames.

"Argel! Ashan!" Frezz shouted as he ran out from behind the tree and sent another fireball flying.

"NO!" One of the giants howled in pain as it stepped through the flames. Looking, Ashan saw it had its eyes locked onto Frezz. It reared back to throw its club at Frezz.

"Frezz!" Ashan yelled as he pointed at the giant. Frezz turned his head as he ran and simply dove to the ground at the last second to escape the club. He rose a second later and ran to Ashan.

"Where is Argel?"

247

"Running away." Realizing that he hadn't seen her running away, Ashan glanced about quickly and found no trace of her. *Good, she escaped.*

"You should run too." Frezz said as he turned to face the approaching giant.

Seeing a giant run was a bit of a terrifying sight and Ashan found himself backing away instinctively. When Ashan arrived, he threw his fist at Frezz and Ashan yelled for Frezz to run; however, Frezz simply stepped to the side and struck the giant in its side. The giant yelled and moved away to its side. The first ball of fire hit the giant in the side of the face and the second, striking while the giant was busy cursing in pain, struck it in the hand it had brought to his face. With a flourish of his wand and a few spoken words that Ashan didn't recognize, small green vines shot up from the ground at the giant's feet. They reached up quickly, spinning around the giant's ankle, and suddenly tightened. At the same time, Frezz ran in a wide circle, leapt upon the giant's back, and clawed wildly. The giant screamed in pained surprise and Frezz leapt away just before the giant jumped up and landed on his own back.

Ashan was still frozen in wonder at the sight when a second giant arrived with its club held high. It swung the club down at Frezz and, as before, Frezz simply stepped to the side to evade the attack. He turned in a casual manner and sent a ball of fire into this giant's face. It screamed and brought both hands up to its face and Frezz ran at it, driving his elbow into its stomach.

Ashan was moving even before the thought occurred to him from nowhere. *Attack while they're distracted.* He brought his sword up over his shoulder as he ran and aimed himself at the back of the giant that was attacking Frezz. Frezz dodged three punches, stepped to the side, and the giant followed, turning its back on Ashan. Ashan slashed the soft tissue at the back side of the knee. His blade landed somewhat close to where he had intended to put it, but only made a small cut. The leg rose then, moved backwards toward Ashan, and

248

caused him to lose his balance. He stumbled to his left and collided with the giant's other leg. The collision caused the pain in his chest to flare up and he lost his grip on his sword before falling.

"Danuk!" a giant's voice called.

It took a moment to steel himself against the pain that rose when he hit the ground and even longer to get himself up to his feet. On his feet again, Ashan glanced around to get his bearings and found his sword some ten strides away. Frezz was still dodging punches from the same giant and, further back, the first to attack was just pulling the last vine from his ankle. *The third?* He scanned the clearing and headed towards his sword. The third giant was slowly walking towards Frezz with its club raised overhead. It seemed it meant to sneak up upon Frezz.

"Frezz! Behind you!"

By the time he picked up his sword, things had changed. Frezz was retreating from the two giants attacking him, throwing balls of fire or having vines ensnare their legs when he had the chance, and the third giant had finally freed his leg. This giant took a long moment to evaluate the scene before deciding to attack Ashan. He almost turned to run, but then stopped himself, realizing that the thing ran much faster than he could. *No, there's another option,* he told himself. He let his sword hang down by his legs and waited instead. He only had to wait a few breaths for the giant to arrive. It swung that giant club down at him and Ashan jumped backward with all the strength he could muster, which didn't feel like that much now. The sound of the club hitting the ground was deafening and the dirt that was thrown stung his eyes; however, Ashan found it easy to ignore both with the certainty that he was unlikely to dodge another such attack. He brought his sword up and swung it at the giant's neck. His arm faltered under the weight of the blade, dropping the blade substantially so that it contacted the man's upper chest. The result was that he made only a shallow cut a few inches across. Panic shot through him at this failure. *I have to...do better,* he thought as he brought his sword back for another attempt.

The giant reacted to this much more quickly than Ashan expected. He released his club and leaned back just in time to avoid Ashan's second attack. After the blade passed, he pulled back one arm, twisted at the waist, and threw a fist forward. Ashan watched the fist coming directly at his chest, let the air escape his lungs in a wild scream, and closed his eyes.

Argel made it as far as the outer edge of the illusion and no further. *You'll never leave this forest alive;* her aunt's words haunted her each time she tried to gather the courage to cross the open space to the forest. Dressed in stark white, she knew the giants would spot her instantly and even if they didn't give chase right away, they would spot her easily in the forest later. After they'd dealt with Ashan, they would catch her. The only way she could think to avoid being seen was to cover her clothing in mud or hide in a ditch, but that would take time she didn't have. It didn't even seem worth the effort in her mind, as she knew that she would not get far before exhaustion set in. Sure, the food Ashan had found had been plentiful and delicious, but it lacked what her body needed to fuel her for a good run. So it was that she found herself watching Frezz and Ashan battle three giants and desperately trying to convince herself that they could win...that they WOULD win; after all, they had to win, or they would all die.

She tried to ignore the clumsy, unskilled way Ashan handled himself and how he barely survived his first attack. Ignoring that was a challenge, but it was near impossible to lie to herself about Frezz's situation. She could see that fighting two of them was taking its toll quite quickly. She was certain that his aim only seemed good because he was so close to them, and he was not utilizing any new magics. Having slain her aunt, fireballs, walls of fire, and vines seemed like rudimentary skills the man should be beyond; after all, her aunt could do far more things than just three. She wondered if he was fighting through an injury that was preventing him from focusing. She watched and tried to ignore how it seemed the fight and her life would soon end.

Her hope for Ashan's survival vanished in an instant when he ran for his sword instead of in Frezz's direction. She had seen the giant rise and study his surroundings a moment before locking it's gaze upon Ashan. Dread and certainty of death came when Ashan didn't run from the charging giant. She gasped in surprise when Ashan jumped out of the club's way at the last second and attacked. When the giant punched him, which sent him flying away with great speed, she gave a silent thanks that his death was instantaneous instead of prolonged. Her aunt wouldn't have been so generous. *At least he won't suffer,* she thought.

Quite to her own shock, Argel stepped out from her hiding place in that moment and reached out to the towering man's arm with one hand. Why she did so, she had no idea, but she couldn't stop herself. She took hold of the giant's right arm just below the elbow and began closing her eyes. *NO!* The weakness in her knees and the cold in her chest matched the intensity of the silent screaming inside. Shame, sorrow, and fear flooded her heart in equal parts as she recalled the many faces of men, women, and children she had murdered these last few years. *Never again!* She commanded her hand to cease, to release, and then she screamed at her legs to give out, hoping that she might fall and roll back into the fake stack of dead plants, but to no avail. Her eyes closed and, despite herself, the accursed red symbols lit up upon the dark canvas of her mind. She replicated the symbols she had seen her aunt make on paper a thousand times before in a flash and opened her eyes. She clamped down upon the giant's arm with all her strength, terrified that it would kill her in an instant, and her eyes began to water. Those red words broke apart like a fresh painting having water poured upon it from high up, leaving behind fresh guilt and darkness. A squirming sensation ran out from her neck to her hand and then into the giant.

She braced herself for the next part. Red tendrils of smoke rose from all over the giant, snaked about in the air, and made their way to

251

her. When the first contacted her, it delivered a torrential flood of-well, she didn't know what to call it. In a flash, her physical pains lessened and her near constant exhaustion faded considerably. The shaking in her hand fled after only a few blinks and the weakness in her knees was replaced by an unwavering vitality that she hadn't realized she had taken for granted in the years before her aunt had taken her hostage. The worst part was that this had always been a fleeting thing, as this strength was always passed to her aunt after only a few breaths, leaving Argel in even worse condition.

She lifted her eyes up slowly and found the giant just shifting his gaze down to her. Anger turned to terror, and he fell to his knees. He raised his far arm up, forming a fist along the way, but she could already see in his eyes that his strength was faltering. He was realizing that he was powerless to follow through with his intentions and he was terrified by the weakness he felt. They all looked that way in their final moments. He worked his mouth as if to speak but fell forward instead.

He doesn't need to die, she plead silently.

Argel bent down and, being careful not to touch him, placed a hand in front of his mouth. Gloriously, she found that air still escaped his lips. It was shallow, but she wasn't sure if that was terrible or okay for a person his size. Looking up, she found that the illusion of a heap of dead plants was gone, replaced by three brambles of berries nearly as wide as she was tall, slightly taller than herself, and each stretching about twice as long as she was tall. They were dead now. All shriveled, yellowed, and falling apart. The same was the case with all plant life in a circle a good twenty strides across centered on herself. Why that was the case, she had no idea, but it made cold shivers run down her spine.

A pained groan then erupted from the fallen giant and startled her such that she screamed and jumped away. She landed upon her right side facing the giant and her eyes automatically found and locked upon the man's open eyes. His eyes shifted slowly, not focusing on anything, and then it took a deep, slow breath. *He's not dead!* A part of her was deeply relieved, but another part was terrified. As she scrambled to her feet, she wondered if he had survived because his body was so much larger than a normal man's or because her aunt wasn't there to push her actions.

"Argel!" Frezz's shout drew her from her thoughts.

She found him retreating from the giants at a full run on the other side of the clearing. As he ran, he stabbed the bottom of his staff into the ground on every other footfall. At first, she thought him injured, but then he jumped, spun about in the air, and cast a ball of fire at the giants. The distance was enough to allow the giants to evade the attack easily, but then he threw something out with his other hand. It was like a small hand of pebbled that fell onto the ground where he had been running. "Argel!" he yelled as he landed.

"Here!"

She started off in his direction and was surprised by the strength in her usually weary muscles; in fact, it was as though her entire body yearned to run, to stretch, and to burn off excess energy. Ahead, Frezz turned, come to a sliding stop, and began waving his staff. She could see his lips moving but heard none of his words. As she picked up speed, she noticed the green of the forest deepen and then the sunlight dim. Looking up, she was only partly surprised to find that a massive, entirely black cloud was moving in overhead. It was just at the edge of the clearing and stood above the trees probably no higher than the height of the giants, and it moved as though a moderate wind pushed it. The thing's belly hung low like a cat days from birthing a litter, and it was dropping rain here and there in short bouts. Thunder rumbled then and the giants ceased their approach to look up at the thing. Just then, the monstrosity boomed angrily and began to pour out water so furiously that Argel's heart leapt in her chest, and she very nearly screamed in surprise.

By the time the rain reached Frezz, thick vines were already climbing from the ground near the giants' feet, each growing about as thick as Argel's arms in mere moments. Blood-red thorns the size of pairing knives shot out all along the vines as they reached Argel's height and they flailed as if trying to reach out and grab the giants, but they quickly ran backward until they were beyond reach. They studied the cloud and the vines for a long moment before shooting Argel and Frezz matching looks of anger. Their attention turned to their friend and they headed that way at a brisk walk, repeatedly turning their eyes back to see if Frezz would attack. When they reached their companion, one of them picked the fellow up while the other eyed Frezz and held his club up defensively.

To her surprise, when the man was brought upright, he lifted his head and glanced about in a daze as one would when woken up rather suddenly after a night of heavy drinking and it soothed her guilt tremendously. He moved his mouth and leaned against the other and they began walking slowly, turning towards the forest as they went. The third stood eyeing Frezz and Argel.

"They appear to be done with us." Frezz said as he stepped up beside her.

"Frezz!" She nearly shouted as she half threw herself at him to hug him. "Where have you been?"

"Following. Trying to reach you two, but constantly blocked by those three. Apparently, they think I smell like something that would be delicious if boiled inside my own intestines for a few days."

"What?"

"They've been following you but would chase me if I got too close. I kept trying to go around, but their sense of smell is...powerful." he explained.

"We thought that shadow-man...took you."

"Can you heal Ashan?"

"I..." She pulled away from Frezz and began frantically searching for Ashan. That punch had sent him flying and she hadn't paid attention to where exactly. *Near the...dead berries,* she reminded herself and began walking that direction.

The three giants' voices rang out loudly then and Argel paused. Looking to her left, she found them facing each other, one angrily pointing his free hand at the one not carrying their comrade. The other pointed back, but in a slightly less hostile manner, as he dropped his club and stepped forward. The injured one raised his hand after a moment and spoke, but his words were as soft as distant rumbling thunder to Argel's ears. It went on a few moments and then all three fell silent, two of their heads falling as if watching their feet. A long moment passed before they raised their heads and shared silent gazes before the one assisting their injured friend turned towards the forest. The third remained still, watching his friends until they reached the trees and then turned back to Frezz and Argel.

"Kelmadi!" He shouted. "Tregtoj...ushqim!" He stood there without moving for a few breaths and then turned towards his fellows. He jogged to the trees, stopped, and turned back. "Sherim." He shouted, held a moment, and then was gone.

Ashan lay upon his back some thirty strides from where he had been punched by the giant. Even before she had reached him, Argel saw the disturbed ground and blood ran in a straight line from where he lay currently to another place a good ten strides closer to where he had obviously landed. He held his sword in his good hand. She let her legs fall out from beneath her and slid the last five strides to his side and wasn't aware that she was yelling him name repeatedly until she felt the strain in her lungs. He was motionless, a bone stuck out from his upper left arm, and his chest didn't seem the correct shape or size below the arm. The blood had made a little pool by his arm and one of his legs was bent the wrong way.

255

"Placet sanavi." Frezz's voice brought her attention up from Ashan and she found him at her side with his staff held high and the small stone atop it letting out a blinding white light.

"Can you heal him?"

"I do not know." He replied. The tone in his voice revealed that he did not hold much hope.

"Don't die, Ashan!" She yelled as she turned back. She put a hand on his chest to feel for movement. "You can't die!"

"Kerathevo!" Frezz almost shouted over her shoulder and the bright white light changed to red. "Ethidorkosi." The red light flickered three times and went out. "Kalnin." The stone flashed green for the briefest of moments. "No."

Ashan's chest jerked, his eyes shot open, and he made a small choking sound. His face twisted with pain and his eyes did not move to her or Frezz but were unfocused as if deep in thought or daydreaming. His second breath was shallow and slow and the gurgling that followed told her that he was drowning in his own blood. "Something pierced his lungs!" She shouted.

"No." Frezz's voice came soft as his face shot down with terror in his eyes. He held his wand with both hands and began speaking in words she didn't know, repeating a small bit of something over and over as if it were a prayer. The stone at the top of his staff let off only the faintest of light for a moment before winking out and she knew he had used up all his power.

He can't save Ashan; she thought as she turned her eyes back to Ashan's face. His chest jerked hard, he lifted his head a hand from the ground, and he spat up blood. His chest expanded as if he were trying to suck in air a few times before he fell to the ground and began jerking rapidly. "No." Argel screamed as she shot forward and placed both hands upon his chest as she scrambled for any bit of information that might help. She found nothing in her memories of medical lessons

256

that was useful. *There has to be a way! Please, don't let my friend die! Whoever can hear me!* She didn't know the gods of this land and, so, could not put a name to whatever gods these southerners might pray to, but she prayed just the same. *If only I could do more than kill people, maybe I-that's it! Mary made me rejuvenate her tons of times!* She suddenly recalled the first time it had been done. Mary had to have been nearing seventy back then and before her death she had appeared as a woman in her early thirties. *Yes!*

"Frezz! Get the bonding ring! Put it back on me and make me rejuvenate him! It made my aunt look half her age and fixed all her old wounds and illnesses!"

"Argel," The willingness to perform the act was there, but there was also regret. "I destroyed it."

The accursed symbols her aunt had made her learn flashed through her mind as she recalled a particularly gruesome man she had been made to kill. That man had been stabbed by Mary's undead soldiers, held down, and Mary had driven a finger into one of his eyes. Mary had delighted in that bit of cruelty, laughing as she taunted the man before having Argel kill him, but he had pulled a small silver knife from his boot in the height of pain and thrust it into her arm just before dying. That small injury had been a small thing however, healed easily in the following Rejuvenation. It hadn't even left a permanent scar. *I could try. It's not like I could do him any more harm and he's about to...*the thought came out of nowhere and she didn't let herself finish it. Instead, she closed her eyes and drew the symbol for Rejuvenation with all the haste she could muster. It was complex though and took time, as each symbol had to be done correctly. The simple depiction of the sun Hakul, the equal scales of trade, and the three crooked legs of Alm'hest – god of life, death, and healing – all had to rest in a triangle above a flat line. On either side resided two simple human figures and above this Argel had to draw the six eyes of judgment and then encircle the entire thing in three unbroken lines. The fourth line had to be broken into six parts with the ends curled around each other somewhat

257

like chains. Why the picture had to be exact, she wasn't sure other than it wouldn't work at all if she made mistakes. One the thing was complete, she paused to make certain it was all correct, wondering at each line. *No,* she reassured herself, *I've seen this a thousand times...but how do I do the other part? How do I put all this energy into him? Was that something Mary had to do? What if nothing happens?*

When Argel opened her eyes, she found Ashan's eyes closing. The red symbols melted away from the dark canvas in her mind and that wriggling sensation moved along her arm, but much more slowly than ever before. Blood rose in Ashan's mouth, spilled out one side, ran down his cheek, and made its way to the ground. The wriggling thing reached her hand and she saw the light in Ashan's eyes wink out.

"No!" She screamed.

"Ashan." Frezz breathed as he knelt and let his staff fall to his side. "I'm sorry."

"No. We have to do something."

"There's nothing left to do." Frezz replied dully. "My stone is empty. I have no tools for mending so much damage."

All her strength vanished in a flash then. A profound hunger sprang upon her and, as she gasped in surprise, her chest began to burn with a bitter cold. She fell to her side and snapped her mouth shut to keep from vomiting as the motion made her dizzy.

"Argel!" Frezz's voice seemed to come from a hundred strides away.

"What did you do?"

"I tried."

"What did you try?"

"Mary's...re...juv...enation spell." The weariness that always followed the performance of Rejuvenation hit her hard and her eyes began to close.

"You look half dead now yourself. You should have explained what you were going to try." he scolded.

"No... time. Besides," she had to pause to catch her breath before going on. "It didn't...work. He's...dead."

"Stay with me, Argel."

"I..." she yawned so deeply that she almost thought she'd fallen asleep in the middle of doing so. "Must." The second yawn was nearly as long, and she saw a dream forming in the back of her mind. She was vaguely aware of a warm pool of water like the one in her uncle's home and the warmth of that place beckoned her to it with a mighty strength. "Sleep." She barely got the last word out before yawning a third time.

"Argel." Ashan's voice came no more loudly than the whisper of a breeze.

FAILURE

The fall from leading a special mission directly under the high-king's watch to commanding his own forces again was monumental. It stung a bit personally to have failed, but the fact that High-king Hotar had announced it by screaming in a room full of other royalty made it all the worse. Rumors would be spreading like wildfire and the family name would be tarnished greatly. Fortunately, he hadn't been stripped of lands or titles, but falling so far could cause the loss of trade partners, political allies, and could eventually cost the family just as much. The shame of it was such that he would never be able to repair his family's honor through regular good deeds, charity, or other mundane means. No, repairing the family's honor required something grand and unforgettable that would stick in the minds of people, and he needed to act soon. The rumors would take several months to congeal into one core story with all the same basic ideas before it would stick to his family, which meant he had a few months to coax that story along in a more favorable manner. A few charitable acts, public services, and maybe a heroic act would go a long way in fighting the initial versions of the story. After that, he expected that the bankers would increase interest rates of any loan to his siblings, acquaintances would begin pulling back their involvement with his family, and his siblings would blame him. There would be yelling and endless complaints where they blamed him for their failed business ventures and personal failings, but that last part would not be a departure from the status quo in the main. Just the same, he had to do right by his family.

It took a few days of thinking to come to the realization that the quickest and easiest way to regain the lion's share of lost honor would be to commit suicide. He could leave behind a letter blaming his failure to king and country on general incompetence or stupidity. If he really wanted to sell that idea, he could throw in a line about how he had become lazy or had turned too heavily to hard drink. He could blubber for forgiveness and understanding, stating that his failures were not family traits, so his living relatives were not tainted by his words. His family would suffer very little socially or financially in the immediate future should he take this route, and, in fact, there were some very good benefits to be found, as his older sister Koraine had cheerfully pointed out. She would spin the situation to highlight the family's "deeply held belief" in taking personal responsibility for their failings, their love for country, king and, above all, their loyalty to the people. *A people she despises,* he thought. Yes, in the end, Koraine would turn disaster into opportunity, as was her gods-given talent. It would go a long way in her designs to marry off her first daughter into another royal family of much higher social ranking than their own, thereby boosting the ranking of their whole family. *Money,* he considered, *is her only love.* "One can never be too close to the throne." she often remarked. "The throne holds power...no matter who sits upon it, but standing beside it is much safer." was likely her second-favorite saying.

So it was that Lord Kairn found himself drunk in the middle of the day as he approached High-king Hotar's main encampment, which lay a stone's throw north of the city's outer wall. He held a half-bottle of strong southern barley beer in one hand, his overcoat lazily in the other, and didn't do anything to hide his drunken lack of balance. The encampment was a massive jumble of tents, wagons, carts, and horses that stretched north several hundred strides and to the east at least ten times as far before wrapping around a small lake. Before the call to war, the only thing that had existed here was a tent city filled with the most wretched, destitute, and desperately unfortunate people in all the north. Where they'd gone was a mystery, but he suspected they'd gone south into the city and either found themselves the random alley to occupy or they had been arrested for vagrancy and currently filled the high-king's dungeons. He doubted he would ever get an answer to that mystery. *There are plenty of needy people to feed elsewhere,* he considered. As he arrived at the camp via dirt path, he found a group of soldiers standing guard just before the first tents and a group of young boys lounging nearby. After a quick explanation of his arrival, one of the soldiers turned to the boys and demanded one of them take Lord Kairn to the high commander. The boy that approached beamed at Lord Kairn.

"Kanin?"

"Yes, my lord." The boy replied as he waved him forward along the path.

He was shocked to find the boy wearing the white uniform of a full messenger, which was usually awarded after years of good service. The things was an oddity because it almost looked like a chef's garment with the overlapped front, the big buttons that ran down the chest, and the fact that it was pristine white, but that was the latest style imported from the Bal Keth region. *A strange people,* he thought as he returned the boy's smile.

"It's good to see you again."

"You as well, my lord. Sure are a lot of soldiers."

"Indeed."

"Have you ever gone to war, my lord?"

"No. House Kairn hasn't even really had a skirmish with any other houses in three generations."

"That's what my master said. He told me that there hasn't been a real war since before High-king Hotar took the throne."

"I suppose that is right. Of course, we have a very particular definition of war these days. Some of the skirmishes between houses fit what people used to call war a hundred years ago."

"This is more soldiers than I've ever seen in one place in my life. Do you think there are enough to go to war and protect the kingdom at the same time?"

"Our people will be safe." he replied without really thinking about it.

"Why do you think they tried to kill our king?"

"Hard to say."

"Lady Emireth told me they want our fish." With that childlike wonder in his big brown eyes, Lord Kairn found it difficult to believe that the boy hadn't already been tied up, thrown on a cart, and sent back home the day he'd come to this place. He couldn't even be twelve yet.

"People kill for many reasons. Royalty more than most. My father often said war is stronger than any bank."

He considered the extensive business records his father, grandfather, and great-grandfather had gone through great lengths to put together. In total, they had amassed nearly a hundred tomes relating to domestic and foreign trade that had occurred during past wars, which was mostly just copied information from other royal houses. The fruits of many spies over decades.

"Lord Turley says that the common folk are the currency of wars. He says that if you must go to war, it should be a small war so that it ends quickly. He says we've brought too many soldiers, that this war is a mistake."

"Lord Turley is a wise man."

When they arrived, Lord Kairn found that the tent was enormous compared to what he had expected to find. It stood three times taller than any other tent in sight and was large enough to house at least fifty horses comfortably. Out front, there stood a cluster of ten personal attendants, a handful of messengers, and fifteen guards wielding swords in matching white uniforms. Kanin gave a wave as he ran over to join the other messengers, the youngest of them easily three summers older than Kanin, but none of them gave Kanin a second look. Lord Kairn gave the boy a smile and stepped into the tent cautiously.

Inside, he was surprised to find no less than sixty lords and ladies, all dressed as if ready to attend a summertime ball rather than a war meeting. A young girl broke from the crowd carrying a silver tray with several cups upon it. Lord Kairn recognized the strain in her forced smile and the stress in her voice as she offered him a drink. She came right up to him and forgot to give the customary curtsy as she lowered the tray for him to look at the contents of the cup and he saw in her eyes that she was very nearly about to cry.

"Good evening, my lady." He began with a soft tone and a smile, giving a slight bow so as not to fall over. There would be time for that later.

Some of the stress melted from her eyes face in response. Unfortunately, what replaced that stress was a measure of suspicion and freight. He glanced over her shoulder and found a young man glowering at her with an intensity he rarely saw. He was perhaps a year younger than Lord Kairn, wore a suit in a light red that looked as if it had been washed with too much soap a few too many times, and his hair was a golden mess that seemed determined to stand straight up. Lord Kairn couldn't place the man's face, but he did have the crooked nose, slumped shoulders, and too-close eyes that were common among the Alma Dorish region. Inbreeders, he hissed as he turned his attention back to the serving lady. "Would you please get me some grog? I need to sober up." he practically whispered to her. Reaching into his pocket, he pulled out a single copper Stater and one golden Rose coin. He pressed the golden Rose into her hand and her eyes shot wide open in shock.

"My lord, you-"

"Can do anything I like with my money, my lady."

"I cannot-"

"You can and you will. I'm far too drunk to argue with you. The grog, if you would please, my lady." He patted her on the shoulder as he passed, eyes on the young lord who was still eyeing the young lady.

"Right away, my lord." she replied.

Lord Kairn intentionally bumped into several other lords and ladies as he made his way through the crowd. It dawned on him about halfway through the gathering that they were all generally looking towards a single table near the center of the tent. When he found a good place to stand, he caught sight of Lord Turley standing at the table and reading over a paper that was so brown that it looked as though it had been dropped into a dirty puddle of mud and left for a day.

"Alright, alright. Quiet down, you lot." Lord Turley scanned the crowd and waited for all the talking to come to an end with a look that said it had better cease immediately. It did, and he cleared his throat loudly. The man wasn't exactly known for giving speeches or dressing up, but here and now he wore his finest red coat with black trim and his decorative golden sword that had been passed down within the Turley family for at least four generations. It was a single-bladed sword with a slight curve to the blade and a straight back as thick as an adult's finger. It had a quillon cross-guard of a slightly darker gold than the blade and it was much larger than an average man's sword; of course, Lord Turley was a mountain of a man, standing at least two hands taller than anybody else in the tent and his size made wielding such a thing manageable. He was also husky for a Turley, which drove people to joke that the Turley family had mixed with giants a thousand years ago and that their current stature was the last remnants of that blood.

"I have received several messages from High-king Hotar today. Primary among the news is this: A small group of soldiers have our assassin on the run in the Forbidden Forest. King Hotar feels it is appropriate to send Lord Kairn off with one platoon to help capture this assassin."

The crowd exploded into cheers and disapproving shouts as heads turned this way and that, searched, and eventually found Lord Kairn, who did not let surprise show on his face. "Disgrace." one man shouted just before another called out "Abject failure!" Lord Turley's face turned sour, and he had to shout several times to restore silence.

"As High-king Hotar has declared," He paused as if to let that point sink in. "When the order comes, Lord Kairn will depart, capture the assassin, and meet back up with us at the old border-town of Karkan and we will continue on to Isirdost."

"He already failed!" Lord Kairn didn't catch who yelled, but several others followed it with "Right!". Arguments rose, but Lord Kairn did not pay attention. Even without his failure, there would be bickering like this as most would want to gain the high-king's favor through such successes. The fact that the king had decided to offer him a second chance was surprising and confusing. Some would see this as an insult and others would see it as the king trying to give Lord Kairn an opportunity to regain favor. It made some sense to give him a second chance, given that house Kairn was one of the wealthiest in the entire nation, but it didn't fit right in the back of his mind.

"The king has spoken his peace on this matter. If you please, there are several other important issues yet to be discussed." Lord Turley called over the other voices. The crowd fell silent after a moment and Lord Turley began listing names as he read from another sheet of yellow-brown paper. "You must shore up the fighting in your camps. I've gotten reports that your soldiers are getting out of hand. Do not make me move your camps to end it." He took a deep breath before continuing. "High-king Hotar has purchased ten thousand *bound* for the war. Due to time constraints, they will remain bound for now. Lord Tevish will be responsible for establishing a location and schedule for the removal of the bonding rings. You will be assigned your portion as I see fit and I don't want to hear any complaints or rumors that they are being sold or traded. The war council has come up with ideas for their use in the war and they request any suggestions be given directly to Lord and Lady Verill." The collective gasp at this caused Lord Turley to pause a moment. "This ten thousand will be the first wave, as there are plans to purchase many more."

"So, the bound are to be *soldiers* now?" Lady Emilia Voth shouted angrily from the other side of the congregation. "Are we to drive them at our enemies like a mad sheepherder driving cattle over a cliff?"

"Lady Voth," Lord Turley gave a deep sigh of frustration. "They will fight, like so many others, to protect the citizens of our country."

"It doesn't sound like they have a choice in the matter."

"No, I don't see that they have a choice in the matter. Our king has decreed that all who fight will earn their freedom. Their debts will be paid by the crown, and they will be set free once the war has concluded." He opened his mouth as if to say more, but then, clearly thinking better than to go on, waited for her response instead.

"They shouldn't be used like this. They are people!" Lady Voth's tone was respectful but only just.

"Many will find freedom after the war and better treatment along the way. Take it as a glimmer of hope in the dark times ahead."

"You may see it that way, but I see it as another measure of cruelty, Lord Turley."

The collective gasp that came was quite loud and several people called out to denounce Lady Voth as a ninny, a traitor, and one man had the gall to shout, "Royal puppet!". Oddly, nobody seemed at all offended by this outpouring of disapproval, but Lord Kairn knew that they saw her words as an attack on their livelihoods. They all stood to lose incalculable sums of gold by having their *bound* freed, as that meant the children produced would not belong to them in the years to come. Yes, the self-reinforcing system would fall apart, leaving these people with a sudden loss in productivity, workers, and a fear that what the high king would pay would not make up for that loss. The entire market would be thrown into chaos and prices could fluctuate so wildly that today's sound investment might be tomorrow's financial nightmare. Half the faces Lord Kairn could see expressed anger and the rest were a mix of fear and excitement.

Lady Voth scanned the crowd with an uncaring expression on her face as if the words were meaningless to her. That was until her eyes found Lord Kairn, who she gave a slight smile. He gave her a reassuring smile and stood a bit taller than before, suddenly embarrassed by his drunken slouching and messy attire. He knew her, but only as well as a northerner could be expected to know someone from the south with whom there were no family ties, trade deals, or old family rivalries to contend with. Her lands were mostly swamps and thick forestry, which meant that she had little to sell in the form of food-crops or livestock. He couldn't recall if they'd actually spoken about anything other than trade, but he couldn't force his drunken mind on that at the moment; instead, his mind found all the rumors that he'd ever heard about her, and he began to wonder how much of it was true and how much was politicking.

"Are you suggesting that the war council might purchase more of our slaves?" Someone called out.

"Yes." Lord Turley answered flatly.

"How many?"

"As many as are required to assist in the war effort." Lord Turley said, annoyed.

"I cannot afford to sell many. My bound make up three-quarters of my workforce!"

"You might just have to hire citizens." Lady Voth interjected.

"You're out of your mind! That would bankrupt my house!"

"These are our king's orders!" Lord Turley's voice boomed. "Our nation got on just fine before you were allowed to have indentured servants and the bound. You will make do without!" Lord Kairn noted the look of dissatisfaction on Lord Turley's face then and wondered if the rumors that his house had never owned other people were true.

"You know they'll just fall into new debt! They'll be dead or bound within months." Lady Voth protested.

"Lady Voth," he gave a sigh of annoyance and knuckled his forehead. "We have all heard your arguments on numerous occasions and I must remind you that if you wish to change the laws...it is the king's ear you must chew. Please, this is neither the time nor place."

"I'm sorry, Lord Turley." Lady Voth replied just after the room fell to silence, to which he replied with a slight nod in her direction.

After this, Lord Turley went on reading orders from a thick stack of papers for almost an hour with only the occasional interruption, but none were nearly as loud or controversial. When, at last, he set down the last page, he raised a toast to wish the nation a lucky summer and then departed the tent with a handful of lords and ladies for a private meeting. The tent burst into loud chatter as people broke apart into smaller groups and began to feast from food atop tables against either wall. Some were likely, he figured, trying to get a head start on privately selling their bound servants in order to get better profits now instead of waiting for the crown to demand the servants at a much lower flat rate. Others would likely attempt to purchase at a

270

discounted rate but would call it a good deal compared to what they figured the crown would offer in the weeks to come.

Lord Kairn accepted a second mug of grog from the same serving lady and stepped out of the tent for fresh air and to avoid being drawn into conversation. *People of action are rarely seen talking,* his father had often told him. No amount of talking with other lords would help him this day, especially since they would be preoccupied with news regarding the *bound* being used in war. Though he planned on dying near the beginning of the war, it was beginning to bother him that his life's efforts had only amounted to...well, it all seemed very little now. Sure, he had increased the family's wealth a great deal, but he had had other plans for his future. After all these years of careful planning and tolerating passive-aggression from his peers and this was the end. A few more months of planning, dealing, and building the image of a young lord falling apart and drowning himself in alcohol. His personal growth was done. Outside, he found several lords gathered with the young band of messengers, each frantically instructing the young men to deliver multiple messages in the high-pitched, strained voices of men stressed to the point of breaking. *Fortunes on the line,* Lord Kairn thought as he took a small sip of his grog.

He tried to imagine what tactics would be utilized with unarmed slaves or how so many untrained, half-starved people might be used to bolster a force's defenses, but his mind refused to focus on any of that; instead, his drunken mind drifted to his father's hidden library and the insane ideas the man had written down. Just then, Lady Voth strode out of the tent with a purposeful stride heading in his direction and a look on her face that made Lord Kairn think the woman was about to attack him.

Emilia Voth wore pants. Worse still, she wore pants made of thick material like those worn by commoners who worked the physical trades and they bore several holes that looked to have been caused by some sort of labor. They stopped short of her knees by several fingers,

271

which would have been called wildly inappropriate for private settings by the other lords and ladies. The fact that she wore such clothing at a formal gathering among other royalty made Lord Kairn wonder if she'd been thrown from a horse as a child and hit her head on a rock upon landing. Above the pants, she wore a long-sleeved, button-up blouse in deep red with big black buttons that reflected light quite brilliantly. Her hair hung down in twisting strands as if she had begun to do something with it and gave up halfway through. He instinctively wondered if she was still angry that he had declined her previous attempt to strike a trade and sipped his grog to hide the look of worry upon his face.

"Lord Kairn." Her words came out with a sharp edge, and she gave him a quick nod.

"Lady Voth." He took another sip of his grog and smiled. "I am surprised to find you here. Rumor was that you had sent a representative in your stead, as you do not take traveling well and generally despise large gatherings of people. I believe I was told that you have a fear of encloses spaces of any size."

"Baseless rumors, Lord Kairn." She snapped as if offended.

"Well, nobody could blame you if you chose to send a representative in your stead on the march to war. Many have done exactly that, owing to their age and lack of children."

"What reason would I have to stay home, Lord Kairn? Do you think me the type to hide until it is over?"

"Because you have no heir? If you were to die, your lands would fall to the crown, if I am not mistaken."

"In fact, you are mistaken. As my only living family, my uncle would inherit everything. And I can hardly be expected to have children at my age, Lord Kairn."

"Many start their families young these days. Why, my older sister had her first daughter at eighteen."

"Lord Kairn, I am twenty-three and the Voth family does things very much differently!" She snapped. "For a Voth, I am too young to have children. Such matters must be carefully planned for, as children must be cared for and looked after for many years."

"What will become of your lands under your uncle's rule?"

"I'd be dead, Lord Kairn." Her voice was flat, devoid of emotion and so Lord Kairn wondered if she were offended by the question. "I doubt very much that I would have much to say on the matter, but feel free to dig me up and ask if you wish."

"My apologies if I have offended you, Lady Voth. It was not my intention."

"Ease up, Lord Kairn. Maybe take another drink of..." she stepped up close, hooked a finger onto the lip of us cup, and pulled it down to peer inside. "Okay, I'm going to need you to drink something made for adults and get on my level. I was joking, Lord Kairn. You northerners are far too serious."

"Which part was the joke? The part about digging you up or your last attempt at negotiating trade last summer?"

She gave a wicked smile to that. "I wanted to talk to you about something else, if you have a moment."

"I have plenty of time."

"I wouldn't say that at your age, Lord Kairn."

"I'm only twenty-six."

She screwed up her face and gave an exasperated sigh. "I wonder if you would allow me to come with you when you are sent after the assassin. My soldiers could do with some education from more experienced soldiers such as yours and I'm afraid I have no viable

273

options when it comes to hiring someone. I fear I may be sending untrained soldiers to war when the time comes."

"I..." His smile faltered and he glanced about to see if anybody was close enough to have heard her words. The nearest people were the guards at the tent opening, but they appeared to be busy conversing with each other and watching those who came and went on the dirt road ahead. *Perhaps the rumors that her neighboring royal families have been covertly interfering in her affairs are true?*

He took a deep breath and stilled himself in preparation for the look of disappointment that would come when he declined the offer. Koraine would probably have a screaming fit and spend several hours lecturing him on just how dreadfully far beneath house Kairn the Voth house was and then recite rumors that she had memorized over the past six years. According to Koraine, the Voth house was nearing destitution, the lands had been cursed so that the animals were diseased and crops failed, and Emilia's parents had committed suicide to escape the shame once it had been made public that Emilia had become barren after the second still-born child she'd conceived with her own uncle, which was allegedly the reason he had sailed to some nation in the south a number of years ago. At least, these were the reasons Koraine had given when arguing against every trade inquiry from the Voth estate sent during the last two years. The only problem with all of this was that Lord Kairn was certain that Koraine had bolstered one of those rumors herself and, after so many years watching her politicking and gaming for power, Lord Kairn knew to trust nothing she did or said to be plainly true.

Images of his imagined death came to mind, and he found that he didn't care what Koraine would say. He felt a weight vanish from his shoulders and nearly gasped at the sudden sensation of freedom that flowed through him. *This could support the image of a chaotic drunkard who has given up on life,* he found himself taking a deep pull of his grog and wondering at the possibilities that flooded his mind.

"I welcome the assistance of your forces, Lady Voth." He said the words very loudly so that they could be heard by anybody within earshot.

HAUNTED

Having eaten her fill of the spiced stew Frezz had made, Argel set herself down on the ground with her back to a tree and let herself fall into a deep sleep. As usual, she dreamed of corpses that walked about aimlessly and of being used as a weapon until the stress of those images brought her back to the world. This time, she did not wake up in the middle of a scream or drenched in sweat; however, she did find her hands shaking and cold with a tightness in her chest. She had to remind herself to control her breathing the way Frezz had taught her to try and find some measure of calm. Even as she tried to calm down, she found herself frantically searching the forest for any sign of her aunt or that army of the dead. *She's dead. I saw her die;* she said the words to herself but found no comfort in them. *I'm free.*

When she spotted Frezz and Ashan in the small open area a good forty strides off, her heart began to calm more quickly. They had been heading that way when she'd fallen asleep and now they were practicing with the wooden swords Frezz had made. *Maybe I will feel peace when I return home...if I ever do.* Images of her aunt killing her or recapturing her came flooding to her mind in a rushed series, blinding her to the world before her eyes. She only found herself pulling away from those thoughts after noticing that they were looping. She found herself breathing rapidly, dizzy, sweating with a chill, and nauseous. Clearing her mind was becoming easier and she didn't know if it was the time away from Mary or the company she kept but watching them practice fighting made it much easier.

"They aren't coming for you." Her aunt taunted her in one of the imagined scenes playing in her mind, in which she was being chased through an increasingly darker forest. This scene wasn't something that had happened, but her aunt's words had been spoken quite often. "They never sent anybody for you. They don't love you. They *NEVER* loved you. You aren't worthy of love." The ground grew soft, and Argel sank to her ankles with each step. Looking down, she discovered blood seeping from the ground beneath each footfall. "You'll never see them again. You will die here, but only after I am done with you." Behind her, her aunt ran on dry ground, closing the distance at a terrifying pace.

"You're dead!" She cursed under her breath.

Argel shoved the thoughts away with all her might and focused on Frezz and Ashan. Without a shirt, it was difficult to tell the difference between the bruises he had gained in practicing with Frezz and the dirt that clung to the sweat that covered Ashan's body. Of course, his right shoulder was still swollen and a mix of red and dark blues, but the rest of the bruises were new. Ashan kept his injured shoulder facing away from Frezz and held the sword in his less-dominant hand, which Frezz said was a good thing to train for emergencies. How Ashan kept going instead of breaking down was a wonder in Argel's mind.

Looking at that shoulder reminded Argel of the exhaustion that had lingered deep in her bones for the days that had followed, which

278

had required a lot of sleep and food to drive away; however, with Frezz's return, her recovery had been much easier and faster than any time before. Learning that rest and food could have cut the recovery time down had brought a deeper understanding of Mary's cruelty. There had always been ample food deliveries to her cabin in the woods, which meant that Argel's recovery could have always been comfortable and fast, but Mary was a cruel person who delighted in seeing others suffer. This new understanding fueled anger in her heart that she felt was beginning to fight that mountain of fear she'd been living with.

Frezz also seemed tired these days and she felt terribly for him as well. He'd been hunting, cooking, gathering wood, fetching water from whatever streams were close, teaching Ashan to fight, and she'd woken up a few times to discover that he patrolled the forest during the nights. While his time with her was less physically strenuous, as she had specifically asked to learn how to cook and identify edible plants, it was still several hours a day that he couldn't sleep or at least rest. How a man could go on so long without proper sleep, she didn't rightly understand. *Perhaps*, she considered, *the dragon-touched don't need much sleep.*

You won't even get up to save your life! Ashan's words came to mind unbidden as memories played in her head. She had begged him for rest, and he had gone off into the darkness alone, found food, and carried her there. *No, he tested it on himself first. He also attacked that giant when there was no hope of surviving.* She tried to imagine what had gone through his head that had convinced him that attacking was the best move in that situation, but nothing really made sense. Frezz had said he had been a slave for most of his live, but that only convinced her that fleeing should have been the first thing on his mind. *He could have run, escaped, and maybe found true freedom.* She began to wonder how different his life had to have been in order to make him the way he was.

Argel shook herself and forced her attention back on the moment at hand to keep from crying. She wiped her eyes, scanned the forest again, and wondered how long she would keep looking for someone she had seen die. She'd seen the fading of terror in Ashan's eyes over the past few days and wondered why she didn't feel that same relief since Frezz's return. Birds sang, a gentle breeze of cool air blew through the trees, and she knew she would have found this setting peaceful just a few short years ago. Now she didn't trust so much silence. She took deep, controlled breaths the way Frezz had taught her and began stretching her arms and legs. Her rag-like clothing itched terribly, and dried mud cracked as she straightened her arms and legs. She was filthy and stank horribly.

"Argel?" Startled, Argel let out a soft yelp and rolled away from the voice. She rolled twice and scrambled to her feet, searching the forest for her aunt yet again. *She's dead.* The reminder rang hollow in her heart.

Ashan stabbed his white sword into the soft ground near where she had been laying, leaned the pretend sword up against its cross-guard, and carefully lowered himself to the ground. He gave her a curious study for a long moment. That studious expression he wore matched a hesitant curiosity in his eyes that betrayed his apprehension when it came to starting conversations or asking questions. This was another major difference between them, as she had never felt shy about talking to people. He waited a long moment before scrubbing at his face with the shirt he carried and then he watched her in silence some more. She tried not to be too obvious in studying the many old scars upon his arms and chest. *How cruel was his owner?*

"What happened?" She stepped forward slowly and sat just before him.

"Oh, we're done practicing." He spoke through the shirt as he scrubbed his head and face again.

"No, I mean...to your chest and ribs."

"Oh." he set the bundled-up shirt on his leg and examined himself. "I was given a bad beating. I think some stuff was broken, but I wasn't awake long enough to know. Or maybe the Day Nirvana made it easy to forget."

"Looks like you were lucky to have someone there to heal you with magic."

His expression darkened and he frowned. "Someone else wasn't so lucky."

"What do you mean?"

"She killed a man to heal me."

"She?"

"Sophia. The lady who saved me with magic. She said she killed him to keep me alive."

"You don't look happy about it. Did you know him?"

"He was one of guards. One of the ones who beat me."

"Sounds like he deserved what he got."

"I..." His expression became dark as if he were angrily struggling with his thoughts.

"It's okay if you don't want to talk about it."

"I try not to think about it. Any of it." He sighed and looked away for a long moment. Seeing him fighting back tears made her want to cry, but she held back her tears. If he could keep himself held together, she figured she could as well. "It's better out here. Easier to...pretend it wasn't real. Like a dream...or a nightmare. Best left forgotten."

"Sometimes talking about bad things helps us get over the pain though."

Over Ashan's shoulder, she noticed Frezz heading the other direction. He was leaving camp again to hunt or checking whatever he liked to routinely check. Her heart skipped a beat in fear at seeing the man going off south again. She immediately thought of the giants. *No, if they wanted to attack us, they would probably do it while we slept.* The thought wasn't comforting.

"I'm sorry for what I said before." Ashan interrupted her thoughts. "About everything I said. I was frustrated."

Argel lost control of the tears. "I'm sorry I tried to kill you." She was suddenly uncomfortably hot. "I'm sorry that I kept running when you fell that first night on our own." Paired forever with that memory was the memory of when she had collapsed from exhaustion some days later. He had been setting a hard pace for days and she had reached her end. *He could have left me. He should have!* He hadn't though.

"I know you didn't want to hurt me, Argel. It was that witch controlling you. I could no more blame you than I could blame an arrow fired at me. I would blame the archer. You warned me. You told me what to do, but I couldn't kill you."

"Y-you almost died. You risked your life for someone you don't even know e-even after I-I-I kept running..."

"You were terrified. We both were."

"But you risked your life with the giants and I just...just...sat there."

"You had something to live for..." Ashan offered with a shrug.

"What?" Her voice came much more loudly than she had intended. "Frezz told me that you have family in Isirdost. There's hope for you. I don't have anybody to go find. I'm alone. Both of you have families. Your lives are worth more than mine." Ashan explained.

Her sobbing turned to uncontrollable wailing. She gasped for air and the sudden need to escape struck her mightily. She tried to turn, stand, and run all at once, which resulted in her sort of rolling on the ground and flailing her legs. *No! I'm worthless!* She crawled to the tree and used it to pull herself up onto shaking legs that felt they would give out at any moment.

"What's wrong?" Ashan asked with only a hint of alarm in his voice.

"Leave me!" she blurted without thinking as she pushed herself off the tree and stumbled forward.

Through her tears, she could hardly make out the slope of the ground or the distance to objects. Everything was blurry and she kicked several dead branches as she went. She ran, not looking back, not thinking about where she was going. After some time, she came to a decline where the ground became a light brown and then slipped on something wet and soft. Her next few steps also found the ground wet and soft, and her arms automatically flailed as her feet repeatedly slipped on increasingly slick ground. She managed to keep her balance just well enough to land on her butt in a half-controlled fall. She immediately planted her hands upon the ground, thinking to push herself back up, and found soft mud that rejected her attempts to make purchase. She decided to roll to her knees and crawl out, but then she began to slide further along the depression in the ground, finding ever softer mud as she went.

She gave up fighting to go somewhere and let her tears flow freely. It took a while to let out her bottled up emotions and convince her eyes that no more tears were needed, but she felt much better for having let it all out. Once her eyes agreed with her, she sat breathing calmly and studied her surroundings. She found herself sitting in a large muddy patch of freshly churned mud. *A natural spring,* she thought excitedly. Aside from the fresh prints she had just made, it appeared as though a family of boar frequented this area. She spread her legs out and dug a hole in the mud with one hand. Sure enough, water began to gather in the hole a moment later. She tore some of the cloth from her right sleeve, dipped it into the water, and began to scrub at her face. The water was almost cold.

Argel spent a long while washing her body and her make-shift clothing and having a good think about everything that had happened. When her clothing was somewhat dry, she dressed and headed back to her saviors. *No, they're friends,* she corrected her thinking. *I have to trust someone and why not these two?* Having run blindly away, Argel cursed herself when she finally found her way back to camp. Upon arriving, she found Frezz cooking some thick slabs of red meat over a larger fire than he normally made, and Ashan was sitting opposite the fire slowly working his injured arm. Both gave her a quick look as she sat with her back against a large rock that was just the right distance from the fire to be warm but not overly so. The smell of the meat, particularly the strange spices Frezz used, reminded her of a dish her older sister made on special occasions. The smell was nearly identical, but her sister's dish had involved diced meat, potatoes, and a strange green vegetable that didn't grow in Isirdost.

She sat and watched the two men in silence. Ashan stretched his arm a while and then pulled his white sword from the ground nearby and placed the handle into the hand of his bad arm. He lifted it, winced in pain, and let the flat of the blade fall back into his good hand. With how swollen his shoulder was, Argel was impressed with how little pain showed on his face. Of course, she was still shocked that he had survived and that most of the injury had been healed. Again and again, he lifted the sword. Finally taking notice, Frezz gave Ashan a disapproving look and sighed in frustration.

"You should let your arm rest." Frezz said as he flipped the slabs of meat over and sprinkled spicing on them.

"It has rested." Ashan replied flatly.

"You could cause permanent damage if you don't let it heal."

Ashan didn't reply. Twenty or thirty more times and he stabbed the sword back into the ground and began raising the arm up and down, which seemed to be less painful but infinitely more frustrating based on his facial expression. Though he had made great progress, he still couldn't lift the arm above his shoulder. A short while later, Frezz fetched wooden plates from his pack and served what he'd been cooking. Halfway through eating, Ashan stopped suddenly and gazed off into the distance for a long while.

"Frezz, why is the night's sky so empty?" he asked.

"Most of everything is empty." Frezz said between bites.

"Why is our world so different?"

"What do you mean?" Frezz sounded stunned by the question.

"The night's sky is mostly empty, but our world is full. Everywhere you look, there are things."

"The gods wanted it that way."

"Why?" Ashan glanced up at the darkening sky, a burning curiosity in his eyes.

"To create something good like themselves."

"They're good?"

"Of course. How could they not be good when they've given life to us and created so much for us?"

"If they are good, why are they so..." Ashan glanced off in the distance for a second as if listening to something. "Capricious?"

"I'm not sure they are. I think they gave us the world and it is up to us to learn and strive to become better."

"They seem pretty cruel in some of the stories I've heard."

Frezz hummed at that and smiled, at least Argel thought it was a smile. "Many of the stories I've read are the same. I couldn't say why but I do believe many stories about the gods are entirely made up."

"I've noticed many stories teach lessons about life in general."

285

"Allegory." Argel offered.

"I don't know that word." Ashan said.

"It's a story that teaches a lesson. My favorite story is The Farmer and The Hare." she explained.

Ashan's eyes widened and he smiled excitedly. "What is it about?"

"You don't know it?"

"N-no." his smile faded quickly.

"Well, on the face of it, it's a plain story about a farmer who spends all summer trying to get a rabbit off his lands instead of tending his crops. He focuses only on the one goal and when winter arrives, he has no food at all."

"So, it teaches us to work hard?"

"It's more about not letting one little problem distract you from your entire life and goals. Had he let the rabbit alone and focused on his farm, he would have had plenty of food for winter." She explained.

"I should like to hear the entire story sometime." He said with an excited smile.

Argel smiled back, took a quick bite, and chewed quickly. "Well," she took a deep breath and wondered where to begin. This would be the first time they had a conversation about something entirely unimportant and she was thankful for it. It was almost like a normal dinner with friends, only she was telling this story instead of her father. "Once upon an early Spring, there came a farmer to tend his field, when he chanced upon an eaten green..."

JUST A SERVANT

Emma watched the mass of nobles with a jealous heart as they drank and danced to a soft composition of a large drum, two wooden flutes, and three women wielding violins. The band currently played one of the newer songs she hadn't yet heard, obviously inspired by the coming war, and she watched the nobles closely from the edge of the massive tent. The high-born ladies wore beautiful, billowing dresses that hid their legs, which made them appear to float, in every possible color and had decorated themselves with fine jewelry and perfumes that Emma could only describe as happy fragrances. Even the attending ladies had dressed well for tonight's occasion, but not so well as to be mistaken as high-born ladies themselves, which really only meant that their dresses weren't as wide, that they wore no jewelry, and that their perfumes weren't nearly as commanding of attention. In a grand departure from normal life, the majority of the lords wore tight-sleeved jerkins or doublets in various shades of black or blue with matching breeches. What made them stand out and apart from one another were their military sashes of differing colors, which signified their social rank or prestige. It was most-certainly the case that those wearing purple sashes were the high-king's favored people, for wearing purple without permission was cause for scandal among their peers. Those men without sashes were attendants, advisors, or merchants whom had found great financial success in life and were held in high enough regard among the nobility to have secured an invitation to tonight's event. Lowly servers like Emma wore plain white uniforms to signify their social rank.

Were she any other place, Emma would allow herself to smile openly, drink, gamble, and enjoy a night of dancing; however, she was serving drink this night, which meant that she had to maintain proper composure. As a server, she had to pay close attention to all that occurred, to focus her attention upon mannerisms that were particularly unique among the high-born, and behave accordingly. She had to wear her long-practiced serious, no nonsense permitting expression that gave people the impression that she did not have time for idle chatter or foolish flummery. Over the years, she had learned how people took her less seriously if she allowed herself to smile too much of the time and they would be less respectful of her personal boundaries. Those boundaries were everything that kept a woman like her from becoming the shameful secret of a king or prince – the barrier to becoming pregnant and murdered by a jealous high-born lady or wife. Most women who chose to entertain such men found their graves in short order and Emma was far too entertained with life to follow that path. So it was that she watched attentively, rarely smiled, and never laughed at their jokes, even when the man was hilarious.

When the current song reached its end, a good majority of those dancing gave their partners shallow bows and departed the center of the tent. As the space was freed up, those whom had been waiting rose from their chairs to join in on the dancing that would begin shortly. Many returned to their family's tables and others headed toward the long line of tables along the far end of the tent, where food and drink

288

were served. As people took their seats, a great number of their hands rose, signaling for a server to come to them. Most requested the standard ale or brandy, which Emma quickly fetched from the other end of the tent, where rows of tables were covered in glasses being filled by station attendants.

About forty strides from where she now stood, High-king Hotar was seated in a massive wooden chair with a high back that she supposed was made to look like a throne but lacked the decorative detailing and adornments that most other chairs displayed. The wood of his chair hadn't even been stained and, in fact, looked rough as though the maker hadn't even sanded it down. He was seated before a moderately large circular table along with ten lords and ladies either dressed in purple or wearing a purple sash. He wore a purple robe and a four-pointed crown made from a pure white metal that almost seemed to glow. He was a very rotund man with thin reddish-brown hair upon his head and face, which appeared unkempt and greasy. Even seated he was nearly as tall as many men when standing, his shoulders were four times as wide as any other men in attendance, and his fingers were as thick as sausages. His skin was sickly pale, his eyes had a beady, sunken in quality about them. He was staring at the rear end of a young lady nearby in a very obvious manner, as if he didn't care who saw him looking; of course, being that he was high king, such manners probably didn't apply to him. He shoveled a fist of mash into his face without looking away from the woman and brought a large silver goblet to his lips. A moment later, he belched loudly and slammed it down upon the table with a force that shook the entire thing. Those seated at the table turned their heads in shock and, either not noticing or not caring, he turned his attention to a pale man dressed in black at his side. He leaned to the man and spoke at length. The pale man shook his head, stood, and departed the tent with an unreadable expression.

Emma delivered drinks to three tables before the musicians resumed their playing. As people took to the center, she dodged through them to return to the side of the tent, rejoining other servers to watch and wait. Two songs played before a hand rose in the distance

289

and she responded immediately, crossing through dancing pairs with speed and careful timing. Once through the crowd, she passed between the tables until she reached the tent wall. She turned right along the edge of the tent and passed six tables full of people before finally reaching the hand. Upon arriving, she was surprised to discover that there were three soldiers sitting there with a singular high-born lord. She had seen several other nobles attempt to bring their personal guards into the tent earlier and get turned away rudely by the high-king's royal guards, which made her wonder how this man had managed to get his men in when they appeared to be no more than common soldiers. Nobody at the table turned to face her and she took a moment to catch her breath and study them. They wore light leather armor, a sword at the hip, and at least two knives each. Their skin was dirty, one wore a bandage on his right forearm that had a tinge of red at the center, and another had a scabbed-over cut that ran from the wrist halfway to the elbow with small threads sticking out here and there. A moment passed before one of them finally turned to give her a look that said he'd heard her approach and didn't appreciate the silence, as though he were offended that she thought she had not been noticed.

"How may I assist you, my lords?"

"Three honeyed teas and... Kairn, are you drinking or are you clear-heading this night?" The soldier's tone shocked Emma to her core. He spoke so casually and didn't even add a title. She immediately expected the lord to turn and hit the man, but he turned about without a care in the world upon his face.

"Well, I think grog for tonight. The weaker, the better!" She had been so prepared to witness anger and violence, that his pleasant tone was an even greater shock than the soldier's overly familiar manner. When his eyes met hers, his face lit up with recognition. "You!" he said with a smile.

She tripped over her words as her mind raced and had to take a deep breath to collect her thoughts. "Lord Kairn, it is good to know your name, my lord. If you desire your money, I assure you that I have not spent any of it, my lord. I understand you may have been drinking a lot and-"

"Let me stop you there. I knew perfectly well what I was doing, and I hope you will put it to good use."

"I, uh, I will, Lord Kairn!" She gave him a great big smile. "Three honeyed teas and weakened grog. Anything else?"

"When you return, please do not say my name. Each time someone says my name, another few people take notice of me and come over to chew my ear." Lord Kairn explained just as a rather large man with a red sash walked up.

"Yes, my lord. My apologies."

As she made her way back across the tent, she watched a cluster of no less than six people crowd up around Lord Kairn and she wondered why so many sought him out. Surely there were better times to meet with the man. Given that grog was rarely requested or because of the limitation of space within the tent, grog was stored in a much smaller tent adjacent to the one she was in. She had to cross through the dancers again, exit the tent, and explain what business she was about to the royal guards. Although considerably smaller, the refreshments tent was still tall and wide enough to fit most commoner houses within; however, this tent housed only barrels of mead, bottles of wine and three men capable of magic. She gave a silent prayer to the gods to protect her from the evil of those who could do magic as she entered but was mindful to keep her face from showing concern. She'd been a few times already to fetch chilled bottles of wine and expected the cold air and the cold eyes of the men therein; however, this time the air was so cold that she immediately saw her breath.

"By the gods!" She cursed as she paused and took in the sight of the room. The ground was covered in a thin layer of white and the three men were huddled around a block of ice tall enough to serve as a chair. One of the men gasped and all three looked up in surprise.

"Pardon us, miss. We was just playin' an' got...a little carried away."

The one who spoke was the youngest by a few years and was just getting the first hairs on his upper lip. His chubby face reminded her of the piglets she usually cared for back home, minus the snout, and there was a certain innocence in his eyes that she almost admired. He wore mismatching rags for clothing, no shoes, and the place on his arm where his bonding rings had been stood out in stark contrast with his healthy tan. He had an earnest smile where the other two wore bitter scowls. The others might have been twin brothers if it weren't for their obvious age difference, for their faces and frames were nearly identical. Both had long black hair that fell to their shoulders, sharp angular faces, and brilliant blue eyes.

"It's just water and cold air." The oldest man explained in a sharp tone, but she caught the pleading fear beneath the bitterness that told her they shouldn't be doing what they were.

She offered them her best comforting smile. "I'm afraid I might need to dress warmer next time I am sent out here."

"We'll let it warm, miss." the youngest offered.

"What are you after?" The eldest asked sharply.

"Weak grog and three cups of honeyed tea, please." She set her tray atop a barrel and rubbed her hands together to warm them.

She tried not to pay attention to the sudden flames that rose up from the eldest one's hands. Though it seemed he were on fire, he did not react as if in pain, which made Emma's skin crawl. He grabbed a cast iron pot from the ground and his younger brother poured a pitcher of water into it. The youngest ran behind them and began rummaging through a crate. The water began to boil a minute later, and they dumped a handful of leaves into it.

"Are you from here? If you'll pardon my asking."

"What do you mean?" the middle one asked.

"I mean to ask if you are from Veysor." They all looked at her as if she were crazy.

"Where else would we be from, miss?" the middle one asked as he fetched a jar of honey from a nearby crate.

"I don't know. I just assumed not from this kingdom since you're, uh, doing magic."

"The king has undone the laws on magic." The eldest hissed. "Now we get the opportunity to fight in the war for our freedom."

"All three of us were raised near Despair Valley. Now we're bound like you."

"She doesn't need to know that, Vessir." the eldest hissed.

Vessir returned the hiss with a flat stare. "It won't do any harm being friendly to people, Garrim."

"Oh. Forgive me, I had not heard."

Vessir took a cup in each hand and held them before the one holding the iron pot. "Are you going to fight as well or are they keeping you as a servant?"

"My owner has not said yet." Emma watched in wonder as the water was poured into one cup. Some overflowed and splashed Vessir's hands. His skin turned bright pink where the steaming water touched it, but he didn't seem to notice it as he set the cups down upon Emma's tray. He added honey to both and fetched the third to fill.

"Maybe you'll be lucky either way." the youngest said as he filled the fourth cup with grog.

"What do you mean?"

"Just that, either way, maybe you'll find luck." he replied with a great big smile.

"Navin, that's not how normal people think." Vessir said flatly.

"Not everybody is normal, Vessir." Navin said with a big smile. "Besides, she's nice!"

"She's *being* nice. Not everyone is nice just because they're being nice for a moment." Vessir explained as he took the final cup to the tray and added honey to it. As he did so, Emma noticed the red areas rapidly turning back to their previous color and gasped at the sight.

"Your hands!"

"What about them?" Garrim's tone came sharp as he stepped toward her.

"He burned them and-"

"I'm fine. I'm quite gifted at healing, miss." Vessir said as he wedged himself between Emma and his brother. He used his free hand to push his brother away, which earned him a sharp scowl. "Don't mind Garrim. He is very protective of us."

"We can't let everybody know what we can do!" Garrim demanded as he gave Vessir a dark look.

"It's too late for that. The high king knows and he's probably bragging to his inner circle." Vessir snapped back, ignoring Garrim as he clustered the drinks at the center of Emma's tray, picked it up gingerly, and brought it to her.

"He probably has others like us already." Navin offered.

"Not like us." Garrim replied with intense anger.

"Similar." Navin replied. "And it's a good thing too. Mother will come to fetch us before the war begins."

"Navin, mother sold us!" Garrim almost shouted.

"She was tricked. She wouldn't sell her own children!" Navin replied instantly, his cheerful smile becoming suddenly forced. The look in his eyes told Emma that he was in denial of a painful truth he wasn't ready to accept. At her side, Vessir pursed his lips and took a deep breath. There was pain in his eyes, but also a deep acceptance that she had seem in the eyes of a thousand slaves before.

"Best be on your way, miss." Vessir's tone was a warning that she gladly accepted.

Emma took the tray and exited the tent as quickly as possible. Outside, the air felt hot compared to the unnatural cold within the tent and she almost wished that she could undo some of the buttons on her server's jacket; however, even if it were a swelteringly hot day, doing so would be considered ill-mannered among the high-born. Instead, she took a moment to adjust to the temperature before heading back to the main tent. The guards let her pass with no more than a nod. Back inside, she immediately took note of the line of people that had formed before Lord Kairn, which had grown significantly in her absence. A lively song filled the air and she focused on it, letting it lift her spirits as she tried to forget what she had seen in the smaller tent. When she arrived, two of the soldiers stepped away from Lord Kairn to intercept her. One pressed a copper into her hand and leaned in until his mouth was practically against her ear. "Should anybody ask, our lord is drinking heavily tonight. Alarmingly so, miss Emma." He backed away and gave her a stern nod before turning to help gather the drinks. They both gave her a quick, but sincere thanks and headed back to their table. Being addressed by name was a great surprise, as few people ever asked or even used a servant's name. She thought on this as she made her way back across the tent to wait alongside the wall with the other servers. She resumed watching for raised hands and considered everything that had occurred the past week.

Just as she began to think back on the day when Lord Kairn had given her the gold coin, her attention was caught by a woman entering the tent's other large opening. It wasn't because this woman's clothing was especially ostentatious, which would be normal, that Emma's attention was caught so thoroughly; rather, it was the opposite that caught her attention and that of many others. Unlike all the other high-born ladies, this woman did not wear a brightly colored hoop skirt and flashy jewelry; instead, she wore a simple black dress that was of a quality not outside a frugal commoner's budget. Her hair hung loose and unmade, as if she were a common housewife just done with her day's work. Bizarrely, she wasn't even wearing shoes. Rumors had spread like wildfire and, because the descriptions had been so spot-on, Emma knew this woman must be Lady Voth – a southern high-born fallen on hard times, if rumors were to be believed. Emma didn't normally put stock in rumors, but it would appear these ones were highly accurate. By the time Lady Voth and her soldier reached the dance floor, half the crowd had ceased their dancing and were openly glaring at her with shocked or disgusted expressions upon their faces. Emma had seen plenty of high-born women crumble under lesser gazes, but Lady Voth continued as if she hadn't noticed the looks or the sudden cessation of dancing. Emma gave the musicians a glance and found that they too had noticed the display but continued their playing as any intelligent member of the lower-class would. Seeing a high-born go about their business without any concern for what the rest of their kind were thinking of them filled Emma with a sense of awe and admiration. If it were up to her, that was what she would have from life; unfortunately, her entire life was built around pleasing her owner and other such high-born. Her well-being and survival depended upon high-born perceptions and judgments on her appearance, the quality of her work and her demeanor.

As Emma watched Lady Voth make her way across the dance floor, she noticed a woman with an expression so full of animosity that Emma wondered if the woman was going to attack Lady Voth. Even seated, it was easy to see the woman was taller than average and of medium build for a high-born. Her oval face was framed neatly with straight black hair combed to absolute perfection and cut so it was longer in the front and shorter toward the rear. She sat at the edge of her seat, back straight to the point of looking rigid from discomfort, and her hands rested in her lap; however, with the icy look on her face, it was difficult to believe that the woman was resting in any way whatsoever.

Emma stepped away from the wall immediately and headed straight for the woman. While intervening in such matters was not technically a server's duty, it was well-understood that the commanders of the camp expected such from the servers and attendants while on duty; after all, distracting the high-born to keep the peace was better done with drink than soldiers, as one usually deescalated tense situations and the other often ended in blood shed or death. While open fighting rarely occurred, it was always a concern when so many gathered and drank so heavily. The high-born folk would say that these affairs were civil, but it was a well-known secret that many of them had knives hidden in their clothing somewhere – some even had special pockets sewn into their clothes to hide small blades or vials of harmful chemicals. It had been a year since the last time someone had died at a grand celebration and while everybody pretended to have forgotten that event, soldiers and common folk were more cautious than they once were.

Lady Voth and her soldier arrived at the rear of the slowly shrinking line of people waiting to speak with Lord Kairn by the time Emma arrived before the lady who looked about ready to rise and attack. Her leg had a tremor in it and her hands were clamped tightly enough to cause her knuckles to turn white, but Emma did not stare long enough to call attention to herself.

"A drink, my lady?"

"What?" The woman turned to face Emma so fast that Emma flinched in surprise.

"I noticed that you hadn't requested refreshment in some time, my lady. Would you like something?"

"Oh, I-" She paused to give Lady Voth another glance and then set her gaze out upon the dance floor again. "Yes, something strong." She flicked her hand at Emma and continued watching the dancers.

"Yes, my lady." Emma gave the woman a quick nod and turned away.

It was a quick trip across the tent to fetch a strong wine for the lady, made all that much quicker due to Emma walking as quickly as she could while not drawing attention to herself. Emma tried not to ponder the reason for the animosity between the two women, as there seemed to always be some reason for the high-born to feud. More importantly, she needed to be focused on her job instead of thinking, which she spent entirely too much time doing in the first place. *That's why I'm not married,* she told herself in her best scolding tone or the best impression of her aunt she could muster in the moment. Yes, that was close enough to the truth. She grabbed a cup of strong, smooth wine and then a cup of the sweet before turning back. She found the lady watching her as she returned, most of the animosity now gone from her face. Unfortunately, that animosity had been replaced with an intense curiosity that filled Emma with a sense of unease. *Perhaps,* she considered with no small measure of hope, *she thinks I am a valuable servant worth purchasing.* The high-born did seem to take a perverse pleasure in buying each other's servants. Regardless, Emma hurried over to the lady while trying not to sway or maintain eye contact.

"Pardon, my lady. You did not say and so l brought you two different types of wine." She gave a bow as she offered both cups.

"Both will do fine." The woman reached out with one hand, took the first cup and placed it upon the table at her side before reaching for the second.

"Will that be all, my lady?"

"No, actually." She gestured for Emma to come closer, and she glanced about quickly as if concerned that someone might be nearby. Emma stepped forward and stooped down just a touch. "I saw you serving Lord Kairn just earlier and I am concerned that my dear brother is developing some rather concerning habits of late. Can you recall what you served him? I only ask because I have had to..." she paused as a

298

man neared and gave him a hard glare to let him know he was interrupting something private.

The man didn't pay them any attention as he scanned the nearby tables, swaying slightly as he turned his head back and forth. Finally, his eyes came alight with recognition, and he smiled wide. "Tharvos! There you are!" He practically shouted and set off to his right side around the nearest table. He kicked a chair halfway around the table and then knocked a second over as he tried to place the first back where it had originally been. He glanced about with an embarrassed expression and when he found Emma looking at him, his face turned bright red. She gave him a big smile to let him know she had found the sight entertaining, but mixed in enough kindness that he wouldn't become angry with her. He smiled back in a way that reminded her of her uncle as he straightened his shirt and stumbled away with a noticeably more attentive care. Emma was thankful for the moment of distraction, for it gave her time to prepare herself. She knew something stressful was coming and had never liked being put on the spot in such situations, but there was little choice to be had when a high-born was involved. She returned her gaze to the lady and kept careful control over her expressions.

"I have had to keep a close eye on him the past year. It shames me to say that I've even had to collect him from an alley or two the last few months. I hate to involve you, but I do have my family's image to maintain, and he knows all our family servants."

"That's...dreadful, my lady! I'm so sorry to hear it."

Emma gave the lady a shocked expression and mixed in just the right amount of pity a moment later. "I guess that makes sense of things, my lady." She glanced around to ensure nobody could hear her words or, at least, that was what she played at doing. If she were any other servant, Emma might balk at having to lie or get so excited about speaking with a high-born that she'd gladly tell the truth. Most normal servants would gush and fawn over high-born, hoping they could move up in life if they were friendly enough or worked hard enough to please one of them. Fortunately, Emma had never been a normal servant, nor had her mother or grandmother. Normal servants knew how to build, clean, or fix something. Emma knew how to lie and manipulate people, which was of much greater value and risk. She hated those parts of her duties, but it did mean that she spared from the more carnal desires of the high-born. Her master was a firm believer that a woman of her trade should be kept safe from those forms of mental anguish. Recognizing the high-lady's pretend concern for her brother and seeing how thoroughly she despised him didn't require an expert. Frowning while attempting to sound scared and concerned were not nearly enough to cover the underlying contempt in her voice when she spoke about the man she called brother.

Emma put on her best worried expression, lowered her voice to a soft whisper, and placed her hand onto the lady's free hand in the way her mother had when consoling her when she had been a child. "I hate to say it, my lady, but Lord Kairn has been drinking a lot. His soldiers must be worried as well because they told me to bring him grog in secret, which I don't think he noticed. I know nothing more than that, my lady, but I could ask the other servers if you like."

"I don't think that will be necessary but thank you." The woman attempted to put on a sad expression with some annoyance mixed in. It might have been enough to fool others, but Emma could see plotting in the woman's eyes.

"I will pray to the gods for your family, my lady."

"Thank you."

Emma returned to her place on the wall and carefully considered what had just happened. She wondered if the guard had been anticipating for Lord Kairn's sister to ask about what he was drinking or if it was a routine thing they kept hidden, which wouldn't be surprising given that most high-born were in the habit of keeping secrets from each other. Bargaining chips, as her own master would call them. Secrets were often worth more than lives in the right hands and at the right time. Knowing that these siblings were having some family issue could have been worth several gold, but she already knew that her master was not interested in this family – she knew all the family names of those her master was interested in and Kairn wasn't among that list in her head. She would report it just the same, as her master sold secrets and there was bound to be someone interested in this bit of information.

It was no secret that high-born families quarreled and occasionally murdered each other for controlling power over their family's estate, but they didn't enlist an unknown servant into their personal matters without purpose. That woman had given Emma precisely what information she wanted to become rumor, but for what purpose was anybody's guess. While Emma did not enjoy participating in such activities, she would do it efficiently and with maximum effect. Not doing so would bring that woman's attention back to her. Give it five days and the absence of the rumor would be noticed and it would not look normal. *Look normal,* she reminded herself as her heart told her to leave the situation alone. She already knew that Molly would be the first person she would tell. Molly was young, naive and she wouldn't need an extravagant retelling. Emma wouldn't even have to attend to the details, as Molly would make them up as she usually did. Molly would be the most convenient and most efficient target for getting the rumor on its feet and running. In Molly's unwittingly capable hands, the rumor would have the usual variants within two days and would spread halfway through the camp within the week. Emma wouldn't feel bad about using Molly for this task as she would with other rumors; after all, there was very little chance that this sort of information could or would be tracked backwards or that it would cost lives. Few high-born became upset with this type of rumor and fewer still went about tracking down the source of such talk. No, the high-born knew that some commoners hated them. All Emma needed was an excuse to get away long enough to find Molly.

A GLORIOUS PRINCE

Lasashu stood with one foot upon the seat of his gold and red chair and the other upon the great feasting table as he gazed out upon a sea of faces. Lords and ladies from across the land, the great war generals, and even the elder sages had gathered to hear his umpteenth retelling of how he'd hunted down the witch. Their adoring eyes were glued upon his face as they cheered him on at the top of their lungs. Each day, people begged to hear the story again and brought him gifts of all manner, as was befitting a man such as himself. Pretty soon he would be wealthier than his own father, but the land given to him already meant that he was the largest landowner in all the nation. His mother, father, and brother stood together at his side, cheering harder than the rest as they rested their hands upon his boots and screamed his praises.

"I ducked beneath the flames the witch spewed from her mouth, fetched the knife from my boot her vile henchmen hadn't noticed, and threw it with all my might. The flames vanished then, and her henchmen charged at me from all sides. As I tackled the first man, I gave a glance and saw her motionless body crumple into a heap. The gods had guided my blade to the very center of her forehead." He paused to drink more of the gloriously rich wine and gave the people a grand smile. "I dispatched the first henchman with a single blow to the head and snatched his sword as he fell. I turned then and the next man, seeing the sword in my hand, fell to his knees and began begging for mercy as he pissed himself. Now, I don't know if it was an enchanted sword or if it was just the will of the gods spurring me on toward *justice*, but I cut through their armor as though it were made from dead grass!" He smiled and lifted his cup to the crowd as if to toast. He gave a glance to the witch's head, which lay upon a serving plate just beyond his bare foot and hummed with a happiness he had never felt before. The crowd exploded in renewed celebration for his victory. Then he looked down upon his family and saw the look of shame in his brother's eyes. He gave Reginald a reassuring smile and nod. It hadn't been his brother's fault he'd been cursed with stupidity.

Lasashu was ripped from sleep by cold water. His first thought was that he'd been thrown over the side of a ship at winter, but after a few shouts and blinks to clear his vision, he found that he was in his bed. The three soldiers with whom he shared the small room stood between bunks, each holding an empty bucket and offering an angry sneer.

"Selfish bastard!" Einholdt, as the others called him, offered the curse at speaking volume, and dropped his bucket.

"How dare you?" Lasashu screamed.

Einholdt turned about, picked up a loaded pack from his bed, and headed for the door. One of the others, perhaps the one they called James, threw his bucket directly at Lasashu. Lasashu rolled to his right to avoid it, but it still struck him in the shoulder. It hit the wall and rebounded to strike his hip with a fair amount of force. He snatched the small knife he'd hidden under his pillow and rose back up. He tried

304

to throw his legs out so that he could stand but found either of his ankles tied to either post with several strands of strong twine. He kicked hard to break free but found that the combined strength of the numerous lines was too much. He then retreated backward against the wall as far as he could and held his knife at the ready. "Cheating cowards!" he yelled.

With the three gone, Lasashu pulled the soaked bedding off himself and threw it over on top of the other lower-level bed. He scooted down to the foot of his bed and began to cut at the first length he could grab, but quickly discovered that his little knife's blade had been blunted. *Bastards!* Realizing that the blade was useless, he began to work at the knots with his fingernails. *I will kill them all*, he swore as he tried to remember their faces to add to his now long list of people he intended to hang after his pending victory over the witch.

"Lasashu?"

Looking up, Lasashu found an older man in a brown robe standing in the doorway. He'd seen this man a few times before, usually roaming the halls with others in robes or during meals in the great hall but wasn't sure of his name or title. The man's expression was curious and maybe a bit amused. He stood there and examined the room carefully before returning his gaze to Lasashu.

"What was all that about?"

"I was sleeping. Those men threw water on me, yelled, and left. So, I'm not sure." he explained and returned to working the knots. "Oh, and they blunted my favorite knife."

"It would appear they went through a fair amount of effort. I wonder where they got the buckets."

The man crossed the room and examined one of the buckets carefully, as if it were some strange object he'd never seen before in his life. He righted the thing and picked a second bucket up to examine. After a moment, he sat the second bucket into the first and fetched the third, which he did not examine before adding it to the stack. With a casual wave of his hand, the stacked buckets slid across the room to the empty corner. He then gathered up Lasashu's soaked bedding, crossed the room, and deposited the lot forcefully into the top bucket with a few grunts of effort. Lasashu finally freed his first leg and began working on the second as the old man sat upon the bed opposite him.

"I'll get them though!"

"Men don't usually put so much effort into anything without a cause." he said softly.

"I don't try to understand the workings of such feeble minds." Lasashu replied angrily.

The man stood, stepped to the edge of Lasashu's bed, and then bent down to look beneath it. The sound of metal scrapping on stone reminded him that he had placed the silver serving tray there before he'd fallen asleep. He tried to recall the name of one of the people who had been working in the kitchen when he'd taken the thing but couldn't even remember their faces clearly. Commoner names were all so similar he could hardly remember one from another anyhow. The man returned to his seat on the other bed, set the tray upon his legs, and began to rifle through the food scraps on the tray.

"Breadcrumbs, apple cores, half a tart, eggshell, and cheese crumbs… Seems you have quite the appetite."

"Those are all mine. I didn't steal anything!" Lasashu nearly shouted.

"And the tray?"

"I was going to return it. I just fell asleep. I asked to borrow it!"

"I see." The man moved the tray onto the bed at his side and cleared his throat. When he stood, he waved a hand in Lasashu's direction. The twine immediately wriggled, and the knots came loose. "Dameran seems to have misplaced a similar serving tray some days ago."

"I asked to borrow it."

"Dameran hadn't lent his tray out to anybody. You see, it's the only thing that remained after some bandits broke into his family's home last summer. They stole everything and murdered everyone. You see, it's got his family crest on the bottom." He flipped the tray to show Lasashu the bottom. The Streykis family crest was a simple bit: a hand in the center of a kite shield with two swords pointing up at either side of the hand. They were, in ancient times, the guardians of justice in all the land, called upon in the nation's greatest times of need. Some said the Streykis family had been near-impossible to kill.

"I told you I borrowed it. If he says it was stolen, he's a liar!" Lasashu yelled.

"Come with me."

"I did nothing wrong. I traded for all of that. It is mine!"

"Come along."

"No, thanks. I have my own business to be about. Leave me." Lasashu climbed from the wet bed and walked over to his pack of personal things in the corner. A cold chill ran through his entire body just then and he felt himself leave the ground. He grabbed for the nearest bedframe but missed by a hand's distance.

"It was not a request, young man."

"What?" He flailed and began to turn in place. When he came about, he found the old man standing with a hand outstretched as if grabbing for something. "Put me down this instant!"

"You do not give orders here." the man said calmly.

"I will have your head for this! Do you know who I am?"

"I have that displeasure, yes."

307

The man turned and Lasashu found himself floating along after the man as if there were some tethers between them. He grabbed at the doorway but was pulled free of it before he could get a good grip. The hallway was filled with soldiers who watched in silence. Not one man responded to his calls to action. He kicked at the wall to slow his progress but wound up spinning instead. When he neared the first soldier wearing armor, he reached for the man's sword, but the man jumped backward out of reach. After that, he grabbed at a sconce, but it broke free of the wall quickly. He threw the thing at the old man, but it came to an abrupt stop a hand's distance from the man and fell to the floor a breath later.

"Help me! I am your king! Obey me!" Nobody acted or even appeared shocked at the situation. He decided right then and there that once he had built his armies up, he would come down on this whole place like a hammer. He would hunt every single one of these men down and kill them. *No, that's too good! I'll cut off their hands and throw them in the streets! And I'll forbid the people from helping them in any way!*

Down the hall they went with people watching and not acting until they came out to the massive open room where soldiers ate. The place was usually empty this early, save the few soldiers who enjoyed being up early and the kitchen staff, but at this moment, the walls were lined with soldiers. The Asp man sat at a table in the center of the room wearing plain shorts and no shirt. Lasashu was finally lowered to the floor before the Asp man, but that cold sensation did not leave him. He tried turning to face the old man who had brought him but found he could hardly move at all. He was like an insect submerged in sap.

"Please, sit." The Asp man said once he finally seemed to notice that Lasashu was there.

"Tell this imbecile to release me."

The old man circled the table, took the seat next to the Asp man, and waved his hand toward Lasashu. The cold tingling about his body vanished and he nearly fell to the floor when his body's weight returned. He wanted nothing more in that moment than to choke the man to death, but decided he best not attempt it since the man could wield magic against him. Instead, he took the seat opposite the Asp man and took several deep breaths to calm his nerves.

"I want this man hung. Now." he directed his gaze at the Asp man.

Just then, three young boys arrived pushing a cart with bowls, cups, wooden utensils, and a large black pot. They set the table, poured cups of water, and began filling bowls with gruel. *Great...gruel again.* Lasashu hated gruel almost as much as he hated...well, everything about the great, big, stupid wall. At least the gruel was served hot, as if to combat the cold malice of those around him. While it lacked real flavor, it was a nice break from the usual meals consisting of slices of indistinguishable white meat and mash. Both were usually flavorless, save for the bitter or rancid taste of oil from having been cooked too hot. Mashed carrots, mashed potatoes, mashed turnips, mashed parsnips, mashed rutabagas...he was certain that this place was home to the culinary masters of the world when it came to mashed foods. *Now, if only they can find someone who knows how to spice food!* Every meal had something mashed, plenty of warm water to drink and at least twenty angry glares aimed in his direction. Today there were more people watching than usual and the attention almost made him lose his appetite. Almost. He started eating as soon as he realized he would need the energy if he was going to hunt down his three roommates.

"This will be the third time you have been caught thieving from the kitchens." The old man began.

"Shut up. Nobody is talking to you, peasant!" Lasashu yelled so loudly that spittle flew from his mouth. The man's brows furrowed.

"I have eight reports that you were seen entering the rooms of other students and leaving with food that did not belong to you." The Asp man began.

"That's a lie." Lasashu pointed his spoon at the Asp man wishing it were a knife.

"Stealing is a crime here just the same as any other place." he continued without concern.

"Lies. I will-"

"This is your last warning about such behavior."

"I will face these liars. Tell me who they are!" Lasashu pounded on the table so hard his wooden spoon broke in his hand.

"I will no longer engage in your delusions. You will be placed on night duties from now on. We have reassigned you to a room alone so that you cannot disturb others."

"Good. A king deserves his own room! Show me the way and send up someone to draw me a hot bath. Where are my scented soaps, by the way? It can't possibly take this long to have soaps delivered."

"There will be no special soap and your new room doesn't come with a private bath and servants." The Asp man spoke a bit quicker than usual now.

"It wasn't a request, Asp. Do as you are instructed, or I'll have you replaced!"

"You are a lost cause." The old man said with shock on his face.

"I suppose extreme situations call for extreme actions." The Asp man said to the elder man at his side.

"I couldn't agree more." the old man replied while glaring at Lasashu.

The Asp man rose then and headed to the hall opposite the one from which Lasashu had arrived. Once he was gone, the old man stood, picked up his own bowl and spoon, and waved for Lasashu to follow. "Come. We'll get you some dry clothing." Lasashu grabbed his bowl and snatched the unused spoon that had been meant for the Asp man.

He turned to follow the man but then, realizing how little food was in his bowl, turned back. He put his bowl down, picked up the one meant for the Asp, and scooped the contents into his own bowl quickly. He then grabbed a cup of water and hurried after the old man. *He will get me that warm bath as soon as I am done eating!*

They took a flight of stairs down three levels and then on along a hall again back the other direction. At least, he thought it was back the other way. As he had learned, getting lost was quite easy inside the wall. The halls were uniform and the layout of rooms from one level to the next were identical. He figured a window here and there would be helpful, but he'd only ever seen one window and that hadn't even been a window, but an arrow loop. There weren't even signs to inform people which level they were on. Decorations would have helped him to learn his way around, but he hadn't seen anything more decorative than a candle holder and even that was a plain piece of iron.

Eventually, the old man stopped at a door that looked like any other door and left Lasashu floating about in a slow circle. He waved his hands at the door and then gave it a push, revealing what seemed to be a storage room very much like the one he'd seen on the day of his arrival, but with a bit more space to walk between the mountains of items. The old man stepped inside, leaning up against a table, and began eating his food as if in a great hurry. When he finished, he put the bowl on a small table and finally glanced up at Lasashu.

The old man gave an aggravated grunt and rubbed at his temples as he turned away and headed across the room. He mumbled repeatedly as he sorted through a stack of clothing. It turned out to be white pants. He pulled three pair out and moved over to a stack of white shirts – the ones with the V-neck and sleeves that only went to the elbows that Lasashu had seen the kitchen workers wearing.

"I will not dress like kitchen staff." He said loudly as he took notice of the items on the table in the corner.

311

There were books, tiny bottles of ink, well-used quills and loose sheets of paper, but not in vast quantities; rather, there were just a few. This was a working desk, used for something other than supply storage. He headed in that direction to see what else he might find since the old man was distracted. He didn't count on finding wax or a leather scroll case, but it had everything else he needed to at least write a letter to his family. The most important thing was to tell his father about how poorly he was being treated. Once he had that, he could figure out how to get the letter delivered. He opened the first small drawer on the left, hoping to find a least a gold coin, but all he found was a pair of writing gloves, a small knife, and a bottle of red ink. The second drawer just had loose sheets of paper and a broken quill. The right-most drawer had a set of keys.

"Have you ever washed dishes before?" The old man called from across the room.

"No, nor do I intend to." He quickly scribbled a note to his father. *They're planning to kill me. Send an army. -Lasashu.* Short and to the point was always best, especially when he didn't have a lot of time to consider what to write. He folded it up and stuffed it into his somewhat dry pocket. His mind quickly returned to the keys. He grabbed them and examined them. They were old, but in good condition. On the shank of the larger one, someone had scratched the word "arms" and the other held the words "garden shed". *The garden shed!* He celebrated the find and left the room as silently as possible.

He continued in the direction he'd been brought, hoping he could find the storage room. He took the first flight of stairs downward and then turned into the first crossing hallway he found. The hall went on for quite a ways without door or connecting hall, but he took the first right turn available and then found stairs that took him down again. Eventually, he found a young boy wearing the all-white clothing that signified him as kitchen staff, asked directions to get outside, and did his best to follow those directions. Once he was sure he was good and lost, he tried to double-back to find that same boy, but then he stumbled upon a group of young men wearing only shorts and shoes. Since they were dressed for morning physical training and not already sweaty, he followed them until they came out of the wall and into the outside world.

Finally free of the wall, he headed west along the wall, thankful that the men he had followed didn't question his appearance or sudden disappearance. He stayed near the wall as he traveled to the shed, praying that nobody would spot him as he scanned every space between the buildings as he went. When he arrived, he quickly undid the door's lock and stepped inside, closing the door most of the way and peeking out to see if anybody had followed him. The tiny town wasn't awake yet and he saw nobody about, but he knew the townsfolk did start their days nearly as early as the wall. Searching the shelves of the little shed, he quickly found what he was looking for – a prying bar!

Again, Lasashu followed close to the wall to reach his target. The barn where horses were kept was a large thing, painted red not that long ago, and the air even a block away from it carried the foul odor of manure. This was normally a very busy part of town, but it was still too early for anybody to have need of a horse and there were no guards now. He quickly made his way into the space between the barn and the building next to it, which he thought might be a banker's place of business with its size and because it was made of brick like most banks. He ran all the way to the rear of the barn before turning to see if anybody had spotted him. The only thing he could hear was the chirping of birds. If it were a normal barn, he would have checked the front door, but he'd seen mages work their craft on that door a few times already when being forced to march with the riffraff. Lasashu used his prying bar to force boards out of place, slowly creating his own door. Once inside, he just needed to find a horse and he would be on his way home. *Brilliant plan!*

Getting the boards free without making a lot of sound took a long while. He had to pry each one free at an agonizingly slow speed

313

to keep the nails from whinging too loudly. Each board was about a hand wide and no longer than the distance from his elbow to fingertips, and they were layered in a staggered manner. Worse, there were two layers, so that he had to take off about twenty of them before he could work away at the second layer. *Lazy work,* he repeatedly cursed. He cut his finger on a nail when he was nearly halfway done with the thing and cursed whoever had built the thing. When he finally pulled the last board free, he squeezed through the opening quickly. Inside, the smell was so horrid that he was sure it had not been cleaned even once since its construction. He found that he had entered an empty stall. He crept out of the stall and over to the next one. The horse was average in size and didn't appear weak by his limited knowledge of horses. *You look like you could take me home quickly,* he thought as he undid the cord that held the stall door closed. He threw the door open and stepped up to the horse, surprised that it wasn't wearing a saddle already.

"It's okay. We're going for a little run."

The horse stepped forward and made a sound. Not knowing what the thing meant by the sound, he stepped closer and reached out to pet it on the shoulder as he'd seen people do on occasion. The thing rose on its hind legs and threw out its front legs as if trying to box him. Lasashu backed away quickly, eyed the thing for a long moment, and then headed to the next stall. Upon opening the second stall, this horse made a wild sound at him and rushed forward as if it were going to slam into him. He dove out of the way and the horse veered off toward the rear of the barn. Again and again, each horse acted in what he could only guess was a hostile manner. The last of the horses was different though. It stepped forward slowly and eyed him for a long moment, occasionally shaking its head gently. Finally, he reached out with one hand and touched its side tentatively. When it didn't react, he gave it a good petting and stepped to its side.

"You smell of shit." He spat.

With no saddle with which to pull himself upon the thing, he set to searching for a stepping stool in the main area of the barn but

314

found no such thing. *I guess I ride it without a saddle.* He nudged the thing closer to the wall between stalls and, placing his foot in the space between planks, climbed up the wall while holding onto the horse with both hands. It made an objectionable sound as Lasashu carefully climbed onto it but didn't move. When he leaned forward and threw his arms around the thing's neck, it moved forward and out of the stall. It turned right outside the stall, walking just a hand's stretch away from the other stall doors until it reached the rear of the building, where it turned left. Finally, it stopped in the middle of the back wall, turned in place, and heading in a straight line towards the massive front doors. It picked up speed quickly and, just when he thought the idiot creature was going to run face-first into the doors, the door sprang open. The horses behind let out a collective neigh and charged forward, most of them passing him by in seconds. While the collective ran straight forward, his horse veered to the right. *Idiot creature,* he cursed while tightening his grasp around the thing's neck. It picked up speed then and turned left after the first building.

The dirt path people called a road curved left slowly and the horse followed it at an ever-increasing speed. After a short time, it straightened out and he saw that it ended at the edge of the tiny town. He began to panic then, as he wondered how he would get the horse to go in the correct direction. Up ahead, the other horses came into view as they entered onto the same path. Guards appeared a moment later in all manner of dress. There were those fully dressed for duty, but the majority wore shoes and shorts as if they had just come from morning training. His own horse was nowhere near as fast as the others and, as they exited the small town, he began to wonder if his was ill and set to worrying about how far it would get him. Walking back home was not an appealing idea.

When the horses slowed to a jog, he began glancing back expecting soldiers to give chase on whatever horses they kept in private barns, but he found nothing each time. After a short while, the horrible little town lay far enough behind that he found it impossible to tell if anything was exiting it and began to urge the horse onward. The thing snorted at his every urging and maintained an ever-slowing pace that made him wonder if the thing was about to fall over and die. The thought reminded him of the time a horse had fallen over, both breaking and trapping his uncle Hori's leg some years ago and he pulled both legs a bit higher up. Ahead, the other horses slowed to a mere walking pace and clustered into a tight knot. Their heads swiveled this way and that, which reminded Lasashu of lost children looking for their parents in a crowded market.

"Move, you idiot!" he cursed his own animal as he gave it a kick in the ribs. It snorted and shook its head in protest.

The group ahead suddenly burst into motion. Some of them stood on their rear legs, spinning in place, and let out wild sounds that made the hair on Lasashu's neck stand up. The majority began to run in wide-arcing circles. A moment later, his own made a sound he instinctively understood as fear, and it came to a complete stop. He kicked its ribs and raised one hand up to give its rear a hard slap when he spotted a cloud of dust a few hundred strides ahead. Dark figures rose from the ground, and, in terror, he recognized what they were. The horse shifted suddenly beneath him and, though he tried to lunge forward and throw his arms around its neck, the thing moved so quickly that he grabbed only air as he fell.

Lasashu screamed and braced for the impact, expecting to break and arm or leg, but the grass was so thick where he landed that it was almost like jumping onto a firm bed. He scrambled to his feet and frantically searched for the nearest horse. He found a number of those that had been ahead coming directly at him. "Stop!" He screamed as he jogged towards the nearest, but it veered away sharply. He immediately looked for the next and ran to get in its path, but it too veered away from him so that he never got within five strides of it. The third horse came soon after but didn't shy away from him. He jumped for it and barely grazed its side with one arm before falling face-first to the ground.

When he reached his feet this time, he found that there were no more horses coming his way. The Noka, or whatever his brother had called them, were approaching directly and it took Lasashu a moment to realize that they were all redirecting towards him instead of the horses. *No. I'm not food!* He turned and ran. Moments later, he heard pounding of feet on ground and his left leg began to burn and threaten to lock up from overexertion. Something struck him in the middle of his back, and he went flying forward into the ground.

"No!" He screamed as he tumbled.

When he came to a stop, he found himself on his back and made to sit up but froze when he found that creature looking down at him with ravenous eyes. Hot, moist air washed over him in quick bursts and the thing sniffed him in a manner like that of a dog. This close, Lasashu found the thing even more terrifying than before. It had a mouth full of sharp teeth longer than a hand and a body covered in white, bone-like material, and the curved claws on each foot came to frightening points. Being at least twice the size of the largest horse, he'd ever seen, he now understood why the horses had turned and run so suddenly. Others surround Lasashu at a distance, each snapping their mouths open and shut in quick repetition, which produced a soft clacking. The one towering above glanced at the ground for a moment before letting out a growl very similar to a dog's, which caused the others to back away a touch.

"No! I'm not food! Go eat the horses!"

"Don't tell them that!" Someone cursed loudly. "They love horse flesh almost as much as fish."

Lasashu turned at the voice and found the Asp man seated upon one of the creatures as it pushed between two in the circle. As usual, the man wore pants that betrayed his lowly birth and nothing else. His face was devoid of thought or emotion and, in that moment, Lasashu understood why people said that the Asp people held no more value than a donkey. If the man had a mind at all, it must have been broken since birth. Seeing such a man riding one of the creatures, things suddenly made terrible sense.

"They're pets?" he practically yelled. "You and Reginald set this all up to scare me?" He grabbed the creature's snout and pulled himself up to his feet. As soon as he let go, the thing snorted and rubbed its snout into the ground vigorously.

"Novae are not pets." the man replied dully. "And don't touch them like that. The only reason you still live is because I was out here feeding them when you arrived. They can be very irritable and unforgiving."

"Sure, sure. Very scary creatures, I get it."

"I assume you broke into the horse barn." the man patted the side of the creature and then jumped down.

"Yes, and now I'll be leaving." Lasashu turned his attention to the creature. It's big eyes, a mix of blue and green flecks without the usual black center. "Fetch me a horse."

The creature shot upright and produced a screeching howl that was so loud that Lasashu had to throw his hands over his ears and step away. The creatures then turned and ran in all directions, leaving just the one behind with the Asp man. The creature strode casually about in a wide circle, eyes searching the world as if it were bored and looking for new prey.

"Have you read the book that was given to you when you arrived?"

"I don't have time for all the books you gave me, Asp. As I have tried to explain to you, this whole thing is a forgery of fate, orchestrated by that witch. I need to find her and bring her to justice. She must answer to the gods for her actions, and I doubt they will take her impersonation of them well at all. You should have received a letter from my brother by now, as he's had plenty of time to get home and check into these matters. They will have had time to see that my stone was replaced by a forgery and will have begun searching for the real one."

"You are delusional. The gods have called you to this place." The Asp man bent down and plucked a few rocks, which he began to juggle as he walked. Like the creature, the idiot began walking in a circle around Lasashu.

"An Asp who pretends to understand the will of the gods?" Lasashu laughed. "Don't be ridiculous."

"It is often a great challenge to determine if someone is blind to reality because they can't face the truth," He turned to examine Lasashu as he continued walking and juggling. *Quite the feat for an Asp,* he considered. "Or if they just want so desperately to convince you of he lie they need you to believe so that they might manipulate you."

"You know, you really are stupid. Do you think you have a mind in that skull of yours?"

"Maybe you are protecting yourself from what you are and how you treat those around you. Perhaps, it is too soon to force you to face yourself, but-"

"Stop babbling and get me my horse!" Lasashu yelled. "I've tolerated enough of your stupidity today."

"You've stolen from the kitchens, from those men who would have and should have become your closest friends, and-"

"Shut up! You do as I say! I am king. Get my horse! Do it now!" he screamed. "You do know what horse means, don't you?"

"You force my hand."

A biting pain sprang up in his lower leg, causing Lasashu to yell and jump back. Even before he landed, he looked down expecting a snake or a massive hornet; however, he found a small dart with small red and white feathers jutting out of the front of his leg. As soon as he landed, he reached down and plucked the thing from his leg. Examining it for a second, he threw it to the ground and looked about for an attacker but found only the Asp man.

"You dare attack your king?" He screamed. "I will have you beaten! I will have your family brought before you and slain! I will have you hung in a cage for all to see as you slowly die from starvation! I will piss on you every day!" The world turned sideways, and the grass came up to meet his face. "I will slaughter your friends...I will burn...your lands...and... you...will..." His face went numb, and he felt his bladder release. "I..." His jaw went numb, and he found himself barely able to move. The Asp man casually walked to his side, rolled him over with a push of his foot, and gazed down at him for a long moment. He bent, took one of Lasashu's arms, and pulled him up from the ground. The man slung Lasashu over his shoulders like he was some fine fur, leaving him to watch helplessly as he was carried back to the wall.

When they arrived, Lasashu found soldiers waiting at the edge of town, some having captured horses and some just waiting and watching. Some gawked like morons and others cheered, but all took notice and took no action. The Asp man carried him into the wall and began taking flight after flight of stairs downward. *No, my private rooms are up,* he cursed the man and strained to lift an arm to punch the man, but barely managed to move a single finger.

Eventually, they arrived in a small, bare room, in which stood three soldiers who looked to have been awaiting their arrival. The Asp man shut the door behind himself and then lowered Lasashu to the floor so that he was half laying and half leaning up against the wall. From this position, Lasashu saw that the three soldiers were standing over a shield that lay upon the floor. It was a dark round wooden thing that lacked ornamentation and was so large that no single man could have lifted it. *No,* he suddenly realized that the thing had leather loops at four sides. The Asp man and three soldiers took hold of the leather loops and, grunting under the strain, lifted the thing from the floor.

They took several steps to the side and set the thing down, exposing a hole in the floor wide enough for an average man to fit into.

A moment later, one of the soldiers presented a rope with a grim expression taking his face as he crossed the small room. The others took hold of Lasashu, leaned him forward, and held him in place while the other tied the rope around Lasashu's chest under his arms. They then pushed Lasashu over to the hole and began lowering him into a deep darkness. He guessed it was forty feet down before he reached a hard surface he could not see and was slowly lowered onto his side. Something thumped on the ground at his side.

"Welcome to the lookout post, soldier." An older man's voice called down to him. "If you see vampires coming, you pull the rope hanging next to the door to alert everyone. You have enough food for three days."

FLIES IN HOT AIR

Lord Kairn sat with his books spread out all over the table in the center of his tent, at the center of his camp, on the far north side of King Hotar's traveling forces. For the first time in days, he had finally managed to schedule an hour alone and, though he wanted to spend that time sleeping, he was going over his notes. Being the point of the spear had kept him very busy. Lords and ladies had been sending him requests at all hours of the day and night requesting an audience where they would mostly complain about his rate of travel, his direction being off ever so slightly, or any manner of ill-disguised excuses to take up his time. They wanted to complain, strike trade deals, or simply talk for hours so they could pretend they were more important than others later.

Currently, he was attempting to connect events in a way so that they made sense. He was ceaselessly nagged by a feeling that there was some connection between the assassin, the vampires at White Rock, and the necromancer's cabin in the forest, but he hadn't been able to put these things together in a way that made sense. Through his network of spies, rumors, and a great deal of bribery, he had learned that there had been a few disturbances in several towns west of White Rock. Most were common events, and a few were no more than reports of odd sounds heard during the night that some people thought were the calls of wolves or ghosts. The company of soldiers at White Rock was difficult to get any information on and remained a mystery, but that wasn't a surprise. Try as he might, there was no information about a necromancer available and no missing people that he could place there even by loose association. He still had people trying to find out more about that, but he was growing doubtful he would find anything.

"Surely someone would have noticed the missing people or someone traveling into the woods repeatedly. She had to have eaten something." He paused while the idea formed in his mind and then recoiled at the idea. "Or just their life energy."

He stood, gave himself a good stretch, and then began to pace the length of the tent. It wasn't the same as his father's study, but what the place lacked in a comforting atmosphere it made up for with fresh air and not being interrupted by his family. Thankfully, they were back home where Koraine couldn't interrupt him in person; however, several of them had already sent letters and were clearly squabbling over who should be in charge in his absence. Koraine was already attempting to take charge and several banks had sent him letters to authorize loans to the family. *Perhaps she is trying to replace that old carriage. She always hated it.* He had already written back to decline and was just waiting for Koraine to have a fit about that. He smiled at that thought. *She can do that once I am dead.* With six assassination attempts in the few shorts days since departing the capital, he did have to wonder why she was in such a hurry. *Focus,* he scolded himself.

He'd already determined that the vampires had come from the west, but how far was the real question. Putting that fact together with the fact that someone had to have warned Captain Reskar of their approach, he figured that Captain Reskar's forces were...*no, that's ridiculous. They were defending their town. They could have just been in the right place at the right time...but that would mean...maybe the vampires were after the assassin?* He played with the events and tried to tease out variables he hadn't considered before.

"Captain Reskar hadn't expected me. He lied to me about when he had arrived. The fire too. Why lie about something that doesn't matter? He could have said a lantern was dropped in the fighting. Maybe the vampires weren't after the assassin at all, but the townspeople. Maybe the fire was to defend the houses like he said? No, I'm sure he was lying."

He walked over to the small table at the side of the tent and poured himself a tall cup of wine. He took a small sip and then splashed it on several spots on his coat so that he would carry the fresh scent. *I need to find a way of questioning slaves who work in the fields between.* He walked back over to his desk and quickly searched for his map of the area. Yes, east of Veysor lay Pine Valley, Deer Run, and Paul's Glen, each a larger town than White Rock and much closer to the capital. Beyond those three towns there were hundreds of acres of farmed land, worked by hundreds of slaves. That whole area was Lord Dorrem's territory up until White Rock, but the man was such a recluse that he hadn't answered anyone's letters in ten years. Going there in person was out of the question. *I'll have to send a spy.*

"Lord Kairn?" his assistant Boyd entered through the front cautiously with a grim expression.

"Yes?"

"It's time, Lord Kairn."

"Already?"

"Yes, my lord. Unless you'd rather I send for the cooks so you can stay in tonight."

"No, I have to keep up public appearances."

"Yes, my lord."

Lord Kairn and Boyd walked together through the camp to the south. There was a long stretch of empty field between camps, which allowed him ample time to clear his mind and prepare for all the social niceties ahead. *Fake niceties,* he thought with a sigh. The big tent had been set up on the south side of this camp, which was swarming with guards belonging to royal houses from all over the nation. Surrounding the big tent were rows upon rows of tables where royals clustered together in groups of five to twenty. He spotted Lady Voth in one such cluster and considered heading directly there. *No, I must start inside,* he scolded himself.

"Lord Kairn." Boyd grabbed Lord Kairn by the arm and redirected him up the path that led to the big tent.

"Ever watchful, Boyd." he gave the older man a smile.

"That's why I cost so much, sir." Boyd gave him a brief smile before letting his expression turn to that of an overly serious man who was about his business. That's how Boyd described it, but Lord Kairn would describe it in one word: Mean. The expression fit Boyd well and the man always used it to his benefit. When combined with his dark eyes, which gave him the air of a man about ready to commit murder, there were many royals who wouldn't bother Boyd even if his hair were ablaze.

They entered a very busy tent. The tables had been arranged into a giant circle with an opening in the center for dancers. Tables covered in food and drink lined both long sides of the tent, the podium for musicians stood in one corner, where there were six people playing and singing one of the new war songs now. Another podium stood in the other corner, where six people sat in large, cushioned chairs wearing white robes. Upon their chests there was the black silhouetted crown that many people painted on their shops or houses, but then there was the watching eye above it. These six were magicians and slaves belonging to King Hotar. *Binders,* Lord Kairn hissed under his breath upon seeing them. Capable of removing or creating the bonding rings, these six were a few of those people nobody ever mentioned in polite company, and all feared more than anything else. Why they were here, Lord Kairn was unsure, but he expected they would be somehow related to tonight's proclamations from King Hotar. The Lords and ladies, having been waiting for his arrival, began to form a line to speak with him.

"Cheers, Lord Kairn." The first arrived with a cup of strong red wine held out for him to take.

Trying to distract his mind from the Binders, he turned his thoughts to the future. The very short, likely painful, future. Having outlined the general plan for his death, he found his happiness diminishing with the passing of each day. Only now was he grateful that he hadn't married and had children. He had courted several ladies and gotten to know many others, but he had determined that they had not been right for him. Many had been beautiful, smart, witty, dutiful, and downright hilarious; however, they had all been interested in the modern version of a royal marriage. They would wed him, give him children, and display a public image that would bolster the Kairn family legacy of honor, integrity, and intelligence. They would not love him though. After they had given children to legitimize the marriage, they would find true lovers elsewhere and keep it a secret from the outside world forever. A lot of marriages were like that these days; in fact, it was downright common, but people kept it quiet. They wanted to draw up contracts, sign them, and get on with the business of fulfilling obligations. His cousin Sarah was in such a marriage herself. She had no love for her husband, nor he her, but they were excellent parents to their children and the joining of their two houses had made both stronger. *Business, alliance...wealth.*

He picked at the food Boyd brought him and sipped at a glass of water that had a large chunk of ice in it. He had heard there were some young mages traveling with the big tent specifically for preserving food and drink and wondered how powerful they must be to make enough ice for people's drinks. Normally, the only way to get ice was to buy large blocks of it from those mad men who sailed to the far north to fetch the stuff and it was damned expensive.

"Lord Kairn? Did you hear me, my lord?" Pulled from his thoughts, he found a familiar face.

"Emma?"

She blushed and gave him a little bow. "Yes, Lord Kairn."

"My apologies, Emma. I was thinking. What was it now?"

"I asked if you wanted more water."

He looked down at his cup and realized it was empty, save a tiny bit of water and the chunk of ice. "How'd you know I was drinking water?" He glared at the cup and realized that he was much more drunk than he had realized. It was all the people wanting to drink with him, to toast one thing or another, which had ultimately become toasting to the grand war ahead. He'd lost count of how many cups of wine he'd drank and only vaguely recalled Boyd telling him to switch to water. Boyd had mentioned something about duty and how much he had to do when morning came again. *Smart man, that Boyd!* He glanced to his left and spotted Boyd about fifteen strides off with his mouth to the ear of a soldier. No, it wasn't a soldier at all; rather, it was Damien, his Secret Finder. To the rest of the world, Damien was Lord Kairn's clothier. It was the perfect title for the man. People didn't expect a clothier to be around very often, as most lords didn't need new clothes made very often. Damien would show up every few months to measure Lord Kairn for clothing and Lord Kairn would drop a few words of praise about Damien for a few days when showing off his new things. From the large pack on Damien's back, it appeared he had just arrived.

"Well, I didn't know, but it's been so busy tonight that I stopped counting on my usual assumptions. Some people will take it as an insult if you assume they have been drinking wine or mead – anything at all really." She smiled and looked at his cup expectantly.

Lord Kairn looked at her for a long moment and then at his cup with the ice in it. People loved chilled wines. Commoners would bury bottles deep in the ground to make the stuff cold, but here they stuffed a chunk of ice in it and let it cool the wine. "That's it!" He nearly shouted as he jumped from his seat. "Thank you, Emma!" He turned and ran. "Boyd!" he shouted as he aimed himself roughly at the opening on the other side of the tent. He collided with three people along the way, shouted his apologies, and continued even faster.

When he reached his tent, he found it surrounded by soldiers in every state of undress. Some wore only their sleeping breeches, and some were in full uniform. In all, there were forty or so men circling his tent with some form of a weapon in hand and a serious expression. When they noticed him, their expressions turned to confusion and relief, some clearly having worried that he had died.

"Who sent you?" A familiar voice boomed from near his tent. He pushed through the crowd and a scream rang out a moment later.

"Let me through!" He yelled.

The soldiers made an opening for him just as Lord Turley emerged from the tent with a scrawny fellow held aloft in one of his hands. The scrawny fellow screamed, and Lord Turley threw him to the ground as though he weighed no more than a child. The man screamed even louder when he crashed upon the ground.

"Who sent you?" Lord Turley screamed at the man as he stepped up to him and put a foot on the man's chest. "Answer me!"

"Lord Turley!" Lord Kairn called as he broke free of the crowd.

The man's right arm a single cut a finger long, his bare chest was severely bruised, his face was swollen badly on one side, and his nose was broken and bleeding. For a moment, he had feared that the man was one of his spies, but Lord Kairn didn't recognize the man once he was close enough to get a good look at the face. Lord Turley turned to face Lord Kairn and gave him a look of concern that quickly turned to relief.

"Pardon the intrusion, Lord Kairn. I came to deliver news and caught this man sneaking into your tent. I have four of my men as witness and several of your soldiers as well." he spoke quickly. "We spotted him from perhaps sixty paces away at the same time as your men. We found no weapons on his person. Do you know him?"

"I do not." Lord Kairn replied dumbfounded. "Was anything inside amiss?"

"Not that I could tell."

"I shall have to look. Did you see anybody else?"

"Just the one man." Lord Turley explained.

"Lord Kairn." Captain Reynar stepped out from the crowd and gave a quick bow. "I have had no reports of anything out of the ordinary tonight. I believe this man has been careful to reach this point unseen."

"Thank you, Captain Reynar." Lord Kairn glanced about at all the men and considered the situation for a moment. "Captain Reynar, take the man and question him. Lord Turley, please join me inside. Everyone else, get back to what you were about." He walked to his tent and tried to focus his drunken mind.

"Three guards at the tent. Jones and Cross, pick this sorry man up!" Captain Reynar yelled.

"Did you have to cut him like that, Lord Turley?" he asked as he stepped into the tent and began scanning for signs that someone had rummaged through his things. Nothing seemed out of place at first glance.

"He acted in violence the moment we entered. If you ask me, I went easy on the man." Lord Turley said matter-of-factually.

Lord Kairn walked over to the small table where he kept whatever cup and bottle of wine he used when he drank and examined it. As expected, he found a small glass vial with white powder sitting just behind the cup. He dug a hole in the dirt with his foot, dumped the vial and then dumped the bottle of wine as well.

"Poison?" Lord Turley questioned as he walked up.

"Looks as though you caught him just in time. A shame too. That's some very good twenty-year-old red."

"I've heard that there have been several attempts on your life recently."

"Indeed."

"Do you know who is behind it?"

"I am fairly certain, but I will deal with it my way." Lord Kairn explained as he began checking the rest of the tent. "Why were you coming here instead of finding me at the feast?"

"You have been arriving late. I expected to find you still here."

"What's the news?"

"The order came in hours ago. You are to break off and head after the assassin as soon as possible. Luckily, with your own men this time."

"That shadow-man finally being useful, huh?"

"I haven't any idea about that thing. I heard you asked Lady Voth for assistance on it."

"I did."

"Her forces are untrained. Mostly young boys her neighbors didn't see useful enough to steal away from her."

331

"I have heard a bit about that...situation." He began checking his notes on the big table, but nothing seemed out of place or missing.

"I couldn't help but notice how she's been getting a lot of attention ever since you asked her to help you."

"Everyone has been scrambling to slop deals together since the announcement of war." Lord Kairn offered as he checked his bed for snakes or poisoned darts. "Perhaps she finally had a successful crop or found a use for some of the swamp beasts in her lands."

"Lord Kairn, are you well?" Boyd asked as he entered the tent with Damien.

Lord Kairn turned back around and smiled. "Ah, Damien. At last!"

"At your service, Lord Kairn!" Damien gave a deep bow, which was almost respectable until he threw his arm back and up into the air like a gleeman or circus performer would.

"Ah, Lord Turley. Should I prepare you something to drink, my lord? I wasn't made aware of your visit, or I would have prepared food and drink." Boyd explained as he took note of the small reddish puddle on the ground. "What happened here?"

"Someone tried to poison me. It appears Lord Turley caught the man in the act." Lord Kairn explained.

"You need new clothes for war?" Lord Turley asked.

"Hardly, but Boyd here tells me that it's cooler up north."

"Nonsense. You need new clothes for war. The clothes make the man, after all!" Damien said with a growing smile and that look in his eyes that said he was about to start singing. "To start with, your fancy wooden buttons don't fare well in the cold, wet winters up north. They'll warp and break within a few weeks and then where will you be? Then there's your cloaks!"

"I don't have cloaks." Lord Kairn said.

332

"Exactly, my lord! You'll need them on the cold nights with winter coming unless you have company in your bed. Then you'll need thicker socks to keep your toes. Most importantly, you'll need something slimming at the waist and something decorative upon your chest to give you a dashing look for the ladies. You are still unmarried, my lord?"

"I'm not even courting at the moment." Lord Kairn explained as he headed to his chest of clothing.

"Have you tried a new haircut, my lord?" Damien pulled a thin, silver instrument out from his sleeve and putting it to his lips, began to play something fast and joyous. Whatever the song was, he only played for a few breaths before going on. "I have some very soft silks from the far south that I think would please you, Lord Kairn."

"You always have a great many ideas, Damien."

"That's because I am a creative man! That's why I became a clothier."

"You strike me as a gleeman." Boyd commented.

"That would be a fine life." He twirled the silver thing around the fingers on one hand and gave Boyd an amused smile. "They earn very little in the way of money though. I've seen them on the streets with their hats out for coin more often than I've see them plying their trade. Smelling of days-old piss, wearing clothing made from salvaged scraps, and losing their minds to drink, anger, and depression... Though rather boring at times, I think the clothing game has a brighter future. People pay very well for fine materials and an expert fit."

"Well, you would fit very well with all the singing and the instruments you have." Boyd commented in an admiring tone.

Damien hummed thoughtfully then cleared his throat. "I can also be at your service, Lord Turley. Even at your size, you'll find my prices quite reasonable. Maybe I could even convince you to try some of the newer styles. The ladies do seem to favor men with feathered hats lately." He

333

stepped halfway between Lord Turley and Lord Kairn and made a real show of examining Lord Turley. With a flourish of his hands, his silver instrument vanished and was replaced with a multi-colored string he used to measure the width of Lord Turley's chest.

"I have no use for a feathered hat." Lord Turley said brusquely.

"Well, the ladies are quite fond of them in Bal Keth, but I imagine they wouldn't look right on a man with your demanding eminence. No, I picture you in something toned down and boldly plain. Nothing flashy. Perhaps black and..." He put his hand on his chin and toyed with his stubble for a moment. "Red accents perhaps. The colors would really bring out your eyes."

Lord Turley glowered at the man openly. "No." He barked the word and stepped up close to Damien with his hands becoming fists. He inhaled through his nose several times, his eyes growing increasingly hard, and did not take his eyes from Damien for a long moment.

"Forget I said anything about it, Lord Turley. I did not mean to offend." Damien offered softly.

"Lord Turley and I have business to discuss. I will find you in a short while." Lord Kairn explained.

"Of course. My apologies, my lord." Boyd gave a small bow and made his exit.

"Yes, yes. You can't rush good clothing." As Damien turned, he brought out the small silver instrument, put it to his mouth, and blew. At first, he played random notes, but switched to something melodic and troubling as he pushed through the tent flaps. "He told her he would return...return, discern, concern." He blew three piercingly high notes and laughed before continuing. "He told her he would return, once the ships he did burn...once the ships were ash, he had to dash."

"Where do you come up with these songs?" Boyd asked as Damien played for a moment.

"Taverns, mostly."

"You heard about the shipyard incident your first day here?"

"News travels like the wind...truth and lies does it blend...like flies in hot air." He seemed to be singing more and more loudly. "This tune makes me think of a song about horse shit I once heard my father sing."

"Very creative, Damien."

"Thank you, Boyd. If only forging trade deals for silk were half as easy!"

"So, what are my orders from King Hotar?" Lord Kairn asked as he went back to checking his trunk of clothing.

"He wants you to head directly east as soon as possible. Follow along the Forbidden Forest's north border to the mountains, where you'll wait for the assassin, who appears to be traveling alongside the mountains. Hopefully, he doesn't mean to cross into the mountains, but we should have updates quickly enough to inform you of future developments."

"How will you get those updates to me?"

"I believe he intends to use that shadow-man. If I understand it correctly, the thing can travel great distances instantly at will."

"He can but getting him to do it was a challenge for me. Advisor Narn told me it had flaws in the intelligence it was given when created." Lord Kairn finished rifling through his trunk of clothing and moved on to his chest of books and writing equipment.

Lord Turley hummed thoughtfully. "Well, I believe someone will be utilizing that thing to get information to you. Perhaps they know how to make it do what they intend."

"I pray it does not cost me further. Dealing with it was a complete disaster." The contents of this chest appeared undisturbed, and he moved on to his last chest, which was sort of a catch-all space for unimportant items. "I think I nearly came to understand it, though."

"I trust that you know we will not be traveling the most difficult terrain in your absence."

"I would expect no less." Lord Kairn said as he took a knee and pulled the lid up.

"I assumed you were hindering our progress in order to get someone to take your place."

"I-" He stopped himself from saying more and considered his words carefully. Admitting the truth could be used against him by interested people and could further diminish his family honor, but he found that he didn't care. *I'll be dead come this time next year.* "Yes. I didn't want that duty. The amount of work that came with it was distracting me from other goals." he admitted.

He spotted the abnormality immediately and faked a yawn to cover for the short inhale he gave out of surprise. His books had been shoved to one side of the chest and a black box had taken their place on the right side. It was a plain thing that bore a thousand fine scratches and dings from frequent use and neglect. The hinges were plain and there was no lock. He wanted to yank the lid open with all the urgency of a child waking up on Garrim Topher's day to find gifts waiting at the front door, but he restrained himself. Whatever it was, it would have to wait until he did not have an audience. He closed the chest and studied the scene for any clues.

Examining the scene carefully, it suddenly struck him as very odd that he was alone with Lord Turley. Instinct guided Lord Kairn to his feet and around his desk, where he knew his hidden daggers were within a moment's reach, but, upon arrival, he found no sense of urgency. He studied Lord Turley and cursed the man's unreadable face, which revealed not even the barest hint of emotion or calculated thought. He wanted to hate the man, wanted to be capable of killing him and saying it was justice for the murder of his father, but he just couldn't. He looked into Lord Turley's eyes and found no guilt, no sadness, and no regret. That absence drove a cold dagger into Lord

336

Kairn's heart and only reminded him that he didn't feel that his father was dead and gone. *Perhaps,* he considered, *that's because he filled my life with good memories?* It was an uncomfortable thing he hadn't admitted to his family. They had all cried, spoken at the funeral, and spent a bit of time just being emotional wrecks; meanwhile, the young man Anvindr Kairn had found himself the only one willing and able to pick up the responsibilities of filling his father's shoes. He had become Lord Kairn on the same day that he had learned of his father's death.

Lord Turley's involvement in the death or Anvindr's father had required very little investigation, as there had been six witnesses to the event. He and six of his soldiers have gone directly to King Hotar, announced that he had drunkenly charged the man on horseback, sending him tumbling down a hill and into a raging river. It had occurred on Turley lands, which ordinarily would have been enough to judge it as a justifiable attack due to trespass; however, Lord Turley had declared himself guilty, remarking murder hadn't been his intention, and promptly paid three times the standard weregild of one-hundred-thousand gold. He had been jailed during the fruitless search for a body and was later released when King Hotar eventually decided not to impose further punishments.

He wanted to hate Lord Turley. He had prayed for that ability a thousand nights, but nothing ever came. It felt like trying to find anger for someone who had done nothing.

"I cannot blame you. Taking responsibility is rarely easy or enjoyable." Lord Turley offered.

Beyond that matter, Lord Turley hadn't mentioned Captain Reskar or his travels through Turley lands, news of which should have reached his ears some time ago. *Perhaps,* he considered, *mentioning it would only remind him of what he has done. Focus,* he berated himself. The vampires had to have come from the capital, which meant someone had wanted the assassin found and killed before Lord Kairn had been given a chance to make the capture. Someone in the capital must have known about the assassin very early on, maybe even witnessed the attempt on King Hotar's life, and didn't want the assassin to give up some bit of information. Perhaps someone in a position of power had hired the assassin and didn't want their identity revealed.

"Tell me, Lord Turley, weren't you there when the assassination attempt was made?"

"No. I was at the execution."

"I see. I haven't heard the story of the assassination attempt but once and it lacked precision in that telling. Do you recall who was there to witness the attempt?"

"I believe Advisor Narn, Lady Daneth, Archbishop Hass, and Advisor Sa'teshka were attending King Hotar. A few servants were there as well, from what I heard later. I believe they were lunching over talks of Lady Daneth's son, who wished to begin courting Advisor Narn's daughter."

"Yes, that's much the same as what I've heard."

"I was there for the assassin's admission and his subsequent beheading."

"And he was human?"

"Yes."

"Does Lady Daneth still hate King Hotar?"

"She always will. You don't kill someone's husband and expect them to take a liking to you a few years later." There was a long pause before he went on. "It almost sounds as though you suspect her of being involved, Lord Kairn."

"No, that would be ridiculous."

"Indeed. King Hotar has kept a very careful eye upon her ever since killing her husband."

"No, you're right. I'm just drunk and tired."

"Well, get some rest. You head out soon and you'll need to have your head on straight." Lord Turley turned and marched out of the tent then.

Over the years, Lord Kairn had learned that when Damien did not want to be found, he would make ascertaining his whereabouts a maddening task. Unfortunately, it wasn't much easier to find him when he wasn't concerned about being found. Tonight, he passed a message through Boyd that he was camping in a tent adjacent to the musicians in Lord Kairn's own camp and that had sounded easy enough; however, when Lord Kairn went to call on him, there was no sign of him and the musicians in the area reported that they had not as much as seen Damien. From there, Lord Kairn had soldiers search his camp, but they found nothing. When Lord Kairn headed to Lord Turley's camp to search there, he was met by a young messenger boy as he entered from the north side. It turned out that Damien had hired the boy to wait there for Lord Kairn with a riddle to his location. *We can't all be lights in the dark, but each of us can look to the northern lights for guidance,* the message would be cryptic to others, but Damien had taught Lord Kairn the secret. The second half of any message was always a vague insult or compliment – in this case, it referred to Lord Kairn's position in the north – and the first half was a cryptic manner of saying his true location was outside of a camp and that he would only reveal himself at night. After getting the message, it didn't take long to find a single fire's light in the darkness beyond Lord Turley's camp in the east.

When he was about half between Lord Turley's camp and the single camp's fire, Lord Kairn heard the soft call of a lute playing. The soft haunting tune gave him chills and he hurried toward that lone little camp. When he arrived, he was surprised to find that Damien had brought a big, square carriage that looked older than the one he kept as a reminder of his father and two horses. It was a plain thing made more for simple transportation than comfort or looks. Damien, of course, pretended not to notice Lord Kairn until he took a seat on the log opposite the fire.

"Good tidings, Lord Kairn." He said cheerfully without looking.

"How are things, Damien?"

"Well enough, my lord."

"That's good to hear." Lord Kairn replied as he gave a glance at the larger camp in the distance. "You could have set up in my camp."

"I have a bit of news I didn't want anybody else to hear."

"We could have spoken in my tent. My soldiers would have provided privacy." He pulled the coin-purse from his belt and tossed it at Damien's bare feet.

"You may be interested to learn that a number of prisoners escaped the slaughter after the dungeon riot."

"Why would I find that interesting?" Lord Kairn tried not to recall the aftermath of the slaughter that he had witnessed that day. "There were so many of them that it would be rather interesting to discover no survivors."

"They are organizing themselves and their numbers are growing quickly. I cannot say who it is, but someone is supplying them with ample coin and food. The food is garnering attention from the poor and they've been using the coin to buy and free bound slaves, who seem to be joining them."

"Who would supply them so much?"

"Perhaps a wealthy merchant." He strummed his lute softly and cleared his throat.

"We've seen such groups form before. They grow quickly and fall apart when their leaders begin fighting for control."

"I dare say that this one is different. Word has spread beyond the capital gates and rumor is that they've already grown to more than a hundred members."

"Time will tell. Have you any news regarding the vampires I asked about?"

"Save the best for last, my lord."

"Okay, but please get to it. I am kept very busy these days."

"I did manage to locate that blacksmith who stole all that gold from you last winter. Unfortunately, his greed was not sated, and he got involved with three fellows who aimed to rob a merchant near Dillon's Falls. They were caught in the attempt. The soldiers there are as crooked as they come, so I doubt you'll get much of the gold back for your troubles."

"We shall see."

"That brings us to the vampires." He strummed his lute and hummed softly for a minute. "You won't like it." he warned.

"I don't like half of what information you bring me, Damien."

"Let me be clearer." He stopped strumming and rested his arm atop the instrument while letting all the joy fall from his face. "You won't believe me."

"You find out some very shocking things at times."

Damien laughed at that. "You just need to get to know more of people is all, my lord."

"So, you always say."

"You didn't believe me about that flute that makes people fall asleep!"

"Out with it."

"King Hotar sent them. Right out of the capital itself."

Lord Kairn waited a moment for Damien to tell the rest of whatever joke he was telling, but the man just looked at him with that serious expression and waited for him to reply. Finally, his expression changed, but not in the way he expected; rather, dread and worry crept into his eyes as he glanced off into the night. The man took a deep breath in and sighed. Lord Kairn got the impression that Damien was in a hurry.

"You're serious?"

"Very."

"How sure are you on this?"

"Dead certain."

"That doesn't make sense, Damien."

"It may yet in time, my lord." He looked out at the camp in the distance and strummed his lute once. "Many things work that way. Like love. I'm sure you'll find it after you've realized what you really, truly need."

"I've courted before." Lord Kairn protested. "I know what I want."

"Do you, really?"

"Yes! I want a woman who wants me and not my family's influence and money."

"And what other thing about you would a woman find desirable, Lord Kairn?"

"I'm intelligent, kind, and I occasionally make a joke that doesn't piss everyone off." He did his best to sound offended, but Damien laughed.

"You're rich and generous. That's why you think you are kind and intelligent – everyone says those things to you to keep you paying them!" He strummed his lute and gave Lord Kairn a solemn look. "I hate to be the one to tell you, but you're ugly. Your hair is too long and messy. Also, your nose is a bit bulbous like a bee just stung it right on

342

the end. Your eyes are too far apart, your smile is lopsided, your lips are too thin, and your ears are too big for your head, which is shaped like a peanut."

"Your eyes are ugly." Lord Kairn retorted with a smile.

Damien gasped and fell backward to the ground. "My eyes? My beautiful blue eyes? That's what you're attacking? Why, sir, that is my best feature! The ladies love my eyes almost as much as…" he rolled himself back upright and strummed his lute twice. "My lute."

"Alright, alright. I'm not witty like you."

"You are royalty. That's not really the way it works. Your kind marry for influence, money, to end old feuds that became wars, and to keep family blood pure no matter how many extra fingers it causes."

"Maybe my life should be about more than all that."

"It is. You just need to take more breaks from all that…work you do and find a woman who can stand you. It shouldn't be too difficult. I mean, there are plenty of blind women with no sense of smell." Lord Kairn laughed despite himself. "Anyhow, I'm afraid I can't take any new requests to gather information at this time."

"Are you quitting the trade?"

Damien laughed. "No, I have to go visit a friend, maybe even save his life."

"Save his life? From what?"

"Well, you see, he's a thief." He strummed two lower notes quickly. "A real amateur too. Fresh to the trade and probably doesn't even know that his victim has sent soldiers to apprehend him. If I don't hurry, it'll be the end of him and that would be a shame because he's got real potential."

"You hang out with some colorful characters, Damien."

343

Damien stood up and gave him a sarcastic look and let it linger before taking a deep breath. "You sure are one to talk. Anyhow, I must be off to save my friend. I'll find you in a few months."

"Thank you, Damien."

"Oh, you are most welcome, my lord."

LIES

As Argel told another of the stories she's been told as a child, Ashan gazed out at the forest to imagine the scenes her words weaved. As he listened, it occurred to him that nearly half the stories she told were set in winter and that snow was sometimes an issue when it came to traveling, which made him wonder if they would run into snow before they reached Isirdost. He'd rarely seen snow in his life, unless one counted the white-topped mountains in the far distance, and he found himself wondering how often it snowed where she had grown up. He also wondered if stories told where he'd always lived were similar or very different from where she had lived. He'd heard a few stories from troubadours during festivals and read stories at the Misty Trail, but none of those had ever mentioned snow. In fact, most of the stories he heard never mentioned the weather or season at all, but seemed to focus on just the one character, their friends, and what plagued the world. Most involved a greedy knight, a vengeful spirit, or perhaps a wizard who wanted to rule or destroy everything.

As soon as the story came to an end, Frezz walked over to the fire and pulled the steaming black pot from it. He set it upon a nearby flat stone he had Ashan fetch from a creek earlier in the day and began filling their three wooden bowls. With the oddity of Frezz's lizard-like features now worn away, Ashan found he could recognize the cheer upon the man's face, and it made him happy that his friend was in such a good mood. Frezz began to hum a song that was quickly becoming familiar to Ashan, and he joined in on the humming while wondering what the words were. The longer he traveled with Frezz, the more he understood that, while very quiet, the man was perpetually at peace no matter what was going on around him. If Frezz had any doubts or was annoyed by anything, there was no outward sign. A moment later, he handed out bowls of food and took his seat to eat.

Instead of taking her food and finding a tree to hide behind as she once had, Argel sat upon a log that Frezz had rolled up close to the fire. She sniffed at the food cautiously, smiled, and began to breathe on it to get the temperature down. Ashan sniffed at his own bowl and smiled to himself. It was some sort of stew with a thick brown liquid, a variety of vegetables Argel had found early the day before, and a generous helping of meat. Following Argel's example, Ashan scooped some up with his spoon and began to blow. As he blew, he gave a silent thanks to whatever gods had decided to grant him his freedom and this new life.

Glancing over, he found that Argel sat a bit taller today than yesterday and even taller than the previous week. She also spoke at greater length and volume, as if she were no longer in a constant state of terror. She almost had the appearance of a normal person now, as she had been slowly shedding more and more of the wrapping as they had traveled. Currently, it almost looked like she wore a sleeveless shirt and shorts. Her golden hair hung loosely halfway down her back and, though it was tangled, it was clean now. Her skin was pale and, though she looked exhausted, her eyes were full of joy instead of drained. She wasn't the same as when they had met.

He began to think about why people and animals came in so many different colors and patterns and recalled a short passage in a book he had read somewhere he could not quite recall. The book had been all about birds and focused mostly upon their variety of colors, shapes of beaks, and other such things. He vaguely recalled being bored to tears reading it and only now wished he had paid more attention, perhaps even had read it twice. He recalled an interesting bit about an unusual bird colored in bright orange and red. Whatever the type was called, he could not remember, but the author had explained that the males were red and orange while the females were a dirt brown. Why the gods had made this so, he could not imagine. Of course, he considered horses then, as he had seen many different types and they all looked very similar to each other. There were no orange and red horses and if male and female horses were usually one color or another, he had no idea. *Perhaps the gods find horses too boring to make them in different colors like birds? Maybe the gods painted those birds to tell us not to hunt them?*

Thunderous drumming pulled Ashan from a dream about the shadow-man chasing him through a moonless night in the forest. He immediately grabbed his sword, scrambled to his feet, and scanned the forest. The faint morning sunlight was barely enough to let his eyes tell the trees from darkness. *They're coming.* He glanced about camp and saw that Argel was fast asleep and Frezz was missing. He turned his head left and right, identified the direction of the drumming, and crept that way. *We should run.* He continued only as fast as was reasonable in the darkness. Up a small hill, down the other side, and then flat ground for a fair distance. Up a second hill, down, then there was the big pond they had passed last evening and a very steep climb up the third hill. The top of this hill was a mass of rock with moss on most of

347

the surface and the other side was steep enough of a drop to call a miniature cliff. When he reached the top, the drumming seemed twice as loud, but he found nothing in the forest below.

"Ashan." Frezz called from his left.

Ashan ducked down with a gasp, raised his sword defensively, and then found Frezz laying on the stone a short distance away. Frezz rose and crept over to Ashan, eyes kept mostly on the forest below as he came.

"What are you doing?"

"I-" a sharp snap arose from the forest below and both turned to face it.

A man appeared in the distance wearing a filthy shirt with long, tattered sleeves and equally soiled britches. Every few steps were made audible by the snap of a twig or the occasional soft ting of metal striking metal. This far away, Ashan could barely make out the dark outline of a sword at the man's waist. Frezz grabbed Ashan's arm and dragged him down to the ground. The soldier traveled in a straight line, as if coming for Ashan and Frezz, but he glanced about the forest in a casual manner. After a minute, the man grew close enough to see that the sound of metal striking metal was caused by a metal plate he held and his fork striking it as he stabbed down into something he was eating. The soldier came to the very edge of the sheer rock face below, set his plate down upon a boulder as high as his knees, and walked to the nearest tree. He yawned loudly as he pulled his pants down, turned, squatted down, and let his back fall against the tree.

"I knew it." Ashan said softly.

"They've been very careful to keep their distance until now." Frezz pulled his backpack off and set it between Ashan and himself. He carefully riffled through a pocket and pulled free a rag and a small glass vial with a cork stopper in it.

"What's that?"

"A truth potion."

"For what?"

"We're going to capture that man and see what we can learn."

"But he has a sword. We'll wake his camp."

"Not if we are quiet."

Frezz dug through another pocket at the pack and pulled free a small leather case, which he placed on the ground before opening. There were three small metal spheres with sharp points sticking out all around and a coiled-up sling. He unstopped the vial, poured half the contents onto the rag, placed the spiked balls into the rag, and rolled them about the rag vigorously. He uncoiled the sling, loaded a ball into it, and slowly climbed to his feet. He spun the sling around one time and sent the ball flying. Ashan couldn't see where the thing hit the man, but the man let out a half-yelp, bolted upright, and pulled his pants up while turning in their direction. A moment later, he fell forward onto the ground. The drums died down to no more than a whisper in the same moment.

"If you see anybody else coming, whistle to let me know."

Frezz opened the main pocket of his pack, pulled out a big coil of rope, and tied it to the nearest tree. He practically flew down the rope and made very little sound in the process. He threw the man over his shoulders, returned to the rope, and was back up in short order. When he reached the top, Ashan saw that the soldier was awake and wide-eyed but did not move or speak.

"Gather my things and follow." Frezz whispered.

He caught up with Frezz quickly and followed in silence as they turned to the south and then followed a creek a few hundred strides. They came to a flat, rocky area at the side of the creek and Frezz set the man down with his back up against a large up shoot of rock. From there, he dug through his pack Ashan held and retrieved a handful of small glass vials. He picked out one full of a clear liquid with an unfamiliar symbol cut into the top of the cork and replaced the rest. He poured the vial into the man's mouth and sat down. Several minutes went by before anything seemed to happen. At first, the man began to move his mouth, but soon after that, he began to mumble. Eventually, his slurred mumbling became words and his eyes filled with terrified awareness of what was happening.

"Please," His breathing became panicked. "Don't...kill me...I... have gold." He looked a bit sideways at Frezz before continuing. "I also have food, so you don't have to eat me. Whatever you are, you don't need to eat me!"

"We aren't going to kill you unless we must." Frezz offered the man a smile. "Who are you?"

"Lord...Jasper of...House...Talrin. Please don't eat me."

"How many of you are there?"

"Fifty."

"And why are you following us?"

"You...tried t-to...kill...king...Hotar."

"Why have you not attacked us?"

"We...are...to follow. Keep you...north."

"Into a trap?"

"Y-yes."

"We aren't assassins." Ashan said.

"So, the king wants us alive?"

"I... don't know."

"Calm yourself, Lord Talrin. I am not your enemy, and the boy speaks the truth. We are not assassins."

"What poison is this?"

"Not poison, exactly. A paralytic and a truth serum. You'll be fine in an hour's time." Frezz explained.

The soldier smiled as if he were in a drunken stupor. "Maybe...maybe we're following the wrong people."

"No, your high king wants us for some reason. You aren't the first group to come after us." Frezz explained.

"Another group? You mean the one led by Lord Kairn, who failed to capture you." His face twisted in confusion. "I was sent, but then he...did something."

"We're escaped prisoners."

"Escaped prisoners? From the dungeon?" Fear took his face for a moment, but then was replaced with a placid, unthinking expression. His eyes grew hard after a few seconds and then it was plain to see that he was fighting off a deep confusion. "Something is wrong. I can't...think straight." The dullness returned to his face and his eyes wandered off to the trees, almost as if he were just about to fall asleep.

"Lord Talrin?" Ashan asked after a second.

The hardness returned to his face and his eyes focused on Frezz in a flash. "We're supposed to be chasing the assassin. Let me up! I can almost see-" His face returned to that dull expression and his breathing became calm.

"What's wrong with him?" Ashan asked.

"I'm not certain. This isn't from what I gave him." Frezz turned suddenly and looked off into the distance with worry taking his face. "They're coming. I can hear it."

Turning his attention, Ashan could hear the drums picking up again as well. "I hear it too."

"Just give me the assassin." Lord Talrin whispered. "Killing us."

"We're not going to kill you." Frezz said. He unstopped the other bottle with red liquid in it and held it to the man's mouth. "This should help to clear your mind."

Ashan ran the rest of the way back to camp, not at all surprised that Frezz outpaced him dramatically. When he arrived, he found that Argel had already woken up and was frantically packing her things. She gave him a glance that was full of worry and determination but went back to throwing things into her pack without speaking. Having discussed what they would do in such a situation, Ashan set himself to gathering his things as well. Once his things were gathered, he kicked dirt onto the fire pit and threw his pack over his shoulders. When he turned back to Argel, she was already twenty strides out of the camp area and waiting on him.

Several hundred strides later, they came upon a hill and raced up it. At the top, Ashan turned back to look for Frezz, but discovered ten soldiers in the distance. They were closing the distance at a terrifying, unnatural rate. He turned and waved for Argel to run without speaking and considered removing his pack to lighten his load. By the time they reached the bottom of the hill, the soldiers were right on their heels. Three of them passed, turned, and held out their swords threateningly.

"I've got you. Lower your weapons and come peacefully." One of the soldiers commanded.

Ashan quickly imagined different scenarios of attack and escape, but none of them worked out in his mind. Each man wore a thick gambeson in dirty white with that silhouetted crown at the center of the chest, which he was certain he couldn't penetrate with his sword. He imagined that there might have been a chance if he had a spear or a thin-bladed sword instead, but even if that were the case, he knew he couldn't take them all on. Their legs and heads were the only real targets he had, but since they were soldiers, he assumed that he had very little chance of breaking through their defenses to reach any target. He figured if there was only one or two of them, he would have stood a small chance in a fight if luck was on his side. Finally, he decided that there was no possible chance of winning and lowered his sword. He had to fight himself to let it drop to the ground, sure that the soldiers would strike him dead the moment he was unarmed. Instead, they came calmly to collect everything from Argel and Ashan and then marched them back along the way they came at sword-point.

When they arrived at their camp, Ashan was surprised at how large it was. There was a wagon full of crates and another with a large cage built onto it, which was where he figured they were taking him and Argel. There were at least twenty other soldiers swarming about the camp at that moment and none seemed surprised to see Ashan and Argel being led in at sword-point. Two men on the north side were chopping wood, five fires were going near the center of the camp, and the whole place was saturated with a savory bouquet of cooking meats. How he and Frezz had not caught the scent was beyond his understanding. Off in the distance stood a long row of medium-sized tents made from what appeared to be a sturdy white cloth and metal poles to give it a round form. They passed the wagon with the cage on it and continued across the camp, where Ashan soon spotted Frezz chained to a tree. From a distance, it appeared that Frezz was asleep or dead because he didn't stir, but when they arrived, Ashan saw Frezz's eyes were open, and he was breathing. What he thought were silver chains turned out to be something more as well. They had a subtle glow about them even in the early morning's light.

The soldiers placed Argel and Ashan with their backs against trees and chained them into place with silver-chained nets like the one restraining Frezz. The moment the chains were in place around his chest, Ashan began to feel a draining of his strength and an exhaustion setting in. The soldiers emptied the stolen packs out upon the ground, organizing everything they found as they searched through the lot.

When they found Frezz's small magic bag that carried far more than it appeared capable and turned it upside down, the avalanche of cold meats knocked two of them off their feet. Ashan expected them to grow upset and accuse Frezz of performing evil magic, but they set to sorting the mess out as if it were an unexpected but completely normal event.

As the soldiers sorted the mess out, organizing it in a manner such that everything could easily be seen, Ashan spotted another group of soldiers approaching from the other side of camp. Three walked on either side of a man wearing bright red shorts that flared out wildly at the knees, a flat off-white short-sleeved shirt, and a blue vest with massive wooden buttons that seemed too small for his frame. He also wore slender blue shoes with white socks that rose to the bottom of his knees with two gray bands at the top. His hair was obscured by a flattened wool beret in black with a massive green feather standing straight up at the front center with a dark eye painted upon it. He held a red tobacco pipe that he puffed on as he walked. He appeared the vision of a public fool, but his face wore a deep frown, and his eyes were filled with a deep hatred that seemed barely controlled. The man could barely be older than Ashan, but he walked as though he had worked a lifetime and the years had done his back in. Behind him a good fifteen strides, there were three additional soldiers escorting the man Frezz had captured. The man looked as though he were nearly asleep.

"Imbeciles." He screamed loudly when he arrived. He gave the scene a quick study before continuing. "You have ruined the plan."

"I am sorry, Lord Farlan." Lord Talrin said softly.

"You really are a sorry sack of shit." Lord Farlan retorted without looking back.

Lord Farlan sucked at his pipe and eyed the supplies on the ground for a long moment. "Which is the assassin?" he questioned. The other soldiers glanced at each other but did not speak. Lord Farlan walked over and gave Frezz a good examination. "I see you've implemented my tools as you were told. I guess you're not entirely useless men." He then walked over and examined Argel, who mumbled at him. He ignored her attempts to speak and poked her stomach softly and with the care of a doctor. He hummed to himself and squeezed her forearm in one hand. He then stepped over to Ashan, sucked at his pipe, and blew the smoke into Ashan's face as he studied his face. Another puff, another soft hum, and he stuck the pipe into his mouth and grabbed Ashan's hands. He forced them open and studied them in silence for a long moment. He hummed, blew smoke again and pulled Ashan's shirt up to his neck. He poked Ashan's stomach softly in two places and dropped his shirt.

"You are but children!" he said loudly. He turned to face Frezz and pointed at him with his pipe. "I could see you as a man easily mistaken for an assassin." Frezz perked up and looked at Lord Farlan. "Fetch my chair and more tobacco."

The man paced, smoked, and studied his captives for several minutes before a big wooden chair was delivered. The thing was plain but appeared sturdy. A short table was delivered moments later, set beside the chair, and a leather pouch came immediately thereafter. The man sat in the chair and grabbed the leather pouch without even looking. The whole thing was almost a show of how quickly and precisely it had gone. The man pulled a strand of metal from the pouch and began cleaning out his pipe. He hummed, studied Ashan, and quickly packed more tobacco into the pipe. A short while later, two soldiers arrived with food and drink. They set a plate with a steak upon the small table, poured something red from a dull silver pitcher into a golden goblet, and waited in silence.

Taking up a small silver knife and fork, the man gingerly and methodically cut the steak up into tiny pieces. Once done, he stabbed a single piece with his fork, brought it up to his mouth, and gave it a long sniff before placing it into his mouth. He chewed rapidly, swallowed, and then took a tiny sip from his goblet. He repeated this until the food was gone and then, with a wave of his hand, the soldiers came to remove all that they had brought. He then stood and lit his freshly packed pipe of tobacco.

"Load them into the cage." Lord Farlan announced. "Send scouts immediately." He turned and headed away, followed closely by the soldier carrying the leather pouch of tobacco.

Once they finished packing up all the supplies, they moved Frezz to the caged wagon with the chains still on him. Next, they came for Argel, who they practically had to carry. They took Ashan last and once he was loaded into the cage; they shut the door and pulled all the silver chains out through the gaps in the bars. As soon as the chains were pulled away, Ashan felt his strength return in full force. Argel's strength came back just as quickly but Frezz took several minutes longer.

"Are you okay, Frezz?" Argel questioned as he pulled himself into a seated position.

"Well enough." he responded as he began studying the camp.

"What were those chains doing to us?"

"It was some derivative of a sleeping spell." Frezz answered.

"They have a wizard?" Argel asked as she began scanning the camp as well.

"Not currently."

"You sound very calm for having been captured and accused of being an assassin." Argel said, the worry in her voice rapidly increasing.

"He didn't exactly accuse me of being an assassin. He said that he could see me as being easily mistaken for an assassin."

"What's the difference?" Ashan asked.

"We are being set up." Frezz replied.

356

"You think they'll kill us before we get where they're taking us?" Argel almost yelled in freight.

"Breathe, Argel." Frezz said softly.

"We're going to escape." Ashan declared as he too began studying the camp.

"What? How?"

"We'll figure it out. We must." Ashan said.

"There's only fifty of them and they're all under a spell. Watch them carefully and you'll notice that they come in and out of a state like sleep." Frezz explained.

"Only fifty? It was more than enough to capture us." Argel said.

"They captured you two, not me."

"You let them capture you?" Argel gasped.

"Yes."

"Why?" She almost shouted.

"We captured that one." Frezz pointed at Lord Talrin who was just standing in place with his eyes on the ground and swaying back and forth. "They need our help."

"They're going to kill us!" Argel's eyes were beginning to water and her breathing was becoming panicked.

"They won't get a chance." Frezz reassured her as he placed a hand upon her shoulder.

"We're locked up, Frezz!" she protested.

"We're just taking a ride, Argel." He said in a soothing voice.

"Free ride." Ashan smiled as he leaned back against the cage's bars.

"Sounds like a dangerous gamble." Argel frowned at them both.

"Life is dangerous." Frezz reassured her with his own smile.

The day passed in relative silence outside the cage as they traveled mostly to the north. Inside the case, Frezz and Argel napped on and off through the day while Ashan stayed awake to study what happened outside. Scouts came and went with news to direct the gathering along the easiest terrain. The soldiers slept on their horses in shifts, leaving only a few awake at a time to lead the formation. Oddly, they would all wake up at the same time whenever they needed to change direction.

Morning brought a steady breeze of cool air, which woke Ashan from a dream of being stuck alone in the cage surrounded by dead soldiers. He found Argel in much better spirits and looking not at all bothered by the cool air, which made him wish he had a better shirt on. Frezz seemed rather content to lay on the floor of their cage, that odd expression that Ashan had come to understand to mean the man was happy permanently on his face. The soldiers rose a short while later, gathered their horses, and set to work preparing to set out again. They moved a bit faster than the previous day, as if sleeping had rejuvenated their bodies, but they still moved about and performed their duties as if still mostly asleep. They saddled their horses, ate dried meat that was being passed around by Lord Talrin, and mounted their horses to wait. When Lord Farlan finally exited his tent, he had two soldiers gather water-skins from the rest, and they headed out of site to the south.

"Is there a river nearby?" Argel asked Frezz as she glared after the men.

Frezz yawned before pulling himself upright to a sitting position. He rubbed at his eyes and then scanned the forest for a long moment before speaking. "I doubt it. I think he's using magic to draw water up from deep down."

"You can do that?" Ashan asked as he stood up and stretched his legs.

"I cannot, but others can." Frezz replied.

"How can you tell if there's water in the area or not?" Ashan asked.

"The air near water tastes cleaner."

"Cleaner?" Argel questioned.

"Yes."

Just then, Lord Talrin walked by with a limp and a blank expression. He clumsily climbed up the side of the second wagon, stumbled over the mountain of supplies therein, and stopped at one of the two barrels at the front. He stood motionless for a moment, eyes on the barrel with a confused expression, and then began prying the lid from the thing with a small knife. When reached in and brought out a small bucket, which he held up and studied as if he didn't understand what the thing was. Finally, he reached into the barrel with his free hand and brought up a handful of dried meat chunks. Once full, he walked back to the edge of the wagon and climbed down again. He glanced this way and that before heading to the caged wagon.

"Lord Talrin, are you well?" The man took a handful of the meat, reached through the bars, and let it fall to the floor. "Lord Talrin?" The man didn't seem to hear him. He dropped a second portion of meat next to the first and headed towards the nearest soldier on horseback.

"What's wrong with them all?" Argel asked as she took a chunk of meat and sniffed it.

"Their minds are dulled. I expect that they are barely aware of what is happening around them." Frezz said as he grabbed a chunk of meat and began sniffing it.

"Frezz!" Argel nearly shouted as she pointed.

Turning, Ashan immediately spotted what had captured Argel's attention. A mounted soldier was sitting bolt upright in his saddle with his arms stretched out at either side. He was shaking and mumbling something repeatedly. Slowly, he tilted backward in his saddle until he came to rest on the horse's rump, at which point he tilted to the side. He hit the ground a moment later, eyes wide in terror as he began to convulse. He spewed blood and let out a guttural sound that he repeated quickly. Ahead, Lord Farlan stopped his horse, turned in his saddle, and watched the scene unfold with a satisfied smile. Nobody else even glanced at the scene and the body became still a few moments later. The men with the water-skins appeared in the distance just then.

"What happened, Frezz?" Argel asked as she looked to the floorboards of the wagon.

"He may have been poisoned or had an illness of the brain that just caught up with him. I'd bet on poison though."

"Poison?" She looked at the meat in her hand and terror spread across her face.

"The meat is fine. I would smell poison." Frezz said as he patted her on the shoulder.

"They're not going to stop and bury him?" She asked in shock.

"I guess not." Ashan stood and watched Farlan turn back around in his saddle and gave the horse a little kick. Not one soldier looked back as they began moving.

"Something is very wrong with these people." Argel whispered.

"Indeed." Frezz replied.

JUSTICE BE DONE

Days came and went in utter silence once Lasashu's voice departed him, betraying him in his time of need – *another curse from that demonic witch!* He'd spent the first three days and nights screaming and throwing rocks at the metal plate that covered the hole in the ceiling and he figured she had heard him and unleashed this latest curse upon him. *Probably because someone was starting to hear me. Yes, the strength of my will was breaking her curse and she had to stop me!* He smiled at that thought.

The room where they had placed him was rather small and lacked the basic comforts a man such as he deserved. In the back corner was a bucket and straw that he now had the shame of having been forced to use twice. *Twice!* For that insult alone, Lasashu had decided that their punishment would be having their fingers removed instead of their entire hands. At least with a stump, they could have had a blacksmith forge them a decorative hand or just a wooden hand they could cover with a glove to appear normal. They could even have hooks, knives, or any manner of attachment made to fit a stump, but with finger-less hands, they would always be reminded of their foul deeds. He would hold a celebration in the capital every year to remind everyone of his victory over such villainous bastards.

"Yes, that's what I'll do!" He laughed to himself as he glanced through the hole in the door.

Outside, there was a torn field that barely grew any grass. A body lay half-decomposed about thirty strides out and black birds pecked at the grotesque figure. If he stood and opened the peek-hole in the center of the door, he would get a better view, but he didn't care to see more than this now. Besides, he'd studied the scene before and knew what he would find. There was a long stretch of land full of rows of spikes shutting up from the dirt, large rocks, and a hundred skeletal corpses strewn across the first hundred strides. Further in the distance stood a red tent that he had heard about from soldiers, where vampires were supposed to be sleeping during the day.

"What would happen if they attacked while I was in here?" he wondered.

Surprised that the thought hadn't occurred to him earlier, Lasashu leapt to his feet and examined the large door. There was a thick, iron-wrought bar serving as a handle upon it, but no locking mechanism that he could see. He gave the door a yank and felt it move a tiny amount before stopping with a loud thud. He set himself to examining the door again for a hidden keyhole, but again found nothing.

"Children of whores, the lot of them!" he cursed and sat back down.

His stomach growled audibly, and he glanced over at the bucket of slop they'd lowered down several hours back. The stuff within had a bunch of green things that had been diced up, orange squares that were mushy, and a few other things he couldn't identify. Whatever meat was in it was stringy and looked to have been tenderized to the point of being nearly as thin as good paper. *Probably feeding me rat meat from the sewers!* He'd refused to eat it no matter how they had made it smell with clever spicing. *They will bring me steak! They WILL!* He screamed it in his head, pouring all his will into making them hear his thoughts if only in their dead, cruel hearts.

"The wicked creatures of darkness have no power to resist the will of the gods!" He said softly and glowered at the hole in the ceiling. "I will find a way. You cannot stop me!"

He glowered at the hole in the ceiling and poured all his hatred into the men he knew were just on the other side and wished them slow, agonizing deaths. He knew nothing of medicine, but he silently asked the gods to create something new and cruel for those men. "They're probably eating steak and laughing about what they've done to me!" he said as loudly as he could with his sore and itchy throat. Hearing his voice come out as little more than a croak stoked the fire in his heart. He climbed to his feet, ran across the room, grabbed his bucket, and threw it at the metal plate covering the hole above. He ran over to the bucket and threw it again. This time, it bounced off, hit the wall, and then rolled along the floor all the way to the big door. He huffed, balled his fists, and walked over to it. Picking it up, he noticed that one of the metal hoops was now loose. He turned and threw it as hard as he could. "Idiots can't even make a good bucket!"

He leaned back against the door and closed his eyes to calm himself. It didn't work and he started slamming his fists into the door and trying to scream. After a moment, the door stabbed his right fist with a big splinter. He cussed softly, pulled the thing out, threw it angrily, and began kicking the door with his right foot. He hoped the constant thud could be heard by the men above and that it annoyed them. He found a comfortable rhythm of kicking and smiled up at the hole as he imagined them not being able to get to sleep from the sound. He laughed. Softly at first, but then hard, which hurt his throat, but he didn't care.

After a few minutes of kicking, his left foot slipped on the floor just as he was bringing the other up to throw at the door. He fell and just before his but hit the ground, something pulled up on his shirt, preventing him from landing on the floor. Looking up, he found that his shirt had snagged on the door's handle, which had bent downward at a harsh angle. He put his feet beneath himself and stood a quarter of the way up, but stopped when he heard a soft clicking. The door handle had moved back up with him. He twisted and freed his shirt with one hand. As he did so, he found that the handle on the door sprang up to its original position. He grabbed the handle and pushed it down gently until a loud click came from within the door. He pulled the door and gazed out upon the field. It took a moment for him to figure it out.

He studied the scene for a long while wondering what he should do. First, he considered going left or right along the wall until he found a way up it or around, but then he remembered that the wall spanned the entire length of land from West to East. *Two days by horse, was it?* That was too long without food. Then he began to consider how stupid everybody at the wall was. *Would they know a vampire when they saw one? This place really is a prison for damned fools.* He pulled the door all the way open so that if anybody ever checked on him, they would know he had escaped their pathetic trap. Triumphant, he stepped out into the warm light of day and headed north, figuring it couldn't be more than a half-day's march to the next town. He'd find a road shortly and, with any luck, he would then be picked up by a trader.

Not twenty paces later, he came upon a skeleton with a shattered skull. He grabbed a knife in the dirt at its side and examined it. It was plain and rusty, but mostly sharp. *Probably someone who fell from the top of the wall, given how stupid everyone here is,* he concluded. Thirty more paces and he spotted what must have once been an expensive silver sword with a broken cross-guard and a heavily chipped blade. He picked it up and continued onward. *Now I can defend myself.* Thirty strides later he came to a row of spikes that stabbed out at a sharp angle about as high as his stomach, where he had to turn sideways to fit through the space between the two of them.

Beyond, there was a small ditch running before the spikes, which was two hands deep and a little bit wider than his feet. It explained the rotting corpse that had been impaled on a spike through the neck a good fifty strides away. He'd heard a story of a soldier who had come out to gather arrows and tripped – *a clumsy idiot!*

In total, there were six rows of spikes and seven little trenches. Between them were randomly placed clusters of spikes forming small circles, boulders, and easily five-hundred arrows scattered about. They were longer, thicker arrows than ones he'd grown up seeing, which he assumed was simply a product of ignorance of the proper way to make arrows. He grabbed one arrow and found it was almost as thick as his thumb, almost as long as his arm, and split down the middle. It was also broken at the end so that there was no head on it. He tossed it over his shoulder and continued towards the red tent.

When he arrived at the tent, he found that there was a small table within. The wooden top had several deep cracks and appeared to have never been treated to survive being used outdoors. It was a good thing too, as the top hadn't been cut square and all four legs were different sizes. He searched carefully and found several broken quills, thick brown scraps of paper, and several empty bottles that might have once held alcohol. Finding nothing useful, he departed the tent and headed north again.

Lasashu was woken by the soft light of morning, and, for a moment, he imagined he was back home and that he'd simply slept on his balcony. He just needed to get up, cross into his room, and call out for his servants. Darla would fetch him something to eat faster than the others. *Was her name Darla or Marla?* His stomach reminded him of how long he'd gone without a proper meal, and he begrudgingly sat up to get a look at the world. He stretched a bit, grabbed his knife, and climbed to his aching feet.

The wall was now far behind, and hills lay to the north. He grabbed his sword and headed north-west and began to wonder why so many soldiers made a big deal about having compasses. *Getting around can't possibly be that difficult. I have been surrounded by complete idiots!*

As he walked, he kept a careful eye out for anything he could hunt or pick from the ground. He was partial to mushrooms, but he would also accept carrots or berries. Now, all he could see was the same grass as yesterday and the occasional patch of dirt. A flock of birds came into view a short while later and he wondered if they would make a good meal, but they did not land; rather, they flew straight south until he lost track of them in the sky.

He walked for what seemed half a day before coming upon a hill that rose five times higher than the surrounding mounds. Hopeful that the height would allow him to see far enough to find a river or town, he climbed the hill quickly. At the top, he found that it was one of three hills, between which was nestled a darkly stained building that might have been as large as his sleeping chamber on the inside, three wagons, and a small, fenced area full of dirt and several buckets.

He ran down the other side of the hill, barely keeping himself upright as he went, and headed directly to the building. "Hello!" he called out, surprised that his voice came a fair bit louder than the last time he had spoken. He stopped before the small building's door and took a moment to compose himself. It was not proper for a king to be out of breath and seem in a hurry, especially when dealing with commoners. He waited until he had full control of his breathing, ran his fingers through his hair, and grabbed the door handle. Pulling open the door, he was assaulted by a stench so strong that his eyes burned, and he had to take several steps to escape it. He stumbled away and dry-heaved at the ground for a moment. When the urge to vomit finally passed, he took a deep breath, pulled open the door all the way open, and walked ten strides away before daring to breathe again. It was dark inside the building, but he didn't need to see what was making that smell, for he had smelled rotting corpses before.

He looked around for evidence of what had occurred and to maybe get a sense of how many bodies were inside that building, but there was little to go on. The door appeared undamaged, and he figured that meant nobody had broken in. *Most murders are done by relatives, friends, and lovers.* He remembered that from his lectures readily, being one of the only subjects he had found interesting. There was a small pen of roughly hewed wood that might have been used to contain four oxen or three horses, depending on their size. The pen's gate stood partly open, and he found that the thing had been secured by a thin cord, which was broken and frayed, much like how his bootlaces would look when they finally broke. He concluded that the animals had gotten free and were somewhere in the grassy mounds feasting. The three wagons were of a standard size, but that didn't give him much to go on. Perhaps there could have been two men per wagon, but traders often traveled with footmen for protection as well.

The first wagon he came to was loaded with animal pelts. There were enough there to make a hundred good winter coats, as best he could tell. He moved on to the second wagon and found it full of casks of different sizes but didn't check them. The third wagon was filled with a wide assortment of goods that appeared to have been thrown in at random. There was a plain chest at the rear that had seen better days, a few rusty swords fit for commoners, a bundle of clothes, a mound of leather belts, a musical instrument that was a circular tube he didn't know the name of, and a barrel.

Lasashu checked the chest first off, expecting it to be empty; after all, money was a great motivator for murderers and thieves alike. Inside, he found several leather bags full of coin, bottles of ink, quills, and a leather-bound book. Opening the book, he immediately recognized it as a businessman's ledger, laid out in a manner very similar to the method his tutors had taught him. As he went through the pages, he noticed the occasional entry with no description of goods;

instead, there were poorly drawn eyes, a sharp tooth, or a hand. They were all associated with large sums of money marked as incoming payments. *Shady dealings.* He reached the last page with entries and studied it carefully; certain that it would off some clue to the approximate time of death for those in the building. There was a notation in the middle of the page that stated "Hunting north of Alguin. Sixty pelts gathered." from a month back. The next entry, being the last, had a sloppily drawn hand and the date, which was two weeks ago, to the best of his knowledge.

Lasashu replaced the book and dumped out the bags of coin, given the lot a careful count. It was mostly silver and copper coinage, which wouldn't buy much, but it was more than he had before arriving. From there, he headed back to the building, but stopped a good ten strides from the door. He removed his shirt and used his knife to cut it into strips. He cut two small squares, stuffed them up either of his nostrils, and wrapped the longer strips around his head so that they covered his mouth.

He stepped inside and breathed gently to test his cloth masking. The smell was still strong, but not overbearing, especially if he focused on breathing through his mouth. Three tables lined the wall to his right, each with cups and bottles set as if in use. Three bodies lay face up in the heart of the room and four more were in the far corner, as if they'd tried to retreat as far away from the door as possible. He walked to the center and checked the three clustered there. One man's skull appeared to have been crushed, while the other two did not present with such obvious injuries. He searched and found each had a small pouch of coin. Their shirts were darkly stained, but he could not make out more. Each had been armed with a good dagger and Lasashu traded out his with the best of theirs.

Moving on, he checked the bodies in the corner. There were several broken bottles on the floor here, which he guessed had been whatever cheap swill they'd been drinking shortly before their deaths. Two had small pouches with copper coin, one had a moderate amount

368

of silver coin, but the last man had a hefty bag of silver coin. He searched the rest of the room but found nothing more than dust and unopened bottles of alcohol. Finally, he grabbed the legs of the body of the man with the richest coin-purse and dragged him around his compatriots – or attempted murderers – and out the door.

In the light of day, Lasashu was surprised to find that the man had died from a neck wound that was most odd. It was a deep wound with jagged edges. The blood had poured out and down his front and back about halfway down his shirt. *It should have gone further.* Lasashu knelt and looked at the man's hands but found them in pristine condition. Not even an unusual scar. One-by-one, Lasashu dragged the bodies out into the daylight and examined them. Each had a chunk of the neck torn out and not enough blood on their clothing or the floor inside to say they had bled to death. They were all very pale though.

He took a few bottles of alcohol from within the building and used the contents to wash his hands, arms and anywhere else he thought he might have contacted the dead before checking the clothing on the wagon for anything that would fit. Luckily, he found a sturdy pair of britches and a sleeveless shirt that was just about approaching soft enough for his tastes. He then checked the barrels and found that one was full of shelled almonds, and another was salted meat. He stuffed himself, opened a bottle from the building for drinking, and walked out of the little nightmare town to the top of the big hill on its west side in search for whatever beasts of burden he might find.

From atop that hill, he spotted them almost immediately. There were two horses and four brown mules gathered around a mound in a group. He headed down after them with a smile wider than that accursed wall. It was a short walk to them, and they didn't seem to mind as he approached. Remembering how most of the horses had reacted to him before, he approached the first mule at its side in case it decided to rear back and kick at him. It made a short, guttural sound, lifted its head and just looked at him as it chewed a mouthful of the green grass. One of the horses gave him a casual look, but the others just kept on eating as if they hadn't noticed his arrival.

"Alright, you. You're going to get me out of here." He reached out gently to pet the mule and was pleasantly surprised that it leaned into his hand eagerly.

Vampires! The realization struck him hard and fast, nearly taking the air from his lungs. His heart began to race then as he pictured how the wounds on those men had been caused and why there was so little blood. *They bled to death, but vampires drank all their blood!* He wanted nothing more than to take off running but held his composure as best as he could. "You want go with me?" he asked as he scratched the ugly beast behind its ear. A second mule finally took notice and walked up along the first and nudged Lasashu's arm with its nose. He gave it a gentle petting as well for a minute and then took a slow step backward. They followed and it took everything he had to keep himself from cheering.

Slowly but surely, Lasashu led the group around the big hill to the path into the nightmare town and to the first wagon. Along the way, he gave each a fair petting and scratching and didn't even care for their foul odor. Getting them harnessed to the wagon was a challenge, as he had never done such before and because they wanted to circle about him and get his attention. He eventually figured out how to get the mules connected to the wagon and then used rope to tie the horses to the back of it so that they had to come along as well.

IN THE RIGHT PLACE

The days after breaking off from the advanced war party passed at an agonizing pace, like honey in the dead of winter. Lord Kairn had gathered two hundred of his best, met up with Lady Voth's forces of roughly one-hundred and seventy soldiers, and headed east. If his life were simpler than it was, he wouldn't have been so stressed the past few days; however, Lady Voth's situation turned out to be much more dire than he had understood.

Lady Voth's soldiers were young, untrained, disorganized, and in desperate need of leadership. They were only roughly organized into teams and half of them acted as though they were the highest authority among their ranks, and they bragged about it constantly. Questioning their rank, training, or experience was an easier way to start a fistfight with them than slapping a northerner's wife in front of him. They were the leftovers and she had barely managed to keep them in her employment. In a desperate attempt to maintain her dwindling forces

371

two years back, she had purchased horses in such numbers that this group of her forces had enough for each soldier. They took advantage of that as well, with not one of them marching unless they needed to stretch their legs, which meant her soldiers were soft and the horses overworked. Some had heavy armor, some light, and some none. Among those with heavy armor, the majority were secondhand or passed down from grandfathers or uncles. None bore banner or symbols of House Voth. Unfortunately, the problems didn't stop there either. Even for southerners, they were especially hot-headed, impatient, and disrespectful even to Lady Voth in front of Lord Kairn.

On their first night to make camp, those soldiers had argued over tent arrangements for hours, which ended with sloppy rows and at least four men with facial injuries that required stitches. They ate in small groups, each cooking for themselves and causing a great consumption of wood and wasted food supplies. The second night had been very similar in the overall picture, but with the addition of a stabbing that, luckily, hadn't been fatal.

So it was that Lord Kairn had to make a show of things. He marched with his men as much as possible instead of riding his horse and working on his notes, letters, and reading his newest books. He made sure he was seen handing down orders to his men and that those men were seen going about the business of carrying out those orders, which often meant they were dividing duties to those below them and holding people responsible for failure and success. It was like a game for them, and they were glad to play. Of course, some of his newest soldiers also needed to see that he would take his own turn at the most unpleasant of duties, like digging latrines. *Never ask a man to do a thing you would not also do*, his father's lessons constantly came to mind, especially when he was doing chores he did not want to do. Eventually, those men employed by House Voth would either give up or fall into the rhythm of how he did things.

For her part, Lady Voth had quickly adapted to the rhythm of life on the march. In the first days, she hadn't been awake early enough and had to scramble to get prepared and would fall asleep in her saddle for an hour. How anybody could sleep while riding a horse, he did not understand. *Must be a southern thing,* he had decided. Lord Kairn had almost grown accustomed to seeing her hair in a tangled mess, but that passed. What he wasn't sure he would grow accustomed to was her manner of dress. Some days, she wore plain brown shorts with a tattered shirt and others she wore a black riding dress fit for a ball. She had trouble starting in the mornings, but she was always pleasant and never complained about the heat, the bugs, or the hour of day.

Today was a brown trousers and tattered shirt day. She went straight from her tent to her horse and caught up with him after giving out orders. Lord Kairn vaguely watched the tearing down of the camp from atop his horse with his notebook in one hand.

"I have to hand it to you, Lord Kairn." Lady Voth commented with a smile. "I have never seen my soldiers so organized before."

Keep your eyes on the road and forest, Lord Kairn scolded himself.

"They just need guidance." He tried to focus on his notes, which he hadn't been able to go over in days.

"Are they not following your orders? Did you not set an example for them?"

"Any fool can bark orders. I ask my men to do things. As for setting an example, sometimes that's not the key to establishing order." He glanced up at her and saw her eyes were full of confusion.

"What do you mean?"

"What is that man's name, Lady Voth?" He pointed to the nearest of her soldiers. He was a young man with a medium build, long brown hair, and an aimlessness in his gait.

"I do not know, Lord Kairn, but why does it matter?"

"It's fine not to know. They are soldiers under your employ, and it is their job to do as you wish just like anybody else."

"Then why do you ask?"

"Because it matters. It matters to them and, given your situation with losing so many to your neighboring lords and ladies, it should matter to you."

"You expect me to learn all their faces and names, Lord Kairn?" she looked almost insulted.

"It's not about what I expect, Lady Voth. It's about how you treat people when you are under stress. They are disorganized because there is no clear structure of authority among them, and you've bought them all horses to try to keep them. So, they're spoiled as well."

"I have had little choice in the matter. Nobody wanted to walk from town to town and I've got fewer soldiers now than in years past. It was either get horses or fail to have soldiers to keep the peace in half my territory. A peace that has been greatly strained by outside forces these last few years, I might add." She explained.

"You could have threatened war against those who were intentionally taking your forces away and, as I hear it, trespassing into your lands to intercept your tax collectors."

"Those-" she stopped quickly, her face turning red with anger, and took a few slow breaths. "Any one of them would have destroyed me in open conflict, Lord Kairn."

"My sources suggest they were destroying you covertly about as quickly as war would have and without taking loses."

"Yes, you could say that."

"I guess you could have pretended you didn't hate them instead." Lord Kairn gave her a wry smile.

Lady Voth twisted, put her hands on her hips, and let her face express her loathing for whichever people she was thinking of expertly. She held her tongue while she visibly considered her reply, which took a long minute. Finally, she faced forward and took several deep breaths before speaking.

"Lord Kairn, I would rather eat a rotting, diseased corpse's unwashed feet than spend my life catering to the politically calculated mechanisms and pretend feelings of such people."

Lord Kairn gave a laugh at the image and nearly dropped his book. Lady Voth looked away quickly, but not so far away that he didn't catch that she was quietly laughing at him. His father had told him something similar about dealing with soldiers who had been disrespectful to him when he was fourteen and, though it took a few years to really settle into his mind, it had done the trick. *Thanks, dad,* he thought, looking up at the sky and wondering if, somewhere, his father was looking back at him. *It's a shame I don't have time to have all those lessons put to paper.* He'd always thought that he'd have time to have it done when he was older, perhaps with kids of his own who would already have taken over the endless responsibility of running the family affairs. Sadly, it was unlikely that any of his siblings would do that work and so it was likely that a great many of his father's teachings would be forever lost upon his death. *I should write the most important ones down.* But how could he write down his father's warm hugs and that loving look in the old man's eyes that had seemed to grow deeper with each year?

"Pardon the language, Lord Kairn."

"Not at all. I find your directness a relief."

"You mean that didn't ruffle your northerner feathers?"

"No."

"I think I get your point though." She said after several minutes passed in silence. "How long before we reach our destination?"

"Another few days if that shadow-man put us where Advisor Narn instructed, but I have my doubts."

She stood up in her saddle and gazed ahead. "Couldn't the assassin just...go east into the mountains?"

"Stories say that the immortal giants live there. Nobody would go there."

"That's just a legend. There are no giants left living. I doubt they ever truly existed." She laughed.

"It may be just legend to people our age, but when there was trade with Isirdost, there were no trade routes that went through there. Stories say there is a lake with water blessed by the gods and that any who drink from it will be healed of any injury no matter how severe." He paused a moment as he recalled the many stories his father had told him. "It is also said that should a healthy person drink it or take it beyond the mountains, they will be cursed with grave luck." He gave her a smile. "I would believe there is a lake. Perhaps with tainted water from mining. Why do you think that trade routes would avoid such a place? Horses and people need water, do they not?"

"Who knows. There are a thousand stories. Like the Maiden of Murray's Lake or the spirit army of Rodrick's Point."

They continued for a few minutes in silence before she spoke again. "I've never been north of the capital in my life."

"I have." Keeping his eyes locked on the horizon, he caught the scent of Lady Voth and tried to ignore the suddenly increased rhythm of his heart. "The great grasslands make the Forbidden Forest look small on a map."

"Did your father take you to Isirdost when you were little?"

"No, but we did come north to the grasslands during spring to watch the great herds gather. I don't know anybody who has been to Isirdost."

"That's because most of your trade is done in the heart of the kingdom. All you lords from the capital stay close to home in everything you do." Lady Voth sounded playful and angry at once.

"No, it's because it's illegal to trade with Isirdost and all of you southerners think we're all stuffed shirts, too full of ourselves to come haggle when really we just don't want to come argue over the price of rice every season."

"You northerners just hate haggling. You think you can march on down and tell us we're going to give you the world for a single copper! Probably with shaved edges too!"

"Well, we do have to recoup the costs of visiting so frequently. You southerners should be grateful that we visit at all during the summer with how little you wash your feet."

Her pretend gasp of shock almost sounded honest. "Why, I didn't know that you northerners could smell someone's feet with your heads shoved so firmly up each other's rear ends." This was the type of southern humor that could start a midnight bar fight that he so missed between visits.

"It smells better than southern homes and the smell washes out much easier."

"We'd love to have you come visit **every** summer! We could use your stuffed shirts to make scarecrows to save our crops." she laughed.

Lord Kairn gave himself a sniff, doing his best to mimic the exaggerated mannerisms he imagined Damien would use in the situation, and then gave Lady Voth his best attempt to appear offended. She furrowed her brows at him in an almost serious manner.

"See! You northerners take offense at everything."

"And you southerners fight over everything."

"Good morning, Lord Kairn!"

The genuine, excited tone of the voice behind those words didn't even register to Lord Kairn until after he was off his horse. He moved his book of notes to his off-hand and drew his sword with his good hand. He ran upon the shadow-man and slashed at it twice before attempting to elbow it in the face.

"Oh, it *is* great to see you again, Lord Kairn. Your sense of humor is so unique." The thing smiled at him as he swung his sword through its smokey skull. "High-king Hotar sent me to help you along to your destination."

"NO!"

Its smile faded then as Lord Kairn swung his sword through its center again. "Please, Lord Kairn. Help is here. Me being here is good for you."

"NO! Don't do anything."

"Apologies. I know the experience is unpleasant for you all."

"Go away. You ruin everything."

"Lord Kairn?" Lady Voth approached from behind the shadow-man with a sword at the ready. "What is that thing?"

"It's Ras'vetra!"

"I don't have a choice. High-king Hotar wants you in place as soon as is possible."

"Why not just send you after the assassin?"

"Trust me, Lord Kairn."

"It's because you'll betray anybody for the assassin, isn't it?"

He felt the cold tingle run through his body and jumped forward to tackle the shadow, but the world spun about and was swallowed by the darkness. Lord Kairn's freshly filled stomach protested after the third change in direction, but he held everything down firmly as he

378

waited for the world to return. When it did, he took care of where the end of his sword was and how he took the blow with the ground. He climbed to his feet immediately and checked for the creature, ready to start swinging as soon as he did. Finding no sign of the thing, he turned his attention to Lady Voth, who was on her side with a shocked expression upon her face. Her sword lay just beyond reach, and she didn't appear injured.

"Lady Voth, are you well?" He knelt at her side.

"I am, but I fear I may lose my breakfast." She groaned.

"It will pass shortly. I'd suggest just not moving for a few moments."

"You've experienced this before?"

"A few times."

He stood and checked the rest of camp to see how many had made it and how many had been left behind. From a quick glance, it appeared that most had been sent along, but it was difficult to get a head count with most laying on the ground or down on their hands and knees. Seeing no injuries and hearing no obvious cries for help, he turned his attention to the world around them. They were in the gap between two tall rocky hills with sparse grass, which sat a short distance before a great mountain with a white cap. After spinning around twice, he headed up the hill, examining the world with a careful eye as he went. Halfway up, he spotted thick, green forestry in the gap between hills in the distance. In the opposite direction, the land was all tall hills with sparse grass and a mix of light brown and gray rock.

Confirmation came in the form of an equally monstrous mountain to the left of the first and the great forest a short distance away. He did not need to see the third mountain to know it was hidden by the one looming overhead. He took in the view of the mountain with both dread and awe. It had been one thing to have been traveling in the great grasslands before, but now they had entered the rumored lands of giants. Having not had time to really write down ideas on how to deal

379

with giants of unspecified size in combat, he felt woefully unprepared, which he could imagine his father berating him for in that tone that had always stabbed his heart with a burning cold.

He considered what his father would say and looked down from that awesome peak above to check the ground for approaching giants, which was suddenly more terrifying an image in his mind than it had been previously. White specks caught his attention two hills over and, focusing on that, he also found pricks of reflecting sunlight.

"Lord Kairn."

Turning, he found six of his soldiers. Sergeant Janal and Captain Gorlich lead the others, each just then sheathing sword or shouldering a bow. Lord Kairn walked over to them at the crest of the hill and glanced down at the forces below. The combined forces were drawing together into a large circle around the supply wagons, horses collected in the center, and multiple scouts were just now riding away at speed. "Deserters, Lord Kairn." Captain Gorlich said grimly. Looking to the west, he spotted at least fifteen soldiers riding away on horses.

"Should we have them brought back?"

"No. I cannot blame them for being afraid."

"And if they return?"

"Think of some creative work to keep them busy. Now, any injuries to report?"

"Nothing serious, Lord Kairn. Scrapped knees, a broken nose or two, and a whole lot of clothing that smells of vomit." Captain Gorlich spoke plainly, as if nothing of interest had occurred.

"Sergeant Janal, get a count going to see if we're missing anybody aside from the deserters."

"Yes, Lord Kairn." The man turned immediately and ran down the hill.

"I want a watch established up here immediately and at least three surrounding hills. I did see something interesting a few hills over." He turned about and pointed to the one he'd noticed.

"Glass? Water?" Captain Gorlich asked as he squinted.

"I can't tell, but it stands out."

"I'll get twenty men ready, my lord."

"Good man." He patted Captain Gorlich on the shoulder and headed down the hill.

Lord Kairn marched down the hill calmly, knowing that he had to set an example after what had just happened. *If you are calm when things are falling apart around you, those who follow you will feel that things are going according to your plans,* he recalled his father's words. He had been describing war situations at the time, but Lord Kairn felt it applied to this situation as well. He had not expected this to happen, but he couldn't let it shake his outward appearance of confidence.

"Lord Kairn!" Lady Voth gave a yell and a wave as he returned.

"Yes, Lady Voth?"

"What was that?"

"Its name is Ras'vetra." He headed to his horse, and she fell in at his side.

"Not the shadow. I mean the fact that everything went dark as night and now we're in an entirely different place."

"Oh. I don't recall what he called it, but he can move people about with magic. You grow accustomed to it...perhaps slowly."

"You   could   have   warned   us."
"I had no idea King Hotar was going to send Ras'vetra to do that." He pulled himself up onto his horse and searched for his book of notes.

381

"Where are you going?"

"To investigate something."

"I'm going with you." She turned and ran for her horse.

"I would rather you stay here, Lady Voth. At least until we have surveilled the area."

"Nonsense!" she shouted as she ran for her horse and practically threw herself upon it. She produced a mess of blue and gold thread from somewhere and began tying her hair into a tight tail at the back of her head. Captain Gorlich appeared shortly with twenty men on horseback, half carrying swords and half with bows. Lord Kairn gave Lady Voth a glance and she gave him a sharp nod that said she would entertain no further discussion about staying behind.

Lord Kairn searched his book of notes, considered the news Damien had given him, and pondered Ras'vetra's abilities. Suddenly it made sense that the vampires had reached White Rock without being discovered along the way there, but the idea that the king could be dealing with their kind was too much to believe.

"What are you reading at a time like this?" Lady Voth asked.

"Just my own thoughts."

"Strategies you've put together?" She smiled a bit. "I have heard that you like to plan things out carefully."

"I do, but these are not related to our task here." He closed the book and put it away.

"Something you don't want to share?"

"Not particularly."

"I thought we were allies, Lord Kairn."

"We are, Lady Voth, but I have a great many plans in the works and not enough time at hand to explain it all. Never enough time." *So little time left before I die.*

"Perhaps later?"

"Perhaps."

They arrived upon the gap between hills that led to their target and found it littered with shattered bones of man and beast alike, but mostly they found long-rotting bodies in demolished armor. They stopped at the first group of dead men in armor and Lord Kairn let Captain Gorlich take the lead on investigating the scene. From atop his horse, he could see patterns among the bodies, but overall, a lot of them had been fleeing something in clusters or waves.

Captain Gorlich examined the area carefully and approached a short while later with a rusted helmet in his hands. Inside the helmet, Lord Kairn found several rings, each bearing outward facing letters and symbols. They all followed the same layout: family name, rank and then a symbol that he didn't understand. One had a feather, another a sword, and most of the rest had hammers.

"Soldiers from Isirdost." Lord Kairn dropped the rings back into the rusted hat and gazed out at the scene in shock.

"At the border, Lord Kairn."

"Indeed." He counted the dead he could see just in the gap and then looked to the hill ahead. "Send two men back for scouts, gather any identification, tally the dead, and keep this quiet until we learn more."

"Identification,   Lord   Kairn?"
"Yes, necklaces, rings, branded helms or shields, and maybe bonding rings if you find any. I want to gather every shred of data we can about what happened here." he explained.

"Yes, my lord."

"Do you really think it prudent to investigate this at this time, Lord Kairn?" Lady Voth asked softly at his side.

"Yes. Whatever killed these soldiers could come for us."

Lord Kairn had constructed several decent ideas about what had occurred by nightfall. Most of the bodies were scattered about on the south and west of the hill, most facing away, and those further away were generally found to be wearing lighter armor. There were parts of smashed wagons all along the north and eastern side of the hill, where it seemed that they had tried to build a defensive wall. Scavengers had picked the field clean of any useful or valuable items long ago, leaving the dead to rot. Well, they'd taken their own dead from the field. Outside of this, there wasn't much to go on. The searching hadn't turned up so much as a single mismatching arrow that might have come from the enemy. It appeared almost as though the enemy had brought a hundred catapults and attacked in unison. After that, they used blunt force weaponry, as everybody bore broken bones.

"How can you tell the time since these soldiers have died?" Lord Kairn turned to Sergeant Janal, who was clearly worried by the furrow in his brow.

"The weather and state of decay, my lord. The weather is cooler up here, which slows decay."

"Disturbing." Lady Voth said.

"Very." Captain Gorlich agreed softly.

Deciding he needed a break from thinking about the discovery, Lord Kairn grabbed the book A Jolly Chant of Death that he'd taken from the necromancer's cabin. Opening it to the first page, he found this was one of the books that offered pictures instead of words. There was a drawing of a few skulls, feet, and eyeballs that appeared to be

384

sitting on a flat surface. On the second page, he found a simple poem of six groups of four sentences each, telling a story of murder by stabbing. The next page contained another poem in four groups of four sentences which read like a letter describing the writer's hatred to the reader. Again and again, he found poems describing murder, the sensation felt by the one doing the stabbing, and another letter detailing the writer's hatred of the reader. Eventually, he closed it and focused on more important matters.

"You look especially troubled, Lord Kairn." Lady Voth said after a while.

"Busy times lately." He yawned and gave her a look. She sipped at her tankard of mead and gave a small, reassuring smile. The fact that she was drinking was understandable, but the fact that she hadn't downed half the bottle already was very confusing for a southerner, especially considering the horrid scene she'd witnessed.

"Is something the matter, Lady Voth?" He tried to indicate the bottle of wine by looking from her eyes to it repeatedly.

"No, why do you ask?"

Seeing the confusion on her face, he realized that she hadn't understood. "You're not really drinking that."

"This?" She hefted the bottle in one hand.

"That."

"Yes I am."

"Well, not much."

"Just a little. Tonight, I just need a little fire in my belly to fight off the chill in the air." she explained.

"I could send someone to fetch you a blanket."

"Not that kind of cold." She scolded.

"Oh. Yes, I suppose a bit would help with that."

"I gather that you love your books and long thinks."

"Well, sometimes life takes a lot of planning and thinking. What about yourself?"

"Hardly. Everywhere I turn, I find that even my allies have," she glanced about the fire quickly and went on with a bitterness to her voice that he hadn't heard before. "Made my options plainly clear to see."

"Allies can be quite...enlightening at times."

"Well, there are a few allies of mine I would love to enlighten right back." She gave him a sour expression.

Across the fire, Captain Gorlich snorted once, scratched his throat, and raised just one eyebrow at Lord Kairn. In return, Lord Kairn cleared his throat and rubbed his forehead as one might when exhausted from a long day. They'd talk later at night about what Lady Voth had just said.

HATRED

When Emma entered the tent to fetch a bucket of ice, she was surprised to find that only one of the brothers was there. Vessir sat on a little wooden stool at the back of the tent before two big metal tubs. He wore white pants that looked to have been left out in the weather for five years and nothing else, which allowed Emma to see the extensive bruising on his chest, ribs, arms, and legs. Oddly, it appeared that his face had been left unharmed. Violent owners, to Emma's understanding, often did not bruise faces for some reason she had yet to learn. He wore a sour expression, as though he were actively planning on committing murder. His eyes moved up slowly as she approached, but he didn't speak. An older man wearing nothing more than torn and faded brown trousers came in from the side opening of the tent carrying a small bucket of water in either hand.

"Morning." the older man offered her a toothy grin as he set the buckets down.

"Good morning." she returned his smile and stopped short of the two tubs. "Good morning to you as well, Vessir."

"Oh, he cannot hear you, miss." The older man explained.

"How so?"

"He and his two brothers did try an escape some days ago, miss. King Hotar, bless his name, wasn't keen on it and had them beaten and this one cannot hear no more."

The man explained it with a grand smile, like he was proud to be speaking or proud to be gossiping. The latter wouldn't have surprised Emma, as many people considered information as valuable as gold, especially if they were able to get that information into the right ears. There were even those who believed that if they found information with high enough value, they would win their freedom. She had never seen that happen, but valuable information often afforded her good treatment from her owner and privileges that normal slaves like the men before her would probably never experience. One of her favored luxuries was soap and the occasional heated bath in her master's home.

The old man grunted as he lifted one of the buckets and poured it into the nearest tub. He was overly thin, lanky, had a hunched back, and a tiny bit of hair upon his head. He glared into the small pool of water with a smile on his face that didn't fade, almost as if he were entertained and in awe with something beautiful. She'd met simpletons who were like that, but this man's eyes had an intense light within them that made her skin crawl.

"Are you okay, Vessir?" She squatted down to look him over and gave him a reassuring smile.

Vessir did not respond. He reached with his right arm and, stretching his fingers out wide, began to hum softly. Moments passed and the older man carried the second bucket around behind Vessir, grunting as he went as though the weight were nearly too much for him, and then began pouring the water into the second tub. The water in the first rippled from a few drops that splashed from the other to it and then, in an instant, the surface became white. Vessir stopped humming, withdrew his arm, and then stretched out the other arm over the second tub.

Once frozen, the old man grabbed an iron bar that was nearly as tall as he was. He lifted the thing with a strained grunt, tilted it, and lunged it a foot forward upon the ground. It took the man four goes before he reached the side of the tub. There, he tilted it until the pointed end was over the side of the tub, before swinging it. Inside, he lifted it and dropped it against the ice, causing it to shatter. It took several goes before the ice was broken into small enough pieces to fit into Emma's bucket.

"Vessir, can you hear me?" she asked as she knelt to scoop the ice into her bucket. The old man hefted the iron bar over and into the other tub without speaking.

"He doesn't talk." the man said, a bit of annoyance in his tone.

"It never hurts to try." She replied.

"Sometimes it does hurt to try, miss. Just ask this lad."

Emma reached out and placed her hand on Vessir's and gave him a comforting smile. He didn't react. She gave his hand a gentle squeeze, stood up, and left without giving the old man any other reason to speak to her. She gave a look back as she pushed aside the tent flap and found the old man smiling at her. Vessir's eyes were unfocused, and his head slowly tilted down. Something about that smile made her skin crawl and she made a mental note to do some asking around about the boy and his two brothers.

She hurried along to the main tent's opening and, giving a polite smile to the two soldiers standing guard on either side, entered quietly. Inside, there were no more than twenty lords, ladies or their servants combined. A few of them sat together in parties of ten or so, but mostly there were individuals sitting far apart. When the big tent wasn't being used to celebrate the war or feed large groups, it was quiet, and anybody was welcome to use the space for any manner of meeting. Lords, ladies, and even merchants often came to haggle, arrange marriages, or just to use the big tables to lay out paper and books for study and the occasional meal. She delivered her bucket of ice to the table of refreshments, where two young men stood watch over the few visitors who currently sat about the tent.

A hand rose almost immediately in the far corner of the tent and Emma set off towards it without delay, her mind still on the three brothers. Halfway there, she recognized the lady as a regular morning visitor over the past week without even seeing her face. A large bag sat in the middle of the table with several books exposed, several set out before the lady, and writing implements sat at the ready upon the table before her. The woman usually spent half the morning here eating, reading, writing, and holding meetings with spice and food merchants. She wore a long, blue A-line pleated dress with two black bands as a decorative hemline that would have hidden her bare feet if she were standing. The bodice was fitted with a square neckline, tailored quarter-sleeves and two matching black hemlines. Her gold-blond hair fell to her shoulders in messy waves, and she wore a simple silver-chained necklace that held a flat oval at her sternum with a tree carved into its face. Aside from the cheap necklace, she was an exemplar of how many poor people imagined royal life was every day. Though she might look the part in every way, Sophia wasn't royalty at all; rather, she was a witch and that made her the property of High-king Hotar.

"Good morning." She announced her arrival with a grand smile.

"And a great morning to you as well, Emma." Sophia returned her smile. "How are you, my dear?"

"Alive and well. How may I be of service?"

"I would die for some of the iced tea I've heard so much about recently, if you would."

"Right away!"

"Thank you, Emma."

Emma turned and headed back across the tent. Halfway along, she noticed Sa'teshka enter the tent. He didn't stop to take in the sight of the tent as most usually did when they entered, and he didn't glance this way or that to locate a companion. As usual, the man wore his slimming, dark clothing with no weapon and arrived alone with that dark glare full of hatred. He marched directly for Sophia, pulled a chair out, sat, scooted himself forward, and planted both hands upon the table before himself. If he'd done the same to her, she thought she likely would have jumped up and run away without so much as a question. Sophia's smile faltered as she opened her mouth, but Emma was too far away to hear the woman's words.

"Please get me a cup of spiced rum." she said to one of the servers. She'd have used a name but wasn't familiar with these two. She'd heard that Sa'teshka favored rum if he drank anything at all from other servers and gambled that it wasn't rumor. She quickly prepared the iced tea with care. She had to break a few chunks of ice down so as not to overload the cup with ice – people often complained that their drink tasted watered down if there was too much ice or wasn't cold enough if there was too little ice. *It's your own fault for letting the ice melt,* she thought with annoyance as she recalled one particularly loud lord's complaint from a few nights before.

Moments later, she was heading back across the tent with the prepared drinks in hand, walking as quickly as she dared. When she reached the table, she set the spiced rum down just before Sa'teshka's right hand and gave him a polite nod before turning to Sophia. He looked from the cup to her and nodded in return. "Thank you." He grabbed the cup and immediately took a small sip.

"You are very welcome, my lord."

When she turned, she found that a chair had been pulled out from the table beside Sophia as though another visitor had come and

391

gone when she hadn't been looking. She walked around the table and sat the iced tea before Sophia, gave a nod and stepped back. Sophia's hand shot out, took her very tightly by the wrist, and pulled her down toward the available seat. Sophia's face became a pleading to sit, a touch of fear, and worry. Emma held back her surprise and took the seat, giving Sophia a reassuring smile. She was accustomed to royal ladies using her as a human shield socially, but she instantly worried how she would hold up against Sa'teshka. He was terrifying even in this moment and, yet, he'd said and done almost nothing.

"Were you not thirsty as well, Emma?"

"I drank a lot over my breakfast earlier. You should try it, Sophia."

Sophia lifted the glass to her mouth and took a deep breath before taking a sip. Emma noticed then that Sophia's pupils were dilated, her skin was flushed, and that she was fidgeting with the spine of the book she held in her free hand. When she set the cup down again, her smile was a bit wider, but not as genuine. There was a troubled strain there.

"The apples?"

Sophia reacted quickly, almost as though startled. She snatched a book from her bag, nearly dropping it, and set it before herself with a loud thud. Opening it with trembling hands, she spent a good minute searching through its pages. "To answer your question: yes, I believe I will have harvested several hundred bushels of apples by the end of the month."

"Good. King Hotar wants them all."

"Very well. I shall see that they are sent to the right place." Sophia replied.

"Good." Sa'teshka practically barked.

He sipped at his rum and kept his eyes on the center of the table as though he were lost in thought. At the same time, Sophia shoved the book back into the bag and brought her cup of tea up to her mouth. She didn't drink from it; rather, she hid behind the thing, eyes locked on Sa'teshka and breathing a bit faster and more deeply than before.

"This tea is quite good, Lord Sa'teshka. You should try it." she finally said. When he looked up at her, she glanced away and put her cup against her lips but still did not drink.

"I already have a drink."

"It is rather lovely, my lord. It's a brand-new blend the chefs came up with. Some southern leaves in it. If you like spiced rum, I think you'll enjoy the full body and bold aroma." Emma offered.

"No."

Sa'teshka turned his attention to Emma just long enough to bark the word. His gaze was intense, and Emma immediately wanted to flee the table and ask her owner if she could be a farmer instead. At the same time, his expression and body language didn't really tell her that he was ready to murder someone at that moment, but maybe that it was merely a task that he could carry out without the slightest of regrets. The silence that followed did not help to alleviate her sense of danger. She and Sophia exchanged looks and Sa'teshka focused on his drink.

"Are you still angry about the Day Nirvana I slipped into your drink?" Sophia asked softly.

There was a flicker of confusion in his eyes that did not touch his face, but Emma noticed it and wondered about it. Sophia picked up her cup, turned to face Emma, and took a very long sip. She opened her eyes wide and gave a worried frown. Emma saw that Sophia wanted to prolong the conversation but was unsure of how to redirect it. He wasn't being very cooperative about it and Emma was unsure of herself.

"I did apologize for it."

"You did not. We haven't spoken since before that happened." His bark was a bit less hostile now.

"I sent you those blue hyacinths." Her protest was meek.

"So?"

"Did you not get them?"

"I did. What about them."

Emma watched as Sophia's mouth opened and shut several times and her brow furrowed. She knew immediately that Sophia thought the man was saying that he did not forgive her for the Day Nirvana. It came to her that she had heard Sa'teshka had come from a kingdom far away and that maybe he didn't know about flowers. *Barbaric!*

"My lord, if you'll allow me, I think I see the problem here. In some places, we use flowers to communicate specific things. Where I grew up near Three Falls, blue hyacinths mean that you have thought about your actions and are sorry."

"People send flowers to say so much?"

"Yes." Sophia said.

"I don't like it." he said.

"What does Day Nirvana do?" Emma looked to Sophia for an answer.

"Kills people." Sa'teshka said.

Sophia's eyes shot open. "No!"

"It is the drug people commonly call Bliss." he explained.

"You gave him Bliss?" Emma glared at Sophia in utter shock.

"Day Nirvana requires large doses and habitual use to become harmful. I gave only a small amount, I swear!"

"For what purpose?"

"He's always so stressed and... terse. I thought it would relax him so we could talk." Sophia looked at Emma as she said it, her eyes searching for understanding.

"You did not seek me out to talk that night."

"I was waiting for it to start working but then you left."

"It was late when I left. King Hotar called for me to see to matters involving the assassin situation." He took a deep pull of the spiced rum and looked off in the distance a moment before continuing. "It kicked in at a most inopportune time, causing me to say things that I should have been able to keep to myself."

"I'm sorry." Sophia said.

Sa'teshka stood. "I trust it will not happen again."

"It won't." Sophia answered sheepishly, eyes falling to the table.

Sa'teshka chugged the rest of his drink quickly and set the cup upon the table with the care of a man barely containing rage. He then looked at Emma and gave her a quick nod of respect. He looked to Sophia then and waited until she looked back up at him to give her a polite nod before departing. He walked directly for the opening of the tent from which he'd entered, his strides long and powerful, as if he were on a mission.

"By the gods!" Sophia shuddered visibly and wrapped her arms around herself. "I thought he was going to kill me." She grabbed her tea and took a good draw of it before grabbing her folding hand-fan from the table. She took several deep breaths and began fanning herself rapidly.

"My word, Sophia! Why would you meddle with that man?"

"I need friends! Besides, he is nice!"

Emma glared at Sophia harshly. "He is *not* nice! Nothing about that exchange was nice. In fact, he is the opposite of nice! He is terrifying!"

"You don't understand, Emma!"

"You better make me understand because I thought he was going to kill us! And why would you drug him to get him to be open with you?"

"He cares about his people! Ever since he was given the Brown lands, he's been turning that place around."

"As in Lord and Lady Brown who were murdered with all of their servants?"

"Yes."

"You know people say he murdered the Browns!"

"Rumors! There was an investigation, and he was cleared of any wrongdoing in that matter! Besides, the Browns treated all their people like slaves and were almost universally hated."

"Most people hate their rulers." Emma argued.

"Yes, but the Browns ruled with strident animosity for the less fortunate. He cut taxes and sent out The Proclamation on Rights."

"Every new ruler has cut taxes and brags about how many rights they grant to those they rule, Sophia."

"He's just recently solved his people's lack of work by allowing Lord Kairn to hire a bunch of them. The blacksmiths, carpenters, and plowmen have work because of that deal."

"None of that changes the face that he's terrifying and not even a little sociable or polite."

"He's just misunderstood."

"Speaking of Lord Kairn, why don't you make friends with him? *That* is a nice fellow!" Emma declared with a smile.

"Lord Kairn is too young for me." Sophia protested.

"I thought you said you were looking for a *friend*, not something more. Besides, he can't be more than two years younger than you!"

Sophia blushed and frowned at her. "Lord Kairn is a good man, but I don't think he's really my type." "You both like to read your books." Emma offered.

"Yes, but I just can't see that working out. I think he would bore me to death."

"He is rather quiet."

"Besides, people say that he is spending a lot of time in his bottles after failing to catch the assassin and I can't stand a drunkard."

When everything was gathered up and the bag slung over her shoulder, Sophia turned to give Emma a hug and Emma saw the watery eyes, the beginning of puffiness beneath them, and the trembling of Sophia's free hand. They hugged tightly for a long moment and Emma decided to say nothing. *The poor fool let her heart fall for someone who wasn't interested. She'll have a good cry and then we'll talk about how silly it was tomorrow over tea.*

WAKE UP

Lord Talrin was Lord Farlan's favorite to use as a stool when climbing on this horse. It took a few days to realize it, but Lord Farlan liked taking the extra time to find the most uncomfortable place to have Lord Talrin stand on his hands and knees before mounting his horse. This day was no different than others, save for the fact that on this day Lord Farlan chose the grass where he had just urinated. Ashan had no love for lords and ladies, but it seemed a foul way to treat someone. *I would rather be hit in the face,* Ashan thought as he watched Lord Farlan setting upon his horse and Lord Talrin climb to his feet clumsily. Lord Talrin turned, and Ashan was amazed at the perfect lack of emotions on the man's face.

He turned to face the south and waited. A guard came and delivered the usual serving of dried meat with a blank expression like he wasn't thinking. Frezz grabbed a piece and chewed casually, eyes on the forest, and waited. His skin had changed a bit, the green sections growing more vivid and the reds deeper, which Ashan figured were signs of improved health but hadn't asked.

Argel and the two who had taken her to find a tree to relieve herself appeared in the distance. The guards held their swords at the ready as they walked. Checking Lord Farlan quickly, he found the man looking that direction with slight annoyance and amusement upon his face. Ashan turned back and waited for the two to put Argel back into the cage. She sat at Ashan's side and waited for the men to depart.

"They do get a bit more aware the further we go, but it's fleeting at best." she said softly to Frezz.

"Mind control." Frezz replied. "Unfortunately, there are many methods to achieve that."

"They refused to go further away at a point." she said.

"Probably because you were nearing the limits of Farlan's reach." Frezz said as he grabbed another chunk of meat.

"Any idea how to break his control over them?" Ashan asked.

"Not any that I can actually deploy."

"So, we sneak out and just run for it?" Argel grabbed a chunk of the dried meat and ate greedily, which was becoming her habit and Ashan knew it was because of the stress.

"I'd rather not fight and kill men who are under spells." Frezz replied flatly.

"It's not our fault they're under someone's control." Argel almost hissed.

"It's not, but I'd still rather not kill them."

Just then, a thud stole their attention. Turning around, Ashan found a man laying upon the ground. From where he lay, it appeared that he had just fallen from his horse. He flailed one arm about wildly as though swatting at a fly, made a sort of short, choking sound, and appeared to be trying to roll over to his side. He ceased a few moments later and, all the while, nobody paid him any attention. Instead, the soldiers began mounting their horses as if nothing was happening.

"I don't want to die like that." Argel said.

"We won't." Ashan said.

"How do you know?"

"Lord Farlan wants us alive." He replied.

"It's not random. It's something to do with the magic being used." Frezz explained.

Ashan watched the body vanish into the distance and gave a silent prayer for the man's soul. So far, one soldier fell dead each day and none of the others ever paid any attention when it happened. Lord Farlan took notice each time, but all he ever did was smile and return to whatever he had been doing, which was usually riding his horse like everyone else. He would hum occasionally, but otherwise he was focused on the business of heading north.

Just then, Lord Farlan began speaking and the sound broke Ashan from these thoughts. He turned and found that Lord Talrin was riding alongside Lord Farlan, occasionally nodding at whatever Farlan said. After a while, they slowed and fell backward alongside the formation of soldiers until they arrived upon the caged wagon. Lord Farlan gave the cage a careful eyeing as if checking for weapons inside and gave them all a smile once satisfied.

"You'll be the last one alive, you know." he said to Lord Talrin, who shook his head in agreement. "It really is a shame it had to be this way. You're a smart man with a beautiful wife, strong sons, and pleasant daughters. Your family is good stock. You could have made for an advantageous ally." Farlan said admiringly.

Lord Talrin nodded again but jerkily.

401

"King Hotar likes me for my loyalty. I've used my many, many, many talents to accomplish his goals. You aren't the first king that has danced on my strings, and you won't be the last."

Lord Talrin's voice came softly. "I will-"

"No." Lard Farlan spat the words as if lecturing a misbehaving dog. He pointed a finger in Talrin's face. "You only say what I want!"

Lord Talrin shook his head in the affirmative.

"You know, if you stopped resisting me, I might be so kind as to grant you permission to wash yourself in the next river we find. Maybe I'd even permit you to change into clean clothing." He smiled wide at Lord Talrin. "What do you say to that?"

Lord Talrin's face twisted with a rage unlike any Ashan had ever seen before. Seeing it alarmed him so thoroughly that he almost threw his handful of dried meat at Lord Farlan. "You will burn in the-"
    Talrin's mouth snapped shut and he mumbled for a second longer, but the hatred on his face did not ease. His eyes burned with hatred and the sight reminded Ashan of Sa'teshka the day the man had destroyed that table in the royal courtyard.

"If you are unwilling to behave yourself, you will continue to stew in your own filth. I'll do you a favor and let you think about it for a while." Lord Farlan smiled at the man and began to hum.

"He's sick." Argel leaned in close and whispered to Ashan.

"Very."

"We have to escape."

"You saw Frezz bend the bars." He reminded her for the fifth time. "The easy part is covered. It's the running away part that is the problem. I still think getting to the horses they put somewhere beyond sight is the dangerous part. He could be using magic to hide them or alert him if they are taken."

"You don't know that."

"I know almost nothing of magic, but it could be."

"Frezz can figure out the magic!" Argel protested.

"Yes, but I think he should do that before we make our move."

"How do you think he will do that?"

"Argel, trust him to come up with a plan that works. Breaking out and just running on foot isn't going to work. Even if they didn't notice us all night, they'd catch up with us quickly with their horses."

"We could just kill the horses."

"That would make too much sound." He struggled to remain quiet. She was growing rather desperate to leave and his patience was growing thin. "Have patience."

They watched as Lord Farlan and Talrin slowly fell back beside the supply wagon. Talrin leaned over and snatched up a handful of meat from the barrel within and gave it to Lord Farlan, who gave Ashan and Argel a big smile before he began eating. "Oh, it's delicious." he called at them and stuffed his mouth. "Pig!" Lord Talrin blurted out. Lord Farlan turned and pointed at him with his right hand, but Lord Talrin sneered back angrily. Lord Farlan then moved the handful of food from his left hand to this right and threw his left hand out at Talrin. Ashan caught a red, gleaming speck of light upon Farlan's hand. It lasted but a second and Lord Talrin's anger melted away in an instant, his expression becoming that blank mask everyone else wore.

"I will try." Argel told him.

A flittering at the corner of his vision caught Ashan's attention and drew his focus to the forest behind them. He found nothing but the motion of trees in the gentle wind, but then a soft drumming began to whisper from the distance. *I'm hearing things, aren't I?* He studied the forest intensely for a few moments before spotting something small and dark in the lowest branches of a tree a hundred strides off. It hopped along a low branch then leapt down into the sunlight. It spread its wings and flew to another tree's lowest branches, disappearing into the darkness there. A few moments later, it reappeared, hopping along that branch nearly to its end before jumping and flying to another tree. Again and again, the bird moved from tree to tree, never getting closer, but moving in a relatively straight line. With fluffy black feathers, a long neck, and legs too short for its squat body, it was unlike any bird Ashan had ever seen.

"I've seen that bird before." Argel said softly at his side.

"Shadow!" Frezz hissed softly as he sat upright suddenly.

"Shadow?" Ashan questioned. His heart raced as he pictured the shadow-man from his nightmares. "He's come?"

"He has and now I think I have miscalculated in allowing us to become captured." He spoke.

"We have to escape right now." Argel said.

"No, not exactly right now, but rather soon." Frezz laid a hand on her shoulder.

"But it is dangerous!"

"Life is dangerous."

The bird threw itself from a tree branch, flew out low over the ground in a straight line, and let out a scream. It was a very human scream that sent a chill running up Ashan's spine. The bird flew directly towards them this time rather than finding another tree but fell to the ground about twenty steps away. When it hit the ground, a great explosion of black smoke erupted, spreading out an arm's width and as tall as Ashan stood in a blink. A scream rang out from the smoke and then there were several voices cursing in surprise.

"Get on with it!" a man's voice came. "Move it!"

Two men stepped out of the smoke then, each with a pole over one shoulder. They wore dirty brown shorts and bonding rings on their arms. After a few strides, a large black box that appeared to have been crafted from highly polished black stone, and beyond that there came two women dressed much the same, supporting the other ends of the bars that supported the box. Behind these women came a man in light blue clothing with a golden crown on his head.

"Lord Tharsden!" Lord Farlan called out enthusiastically as his horse carried him towards the new arrivals.

"Yes, it is I, Lord Farlan." Lord Tharsden sounded rather annoyed.

Ashan caught that flicker of red light upon Lord Farlan's hand as he waved toward his soldiers as if snatching a fly in the air. The soldiers brought their horses to a halt and sat motionless, not even one of them interested in seeing what was happening behind them. Lord Farlan turned his horse about and waited for the newcomers to approach with a wide smile upon his face. Lord Tharsden walked right up to Lord Farlan and gave a short bow while the bound slowly walked along the large chest. As they neared, Ashan saw the bruises upon their bodies and the masked pain in their faces and he grew both angry and fearful. *They don't even have shoes!*

"Has there been a change of plans?" Lord Farlan asked with eager anticipation.

"Yes." Lord Tharsden replied. "Mary wants the girl now."

"Excellent. Where are we meeting her?"

"We're bringing her here."

"NO!" Argel blurted loudly. "No. No! You killed her, Frezz! This can't be happening. She's dead! She's dead! I saw her die!"

"Argel, calm yourself."

Frezz tried to grab her by the shoulder, but Argel jumped up and began yanking on the cage door. When it didn't give, she began kicking it instead, her breathing becoming erratic. Tears began falling from her eyes as she screamed, and her face turned white. "NO!"

"Ras'vetra!" Lord Tharsden commanded after a moment.

The shadow-man appeared suddenly at the man's side. "Yes, Master?"

"Bring Mary here now."

A biting chill ran down Ashan's spine at the man's words and his stomach threatened to turn. His balance shifted as if the land were quaking wildly, and he felt a tingling in the back of his skull right where the connection to Erekej had once been. For a second, he wanted to obey. He wanted to tear a hole in the world and bring Mary through it. It passed after a few breaths, and he realized that Argel was screaming at the top of her lungs at his side. Frezz was standing behind her with a hand on one of her shoulders and a hard look of determination on his face. No, it wasn't determination, it was anger. He'd never seen Frezz angry before and he didn't like it now.

"Yes, Master." The shadow-man turned and began to walk away slowly.

"It will be glorious!" Lord Farlan cheered loudly.

"NO!" Argel's screams grew more intense.

"-servant of the Isles of Fire, call upon Rue the Seeker-" Frezz had closed his eyes and seemed to be chanting.

"SHE IS DEAD! I SAW HER DIE!"

"-for your protection of these young ones-"

"Shut up, girl!" Lord Farlan screamed back at Argel.

"-me your favor in this battle, should I be worthy-"

406

The shadow-man exploded into a cloud of darkness about twenty strides away. The dark cloud roiled like the eye of a thunderstorm and then voices came from it. "Kill me! PLEASE!" a man screamed. "For the love of the gods, let us die!" another added. "Move along." A calm woman's voice came from much closer. "Please, kill us! Please!" Sobbing and agonized screams rose into a cacophony. "No! Come back! Kill me!"

"I do not have all day, Ras'vetra."

"This way." Ras'vetra's voice came softly.

The woman who stepped out from the dark cloud was the same witch who had commanded the undead and Argel, but she was dressed very differently than before. She wore brilliant white clothing that was like a butcher's gown instead of the dress and jewels. There was a sprinkling of blood on the front of her clothing, her hair was also done up into a tight bun at the top of her head, and she appeared younger in the face than he remembered. Recalling how she had died, Ashan glanced to her throat and found three lines of white scar tissue. It wasn't fresh though; rather, it appeared as though she had been injured many years ago. Argel screamed all the louder and more frantically at the woman's appearance.

"-my darling. I've missed you so-" Mary smiled and there was a dark twinkling in her eyes as she approached the cage.

Screaming so loudly that it hurt Ashan's ears, Argel ran to the other end of the cage and began trying to crawl out through the space between bars. Ashan rose and backed away from the door just as Frezz stepped up to it, raised his arms and posed as if he were preparing to fight the woman. Mary laughed and shifted her focus to Frezz, giving him an amused smile.

"You were rather lucky last time, but what will you do now without any of your weapons?"

"I will make certain that I finish the job this time, necromancer!" Ashan found the venom in his voice quite surprising.

She laughed and turned her eyes upon Argel. "I hope you enjoyed your little stroll through the forest, Argel. Where I'm going to put you, you'll never see the light of day again."

"Put it down." Lord Tharsden commanded his four *bound*.

"Soldiers, remove the girl from the cage." Lord Farlan commanded.

The bound lowered the chest to the ground and knelt on their hands and knees as Lord Tharsden approached. With a wave of his hand and a flash of red light, Lord Farlan's soldiers dismounted their horses, gathered around the cage, and stuck the tips of their swords between the bars threateningly. Mary backed away as Lord Talrin approached with a ring of keys.

"This has been a lot of trouble for a missing amulet." Lord Farlan said as he approached.

"We don't have it." Ashan blurted out.

"Yes, we've figured that much out already." Mary replied. "You did have it at one point. We assumed that you opened the package and had hidden it to sell it later or trade it for your freedom like the rotten little slave you are." She sneered.

"Wait, you sent me all the way out here in the middle of nowhere for nothing?" Lord Farlan protested.

"No, Lord Farlan. I needed that girl and King Hotar needs *the assassin* to be caught by Lord Kairn, who will then bring the assassin to justice. You can work your magic on the assassin to make him confess his crimes in front of an audience, an audience who will spread word of what they witnessed, because King Hotar needs his armies." Mary explained.

"That's a lot of effort."

"Not in the big picture." Mary explained.

"Couldn't you have sent someone else to chase them into your trap? You do know I have my own-"

"No." She snapped. "I need your skills. I need *the assassin* to admit he is an assassin in front of a large audience. Someone must admit they were sent on behalf of Isirdost to kill our king. I swear, you don't pay attention at all!"

"So, why couldn't I do that after Lord Kairn delivered them to me?"

Mary took a deep breath and glared at the man as if she wasn't sure if she was going to explain or slap him upside the head. "I already told you this!" she finally shouted. "You are supposed to do the same to him. I want him as a puppet too! What is wrong with you?"

"I didn't take anything and I'm not an assassin!" Ashan protested.

"Obviously, you idiot." She yelled and gave Ashan a spiteful glare.

Lord Talrin finally found the correct key but didn't unlock it just yet. The soldiers shifted their swords about threateningly, driving Frezz and Ashan towards the back and Argel towards the door. Lord Tharsden approached then with Ras'vetra at his side and a self-proud smile upon his face. Switching focus, Ashan found that the man was carrying a large, red orb against his chest with both arms wrapped around it. The thing seemed to be made of glass with a thousand pinpricks of white just below the surface. Though it was difficult to make out the more detailed features upon the shadow-man's face, Ashan thought it wore a troubled expression.

"Alright, let's get on with this." Lord Tharsden announced. "Bind the girl to Mary."

"Yes, Master." The shadow-man replied softly.

Argel let out a piercing scream and Ashan spun to face her, being careful not to run afoul of one of the swords nearby. She

409

screamed and grabbed at the rings, pulling at first and then trying to dig her fingers between them and her skin, but they held fast.

"Good work, Lord Tharsden. Now, bring her out so that I can-

A thump and yelp of pain brought Ashan's attention back to Mary and he found an arrow sticking out of her shoulder. She let out a string of curses while glancing about and then dove to the ground just as another arrow came. Ashan instinctively looked in the direction the arrow had come from and spotted two figures a hundred strides away. One wore a dark green traveling cloak with the hood up and the other wore a full suit of armor with a sword like Ashan's in either hand. The archer let another arrow loose and it flew through the shadow-man's head and then off into the forest beyond. The shadow-man spun about to face the archer as if surprised by the event.

Mary rose, took hold of the arrow in her arm, and yanked it free with a howl of pain. Seeing her smile fade then filled Ashan with a great deal of satisfaction, one that he then realized would only come second to the satisfaction he would feel when the woman was truly dead. It vanished instantly when she pulled a starkly white rod out from one of her sleeves and threw her arm out in the direction of the two strangers. Lightning burst out from the end of the rod and raced towards the two, the sound of thunder that followed was loud, but anemic when compared to real thunder. The robed archer dropped the bow and flung an arm out in a wide circle, apparently throwing dirt. The lightning arrived a second later, branched out into a thousand arms, and stuck the cloud of dirt.

"Who would attack at a time like this?" Lord Tharsden questioned as he stepped backward and turned to look.

Mary flung her arm again and so did the archer. The scene replayed exactly as it had before and Mary screamed out several profane words while shaking her fist at the two. The armored person turned away then, marched over to what Ashan had thought was a large rock, and bent down for a second. When the figure rose back up, it was holding six black rods with clear orbs on their tops and pointed bottoms. The figure stabbed one of the rods into the ground, took fifteen steps, placed a second, and continued. The figure set the poles in a circle before returning to the rock and picking up the two swords again.

"You will lose!" One of the figures yelled.

"DIE!" Mary screamed and flung her arm again. This time, the archer stood there watching in a calm stance. The bolt of lightning became two and each connected with one of the orbs, which lit up in a brilliant white light for as long as the lightning touched it.

"Idiots, that's who." Lord Farlan said with a smile. "Twenty soldiers. Attack!"

Lord Farlan waved his hand as if casually throwing something at the two figures. Again, Ashan caught the glimmer of red light on his hand, but this time he saw that it came from the center of the backside. Twenty soldiers withdrew their swords from the cage, circled around the cage to form a group, and headed towards the two figures somewhere between a jog and fast walking. The archer launched another arrow, but this one was aimed at Lord Farlan, who screamed and dove to the ground when it flew by his head. Another arrow came a second later and sank deeply into Lord Tharsden's neck. Ashan almost cheered at the sight, but Lord Tharsden didn't even flinch at the attack; rather, he shifted the red orb to his side to hold it with just the one arm while he pulled the arrow from his body like it was no more an inconvenience than a splinter in the foot. The wound let out a trickle of blood before it closed.

Lord Farlan crawled up to the wagon's wheel and peered around the side while yelling a few mild profanities at the archer. "Attack!" He finally screamed at the archers while waving his arm wildly in the direction of the two in the distance. The rest of the soldiers surrounding the caged wagon pulled their swords back and followed their companions. Mary walked between the two wagons and began flailing

411

her rod overhead, which resulted in a ball of fire springing to life in the air a foot above her. She finally threw her arm forward and down and the ball of fire, which had grown to be about as large as her head, went flying towards the strangers.

Frezz ran to the front of the cage, grabbed the door's hinge side with both hands, and tore it free as easily as a man might tear an old shirt apart. He jumped out of the cage at Lord Tharsden and slashed at the man with his claws. Lord Tharsden yelped when the first strike cut his shoulder, but he was quick to react and dodged the two that followed if only by a hand's reach.

"Defend me!" Lord Tharsden screamed as soon as he had managed to put a few feet between Frezz and himself.

Ras'vetra appeared in the space between and grabbed hold of Frezz by the arm, who immediately snapped his mouth closed around Ras'vetra's neck. His teeth, unlike the arrow earlier, sank into the cloudy surface of Ras'vetra's body and Ras'vetra cried out in surprise. The two fell to the ground with Frezz on top and he was slashing at Ras'vetra's chest wildly, which seemed to make contact, causing small ribbons of smoke to float away from the shadow-man.

Surprised that Frezz had attacked rather than opting to run away, Ashan stood there for a moment wondering what to do. He turned to face Argel and found that she was staring in horror at the binding rings upon her arm and had seemingly given up on trying to pull them free.

"Guards! Protect me!" Lord Farlan said at the back end of the supply wagon.

When Ashan turned, he found that about ten of the soldiers, who had closed nearly half the distance to the two strangers, were beginning to turn back around. Terrified, he glanced about and considered which direction he should run to avoid danger. Then he remembered how quickly the soldiers had caught him and Argel the last time they had tried to run away. *All you do is think about running*

412

away. It's time to act! Even if I die? Even if you die! As he screamed at himself inside, he recalled where the soldiers had placed his sword. As he ran for the supply wagon, Lord Farlan took notice, yelled in surprise, and ran away from it. Ashan began grabbing packs and throwing them over the side of the wagon. He had to remove five of them to find his sword and, as he grabbed it, he spotted Frezz's staff. As he took hold of it, he glanced up and found that the ten returning soldiers were nearly upon him. Hands full, he turned and ran towards Frezz, who was now standing and trading swings with the shadow.

"Heal me!" Lord Tharsden shouted.

Looking in that direction, Ashan was horrified to see that Lord Tharsden was on his knees now with three arrows sticking out from his chest. He had one hand upon the red orb and the other was pulling one of the arrows from his chest slowly, his face twisted with agony. Ras'vetra appeared at the man's side and snatched an arrow out of the air just before it would have contacted the man's face.

"Yes, Master." Ras'vetra's voice came ragged and full of disgust as he glanced about the forest.

"Good thinking!" Frezz's shouted words drew Ashan's attention and he turned just in time to see Frezz arrive at his side. He snatched his staff from Ashan's hand and ran onward, moving at incredible speed. He jumped just before he would have collided with the supply wagon and screamed something that might have been words. The supply wagon exploded, the light of day faltered, and rain began to fall. Looking up, Ashan found that the shadow of a single cloud was just beginning to creep over the area. The cloud screamed and flashed wildly as heavy rain began to fall.

Vines as thick as Ashan's arms shot up from the soil all around where the wagon had been and began to ensnare the coming soldiers. They didn't shout out in surprise as they were snatched and slowly dragged to the ground. *Frezz, you are amazing!* Ashan cheered and turned away from the soldiers to find Lord Farlan. He found the man

413

hiding behind a tree some fifteen strides away with loathing eyes locked upon Ashan. As Ashan took his first step in that direction, Lord Farlan came out from behind the tree, drew his sword, and gave Ashan a pleased smile.

"You dare challenge me, slave?"

"I'm not a slave." Ashan was surprised to hear himself speak.

"Once a slave, always a slave."

"No man need be born a king to kill another." Recalling Tark's words gave him a touch of courage.

"Brave words. I've had years to study the art of sword-fighting. You don't even know how to hold that thing correctly. You're embarrassing yourself, boy. You should just run away." Lord Farlan smiled as he took a fighting stance that was very similar to one of the ones Frezz had taught him. *Very aggressive,* he thought and tried to remember what Frezz had taught him about countering aggressive stances with defensive ones. *No, use a stance that allows for quick and easy retreats.* "That was a gentleman's fair warning, boy. I'm going to cut you a thousand times before I make you into my puppet."

A scream of pain rang out just then, drawing both Ashan and Lord Farlan's attention to the side just as Mary came running past with two arrows sticking out of her back. Frezz followed closely behind her with a ball of fire forming at the end of his staff. Mary ducked behind a tree just in time to avoid the ball of fire. She seemed to take a moment to breathe before jumping out and flicking her wand at Frezz, which sent a green bolt of light directly at his chest. An instant later, an arrow struck her leg just above the knee. She screamed and fell backwards at the same time Frezz ducked the green light she'd sent his way.

"Kill the lizard-man!" Mary screamed.

"See? None of you will survive." Lord Farlan said, drawing Ashan's attention back to him. "It's hopeless!"

414

Lord Farlan stepped forward and lazily thrust his sword at Ashan's stomach. Ashan brought his sword down hard on Lord Farlan's and stepped backward quickly before bringing his sword back upright. The speed of this caused his shoulder to ache with renewed pain from his earlier injuries. The man laughed and repeated the move, offering no more speed than before. Ashan slammed the sword down again and stepped back just the same as before but didn't pull the sword up as quickly this time around.

"Something wrong with your shoulder?" He sneered.

Lord Farlan stepped forward as though he was going to thrust for Ashan's stomach again and Ashan brought his sword down as he had before; however, this time Lord Farlan pulled his sword back in a flash and came in hard with his shoulder against Ashan's chest. The blow knocked Ashan to the ground. Rather than attacking, Lord Farlan laughed and waited for Ashan to return to his feet.

"You are going to be so much fun to torture." he said with an excited smile. "Maybe when Mary is done with your friends, I'll have you kill them. I'll leave you just conscious enough to understand what's happening."

A wall of fire shot up between them and Ashan watched Lord Farlan run away from it cursing. Turning about, Ashan found Frezz running in his direction with Argel trailing behind him. It took a second to notice that Mary was behind Argel, now free of any arrows, and waving her wand about frantically. A blue ball of light formed, and she sent it flying after Frezz, who jumped high into the air to avoid it at the last second. When the blue ball hit the ground, it exploded and spread out over the ground in a manner very similar to water, but then it turned white. *Ice?*

Further in the distance, the armored stranger was trading blows with three of Lord Farlan's soldiers. A few of them were strewn about on the ground there, but Ashan saw no arrows sticking out of their bodies. The archer fired a shot at Mary just then, but it missed and then

415

the archer tossed something at a small group of soldiers that were closing in. A loud bang sounded, and white smoke swallowed them up. A second later, three of the soldiers stepped out from the smoke moving sluggishly and waving their arms before their faces. One dropped his sword, and another swung blindly into the air before himself. After a few swings and misses, that soldier fell sideways to the ground and his fellows slowly bent over as if their suits were growing too heavy to stand.

"Ashan! Help me!" Argel called out.

"Yes! Come help her, Ashan." Mary yelled mockingly. "Come taste death, boy!"

Argel was chasing Frezz and Mary followed while throwing balls of fire or the occasional blue ball at Frezz, but Frezz was moving so fast that none of the attacks were getting close. *It's a trap*, Ashan told himself as he watched them continue. An arrow took its place at Mary's hip, and she screamed in pain as she came to a stumbling halt. In that moment, Frezz doubled back on the route he had taken, darting around Argel along the way, and came in for a physical attack. He ran up, slammed his staff into Mary's face, and slashed at her midsection with his claws. His attack seemed brutal to Ashan, but Mary didn't seem all that bothered by it; rather, she stepped back and brought her wand up over her head. A blue sphere formed, and she brought her arm down fast like someone using a hammer, bringing the blue sphere along. Frezz thrust his staff upwards into the sphere and it simply vanished. Mary took the moment to whip her wand around in a tight circle, forming a ball of fire, and slammed it into Frezz's midsection. The flames fanned out around his body, and he screamed, but he didn't stay put. He jumped directly up into the air and sent a fireball of his own down at Mary.

"Kill him!" Mary yelled as she vanished behind flames. Argel came running.

"Boy!"

Lord Farlan came with his sword high and to the side. Ashan braced himself to block the blade with his own and immediately tried to recall what Frezz had told him about how to handle charging opponents. Nothing came and so he simply braced himself to absorb the force that was coming. Frezz appeared at that moment and tackled Lord Farlan from the side.

"Kill him!" Mary yelled.

Ashan turned and found that Argel was running directly at him instead of Frezz. "Run, Ashan!" She yelled and he obeyed. He darted left and right around a few trees before allowing himself to look back and beg the gods for a plan. Up ahead, Lord Farlan's soldiers were running towards him – at least those still on their feet – and plotting a course that kept him away from them took a few moments of thought. He looked back and knew that Argel would catch up with him soon if he had to take too many turns.

Suddenly, the shadow-man flew past him. He'd been within an arm's reach but hadn't even made the attempt. A feeling in his gut drove Ashan to follow the shadow-man to the left. Moments later, the shadow-man reached the archer and tackled him to the ground. When they landed, the shadow-man vanished from that spot and reappeared ten strides over near the armored stranger. The shadow-man tackled that person to the ground and vanished again., reappearing above the archer.

"No!"

Argel's voice caught his ear just as he felt the hairs on his head rise. The pain that followed was beyond any he had ever felt in his life. It felt as if he had been stabbed in the space between his right shoulder-blade and spine with a blade that had been pulled from a blacksmith's forge right when it was almost hot enough to turn into a liquid. And then it did. Like a flooding river, it followed his spine, shot out in the center of his arms neck. It ate his flesh away into smoke so slowly that he noticed every tiny piece scream out in agony for ages before

417

becoming nothing. Then he felt the pain of the absent parts of himself. When it ended, he found himself in the air. He crashed face-first upon the ground. Pain melted away an instant later and his heart began to race. He rolled to his back and spotted Argel coming at him with dread upon her face. "Run, Ashan!" He rolled away from her, came to his feet in a flash, and ran.

Ahead, the archer and his companion were struggling to stay on their feet with the shadow-man attacking them in turn. He knocked the archer down, tossed the bow away, and then vanished over to the armored warrior. The shadow-man stole one of the warrior's swords, tossed it away, and ducked as the warrior swung the other sword. The shadow-man snatched the second sword and threw it before shoving the warrior to the ground.

"Ashan!" Argel's voice came distantly.

Looking back, he saw that she was still chasing after him, but she had fallen behind a good twenty strides. Mary was coming along as well and appeared to be closing the distance much faster than Argel. She threw her wand out before herself and that familiar dancing line of white light appeared. He tried to pull his legs up in hopes that his weight would bring him down and out of the path of the lightning, but it was too late. The lightning came to meet his shoulder and he screamed as that hot knife sank into his flesh again.

When the agony vanished this time, he did not feel pain at all; rather, he felt rejuvenated, as if just waking from a full night's slumber. Confused, he scrambled to his feet and found his sword as quickly as he could. Finding it, he ran for the circle of orb-topped poles, hoping it would protect him from another of Mary's attacks. *People sometimes aren't aware of their injuries when they're dying*, he considered. Frezz came into view at his left side, and they arrived upon the shadow-man at the same time. Frezz slashed at the shadow-man just as Ashan punched at it with his free hand. Ashan went through the shadowy figure as though it weren't even there, stumbled, and fell.

"Ashan!" Argel yelled again.

Standing, Ashan took in the scene. Frezz was engaging the shadow-man, the archer and warrior were reclaiming their weapons, Argel and Mary were fast approaching, and Lord Farlan's remaining soldiers were approaching slowly. Lord Farlan and Lord Tharsden were way back by the remaining wagon. He considered them and wondered. He couldn't even match Lord Farlan with the sword and Lord Tharsden had that orb that seemed to be a tool to control the shadow-man. He couldn't fight the shadow-man, Mary, the soldiers, or Argel. *But I can steal that orb from Tharsden! But how to get there?*

The idea came immediately, and Ashan waited for Mary's next lightning attack to be absorbed before he ran. He snatched one of the poles as he went, moving just as Argel arrived and dove at him. Mary targeted him immediately, launching bolt after bolt of light at him, but each touched the orb he carried.

"Fool boy!" Lord Farlan called as he charged to meet Ashan.

Ashan blocked the first attack with the pole and retaliated with his own sword, but Lord Farlan was too fast. He dodged Ashan's attacks with ease, but Ashan used the pole or his sword to defend against the man's intensifying attacks. "Soldiers, protect me!" he called when he tricked Ashan into blocking, but then pulled his sword away. He slipped in and gently ran the blade across Ashan's arm below the shoulder. It was a small cut, but it stung and frightened Ashan into retreating.

"Run away, boy!" Lord Farlan leapt forward and lazily slapped his blade against Ashan's. Ashan stepped back and got into the proper stance Frezz had taught him. The little cut let out a few drops of blood and he felt himself become distracted by the feeling of them running down his arm.

"No." Ashan said loudly.

Lord Tharsden turned away from his study of the battle in the distance to watch but said nothing. *Don't get distracted. Focus on the moment. Focus on your breathing.* When Lord Farlan came in, he came in slower than before and struck the staff so hard that Ashan had to let go of it to keep the weight of it from causing him to stumble. Lord Farlan didn't stop there; instead, he stepped up close, kicked Ashan in the hip, and then casually brought his sword up so that the tip caught Ashan's lower leg. Again, Lord Farlan waited for Ashan to regain his footing with a smile.

"How many cuts before you give up, boy? Ten? Twenty?"

Ashan charged and swung for Lord Farlan's sword and immediately thought he had done well, but Lord Farlan did something Ashan could not have anticipated. He let the force push his sword, turned with it, and came around to slam his sword into the middle of Ashan's. He almost lost hold of his sword as it was flung to his right side and, in that moment, Lord Farlan brought his sword up to Ashan's arm, stepped backward, and dragged the blade lightly over the skin a finger's width below the other cut at the same angle. Ashan stepped away, turned, and swung his sword wildly at the man's neck but missed by half an arm's length. Lord Farlan brought his sword up before his face and gave Ashan a wicked smile.

"How many more?"

Ashan spotted three soldiers coming along. It wouldn't be long before they arrived, and he knew that would be his end. "Kill that archer!" Behind Lord Farlan, Lord Tharsden spoke to the red orb he held in both hands. His attention had returned to the battle in the distance. *Good.* Ashan got the urge to smile back at Lord Farlan, but held it in. Tark would have called it a tell. *Let your enemy think you are weak and afraid no matter what,* he had explained. When asked what to do if you really were weak and afraid, Tark smiled and replied *All the better.*

Ashan used both hands to raise his sword high over his head, took a deep breath, and charged. Lord Farlan dropped his sword to the side and, smiling, stepped out of the way. He brought his sword up at an angle so that the tip of the blade nipped at Ashan's arm, but Ashan paid no mind. He charged on and brought his sword down with everything he had. The blade connected with the red orb and sent it flying out of Lord Tharsden's hands. The man shouted in surprise as he glanced to Ashan. Ashan released his sword and drove his shoulder into Lord Tharsden's chest. The man yelled as he fell backward, and Ashan chased the orb for a few strides before diving after it. A tingling sensation shot through him, and he felt what it meant.

"Free Argel!" he yelled at the orb before bringing his second hand up to secure his prize. *Yes, Master,* a voice replied in his own head. Ashan wrapped his arms about the orb and climbed to his feet awkwardly.

"NO!" He heard Mary scream in the distance as he turned to face Lord Farlan and Lord Tharsden.

"Get it!" Lord Tharsden screamed at Lord Farlan.

"Protect me." Ashan said.

Ras'vetra appeared in the space between Ashan and the two lords. When Lord Farlan came, Ras'vetra kicked him in the chest and sent him flying into a tree. "NO!" Lord Tharsden came at Ashan with desperation in his eyes, but Ras'vetra grabbed the man by the arm and swung him around twice before releasing him. He hit the same tree as Lord Farlan and the sounds that came from the impact convinced Ashan that the man was dead.

"Is Argel free?" Ashan faced Ras'vetra and saw him in a new way. There was sorrow and joy upon the shadow's face he had not seen before, and he could make out so much more detail than before. There were worry lines that darkness and a sad smile.

"Yes, Master." Ras'vetra replied.

Looking down at the red orb, Ashan was suddenly full of regret for having touched the thing and revulsion for having used it. *Magic,* he cursed. He became aware of the connection between Ras'vetra and himself in the back of his mind, but it was different than what he had known before. Instead of feeling Erekej's barely contained rage and the ever-present power of the bond that could crush Ashan into almost nothingness, Ashan felt a vast power that just wanted to be utilized. Good or evil, it didn't matter so long as it was used.

"What are you?" He asked the shadow.

"A tool, Master." Ras'vetra replied softly.

A sudden light came and when Ashan turned to face it, he found Mary standing a short distance away with her rod raised. Lightning came for him, and he stepped back in surprise. Ras'vetra reached out with a hand at the last second and the lightning followed his body to the ground in a thousand smaller bolts that illuminated him from the inside. *Master, look out!* Ras'vetra's voice in his head gave him the shivers and he turned to find what the shadow-man was warning him to look out for and found that the three soldiers were now very close.

"Send these soldiers-"

A hand clamped down over his mouth from behind just as another and wrapped around his chest from over his shoulder. He was pulled backward against someone's chest and then lifted off his feet. They fell together and he landed upon the other person. He tried to yell out but the hand over his mouth was clamped down tightly. Above, Lord Tharsden came into view with a deep frown and both hands reaching down. He took hold of the orb and pulled at it. His superior strength won the fight quickly and then the man holding Ashan from behind tossed him to the side.

"Attack this boy." Lord Tharsden shouted.

"Kill the boy." Lord Farlan shouted even louder.

By the time he got to his feet, the three soldiers were upon him, and Ashan had to dive to escape their swords. "NO!" He shouted as a hand clamped onto his ankle and dragged him along the ground. He was lifted off the ground by his ankle and spun around. Something gave off a loud pop and then there was smoke all around him. His ankle was released, and he fell to the ground.

"Damn you and your arrows!" Lord Farlan shouted from behind.

Ashan jumped up and ran. He came out of the white smoke a few strides later and turned to find his bearings. Lord Farlan ran out from the smoke a moment later and, seeing Ashan, raised his sword. Frezz appeared just behind the man, closed the distance, and tackled him at the waist. The man lost his sword in the fall. "Die!" He screamed as he tried to roll over beneath Frezz. Another explosion sounded, the white cloud thickened and began to expand. *The sword! Get the sword!* Ashan glanced down at Lord Farlan's sword, wondering what was happening within the smoke, and then took a step forward.

"Go kill that boy!" Lord Tharsden's voice came in a panic.

Ras'vetra stepped out from the smoke, locked his gaze upon Ashan, and stepped forward. His movements were slow and jerky, as though each step was a great struggle, and parts of his body were fading in and out of sight in turn. Behind him, two of Lord Farlan's soldiers came out of the smoke coughing. It took a moment for the two soldiers to get their bearings and, when they did, they headed in Ashan's direction. Ashan ran, scooped up Lord Farlan's sword, and paused as he wondered what to do. The flash of red light in Lord Farlan's hand was all he needed.

It took four swings to strike his target and when Lord Farlan's hand departed from the wrist, Ashan was less than surprised when the soldiers began falling. One fell only to his knees and began screaming. Others began screaming in the distance as well and he began to worry that he'd sentenced them all to death.

"Run, Ashan." Frezz yelled as he rose from the wailing Lord Farlan and charged after Ras'vetra, who was still moving slowly.

"Kill Lord Farlan!" a voice rang out above all the others.

"Slaughter Farlan!" another voice replied.

"Retreat!" Mary screamed. "Lord Tharsden?"

"Here!" Lord Tharsden appeared from the smoke with the orb in his arms and three arrows in his back. "Here!" As he yelled, an arrow shot out from the smoke and sank into the back of his leg just above the foot and he fell.

Not thinking, Ashan ran for the man. When he arrived, he dropped onto the orb, grabbed it with both hands, and slammed his feet into the man's face until he felt the orb come free. "Help me." He rolled away from Lord Tharsden, climbed to his feet, and threw the orb forward as hard as he could. As he did so, his sword appeared in the air just before his hand and he grabbed it. He turned around, expecting Lord Tharsden to be where he had left him, but found the man only a few strides away. Ashan swung his sword at the man's middle, but he didn't even shy at the sight of the sword, and it made contact. He felt the blade slice into Lord Tharsden, but the man didn't even respond.

"Mary!" Tharsden shouted as he dove at the orb.

Ashan came down upon the orb with his sword. The blade bounced off and a dull thrumming filled the air for a second. Lord Tharsden rolled away with the orb held to his stomach and rolled to his feet. "Kill the boy!" he screamed as he turned away. Mary exited the smoke then with several soldiers and the black-armored warrior chasing her just then. Ashan turned and charged after Lord Tharsden.

"Stop the boy! Then use magic to get us out of here." Lord Tharsden yelled.

Ahead, a dark cloud sprang into existence and Lord Tharsden turned towards it. "Come to me!" he screamed at the red orb. Ras'vetra

424

appeared beside the dark cloud ahead, but his body was a faint gray fog instead of the usual black clouds. Ashan's legs begged him to stop running, but he pushed all the harder to close the distance. "Kill the boy!" Tharsden screamed at Ras'vetra.

"Tell it." Mary shouted between deep huffs. "To get." Looking back, Mary was falling behind and had a hand on her side where her clothing was a deep red. "My wand."

"Get her wand." Lord Tharsden shouted.

"I'm too weak." Ras'vetra said as he walked jerkily to intercept Ashan.

"Kill the boy with lightning!" Lord Tharsden screamed as he came to a halt beside the dark cloud. "Run, Mary!"

"I'm too weak." Ras'vetra replied.

Ashan jumped to his left and dodged Ras'vetra, who jumped at him and missed by several arms' lengths. A few steps further and Ashan raised his sword up, bringing it down with everything he had. Lord Tharsden's eyes opened wide, and he raised an arm up to block the sword. A loud hum filled the air and a crack appeared on the face of the orb.

"Heal me, Ras'vetra!" He screamed as he turned to run.

An arrow passed so close to his head, that Ashan felt the wind of it move the hair on his neck. It plunged into Lord Tharsden's back and the man went down. A second arrow sank into his hip, and he began dragging himself towards that black cloud. Mary passed Ashan then and he almost smiled when he saw six arrows sticking out from her backside. She jumped into the dark cloud with a scream and was gone. Another arrow came and planted itself in Lord Tharsden's neck, but he still pulled himself forward.

"Get rid of him!" Tharsden's voice came softly.

Ashan took a deep breath and charged Lord Tharsden as quickly as he could. His knees threatened to give out on him, his leg muscles refused to move the way he wished, and his side ached something awful, but he pushed through the pain. He raised his sword and breathed deeply to gather his strength. Ras'vetra appeared before Lord Tharsden so faintly that Ashan wondered if it was only his imagination.

"I'm sorry." Ras'vetra said.

Ashan brought his sword down and Ras'vetra's hands closed on his shoulders. The sword made contact and a terrifying chill swept through his body. Ashan found himself unable to move as he gasped for air and felt parts of his body ceasing to exist. He felt his heart slow as his hands released the sword. Before him, he saw the now barely visible shadow-man's eyes looking into his own. There was sorrow in those eyes. Below, Lord Tharsden's face wore twice as much shock, but his eyes were glued to the orb instead of Ashan.

"It's...it's broken." Lord Tharsden looked from the orb to Ashan repeatedly.

"Yes." Ras'vetra whispered.

"You'll cease to exist."

"Yes." Ras'vetra whispered back.

"No!" Lord Tharsden screamed and began slowly lowering the orb to the ground. Small chunks began falling from the orb. "MY POWER!" Lord Tharsden screamed again, and the main body of the orb began to come apart along the three cracks that ran through it.

"I'm sorry." Ras'vetra whispered to Ashan. "I have to fulfill my last command."

"It's...okay." The cold had already done its work anyway.

As the world became dark, Ashan watched Lord Tharsden crawl toward the black cloud. Several arrows landed in the ground about him, he screamed, and then vanished into the darkness. With nothing else to look at, Ashan returned his focus to Ras'vetra's eyes. A moment later, darkness swallowed the world.

Made in the USA
Coppell, TX
30 June 2023

18644653R00252